CLAIRE KANN

THE MARVELOUS

Swoon READS

NEW YORK

A Swoon Reads Book

An imprint of Macmillan Publishing Group, LLC

120 Broadway, New York, NY 10271

Our books may be purchased in bulk for promotional, educational, or business use. Please contact your local bookseller or the Macmillan Corporate and Premium Sales Department at (800) 221-7945 ext. 5442 or by email at MacmillanSpecialMarkets@macmillan.com.

Library of Congress Cataloging-in-Publication Data is available.

ISBN 978-1-250-19269-1 (hardcover) / ISBN 978-1-250-19270-7 (ebook)

Book design by Liz Dresner

First edition, June 2021

10 9 8 7 6 5 4 3 2 1

fiercereads.com

I'll always be with you

Goldspiracy Forums

Transcript #947
Original <u>Golden Rule diary entry</u> by Jewel Van Hanen
March 14, Year Three
🗨 Transcribed by **SilentStar**

ANNOUNCEMENT | Watch until the end.

Hi. Hello. I've been gone for a while, I know.

[sighs]

I needed to take some time to think about what I was doing here. What my goals were. How close I had gotten to achieving them before I began to grow complacent with the status quo.

A couple of days away from Golden Rule to clear my head turned into weeks turned into months, and now here we are one year later.

[pauses]

I created Golden Rule to be an escape—a safe place to revel in the minutiae and greatness of real life, not hide from it while hoping for something better. A place for authenticity and kindness and support. A place to plan and grow, to figure out what your best life would look like, and how to get there. A place for stories. Yours and mine.

This app saved me, and I know it saved a lot of you too. It organically grew into something so beautiful I almost couldn't believe it. Everything Golden Rule became absolutely exceeded my wildest dreams. I genuinely thought moving beyond the screen, inviting some of you to my estate for Golden Weekend, was the natural next step.

There is always a price for getting everything you want.

[audio distortion/unacknowledged by subtitles]

While I was away, my app continued to thrive and evolve without me. A few new users broke engagement records that were never supposed to exist. Golden Rule stopped being a community and became a glorified popularity contest.

While I was away, I spent a lot of time thinking about the nature of expectations. Our lives follow patterns. We seek the familiar, and our brains make sense of it. It transforms what we see into something recognizable and digestible, even if that's not what it really is. It's comforting to know how something will go, how it will end. Everybody loves watching a train wreck because it's a guaranteed release. You see it coming, and then you see it burning.

[audio distortion/unacknowledged by subtitles]

I wasn't ever going to come back.

And then a very precious bespectacled beauty said to me, "Are you really going to leave without saying goodbye? You? Jewel Van Hanen?"

Me. Jewel Van Hanen.

[pauses and smiles]

Did you know today is White Day? Shall I give you chocolates, or would you like something much, much sweeter?

[pauses]

One more time. One more group. One more Golden Weekend. I will follow four users for three very different reasons.

Additional Video Notes by **SilentStar**

> *Jewel is sitting close to the camera. Torso completely in frame. Background is the Pink Room and appears to be unremarkable. Audio distortion*

appears at 00:02:47 and 00:03:20. No clues present in autogenerated or user-corrected subtitles. The video also appears to be edited, as several jump cuts are present throughout. Since Jewel is known for filming in one take, this is cause for documentation. Replies were disabled on the video.

PART I

SOME ASSEMBLY REQUIRED

*"When the world burns,
at least I'll die in comfort."*

—JEWEL VAN HANEN

SILENTSTAR

After school, Luna sat alone under her favorite tree on the front lawn, eating the rest of her lunch while waiting for her ride home.

And then she started choking.

Her mouth opened and closed like a fish gasping on land. She blinked in disbelief, eyes watering as she pulled at her collar. Air could get in, whistling past the lump of mush bulging in her throat, and luckily, it was just enough to keep her alive. She took a final breath, clenched her core muscles, pushed on her diaphragm, and coughed like her life depended on it. Because it did. She spit the food out into a napkin and collapsed on the grass next to her phone.

Really, eating and reading were two activities that Luna had no business doing at the same time. The girl simply was not built for that kind of multitasking. But in her defense? The gaspworthy news was *probably* worth dying for.

Jewel Van Hanen had finally returned to Golden Rule.

Everyone had speculated and wondered, but Luna *believed*.

She took a moment to relish the feeling of breathing. The crisp fading-winter air smelled like pine needles and felt just as sharp in her lungs. Sunlight streamed through the leaves, making shadows on her hands. The wind fluttered softly through her hair. She had half a mind to make a new video for Golden Rule and title it something like *Resurrection in Green* in honor of not choking to death and Jewel's return.

Videos on Golden Rule were technically called diary entries, and Luna's always kept her face in frame—the app wouldn't record otherwise—but she never spoke. Her silence got filled by the roaring wind on blustering days, the panging echoes of emptiness when her sister left her alone on weekends, the cacophony of her loud classmates, and the like. Crickets at the park were her costars on good days, as were the sounds of speeding cars while she stood on a bridge on bad days.

True to her screen name, Luna was *the* SilentStar of Golden Rule and one of the Founders of the Goldspiracy Forums.

A steady thrum of too much bass peeled around the corner. Luna rolled over, smiling as she packed up her stuff, and ran for the sidewalk.

Alex always drove like a getaway driver fleeing the scene of a bank heist—with a car full of money, riding the hubristic high of making it out alive. He'd never been late, never missed a day, and never slowed down in front of her school, choosing instead to come to a tire-screeching halt. Inside the car, Luna immediately turned back to her phone. The forum had gone feral with excitement when Jewel had announced Golden Weekend X—the tenth time she would host the event. And as promised, she had followed three of the four users:

JadeTheBabe
BelleLow
StreetcarBouvier

One. More. Spot. Left.

Luna could *not* let herself think about that because if she did, she would get her hopes up, and once they were up, they'd be inevitably shot down when she wasn't chosen. So, instead, she concentrated on her work.

The Goldspiracy was *real*—Luna had coined the term after figuring out *everything* Jewel did in the app had purpose. Her idol was also a low-key genius, planting clues and Easter eggs in all her videos, essentially challenging the community to figure them out without ever acknowledging any of it. Sometimes Jewel even roped in Olive, her bestie, and Ethan, her brother, by hiding clues in *their* videos too.

Most of her challenges could be solved with an internet search or two and strung together to create a message, but that wasn't the hard part. What stumped most was discovering the meaning *behind* the message using the Easter eggs.

No one on the Goldspiracy Forums was better at interpreting Jewel than SilentStar.

Alex cleared his throat, drawing Luna back into real life. She looked up, noticing for the first time that he hadn't sped off the way he normally did. The car idled, engine vibrating under her feet.

"Moon Princess," he said.

"Alex." She gave him her full attention, turning her phone face-down in her lap.

"Notice anything different about me?"

"No?"

"No? Nothing at all?" He lifted his chin, looking down his nose at her.

She assessed him quickly. Hair: same reddish-brown. Face: frustratingly smooth and blemish-free. Eyes: a little red for a likely reason Luna refused to even consider because she didn't want to think Alex would do that to her. Private school uniform: pressed and starchy.

The silence stretched between them. Nothing to say, nothing to add. She knew what he wanted, but held back . . .

"Nothing. At. All." Alex turned his head to the side—ah!

"You pierced your ear!"

A gold stud stood out beautifully against his dusky skin tone. "Ears," he said, showing her the other one. "I've been thinking about stretching. Gotta start small. What do you think? Do they look good?"

He checked his reflection in the rearview mirror for probably the umpteenth time.

Luna didn't feel one way or the other about it but liked that they seemed to make him happy. "Yeah. Sure."

"Yeah? Sure?" He scoffed as he put the car in drive. "Just recklessly breaking my heart, as always."

She laughed, shaking her head at him. "Your heart or your ego?"

"Same difference with me." He gave her the sly smile that could brighten the most terrible of days.

Alex claimed the honor of being the third person Luna had met after moving in with Tasha—her half sister from their dad's first marriage. He attended an elite private school on scholarship—sports and academic because he was amazing—but they lived in the same apartment complex. His mom, Cynthia, had volunteered him to be Luna's school chauffeur. If it bothered him, he never showed it.

"Did you skip school to get that done?" she asked.

"Hmmm?"

"You didn't have them this morning?"

"What?"

"Uh-huh. Your mom's going to kick you out." She grinned at him before looking at her phone again. Her smile didn't last, fading as she watched the number of her notifications continue to climb. Luna's mentions were in absolute shambles—inbox bursting with messages asking her thoughts, and she'd been tagged in literally hundreds of posts. The other Goldspiracy Founders were no different, speculating in their private chat and yelling for her to respond in all caps.

"*Threaten* to kick me out," he said. "There's a very loving difference in there."

They didn't live far from her school—about a twenty-minute drive. Alex pulled into their parking lot, finding a space in between their respective apartments. Painted a drab cream color with mellow brown accents, they weren't much to look at it. The interior of her apartment was even plainer—a tiny two-bedroom, one-bathroom apartment that cost more than it was worth, and yet the price went up every year.

Tasha had done her best to decorate with what she could find at thrift stores. The result was a mishmash of colors and styles that clashed horribly but still felt cozy. She loved pictures, filling the walls with a growing collage of prints of her friends, their family, and most important, her and Luna together. Selfies, stills from videos, the experimental portraits shot for fun at a park one day—almost every photo they had ever taken together eventually ended up on the wall.

When Luna's mom had decided she didn't want to be a mom anymore, Tasha had said, "Look, I don't know how to be anybody's parent, but I think I can be a guardian. I can do that." Two weeks later, twelve-year-old Luna had moved in with her half sister, who was a whole ten years older.

And it had changed Luna's whole life.

As usual, Tasha was at work or school or both and had left a note on the fridge.

Warm up one of the frozen lasagnas for dinner.
It'll take about an hour to cook. Home by eleven ♥

Luna folded the paper in half, sticking it in her pocket for safe-keeping until she could put it in her journal with the other notes she'd saved, and then, messaged Tasha.

Luna: HOME!!!!! OH AND
JEWEL'S BACK! AHHHH!!!

"Lasagna tonight," she said, placing it in the oven.

"Amazing," Alex said. "Your room or the couch?"

Luna sighed quietly, thinking of the "concerned" texts she'd gotten from his girlfriend, Melody. It was funny because Melody *was* nice, like, seriously on par with a Disney Princess. But something about Alex spending *every* afternoon at Luna's house upset her.

Eventually, Melody decided it would just be best to meet "woman to woman." At the end of their talk—which wasn't so much a conversation as being forced to listen to Melody for twenty minutes—Luna had promised to abide by the "Girlfriend Boundary."

She didn't understand it. But she promised.

"Couch," she said.

By the time she joined him, he'd already dumped all his homework on the coffee table for show. He never actually did any of it when he was with her, usually choosing to watch anime on his phone instead. She sat next to him, deciding to close the forums and open Golden Rule.

A sparkling golden background filled the screen. At the bottom, a progress bar began to fill from left to right while a thin black line drew a prismatic oval on a stand. Gold faded into white, and two options appeared: CREATE AN ACCOUNT or SIGN IN. Watching the app load calmed her like it always did. She'd found it and Jewel during the darkest moment of her life, and to this day, they both continued to soothe her anxious nerves just by existing.

Since she never spoke in her videos, Luna's Golden Rule inbox had remained blissfully empty. Most users knew she'd never reply. Videos tagged #GoldenWeekendXChallenge clogged the front page—users were already shooting their shots by the thousands because Jewel still hadn't followed the fourth user.

No one knew the specifics of what happened at Golden Weekend, but it was common knowledge that Jewel swooped in like a fairy godmother, granting every attendee one wish. When they left her estate, suddenly they all had enough money for college. Or they could quit their job to pursue their dream career. Or they started traveling around the world, posting pictures of their adventures.

In exchange, the attendees had been forbidden from publicly talking about their time with Jewel. Even more scandalous than that?

They all had to leave Golden Rule by a specified date. No warning, no goodbye video—they just abandoned their accounts and platforms.

Luna always got goose bumps thinking about it. Golden Rule meant *everything* to her, but she'd give it up, her Goldspiracy Forums too, for a chance to meet Jewel and use her wish for Tasha. But that was never going to happen.

"How's your brain?" Alex asked.

"In my skull and functional," she answered with a curious smile.

"Oh?" he teased. "But Jewel's back, right? Must be a big day for you."

"The biggest," she said. "She isn't going to pick me, though. She probably doesn't even know I exist."

"Uhhh, don't you have over a hundred thousand voyeurs? I'm sure she knows you," Alex said.

Jewel had decreed that since videos were diary entries, it made the most sense for followers to be called voyeurs. Luna *loved* that—those tiny touches of Jewel's creativity and personality.

"I seriously doubt it. Everyone who's ever been invited to Golden Weekend is exceptional in some way."

"You're exceptional," Alex said, sounding offended. "No one on that app can hold a candle to you."

"You don't understand," she said, shaking her head. "You don't use the app, so you don't get it. I'm not putting myself down or anything like that. Promise."

Jewel had clear favorites on Golden Rule—the users she replied to almost always had their videos promoted to the front page. She'd never done that for Luna. Not even once.

But Luna refused to let herself dwell on that. Mostly. Besides, it all played into the Goldspiracy, so in a way, she was a part of Jewel's plan too. Sort of. Kind of.

Anyway.

Objectively speaking, the users Jewel singled out had a natural camera-ready radiance about them. She had chosen to amplify their platform because of it, often using their videos in ads to promote the app. And then one by one, they all received invitations.

Luna thought back to Jewel's announcement video: *One more time. One more group. One more Golden Weekend. I will follow four users for three very different reasons.* It was the same story, the same challenge, but with different players. She continued, "Want to hear my theory for the GWX Follows? I haven't posted it yet."

"You know I love being first. Lay it on me," he said, and then quickly added, "*I* still think you're exceptional, by the way."

"Okay, so, JadeTheBabe was an obvious choice. During Jewel's sabbatical, Nicole, that's her real name, became the most followed person on the app, second only to Jewel herself in less than six months. Her rise to the top *without* being promoted by the Golden Rule staff in any way blew everyone else out of the water. No one can figure out how she did it, but on the other hand no one really cares because she's an *absolute* superstar in the making. If I were Jewel, I'd be dying to meet Nicole too.

"Next is BelleLow. This one is a little tricky because while she's a well-known quicksilver—meaning she talks *incredibly* fast in one continuous take—in the past, she made anti-Jewel posts under a different username. A lot of people don't know that." Luna scrunched her face in discomfort.

"But you do," Alex said with a laugh.

"Of course. It's like my job to know." Her phone chimed—a new Golden Rule notification. She picked up her phone and navigated to her inbox, practically on autopilot. "I haven't told anyone that I know, and I'm on the fence about outing her. I don't really want that kind of spotlight on *me* right now. People can change, you know? Maybe she did?"

"You're way kinder than me," he said. "And number three?"

Luna took a deep breath. "No clue," she admitted. "StreetcarBouvier only has one video, and it wasn't even that good. Interestingly, she joined the app two days ago, which I think is key. I just need a bit more time. I'll figure it out eventuALLY OH MY GOD!" She threw her phone at him like it was on fire, yelping like a startled puppy.

"*What!? What is it?*"

"M-m-m-message! Message!" She pointed at the phone as he picked it up.

One new video message: from Jewel Van Hanen.

Alex grinned, mischievously evil and triumphant, as he pressed PLAY.

"*Through all your researching and rewatching, and posting and predicting, did it ever occur to you that I might be watching you back? Hello, Luna.*

"*In any case, you have proven yourself worthy. You are hereby invited to Golden Weekend. Please use the links below to access your invitation, read the terms and conditions, complete your paperwork, and enter your contact information. An agent will be in touch shortly to arrange your travel—all expenses paid, of course.*

"*I hope you're able to accept. I'm very much looking forward to meeting you.*

"*Oh, and because you're only fifteen, my lawyers would like for you to bring a chaperone. Preferably eighteen or older, but we can accept sixteen if you both have parental approval.*"

JadeTheBabe

Outside at 3:40 A.M., the cold air bit at Nicole just like every-thing else. Shoulders hunched near her ears, she speed-walked to her car, work apron hanging out of her coat pocket.

"Off to work?" a voice asked.

If Nicole were a different person, she would've jumped out of her skin. Instead she unlocked her car while turning her head to say, "Yeah," and placed a finger on the trigger of her key-ring pepper spray.

Her neighbors two doors down, three dudes who shared an apart-ment, seemed to have parties every night. And one of them always magically seemed to be outside when she left for her early-morning shifts. This one, Fred, had the look of a stereotypical small-town mechanic—greasy everything, tan skin smudged with oil and grime, and just handsome and tall enough to make you think about him twice.

An evolutionary and genetic mistake designed to get you caught up.

"Oh wow, you're actually talking to me today," he said.

"Not really." She opened her door.

"Can I ask you something?"

One foot in. "As long as you stay over there."

"Harsh." But he laughed. "I know you're not cool coming to our parties, which I totally respect, but my sister is having a get-together at a restaurant for her birthday. I thought you might want to come."

His sister, Daphne, was the only decent thing about him. They'd met by accident in the laundry room and hit it off immediately. Unfortunately, getting close to girls who had skeevy brothers was always a tragedy waiting to happen.

A tragedy of the "Well, what were you wearing?" variety.

Besides, Dinner Parties cost at least thirty dollars and some were shady, making everyone split the check equally regardless of what they ordered. Disposable income was a thing for other people to enjoy. The bulk of her money went to her astronomical rent—a studio apartment in a decent-ish part of town that cost nearly 70 percent of her total pay per month.

"I can't. Just paid my rent, and I kind of want to stay home to enjoy my purchase."

Fred nodded, still watching her as she slid into her seat, closing and locking the door immediately. He kept watching as she started the car, placed her phone in its holder, and reversed out of her space.

"Creep." Nicole frowned as she turned the heater on full blast. Her phone chimed—someone had sent her a private message on Golden Rule.

Except that should have been impossible.

Nicole had disabled her inbox the second she broke five hundred voyeurs. If they wanted to talk to her, it had to be public. Every interaction, upload, decision, and move she made inside Golden Rule had to count toward engagement. JadeTheBabe didn't become the most followed account on the app by sheer luck.

Well, being fair, of course luck and timing had a little something to do with it, but everything else? That was all Nicole.

And now Jewel Van Hanen had sent her a message.

Nicole waited until she reached a red stoplight and clicked on it. She passively watched the video—Jewel gushing about how much she loved JadeTheBabe's videos before inviting her to an all-expenses-paid trip, Golden Weekend X.

When it was over, Nicole didn't even have to think about her answer. She pressed the RECORD button, right then and there, and filmed her quick reply: "No, thanks."

Salty Sea & Co operated twenty-four hours a day, rain or shine or holiday, but the lobby didn't open until 6:00 A.M. When Nicole arrived at work, she rang the bell and waited to be let in.

Her coworker and friend, Charlie, grinned when he saw her. An absolute mess of inky black curls, even darker eyes, and a riot of color on his pale, tattooed arms, he ran from behind the counter toward the door. "Password," he said through the glass.

"My nipples are about to fall off." She laughed at the face he made.

"For the record," he said, holding the door open, "I don't ever want to hear about your nipples."

"They're a normal part of the human body." She shrugged. "You know I poop too, right? Because I poop. All the time."

"Ahh! Stop! My toxic masculine sensibilities can't handle knowing that!" he yelled, running back toward the drive-through window. "Thank you for choosing Salty Sea & Co—how can I help you on this beautiful, dark morning?"

No one was smoother with the mic switch than Charlie. One second, he could be telling the raunchiest not-safe-for-work joke in existence, and the next he'd take an order with enough customer service shine to get a five-dollar tip on a three-dollar drink. They'd met at Salty Sea. She helped get him an interview at Chloe's Country Diner—her evening waitressing gig—and he landed the job all on his own. Now they saw each other just about every day, twice a day and more if they could make it work.

Nicole swapped her jacket for her apron and clocked in. "No manager today?" She cleaned her headset with a disinfectant wipe and slid it on.

"On our own till seven," he said while pouring milk into a pitcher to steam it.

"Nice."

"I know, right? I'm starting to think they schedule us like this on purpose. We're too trustworthy."

"I want a raise, then. Manager duties means manager pay."

"I'll let you talk to Bri about that."

"Nah, I'll just call the labor board. I know my rights."

"And that's why you're the brains of our operation."

"Don't get smart with me." She side-eyed him. If they had an operation, Charlie would be the brains, not her, and they both knew it. She leaned more toward the savvy side of life—observant with a good instinct for figuring out how things (and people) worked.

"You say that like I have a choice." He leaned against the counter next to her while the espresso shots pulled. "You look tired."

"Am tired. Am." Between near-constant nightmares, working two jobs, and school, her body had defied physics, figuring out how to run on fumes, and it always showed.

"Oh, I watched your video. That shit was fucking hilarious."

"I know." Nicole pulled her phone from her apron pocket. They weren't supposed to use their phones on shift, but their store had an unofficial rule. As long as customers didn't see it, no one else did. "I designed it that way."

"Humble, as always." He laughed, finishing the latte. At the window, he handed it off and then made his way back to her. "You made it to Twitter."

Nicole's mood perked up immediately. She had a lot of loyal voyeurs on the other side of the planet who gave her delightful early-morning surprises—like helping her go viral within hours of posting a new video.

Conquering Golden Rule had taken time. Before posting her first video, Nicole had spent about a month researching the platform. She read the terms and conditions twice, inadvertently memorized the script for the welcome video, decoded how the replies played into the system, took notes on the more popular users and their stats, and most important, watched every video the app suggested.

Golden Rule's algorithm never stood a chance.

Her phone chimed again. Another message from Jewel:

It's cute how you think you have a choice.

Nicole blinked at the screen, laughing in disbelief. Rumors about how unhinged Jewel was still floated around the app, even though she'd mysteriously disappeared from it, and the public eye, a year ago. Her legacy had already been cemented—Jewel Van Hanen would always be known for founding and creating Golden Rule, one of the most popular video-sharing apps in history.

Charlie hovered over her shoulder. "That is wild. I can't believe she's really back. I'm not surprised you got an invite to Golden Weekend X, though."

"I'm not going. I graciously declined."

He flicked her forearm. "No," he said, with the full conviction of being right. "You didn't."

"Yes, I did, because something is seriously wrong with her."

"You know what they say," Charlie teased. "She sold her soul to the devil for fame, joined the Illuminati, is the Antichrist who decided to focus on social media instead of politics."

"Hmm, you said it, not 'they.'"

"No, but seriously, you need to go. You have to."

"I don't."

"Why not? This is an opportunity of a lifetime. It could be your big break. Isn't that the point of all this?"

Nicole turned her phone off, placing it back in her pocket. "One: I can't miss work. Two: I don't trust her. Three—"

"One," Charlie interrupted. "You can miss work if you get coverage, which I will find for you. Two: Of course you can't trust her, but that doesn't mean you can't use her connections."

"Three: If I do go, which I'm not, I'll get there and she'll probably force us to fight to the death and broadcast the whole thing on some new app. Didn't you watch her announcement video? She's high-key pissed and not exactly trying to hide it."

For Nicole, an integral part of learning how to be an actress had been figuring out how to read people and how to trust her instincts. She couldn't mimic what she didn't understand, and she had understood Jewel loud and clear.

"Why do you always have to be so dramatic?" Charlie asked with a surprisingly straight face. She was a theater major—drama was what she did. "She wouldn't do something like that. She'd go straight to jail."

"Until her money bails her out and she flees the country. Consequences don't exist for rich people." Not to mention, Jewel would probably end up surrendering herself to make some kind of warped martyr statement about fame. "Meanwhile, I'm still dead."

"If that did happen, there's no way you'd die." He laughed. "Anyway, she's still Black, even though people like to think she isn't. The government would put her under the jail just to make a point. Having money doesn't change that."

Sometimes, Charlie's woke-white-boy routine made Nicole uncomfortable—like a sucker punch in the stomach. He was right, but that didn't mean she wanted to hear him say it. Still, she couldn't shake the feeling that she was right too. Something about Golden Weekend X seemed . . . *off*. Her instincts, her brain, and her heart were all solid as a doomsday meteor in agreement: Something bad would happen if she went to that house. And she'd had enough misfortune and tragedy to last her several lifetimes, thank you very much.

"Maybe not a fight to the death, but Jewel has to be planning something," she said. "Why in the hell would she bring four strangers to her house to just hang out? If you really stop to think about it, you'd realize none of this makes sense." She sighed. "And finally, four: I absolutely cannot miss work, because I need the money."

"Four: Well—we'll figure that out."

"Nothing to figure out because I'm not going."

"Five," he said, standing in front of her. He was impressively a few inches taller than her towering six foot one, looking down into her eyes. "You work too hard. That's literally all you do. You deserve a break. A couple of days won't hurt you."

Nicole gently pushed his shoulder—her sign that she wanted space.

He stepped back immediately and said, "If I can't cover your shifts, then I'll find someone to cover mine so I can work yours."

"Charlie. No."

"Nicole. Yes. I want you to go. I have a good feeling about this."

The drive-through signal beeped in their ears.

"I got it," he said, hitting his mic switch.

The morning became a flurry of pastries, warmed breakfast sandwiches, and coffee with too much syrup and not enough milk for Nicole's liking. Staff were allowed one drink and one food item for free per shift—thank the corporate coffee gods—so she scarfed down what would probably be her only meal for the day on her lunch break. After work, she drove to the library and found a window-facing table in a quiet back corner of the reference section to work on the essay for her economics class.

Midday coming off a night with little to no sleep liked to kill her. She popped a caffeine pill and rolled her neck to work out some of the kinks, while pulling her supplies out of her bag. Her hand brushed something soft—a sandwich from Salty Sea.

Charlie.

He'd given her his free sandwich and snuck it into her bag before his shift ended. Smiling, she sent him a quick thank-you text and then stared at her phone.

Six missed calls from a number she didn't recognize that had called once every fourteen minutes. The only people who had the audacity to assume she'd answer the phone were bill collectors, but she wasn't behind on anything. Yet.

Charlie: I have no idea what you're talking about but you're welcome anyway

Nicole yawned as she opened her laptop. She'd set the wallpaper to the last picture she'd taken with her parents before they died—a quick and easy serotonin boost she relied on every day. It never hurt to look at pictures of them. Instead of the cold ache of grief, warm light filled her heart. They were with her, always, in everything that she did and would do. Dead but never gone, their legacy would live through her.

Her phone vibrated again, and she exhaled in an annoyed huff. Not even telemarketers were that insistent. Hesitantly, she answered, bringing the phone to her ear and listening before saying, "Hello?"

"Hello, Jade."

Her eyebrows hit her hairline. She recognized the voice, the same greeting and tone and cadence from the video invitation, but her brain made her ask anyway, "Who is this?"

"Jewel Van Hanen, but I'm sure you're smart enough to already have figured that out."

"How did you get my number?"

"But also not smart enough to not ask that question." Jewel sighed. "Really, Jade, I promise the surprised act isn't necessary. Let's just skip to the good part, okay?"

"My name isn't Jade," she said with a laugh.

"I'm aware," Jewel said. "Such an *interesting* choice for a username. Jewel. Jade. A purely coincidental perfectly matching pair."

Nicole looked over her shoulder, worried. Librarians could be sneaky when they wanted. One would appear and ask her to take her call outside while also volunteering to watch her stuff. Good wholesome eggs, all of them.

"What do you want?"

Jewel laughed. "I'd like to think I'm being quite obvious here—I don't just want you at X. I need you. Opportunity is knocking: What will it take to make you say yes? I hope it's not something as trivial as money."

"*Trivial?*" Nicole scoffed. "Only someone with enough money to buy a country would say something like that."

"Not true. I'm in the camp that believes money can and will absolutely buy happiness. But I also have a knack for people. Sure, I could give you a million dollars, but then what? The thing about money is that once you have it, your ambitions will either become front and center or die of neglect until you go broke and get desperate again. When I watch your videos, I can see how hungry you are. Every inch of you is starving under those characters you insist on playing."

Nicole's hand began to tighten around her phone.

Jewel had struck a very frayed and fragile nerve. She continued, "Tell me, whose app do you think you're using? Golden Rule made you because of how I designed it. It's successful because it forces people into accountability. I ripped anonymity away and made them wear their true faces. If I delete your account, do you honestly believe you'll be as successful starting over on another platform? That you'll be able to cope with the literal thousands of anonymous hate comments, insults, and death threats that I can guarantee you'll get?"

Being Black on the internet could be a dangerous game. Black and female and fat and outspoken—the odds had never been in Nicole's favor. Not until she'd found Golden Rule, where the users had to show their faces, and hate speech and bullying were banned. Finally, there'd been a way for her to safely grow her platform, to let her talent speak.

The plastic phone case dug into Nicole's palm, her fingers bending against the hard screen. What would it take to crack it? She could *not* afford another one. Breathing in and out with deep inhales and long exhales, she forced herself to relax.

Every day her life felt like it was controlled by someone, something else. If her jobs cut her hours, she couldn't pay her rent, and she'd get evicted. If she didn't get financial aid, she wouldn't be able to go to school, and she'd never be able to get a degree to get a better job.

Growing up had been coated in an illusion of autonomy and sold to the highest bidder.

Nothing belonged to her.

Nothing.

Nothing except her videos and her platform. She created those on her own, and they meant everything to her. But Golden Rule had been an illusion too.

Jewel had her number, all right, and seemed hell-bent on pushing those buttons until they broke. Nicole closed her eyes. Focusing on her breathing, she pushed the feelings of despair always lurking at her edges back into their corners.

She would *not* let Jewel get the best of her.

She would *not* let Jewel make her feel desperate too.

Leaning into her calm, Nicole said, "I know you're used to people throwing themselves at you, doing whatever you want, but the world doesn't actually work that way. I'm not going to disrupt my entire life because you say so."

"Maybe you didn't hear me the first time," Jewel said. "I hate repeating myself, but I'll do it just this once for you. I *need* you. There's no Golden Weekend X without the *Reigning Superstar of Golden Rule: The Six-Foot, Plus-Size Beauty Queen.* That article was brilliant. I'd noticed you before—it would have been impossible not to—but that article sealed it for me."

Nicole rolled her eyes. A few weeks ago, a journalist had contacted her to do a feature and that was the title they went with. The reporter asked if she had ever modeled before (most people did, really), and she'd made the mistake of telling him about the one local pageant she had entered and won. But the reporter had also christened her the "wildly unpredictable and talented love child of Kristen Wiig and Eddie Murphy" and called her impressions "sublime," so she decided to forgive him. If her sketches landed her an audition for *SNL*, she'd give him her firstborn child.

The only downside to Golden Rule was it paid in social capital. She couldn't survive on exposure, but she'd invested in the app to create a highlight reel as a means to sell her one-woman show.

Jewel spoke slowly, enunciating each word with careful, measured precision. "What will it take to make you say yes?"

Outside, the sun shone on the trees and grass. Cars drove up and down the street. Kids ran around the small playground.

And inside, Nicole stared at the picture of her parents, phone pressed to her face, heart beating quietly inside her chest.

StreetcarBouvier

Stella watched the invitation from Jewel Van Hanen in stunned silence.

There was no way in hell her parents would let her go to Golden Weekend X. The name alone suggested debauchery of the highest order.

"I have to convince them. I *have* to. There simply isn't an alternative." Stella rolled off her bed and began pacing the length of her bedroom. "What do you think, Asriel? Should I go for it?"

Resting in his oversized bed, her ancient and lovable bloodhound turned his drooping, baleful eyes on her. He made a soft *woof*, which obviously meant *girl, don't do it.*

"You know, it costs you nothing to humor me," she said, beginning to pace again. "How can you expect me to let this amazing opportunity slip through my fingers? I owe it to myself to try, right? Even if they say no, which in all likelihood they will, I'll regret not giving it my all."

To that, Asriel had nothing to say.

"I'm going to Golden Weekend X," Stella said with finality and purpose. "There, I've said it. I've put it out there. So be it. See to it. Let's do this."

Downstairs, her parents were in the middle of making dinner. They *always* made dinner together, every night, as if it were a date.

Soft jazz music floated from the kitchen, and Stella smelled the tomato sauce simmering on the stove before she even got to the door.

"Parental units," she said, waltzing into the kitchen with her tablet, content to ruin their moment. She stopped in front of them on the other side of the island.

"*What* did I say about calling us that?" Lloyd said. Stella had inherited her beady eye shape and poor vision from him. He wore rounded, thin metal-framed glasses that always slipped down the bridge of his nose. He also had an exceptionally loud face—the only thing on the planet that could make her shut up in midsentence.

"Starting today, I promise to banish it from my lexicon," she said. "I have an announcement to make."

"*Aht, aht*, before you do anything, have you finished your schoolwork?" Diane asked. Stella favored her—same height, same shining brown skin, same shoulder-length microlocs that they'd gotten installed at the same time—and no one would have any doubts about their genetic lineage.

She held back her grumbling complaint. "Yes."

"And you finished unpacking your room?" Lloyd asked.

"Also, yes," she lied with a brilliant smile.

They had moved into their shiny new house that resembled every other house on their shiny new suburban block a week ago. Lloyd worked remotely 90 percent of the time, allowing Diane to follow her nonfiction author dreams across the country, dragging Stella along for the nightmarish ride. Always moving and always being the weird new girl on the block who never goes outside, never having roots, never being allowed to do anything, never having a life that felt like her own.

Until today.

"Want to try that again?" Lloyd had begun to use the rolling pin on the dough.

"I'm *working* on it. Unpacking is a very delicate process. It can't be rushed," Stella said. "But I promise I will finish soon."

"Two promises back-to-back?" Diane asked with an amused, knowing smile. "You only do that when you want something."

Lloyd asked, "All right, what is it, kiddo?"

"I've been invited to a special event. A very exclusive, very safe event," Stella said. Time to pop the Golden question. She propped her tablet up on the counter between them so they could watch the personalized invitation video Jewel Van Hanen had sent.

A steady, nervous ticking counted down in Stella's brain, winding up her intestines into something wholly recognizable as fear. Exactly thirty seconds into the video, Diane's contrary gaze flicked up to Stella. And when it ended, her parents exchanged a look: Diane shook her head, and Lloyd sucked his teeth.

"Letting me go to Golden Weekend should be well within legal limits," Stella said. "Jewel has an extensive security detail in place, and the flight is four hours each way, which gives me plenty of time to do my homework and extra studies while trapped in a metal tube at an ungodly altitude."

Diane's gaze evolved into something dedicated to being unreasonable.

Stella continued, "The attached email said you can schedule a meeting to talk to Jewel or her lawyers if you need to."

"Lawyers?" Of course, that caught Lloyd's attention.

"I have to sign a nondisclosure agreement to prevent me selling the raunchy details of my weekend to some scummy news site—I'm kidding! About the raunchy part, not the NDA. I do have to sign that."

"No," Lloyd said. "Absolutely not."

"What? Why?" Stella had to watch herself—she couldn't appear too disappointed. Lloyd hated whining and wouldn't tolerate petulance. A temper tantrum would win her less than nothing. She needed to spin the conversation in a different way. "You're always saying I need to get out more instead of lazing about in the house," she said, shifting again. "This is out!"

"We meant taking the dog for a walk," Lloyd said. "Not crossing state lines."

"Going outside reminds me of all the things I'm not allowed to have," Stella said, sharpening her honesty into a shank. "Oh wait. Sorry. I forgot I'm not supposed to bring that up. But you know me, I'm always up for a spirited debate about my rights to have a social life."

"You know the rules." Lloyd sighed.

Her parents had rules for *everything*.

Studies came first—homeschool studies, to be specific. Her internet usage, email, and bank account were all monitored. No sports, no clubs, no TV, and no friends to distract her from the goals they'd set. The only reason she'd been allowed to use Golden Rule (for thirty minutes, every other day) was because her therapist, Joan, had made the recommendation and put in the work to convince her parents.

The app advertised itself as a video-sharing platform that gave users an opportunity to tell their stories, like a virtual diary. Extremely community driven, Joan hoped it would give Stella a place to express herself as well as make friends in a safe environment, because Golden Rule was like Big Brother on steroids.

All facets were heavily monitored. Users were required to show their faces in their videos, it had a strict zero-tolerance policy for hate speech and bullying, and users were warned nothing on the app was truly private. Followers had even been dubbed "voyeurs" to ratchet up the cult factor.

Stella had used her first thirty-minute allotment to make the obligatory welcome video, choosing the same username she always did—StreetcarBouvier. It had come from a joke she made one day when her English tutor showed her a cartoon as a fun way to examine parodies and transformative works. Fifteen minutes ago, she'd logged in and had received her very first message: an invitation to Golden Weekend.

"Indeed I do, Daddy-o," Stella said, "which is why I never ask for anything—"

"You ask for things all the time," Diane said.

"Yeah, but you never say yes, so those things don't count." Stella pretended to wave the "things" away with her hand. "Clean slate. This trip could be the one you finally say yes to and make all my newly formed dreams come true. It's literally a trip of a lifetime. Think back to when you were a kid, decades and decades ago—didn't you have a favorite celebrity you would've voluntarily given up some of your rights to hang out with?"

Diane's frown miraculously softened; however, Lloyd continued to be an immovable iceberg, saying, "You didn't even know who this Jewel girl was before two days ago."

"That's beside the point," Stella said, also waving that away.

"If that's beside the point, then what is the point?" Lloyd asked sharply.

Stella nearly flinched at her misstep. Damn. No one else could make her sweat like her dad. He kept her on her toes so much, they should've been permanently bruised by now. She was losing them. Her tiny battleship had barely been in the water ten minutes, and it already had a gaping hole in the bottom, water flooding in to kill her crew and her freedom-tinted dreams. But she refused to let her despair leak into her argument. Fists next to her thighs, she pressed them into her body, thinking and making and discarding ways to turn the conversation in her favor as fast as her brain would allow.

A weekend away without her parents and with people her age—people who could maybe even become her *friends*—that's what mattered to Stella. She couldn't tell them about the way her heart leaped and her hands shook when she got the video invite from Jewel. She didn't trust them to understand how scared and nervous and excited she was to meet the other Golden Follows. The sheer ache of possibility nearly left her breathless. If her parents knew the real reason she wanted to go, they'd never agree.

Unless.

Perhaps.

She *did* make it about Jewel.

"Life experience," she countered, argument forming at the speed of light. "As in, I don't have any."

31

When they didn't respond, instead exchanging another look that resembled confusion, Stella continued, "Think of the college personal-essay material this could potentially give me. Everyone else is going to write about their community service or well-spun tales of their family histories or how being on a rowing team taught them indispensable lessons about teamwork, while we all know they were never on that team to begin with. I can't match that. All I have is I've moved around a lot and studied so hard my brain mass increased.

"But if I write about spending a highly publicized weekend with a famous recluse who built an empire before she turned twenty-one?" She stared at the stove for a moment, giving her brain time to squeeze out some raw potential. "From what I've researched, Jewel had a hard time in school and barely graduated before striking it rich in the acting game. Then she bankrolled that success with her family's money to create a start-up that led to a probable billion-dollar company. Check this out: "The Fame Monster: The Importance of Being Educated." Who is she really? A puppet or a self-made genius? And how did knowing that and meeting her in the house that social-media technology built affect me and my goals for the future." Stella took a calming breath. "It's a little rough, but give me time. Like, say a whole weekend to gather inspiration and source material."

Diane sipped her wine, eyeing Lloyd. "That would be a compelling and unique subject for an essay."

Dear God, I'm amazing, Stella thought, careful to keep her smugness off her face. She had just struck golden-plated familial pay dirt, wholly by accident.

Lloyd worked at a law firm specializing in criminal and entertainment law but was also a published author of bestselling supernatural crime novels. Diane, a prolific writer with several nonfiction books under her belt and more on the way, moonlighted as a visiting creative writing professor at whatever university paid her fee and was near her current research subject.

Of course they'd want their only child to follow in their authorial footsteps.

But then Lloyd said, "You've never traveled alone before. That's too far for your first time."

And Diane immediately waffled. "And we don't know anything about this Jewel girl or her home. I don't think I would be comfortable with you staying there without us."

Stella pasted an amicable smile on her face while her brain screamed, *DAMN IT*, and decided to go for broke. Hit them right in the parental feels. "You know, if it doesn't work as an essay, I could always try my hand at writing a book. Keep the family business going, and all that."

"*Oh*," Diane said, surprised, as if the thought hadn't occurred to her. She looked to Lloyd.

Stella set Diane in her sights. "We could even work on my book together," she said. "You *have* been saying we need to have more mother-daughter time, and your expertise would be invaluable."

"That'd be wonderful," Diane said softly.

Lloyd *hmph*-ed, powerless in the face of his love's hopeful, wide-eyed look. "Well. I can't remember the last time I've seen you this hype about something, Stella. Other than getting a cat—"

"Still want that," Stella said quickly.

"And getting on our nerves," he finished with a rare, teasing smile.

"Hey, when I do that it's out of love. And boredom," Stella said. "Clearly I'm crying out for stimulation, which this fabulous all-expenses-paid Golden Weekend will provide me with. Joan would agree with me. Maybe we should call her. I think this constitutes a family emergency."

Her parents exchanged another look. "Okay. We'll talk to the lawyer," Diane said. Lloyd looked away, a heavy sigh of defeat filling his chest.

"Soooooo, that's a yes? I can go?"

"It's a maybe," Diane said.

"A strong maybe?"

"A regular one. We'll talk to them."

Stella had to grab the counter to stay upright and still. Was this what happiness felt like? She marveled at the burst of lightness in her chest and the extra energy making her want to jump up and down and dance. She'd won. They'd actually listened, and she'd convinced them—what a concept.

Lloyd said, "If the call goes well, you can go, but you will not be going alone."

"But I—"

"That part is nonnegotiable. I don't want to hear it. Either we go with you or you don't go at all."

PART II

SATISFACTION GUARANTEED

"I find it funny that when I tell people I'm building an empire they laugh awkwardly, as if they don't have the heart to tell me I'm delusional. It genuinely tickles me when people don't take me seriously."

—JEWEL VAN HANEN

THE WINERY
AT MIDNIGHT

THURSDAY, 11:45 P.M.

S ettled in a quiet nook straddling the line between Sonoma and St. Helena, California, with green rolling hills and barely treaded trails, their destination was surrounded by acres of grapevines and clusters of trees dense enough to be pocket forests.

The car slowed to a near crawl down the gravel road, symmetrically and systematically lined with tall trees on either side. Overhead, their bare branches reached out across the divide, interlocking as if they conspired to block out the moon. But someone had taken the time to decorate each tree trunk with a spiral of white lights to ensure the dark wouldn't win.

Luna rested her forehead against the chilled window and muttered, "I could walk faster than this."

"Too dark. Too cold," Alex said. They'd barely slept on the plane, too hopped up on excitement, complimentary soda, and cookies. He was fading fast now. Close to midnight, his eyes looked bleary and unfocused. "Which house is this?"

"Winery." Luna hadn't been 100 percent sure where they would spend the weekend until they'd driven through the towering main gates.

The Winery at Midnight.

A moment so iconic the Founders were boiling with jealousy, flooding the group chat with keysmashes, and rage and crying emoji.

Jewel had multiple houses sprinkled here and there across America, and Golden Weekend had always rotated locations, seemingly at random. As far as Luna knew, and she knew quite a bit, it had never been hosted at the Van Hanen Winery.

The Founders had theorized it was off the table because it was the most well-known and personal to Jewel.

Luna continued, "It's her family's house. She grew up here. In one of her early videos she said it 'had been built to function as an overbearing display of Van Hanen wealth.' Direct quote."

Alex wrinkled his nose. "I hope she's not as pretentious as she sounds."

Was it possible to grow up on an actual estate and be down-to-earth? To go to private school, star in hit TV shows and blockbuster movies, and still be a normal, unaffected person? Probably not. But Jewel tried her best anyway. That counted.

"She's not," Luna said, confident in her beliefs. "She just talks like that for the camera, I think."

Aerial shots of the winery were easy enough to find online. A few interior ones of the mansion too, if someone knew where to look, which Luna would never *intentionally* do . . .

So, technically, it wasn't her fault the images ended up on Goldspiracy or that she clicked on them without realizing. And then kept clicking, because what was the point in pretending that she hadn't seen them when she had. Damage was done.

Before, during, and after construction, the mansion had been dubbed the heart of the entire estate, with its three levels, seventeen bedrooms, an excessive number of bathrooms, two kitchens, a massive ballroom, two libraries, several dens, storage rooms, and a sprawling attic. And that's just what was on paper.

Rumor had it that the blueprints mysteriously didn't match the actual layout.

Luna was sure she'd die if she didn't get into that house soon. Was dying of anticipation an actual thing? Could be, judging by the pulsating pains in her chest and back and arms, her sweaty palms, and the way she couldn't stop fidgeting. It was like she'd touched a live current and all that extra energy decided to take its slow time zipping and zapping its way through her body instead of killing her outright.

When the car finally rolled to a stop, the driver wasted no time hopping out and slamming the door behind him.

"Guess this is us," Alex said, smiling a little. "Ready?"

Luna nodded, adjusting the giant gray wool scarf around her neck, pulling it up near her jaw. She tucked her chin inside, so the edge stopped right under her nose, inhaled, and held her breath for five seconds. It still smelled like Tasha. She hoped the scent would last the weekend. After Luna had picked which scarf she wanted to borrow, she'd gone to town spraying her sister's perfume on it.

Sometimes, she got a little overwhelmed. A lot overwhelmed, actually. A while back Tasha had helped her figure out a couple of ways to calm herself down. Writing or making lists worked sometimes. Squeezing stress balls or running in place could get the job done. Her best bet was usually comforting smells, like Tasha's perfume. If home and safety and rainbows had a smell, it would be her.

The driver opened Luna's door and offered a gloved hand to help her out of the massive SUV—she took it and jumped to reach the ground. Alex slid across the seat behind her. She watched him, not at all jealous of his long legs. Not one bit. Whatsoever.

Alex asked, "Why are you frowning?"

"I'm not." She was.

He leaned in close. "It's your happiest place on Earth. No frowning allowed."

"Then stop being so tall," she muttered.

She loved Alex's laugh. All of them, really. This one was a closed-mouth chuckle, knocking around low in his throat. "I'm not tall. You're just tragically short."

"I am not! I'm still growing. There's still hope."

"Sure," he said. "Anything's possible."

The driver said, "Your instructions are to wait here with the others. Your bags will be brought inside for you." He nodded toward three people standing at the foot of the porch with a considerable amount of stone steps.

When Luna realized she hadn't seen pictures of the steps before, her breath caught in her throat. It was real—the house with giant double doors and curtained windows, the illuminated courtyard, the beautiful fountain and its tinkling water and underwater lights—everything was *real*. She wasn't dreaming in lucid, vivid Technicolor. Her gaze traveled up, up, up toward the roof and then to the left until she reached the edge of the house. She turned to Alex to make sure he was seeing what she was, to really make sure she wasn't hallucinating.

"Outside? For how long?" he asked the driver. "Don't know if you've noticed, but it's cold as hell out here."

"Pretty sure hell would be hot," the driver joked as he opened the car door. "Not long. Go on."

Alex waited until the car rounded the fountain before asking, "Ready?"

Luna nodded. The Others, as the driver had so aptly put it, huddled together, openly staring at her and Alex. If their breath didn't plume in front of them when they exhaled, she'd have thought they were weird statues, misplaced and mismatched with idyllic scenery.

White lights in the ground dotted the edges of the circular courtyard. The bushes had been dressed up with their own lights, evenly spaced dots shining like pearls, and the moonlight settled onto the gravel crunching under their feet as they walked. Everything reflected and refracted and beautiful.

Everything except the double doors at the top of the steps. No floodlight. No porch light. Not even the pinprick of a doorbell. The darkness there seemed unreasonable and out of place. Like a warning.

Or a message.

Alex spoke first. "Hey. I'm Alex, and this is Luna."

Luna had to force herself to stop looking at the doors, to stop prematurely theorizing and be present. It practically hurt to turn her head toward the distraction.

"We know. Hi, Luna," said BelleLow, a maybe-white chubby girl smiling through her shivers. Whenever someone asked her ethnicity on Golden Rule or Goldspiracy, she infamously never answered for some reason. "I don't know if you know, but my name's actually Harlow."

"Oh hey. It's nice to meet you," Luna said.

"*Oh*," Nicole said, tone light. "She speaks."

Luna would recognize JadeTheBabe's voice anywhere—sultry and raspy, all feeling and probably no cigarette smell. When Nicole had first hit the Golden Rule scene, Goldspiracy had spent months analyzing her videos to see if the rumors were true, to find any clues to see if she was a plant, "fated" to rise above the wasteland created by Jewel's absence.

The results of their investigation had been inconclusive.

The Founders were going to lose their shit when she reported back that Nicole was even prettier in person. Not just photogenic—but beautiful. Talented *and* funny *and* popular *and* gorgeous *and* tall.

Life was truly devastatingly unfair.

"I do that from time to time," Luna said, before ducking back into her scarf.

"I'm Jade online, but you can call me Nicole," she said with a dizzying smile full of perfect teeth.

"We know," Alex said with a grin, and thank God he did. Luna probably would have said something Not Great™ in response. "So, that must make you StreetcarBouvier?"

"I prefer Stella. At all times." Her tone didn't leave room for argument, questions, or anything. Stella spoke like a judge with a demented sense of humor, smiling while sentencing you to death. She still hadn't posted anything besides the introductory diary entry on Golden Rule, so Luna hadn't been sure what to expect. There hadn't been any worthwhile theories on the forums either—Stella was still *the* mystery guest of the weekend.

"Have you guys been waiting long?" Alex asked.

Stella exchanged an amused look with Nicole—right over the top of Harlow's head.

"Not me. I got here like ten minutes before y'all did," Nicole said, grinning just enough for a wicked dimple to appear in the center of her left cheek. Her round cheeks and chubby face softened her a little, made her look younger than she most likely was, and judging by her videos she knew exactly how to use that to her advantage.

Luna moved closer to Alex.

"Speaking of chaperones," Stella said.

"No one said that." Harlow looked confused.

Stella shushed her. "Where's yours?" she asked Luna. "You look a bit—small."

Nicole added, "I would've said *young*. Aren't you, like, fourteen?"

Luna's ears began to burn, face flushing from the hearty hellfire of embarrassment. "I'm fifteen. Not that it matters."

"Your parents let you come here alone?" Nicole asked.

"Yeah. Um, well, my sister did?" Oh no. The questions were starting. She breathed through her scarf. Why couldn't the words that came out of her mouth ever match the tone in her head?

"Your sister is your legal guardian?" Harlow asked, curious.

Luna nodded. Tasha had been worried about her leaving, but ultimately let her go.

Alex said, "And she's not alone. I'm here."

"And you are?" Stella asked. "Brother? Boyfriend?"

"No," Alex and Luna said in unison before looking at each other.

"Ooh, someone has a miscommunication plotline going on." Stella laughed. "Those can be fun. Or annoying. To each their own, I suppose. Personally, I prefer a more direct approach."

Harlow sighed. "Why do I get the feeling you wouldn't know how to be subtle if it whispered *exact* directions in your ear?"

"Look at you, being all witty," Stella said, proud and complimentary, but it didn't last. Her Judge tone returned as she said, "Try it again. Let's see what happens."

Harlow didn't respond, but Alex laughed nervously. "Remind me not to get on your bad side."

Stella grinned. "Not possible. I don't have a bad side."

Deep, mournful bells began to ring throughout the courtyard. Luna slammed her hands over her ears. It was midnight in the not-quite middle of nowhere! People, if there were any, were probably sleeping! Alex and the Others had covered their ears too, shoulders hunching and grimacing against the volume of the bells.

Luna squeezed her eyes shut, gritting her teeth. Something about the melody felt familiar, but it was so loud and jarring she couldn't think, couldn't concentrate long enough to follow the rhythm to guess what notes would come next.

The song ended as abruptly as it began, replaced by a single bell chiming twelve times.

"Okay," Harlow said, a little loud. "Okay, good, I can hear myself."

"Did that sound familiar to any of you?" Luna asked, hopeful for help.

"Yes!" Harlow's eyes widened with excitement. "But I'm not sure where it's from. And twelve chimes definitely didn't make sense. It's not noon."

Stella frowned at Harlow and said, "Oh, this is going to be a long weekend."

"Maybe the clocks are broken or work in reverse. Vampire hours. There's a rumor about that, right, Luna?" Nicole asked.

"Ah, not you too," Stella whispered.

Luna froze, hand wrapped around her phone as she was about to pull it out of her pocket. Unlike Harlow, who seemed excited and ready to theorize, Nicole, while not exactly mocking, definitely never joined Goldspiracy. Her question was a challenge, but not a good one.

Certain rumors about Jewel had been classified Persona Non Grata—meaning they were only talked about inside the forums with trusted members. No outsiders allowed. The rumors were fantastical, improbable, and didn't always make sense, but they were *fun*. Outside their space, they lost the magic of secrecy and possibility.

Nicole was just trying to bait her like some of the kids at school had done before. Sarcasm and subterfuge undetectable until it was too late. She definitely couldn't be trusted.

Besides, the vampire rumor was *years* old. Jewel clearly and undeniably aged, so it had been ruled out.

Luna shivered from the cold and the challenge. She didn't like to lie, so chose another way out by shrugging and then looking at Harlow, who gave a subtle nod before looking away.

Good. An actual ally, she thought. They would definitely talk later. Hopefully, she'd be able to count on Harlow as well as Alex during whatever came next. Because something was coming.

Jewel would *not* let her down.

The front door clicked.

Silently, they all turned toward the sound on instinct, but Stella whispered, "Finally."

It clicked twice more before the left door began to swing inward. A familiar figure wearing red glasses and a beautiful sparkling blue gown glided out of the darkness. She walked to the edge of the porch, all smiles as she looked down at them. The skirt and bodice twinkled with crosshatched golden lines as thin and intricate as veins. A perfect match to the courtyard and divine on her light brown skin.

Luna wanted to say something. She knew she should say something. Everyone else's gawking, wide-eyed stare was *embarrassing*, but all she could do was exhale in an exhilarated huff.

Olive. Was Standing. Right. There.

Olive—Jewel's very best friend in the whole world. The beloved *Siren* of Golden Rule, whose prerecorded instructional video welcomed every user to the app. A musical goddess, she also created the songbird-style, where users sang in their diary entries, often making up original songs to tell their stories.

"Good evening," Olive said, and then laughed. "Well, I guess it's good morning now."

"Nice dress," Stella said with a mocking smile. "I wish I had known there was a ballroom dress code. I would've asked Diane to buy me something more royally appropriate."

Nicole asked, "Who's Diane?"

"My mom."

"You call your mom by her first name?"

"Not to her face." Stella shrugged.

"Don't worry," Olive said to Stella. "You'll have plenty of chances to dress up later if you choose to stay."

"*If?*" Harlow asked. "Why wouldn't we?"

"We've planned a pretty eventful weekend for you guys. I think you're going to have a really good time." She nodded, smiling. "But in order for it to work, there are nonnegotiable rules you must agree to. Everything is totally voluntary, I promise. You'll always have a choice. Like right now." She took a deep breath, smile giving way to solemnity.

Luna shivered again, from cold and anticipation this time, and balled her hands into anxious fists.

"Rule Number One," Olive began, voice still warm but firm. "You may not leave. If you accidentally take one single step off this property before the weekend is over, you will be sent home empty handed. No exceptions."

That rule pitched the already-quiet courtyard straight into a void.

"Think carefully before deciding on your answer," Olive continued. "If you choose to leave, stay right here and a car will take you back to the airport. For those who choose to stay"—she smiled, hesitant but encouraging—"I'll see you on the other side." She turned around, gliding back into the dark house, leaving the door open behind her.

THE GOLDEN RULE TRINITY

When Olive had been out of sight for a beat, Nicole let out an awkward laugh.

"Okay," Alex said, clearing his throat and turning to Luna. "I'm assuming we're in?"

Luna nodded. "One hundred percent." She didn't beg, cry, and bargain with Tasha, and then travel twelve hours to just . . . turn around and go back home. Besides, she hadn't even met Jewel yet.

"Sounds exciting to me. A little weird and like a horror story waiting to happen, but exciting," Stella said. "Lead the way, Napoleon."

"Napoleon?" Luna asked.

Alex said, "It's because you're short," and Luna frowned at Stella so suddenly, so hard, her eyes started to hurt. It was a tiny miracle that she hadn't given herself whiplash too.

"It's also a vote of confidence." Stella laughed around her words. "Before he got cocky, Napoleon was a despotic badass. Stay humble, little leader, and we might just make it out of here alive."

"Death jokes. Nice," Harlow said to Stella with obvious contempt. Her gaze slid to Nicole, who remained impassive.

Luna let herself calm down, but not before tossing a final warning glare at Stella, who continued to smile at her. Clever and crooked, like a devil waiting to trick her into falling. She glanced at Alex to check in with him—his worried grin was a sight to see. She didn't think anyone could have pulled that off like him. Cute but wary. Supportive but hesitant. She grabbed his bare hand, holding it with her gloved one to give him strength, just in case he really was scared.

She'd discovered that he liked touching while on the plane. He didn't tell her he was scared of flying until he was two seconds away from hyperventilating during takeoff. Out of nowhere, he asked to hold her hand, and she agreed of course, and he just closed his eyes. It was enough.

Somehow, *she* had been enough. And she hoped holding his hand again would have the same effect. When she stepped forward toward the stairs, he followed with no resistance.

Right then, at the exact moment Luna ascended the stairs to Jewel's childhood home, her internal life soundtrack kicked in. Something about a stairway to heaven and knocking on heaven's door. Maybe it was a couple of songs mashed together.

Before he died, her dad liked to listen to classic rock. He was a musician, a guitarist in cover bands that played Motown hits and popular R&B and pop songs from the 1980s and '90s, but he had taught her that you couldn't be a great musician if you didn't listen to a little of everything. You could be good, but you'd never be *great*.

Luna thought of him, his full belly laughs, his tired but patient eyes, and their shared love of mysteries as she crossed the threshold of no return. He would've *loved* this. She kept walking into the dark room until the outside light faded. Until it was impossible to see in front of her face.

Stella sidled up next to her. "End of the line?"

"Can *you* see in the dark?"

"Ooh, feisty. Also, you're cute when you're angry. You really shouldn't have reacted like that around me."

"Why?"

"You'll see."

"I—I don't think I want to?"

Stella shot her another quick smile and turned around, facing Nicole, who stood right behind them.

"I'm just glad it's warm in here. I thought California was supposed to be hot," Harlow said, unzipping her jacket.

"California has three seasons," Nicole said. "Winter, spring, and fire."

"Where do you think Olive went?" Alex asked. He let go of Luna's hand and stood behind her, close enough for his chin to bump the top of her head. She looked up at him, tilting her head to the side, but her hopefully reassuring smile went unnoticed. He scanned the room, frowning as he tried to see what lay ahead.

The front door slammed shut, plunging them into darkness.

Someone screamed, shrill and horrified, and Luna whipped around toward the sound. Instinctively, she reached behind her, grabbing Alex's jacket to keep him close. The hairs on the back of her neck prickled. Her heart beat in her throat. She took a quick hit of her scarf and pressed in close to Alex.

From somewhere in the dark, a voice mocked them. "Oh, come on now. What are you all so scared of?" His voice didn't echo or carry, but somehow came from everywhere, surrounding them, making him impossible to find.

Luna swallowed hard at the same moment Harlow gasped and whispered, *"He's here too?"*

The voice continued, "Jewel would at least give you time to adjust to your new surroundings."

And then, there was light—from dim to full power in a handful of agonizing moments.

If Alex hadn't been in her way, Luna probably would have turned in a full circle, jaw completely unhinged. Making the leap from online pictures to real life was almost too much for her brain to handle. The double staircase. The massive framed portraits. The marble floor gleaming with the reflection of golden chandeliers hanging in the domed entryway. The vases, verified by Goldspiracy to each be worth more than a new car, casually hanging out on top of polished black round tables with elaborate bouquets of white flowers inside.

Luna had truly made it to the inside of Jewel's house.

Her soul would make a break for it any second.

"*Oh my God.*" Harlow's whisper trembled with excitement for a very different reason.

Ethan stood against the front door, hands behind his back, a vision in a royal-blue suit with a shimmering gold tie and a wreath of gold leaves nestled in his short, dark brown curly hair. Four thin gold lines had been painted on his left cheek, standing out against his entirely freckled face.

Ethan—Jewel's adored younger brother and trusted business partner. The infamous *Warden* of Golden Rule, in charge of leading a legion of moderators who kept the app safe for everyone.

"However," Ethan continued, "once you've adjusted, all bets will be, for all intents and purposes, off." He walked past the group. "That's how it works, right, Luna?"

Luna's stomach roiled. Nicole had asked the same thing.

Right, Luna?

Was he—was he trying to tell her something?

"Uh, sure?" she answered.

Ethan was still watching her. Face revealing nothing, he said, "Are you ready for Rule Number Two?"

"I am!" Harlow chirped, moving closer to him. "I'm game for whatever."

Ethan gave her a curious look. "Word of advice: Don't say that again and don't let Jewel hear you. I love my sister, but, uhh . . . well, you know how she is," he said. "Real talk, I would watch everything you say. Everything on the estate—inside, outside, everywhere—is recorded by the security system, audio and video. Cameras in bathrooms and changing areas have been disabled, but other than that? It is what it is. Rule Number Two: By being here, you consent to being recorded. I can't let any of you go any further until you all verbally agree."

"Tricky, tricky. Wait a minute." Stella smiled at him, looking moments away from bursting into a full cackle. "So, if one of us disagrees, we're all out? We all go home?"

"Afraid so." He grinned back at her. "Hope you like group work."

"I'm homeschooled. I've been dreaming about it for *years*." She laughed. "Plus, I'm used to being monitored, so this rule actually means nothing to me. I'm in."

Everyone stared at Stella—who didn't seem to realize what she said was kind of weird.

"Monitored? Like you're on house arrest or something?" Harlow asked.

"Sure. Guilty of the crime of being born. I'm assuming *you're* in and eager," she said, moving on. "Nicole?"

"Oh. Um. Well." Nicole looked toward Luna, who said, "We're in. We don't care."

"Actually," Alex said softly and quickly, "I do care, a lot, but yeah, I'm in. I guess."

Luna smiled up at him and whispered, "It's fine. Don't worry."

"Okay," Nicole said, and asked Ethan, "And we're *only* recorded for the security system?"

"We're recorded *by* security," he said. "A live feed to a secure network and stored on an equally secure server. We've had some incidents on the property."

"What kind of incidents?"

"The kind that resulted in us installing a twenty-four-hour surveillance system. Anything to keep my sister safe."

"Is she okay?" Luna asked, concerned. She hadn't heard *anything* about that. Not on the news or on the Goldspiracy Forums or from Jewel herself. Which was really strange, considering Jewel usually shared everything about her life with Golden Rule. That was the entire point of the app—to truly connect with people who loved her.

Ethan gave her a warm smile and nodded. "Yeah. You know how she is."

Nicole exhaled into a sigh. "Okay. That makes sense. Since it's necessary to keep everyone safe, then yeah. I agree," she said.

"Five for five twice in a row," Stella said with a taunting laugh. "I wonder what's next."

Ethan stared at her for a beat, then said, "Let's go find out. Walk with me?"

"And you're offering me your arm?" Stella mock-gasped, and looped her arm through his as he led her away. "What a gentleman."

"All together now," Ethan threw over his shoulder as they hurried past the double staircase toward a hallway on the left.

Luna didn't need to be told twice. She grabbed Alex's hand, running to catch up. He easily matched her pace as they made a right at the corner and walked under one of the many sets of carved triple arches.

"What do you think so far?" Alex whispered to her.

"I hope we get to meet Jewel soon," she replied. "Like, now kind of soon."

Ethan and Olive were great, definitely, but they weren't *Jewel*.

"What do you think they're planning?" he asked.

"Too early to say. I've only noticed one thing so far, and it might not even be anything," she said.

Right, Luna? Ethan focused on her a lot too, but now he was walking with Stella. Did that also mean something?

As a group, they rounded one last corner and entered the only room at the end of the hall. Luna's soft gasp took her by surprise—*the* pristine and monochromatic White Drawing Room. Jewel had made the infamous *Fourth of July Family Fiasco* video in there!

Luna recognized the long white couch with the swirly pattern on the left wall, the matching pillows, throw rugs, chairs, and love seats scattered around the room. More chandeliers, mixed-matched and encased in glass, hung from the ceiling by thick silvery-white cords. Not even the fireplace dared to have a speck of soot anywhere near it to ruin the effect, but she knew it had been used before.

"Sit wherever you'd like."

Luna would never forget that moment, the feeling of her heart seizing and then going still. Dressed in a purple, strapless, and sparkling ball gown, Jewel sat in a high-backed white chair at the head of the room.

Jewel Van Hanen—the undisputed *Queen* of Golden Rule.

This wasn't a dream. Luna wasn't using the app. She wasn't curled up in bed watching one of Jewel's videos for the millionth time.

Her lips wouldn't move.

Her brain couldn't even function long enough to tell her mouth what to say.

Luna's soul had truly left her body and begun its ascent to an astral plane. She saw herself, an empty, enraptured meat sack of a human with her idol, her love and obsession, sitting across the room from her with a brand-new haircut.

Oh *God*, she was going to cry. Tears began to sting her eyes, pooling in the corners.

Jewel *always* kept her hair on the longer side, nothing above her shoulders, but now she'd gone drastic fantastic pixie. The delicate point of a bejeweled diadem touched Jewel's forehead while the rest of it circled her head. With her large brown eyes, super light skin, and dark brown freckles that dusted her cheekbones and nose, she honest-to-God looked like an elf straight out of a fantasy story—if the creator cared enough to include Black elves. But unlike Luna, whose skin skewed warmer, most people couldn't tell Jewel and Ethan were Black, anyway.

One of the first things Luna loved about Jewel was her hair. They were the same—both had a white mom and Black dad and more intensely curly hair than they knew what to do with. But this new cut was perfect for her.

Perfect. Everything was just . . . perfect.

Never in her wildest dreams did Luna ever think she'd have a chance to meet Jewel. She just didn't have that kind of luck. But there she was and there they were, and they were breathing the same air—

"Come on," Alex said, tugging her forward. Ducking behind him, Luna wiped at her eyes, hoping no one would see. She took a deep, shaky breath through her scarf as she sat. Alex had chosen the love seat closest to Jewel for them. Harlow chose a solo cushy-looking chair, while Nicole chose to sit next to Stella on the long couch. Right, right next to her in a room full of empty seats.

Olive, who stood next to Jewel's chair on the right, leaned down and whispered something to her. Jewel laughed as Ethan took up the empty space on her left.

The Golden Rule Trinity. Live and in person.

"Breathe, Moon Princess," Alex murmured, taking her hand again. A gentle squeeze to ground her. Another asking her to come back.

Luna nodded. "I'm okay," she said quietly. "No, I'm not."

Alex laughed, breathy and unsurprised. "I know. I got you."

"First, I want to say thank you for coming to Golden Weekend X: the tenth and final time I will host this event." Jewel's face brightened with a wicked smile. "My house is your house. Nothing and nowhere is off-limits. My staff has been instructed to treat you as they would me. Your rooms are ready, and your belongings are upstairs waiting for you."

Olive left her post and walked toward the wall on her left. She placed her right hand against it. Three beeps sounded, short and quick like Morse code.

Luna dug the fingers of her free hand into the seat cushion. She didn't blink, didn't breathe, and had to press her lips together to contain the excitement threatening to shout its way out of her as a panel in the wall next to Olive's hand slid upward. She removed a stack of flat, rectangular objects from the hidden compartment. One side had been bedazzled with crystals.

Oh my God, oh my God, oh my God. Luna's brain accelerated into a repetitive overdrive.

Olive handed the shimmering blue one to Jewel, who continued, "The only thing I want in exchange for my more-than-gracious hospitality is for you to participate in a game that will last the duration of the weekend."

"What kind of game?" Nicole's question snapped with surprising anger.

Jewel continued to remain wickedly calm. "The kind of game that lets the winners walk out of here one million dollars richer."

Luna felt like someone had kicked her to the ground and she'd landed straight on her back, clean knocking the wind out of her.

"A million dollars." Harlow had locked Jewel in her sights, voice firm and ready to believe. "Are you serious?"

"I'm very rich. Trust me, I'm good for it," Jewel deadpanned. "There will be two winners. Five hundred thousand dollars each, payable immediately."

THE CRUELEST JEWEL

"I think I'm having a stroke," Luna whispered. Alex immediately touched her back, but he wasn't doing much better, looking as shocked as she felt.

"Be Fast." Stella laughed. "And here I was just hoping I'd be able to get drunk for the first time. Five hundred thousand dollars. Wow. Color me impressed."

"This is a sober house," Jewel said. "Yes, I know it's connected to a winery. Still a sober house."

"Well, there goes my inaugural wild child weekend. I'd like to go home now, please and thank you," Stella said. "I'm kidding. I know, I know, leaving is against the rules. Harlow, fix your face."

Jewel laughed, glancing at Olive. "See what I mean?" she asked before turning back to the room. "Let's get down to business, shall we? Rule Number Three: Lose the tablet, lose the game," Jewel said. "Same will be true if it's damaged in any way. You must also keep it on your person at all times."

Olive walked around the room, passing them out one at a time along with an adjustable belt. Luna received hers last—pale green. Alex had gotten pink. She ran her fingers along the edges of the tablet and over the glittering crystals. Nothing special about it, other than the added loops to connect the belt. And yet, they were a big-enough deal to have an entire rule to ensure their safety.

Interesting.

"Oh, Nicole?" Jewel asked. "Would you mind doing me a small favor?"

"Depends on what it is." Her tablet looked white but had the faintest hint of yellow.

"Player six was unfortunately delayed. They'll be here bright and early tomorrow. Would you mind holding on to their tablet until then?"

"Sure." Nicole shrugged, accepting the purple tablet.

Six? There'd be a sixth person? After Luna received her invite, Jewel promoted all five Golden Follow profiles to the home page for the app—she had even forced Alex to make an account as a part of his acceptance.

Five. Not six.

"Go ahead and turn on your tablets," Jewel said. "We're going to cover the remaining rules for the game, regulations, all that wonderful and law-abiding stuff."

Luna's screen blinked to life. After powering up and breezing through the company logos, the screen shimmered with gold. The background remained solid white, but golden flecks rained from the top of the screen to the bottom. Black text began to scroll behind the glitter, from bottom to top.

A twister brought Dorothy to Oz
And Wendy flew to Neverland.
Wonderland taught Alice nonsense,
But Narnia failed Susan in the end.
Here, my doorways will take you
To places unknown and unseen
But above all, always remember
Everything is exactly as it seems.

From my dreams to yours, welcome to
Golden Weekend X:
The Cruelest Jewel
Press here to begin . . .

"The Cruelest Jewel," Stella said. "That sounds lovely and not at all ominous."

"Because it is," Jewel said, distracted by her tablet.

"Lovely or ominous?"

"Hmm?" Jewel looked up and around the room. "Oh. Just think of the game as a thorough and fun way for us to really get to know one another."

"You didn't answer the question," Stella said.

"Didn't I? Hmm. Curious." Jewel tapped her screen with a flourish, raising her hand in the air after finishing. "If everyone can press the blinking button at the bottom of the screen, we'll begin."

Stella laughed. "Imagine that."

"Imagine what? Care to share with the class?"

"Not yet."

Jewel narrowed her eyes and stared stone faced for a couple of heartbeats before her expression brightened into a killer smile. "I can respect that. Moving on."

Luna made a mental note of that exchange. Stella mirrored Jewel but with a worrisome frosty edge. Jewel was the queen of constant cunning with a heaping dose of weird. Smart, sassy, and strict, not harmful.

Stella, on the other hand, definitely seemed to have a bad side, and Luna didn't want to be on it. Underestimating Stella, the newcomer to Golden Rule, would be a mistake.

"The game is very simple, but please pay attention for the sake of my last good nerve," Jewel said. The tablet screen changed to a solid black background. Large white text in a beautiful cursive font moved in time with her as she spoke, like a slide show. "To win, all you need to remember is C-P-R."

*By completing **challenges**, you will earn **presents**, which will help decipher the **recipe**.*

"Everything is exactly as it seems," Jewel continued. "Everything is connected."

***Challenges** are prescheduled. For some, you will receive a notification and instructions through your tablets at the designated time. If asked to enter a challenge room, once inside you must locate your envelope. Some challenges might be harder than others, but all will be unmistakable. Be mindful of your time.*

"*Oh,*" Luna said softly. So that's why they had to keep their tablets on them at all times! Mystery solved.

***Presents** will only be gifted to specific players. You may not steal someone else's present. You may not sabotage* *another player. Everyone must play, but only two will win.*

"Make of that what you will," Jewel said.

*The **recipe** will unlock, in its entirety, this morning at 6:00 A.M. You will have until the final hour of Golden Weekend to solve it. You may use whatever means available to you in your efforts. Some will have an easier time than others.*

"You should also know that if you fail your challenges, which is very possible, by the way, you may be disqualified," Ethan said with a smirk. "Olive and I will determine your penalties based on your overall performance during the game."

"I have a question," Nicole said, slightly raising her hand. "What will we have to do during the challenges? Will it be like a dare? Or . . . ?"

Jewel stared at Nicole, unmoving and not speaking for five whole seconds before looking away. "Any other questions? No?"

"Wait, wait," Olive said. She moved, standing slightly in front of Jewel, hands up. "I'm sorry, but we really can't answer that. So, to be *fair*, we're going to give you one last chance to change your mind. All the information you have is all you're going to get until the game officially starts. If you'd like to leave right now, you absolutely can. We don't want you to feel like we're forcing you to be here."

Jewel sighed theatrically, gaze fixed on the ceiling. "She's too good. Too pure." She shook her head and brought her attention back to the room. "Fine. I'll give you a few minutes to figure out if you really want to be here. I'd recommend going over the official rules while you're at it." A few taps on Jewel's tablet later, Luna's tablet changed again to a list. "Discuss amongst yourselves. If you must."

Olive turned around and mimed flicking Jewel between the eyes. She didn't even flinch. "Don't be a jerk," Olive said. "And thank you."

Stella laughed suddenly, pointing at her tablet. "Ten Golden Rules. Ten Commandments. Beware false idols and golden gods." She *snorted*. "The religious imagery is a bit much, but I can appreciate a struggling artist when I see one."

"Struggling?" Jewel nearly choked on the word.

"It's nothing to be ashamed about," Stella said, completely serious. "Everyone has to start somewhere."

Jewel scoffed but recovered quickly. "Two minutes. Use them wisely."

Alex sucked in a breath and exhaled, puffing out his cheeks. "Well, this is a lot."

The first three rules were exactly what they'd already been told. There were also official rules, Numbers Four and Five, about sabotage and required participation, plus five more:

VI. Discussion of challenge room mechanics may result in disqualification.

VII. During challenges, once BEGIN is initiated, a red ABORT button will appear on the players' tablets. Engaging the ABORT function will result in a penalty.

VIII. If a player is disqualified, they will be sent home empty handed. Their Presents will be redistributed to the remaining players.

IX. Players may not ask House Staff for assistance regarding any facet of The Cruelest Jewel.

X. Jewel Van Hanen reserves the right to create Addendums to this list.

"I know," Luna hush-whispered, "but it's amazing, right? Five hundred thousand dollars? I can't wait to tell Tasha. She'll probably start crying. Tasha never cries."

"We only get it if we win."

"Which we will? I mean, you want to play, right?"

"Yeah. We're here, so might as well, but . . ." He tapered off.

"But what?"

Alex moved closer, ducking his head. She mirrored his movements as if they could cast a spell to create a protective bubble around them. Voice low, he asked, "Don't you think it's a little suspect that Olive keeps trying to give us a way out?"

"Not really."

"Or what about when Nicole asked about the challenges? It's like Jewel got mad. I kind of wished I'd backed Nicole up because we don't actually know what we're agreeing to."

He had a point. A very good point, and it would make her a bad friend if she dismissed it as him worrying too much.

Luna chewed on her lip while she thought. She had faith, he had doubts, and together, they made a balanced team. It was way too easy to imagine herself getting caught up in the game and majorly messing up. She knew her limits—and knew that she'd shoot straight past them if the right opportunity knocked.

Alex wasn't like that. He was calm, thoughtful. Only took controlled risks. Almost like he had to have a guess of what the consequences would be before he acted.

Get caught skipping class? Get Saturday school.

Get caught speeding? Get a ticket (and some hellfire wrath from his mom).

Signing up to play a game with no specifics made him nervous. Trying to convince him to focus on the money wouldn't get her anywhere, because $500,000 didn't mean much to him if he didn't know what he'd have to do to get it.

"It's just a game. I'm sure it'll be fun," Luna said confidently. "Everything will be fine. I promise. And if it's not, I—I'll take care of it." She paused, shocked by what she'd said. Alex was too, judging by how high his eyebrows jumped. But it was true—she could feel the roiling, ferocious truth of it in her stomach. She was so, so lucky to have him there, her perfect counterbalance. The least she could do was to make sure he felt safe enough to at least try playing the game. She would take care of everything else. Of him.

"Think about it," she continued. "We're the only two people here who actually know each other, and there will be *two* winners. That automatically makes us partners. And partners mean we watch each other's backs. No matter what happens, we'll protect each other and make it to the end together."

"You'd protect me?" Alex sounded skeptical, but the good kind, like it made him happy, which instantly made her happy and wow, why was her face suddenly so hot?

"Of course I would." Right then and there, Luna made a promise to herself to never leave Alex behind, never betray him, and never do anything to put him in danger. "I will."

"Time's up," Jewel said. "Everyone in, yes?"

To Luna's surprise, no one objected.

"Perfect." Jewel grinned as Ethan handed her plastic bags. "Moving on to Addendum One: Turn in all watches, phones, music players, and any other electronic devices in your possession, excluding your Cruelest Jewel–approved tablets."

Alex sighed deeply, but Luna had suspected this was coming.

The reason why she didn't have an impromptu photo shoot in the courtyard the millisecond her feet hit the gravel? Because she had signed away her right to take pictures outside the house, among other requirements Tasha had worried about before she agreed to let Luna attend Golden Weekend X. Luna figured they just wouldn't be allowed to have phones, period, to ensure nothing leaked.

"No," Stella said. "That's not happening. That wasn't mentioned as part of the deal *anywhere*."

"I'm mentioning it now. So," Jewel said.

"I'm not giving up my phone," Stella said. "If my parents don't hear from me, they will show up with the National Guard *yesterday*. Risk their wrath if you want to, but leave me out of it."

"That sounds like a very personal problem."

"I'm only ever serious about three things in my life, and this is one of them." No taunting half smile, no quirked eyebrow. Nothing to make it seem like Stella was being anything other than 100 percent genuine. "This isn't a curious case of hyperbole. My parents will literally storm your gates to come get me. If they even *think* something has happened to me, you can kiss life as you know it goodbye. They will *ruin* you."

"Yeah, my mom is overprotective too," Alex said. "I don't think she'd be okay with not being able to reach me."

"Too? What *too*? I didn't say overprotective. That's not what I'm talking about. They are my jailers. My parole officers. I'm on a get-out-of-jail-free card that they will promptly revoke if I miss a single check-in. You've talked to them," she said to Jewel. "Do they seem like rational, levelheaded people to you?"

Jewel fidgeted for a moment, tapping her foot, eyes on the ceiling. "Fine. Tell them I will arrange for someone on my staff to provide your legal guardians"—she glanced at Nicole—"or emergency contact with an email and phone number they can use to contact you through your tablets, if they'd like. Be aware that all correspondence will be screened and monitored."

Everyone did as they were told, texting updates to their people. Luna messaged Tasha first.

> **Luna:** I was right. We're not allowed to have our phones, but they're giving us an email to contact you. I'll write soon! Having a great time—I love you!

And then the Goldspiracy Founder group chat, which was filled with unread messages.

> **Luna:** Phones are being confiscated now. "See you on the other side!"—actual quote from Olive that I heard with my own ears tonight. Ethan is here too. Totally cried when I saw Jewel ahahahaha OKAY BYEEEEEE

And lastly, she opened the Goldspiracy Forums and went to her drafts. She'd written her final message days ago, a goodbye of sorts. When she returned from GWX, she'd be changed. Different. SilentStar would be no more—a reinvention would be mandatory. She hit POST, breathed through her scarf, and turned her phone off before handing it over.

"And that's a wrap for now." Jewel clapped her hands twice. "Ethan will take you upstairs to your rooms. And if you're lucky, he'll answer some of the questions I can see burning in your eyes."

"They're not lucky," Ethan said with a grin.

"Oh stop." Jewel's quick frown was adorable, the kind of frown an older sister unconsciously mastered after a lifetime of gentle annoyance.

"I'll go too. You can ask me questions instead," Olive said, speaking to the room, but gazing up at Ethan.

"If you must. Everyone follow them, please, except for Luna." Luna's heart skipped a beat when Jewel looked at her. "I need you for a few more minutes."

Luna's stomach began to undulate like a boat caught in the middle of a typhoon. Her excitement had a harsh, buzzing edge to it. Razor sharp and whittling her down one raw layer at a time. She didn't know it was possible to be so excited it hurt, and this was a hell of a way to find out.

"Do you need me to stay?" Alex whispered, concern written all over his face.

"I'm okay." Every time she made a fist and then stretched her fingers, they crackled with knotted energy.

"Deep breaths." He inhaled and exhaled to show her. "Don't pass out on me."

"Okay. Okay."

He looped his arm behind her back and began to rub from the base of her neck down her spine in a tight, soothing oval. With his face so close, she zoomed in on his eyelashes. She'd never noticed how long and curly they were. Wispy and perfect, protecting his deep, dark brown eyes.

"My mom used to do this when I got too wound up as a kid."

"It's nice," she said absently. "Thank you."

"You're welcome." He smiled and his eyes softened.

"Everything all right?" Jewel was standing in front of them, watching with a curious look on her face.

"Yep." Alex hopped to his feet, holding out his hand for Luna to take. She instinctively took it—and then wished she hadn't. She didn't need him to help her stand. "We're just pretty tired."

Jewel smiled at him. "The others are waiting for you."

"Right." He leaned close to Luna, grinning with intention. "Moon Princess."

Alex could have said anything right then, but he'd chosen to use her nickname. He'd be waiting for her, same as always, even in that impossible place. The buzzing energy began to dull, overpowered by a sensation too soft to ever keep.

"See you," she said, and watched him go.

Alex.

Jewel turned to her and asked, "So?"

Luna waited a beat, eyes wide and searching the empty room for help that wasn't there. "Um, s-so?" she asked, and then promptly wanted to throw herself out a window. The first words she had said to her idol were *um* and *so*?! Her despair was so swift she was shocked her knees didn't give out and let her collapse to the floor in a panicked heap.

"What do you think so far?"

"Of?"

Jewel's head tilted downward in disappointment. "You have so much to say on your little forums, but in person this is what I get? I don't know why I expected anything different."

"I'm sorry?"

"For what, exactly?"

"Uh, I don't know?"

"Then why did you apologize?"

"It's just something to say, I guess. You know, if I do something . . ." She trailed off. There wasn't another word for regretting being an inconvenience or not living up to expectations you didn't even know about. *Sorry* was a terrible catchall with multiple meanings and few alternatives. "You're really different than you are in your videos," she said quietly.

Jewel cocked her head to the side, curious. "How so?"

"Upset? And kind of guarded. When people ask you questions, you answer them, but it's like you're hiding something. But in your videos, you always seem so honest, I guess. And vulnerable, I think. It's like you're not talking to the camera. You're talking to yourself and letting us watch. I used to think that's why you never followed anyone back or responded to replies on your videos. Because you never wanted to have a conversation in the first place."

When Luna looked up, Jewel stared down at her with an expression she couldn't read, but it wasn't a good one. She shrank back. *Why did I say all of that? Now she's going to think I'm really some obsessive fan and hate me. I was way too invasive and presumptuous.* "Sorry." She pressed her lips together, wishing she had thought of that ten seconds ago.

"Do you know why I wanted you to come here? Over everyone else that participates in the Goldspiracy?" Jewel asked.

Luna shook her head.

Jewel stepped closer, leaning down until they were eye to eye. "Because you're the only one who gets it right. Every secret, every code, every single time I thought I was being clever, there you were with the answer. It's annoying, and I hate it," she said. "And I had to meet you."

All Luna's nervous energy synergized into a giant bolt of vindicated lightning.

"I've wanted to talk to you for some time, but you obviously didn't want to talk to anyone inside Golden Rule," Jewel said. "And it wasn't my place to join the forums. Players belong there, not the Gamemaster."

"You could've emailed me."

"Neither of us would have been satisfied with that, and you know it," Jewel said. "But now that you're here, I want you to promise me something. Yes?"

"Anything," Luna said with no room for regret.

"No matter what happens, you'll meet me at The End," Jewel said. "I want you to win The Cruelest Jewel."

TOTALLY SUBTLE / DELIRIUM

To play or not to play. That was the question knocking around in Stella's head.

Ethan (with Harlow on his heels trying to usurp his shadow) decided to play tour guide, navigating and relaying behind-the-scenes bits about the house as they walked to their rooms. He also explained how to use the interactive map built into their tablets. The interface resembled blueprints of the mansion's floor plan. Each room name had been written in white, and a sidebar allowed the user to select a floor level. A cluster of blinking gem emoji moved forward together on the map—a different color for each player and two blue gems, presumably for Ethan and Olive.

Stella could respect a thorough plan.

For all her strengths, a good sense of direction wasn't one of them, but it was unlikely a newly implanted house guest would be able to find their way around without getting lost. The map on their tablets took care of any directionally challenged mishaps.

Stella glanced at Olive, who had interestingly ended up walking next to her. Barely more than a smidge bit taller than Luna, she was a close second for the Cute as a Tiny Button award. "What? No crown for you, cutie?" she asked.

"Cutie?" Olive giggled, scrunching her nose like an adorably embarrassed rabbit. "It clashed with my glasses. Not really my style, anyway. This"—she gestured to her dress—"is all Jewel."

"I see," Stella said. "I can't help but wonder: What's the point of this? Why bring us all the way here to play a game? Doesn't she usually play them online?"

"I've been thinking about that too," Nicole added, joining Stella's party of two. "I don't get it."

Stella smiled at her new leggy acquaintance, pleased to have backup. She didn't want to seem too pushy right out the gate, but the questions gnawing at her were getting restless.

Olive made a flat *hmmm* sound, lips pressed together. "The Cruelest Jewel is a story," she said, eyes on the group of three at the front. "I can safely tell you that much. Everything means something. Everything has purpose." She pushed her glasses up the bridge of her nose. A little line appeared in between her brows as she frowned. "And if everything has a reason, it's easy to get it wrong. The answer to your question is everywhere, but Jewel is clever. That's why you don't get it."

"Orrrr," Stella said, dragging out the word, "we haven't been given enough information yet."

"If you find the key, you can unlock the game." Olive shrugged. "Or Ethan was right. You're not lucky after all, Stella at all times." She skipped away, joining Ethan's group.

Meanwhile Stella watched her go, eyes narrowing. "Well," she said. "*I* won't be trusting that tiny terror."

"I think I must have missed something." Nicole poked her in the arm.

"You did. She called me 'Stella at all times,' and she wasn't around to hear me say it. They were watching us while we were outside."

"Huh." Nicole crossed her arms. "And if everything means something, that must have been a clue. But about what?"

Stella closed her left eye and stared at Nicole with the right.

"What are you doing?" Nicole laughed.

"Thinking very, very hard." She grinned as she opened her eye.

Jewel had lined them up like ducks in a perfect row. At her mercy with nowhere to go but home. Dangling a $500,000 carrot in front of them was a near-perfect way to ensure compliance. Everyone had to play, but only two would win. Group work until it wasn't. Disqualification was also on the table, so elimination rounds weren't out of the question. Everyone seemed game, but to what extent?

Winning the prize money for The Cruelest Jewel could potentially be life changing—for someone else. If Stella won, her parents would simply take it and put it in a trust fund or something equally inaccessible to her. Maybe she'd get access when she was twenty-one. Actually it would probably be closer to twenty-five. Anything to keep her under their thumb because she didn't need her own money since they had so much of it. It was hard to hate the people who literally gave her everything, and yet, somehow, she found a way.

If money were the only goal, what would happen to Stella, who didn't really care? Would she be the first one in the group sent packing?

Unacceptable.

Stella decided she needed a partner. Someone invested enough to cover up her disinterest. Someone interesting enough to keep her attention.

Alex and Luna seemed to be a package deal. Harlow *felt* annoying—a sycophant like that could never be trusted. And mysterious player six wasn't an option yet.

"Does this game matter to you?" Stella asked Nicole. "Any of it?"

"Yeah. Winning would be better than the best get-rich-quick scheme I'd ever be able to think of. I mean, I'm not willing to do *anything* to win, but as long as it's chill, I don't see the harm in trying. You know, when in Rome and all that."

Nicole could be the last player standing. Stella could be the one to help her get there. A new companion, and she'd get to stay the whole weekend. What better way to cement a friendship than having a hand in helping them become fabulously wealthy?

Now all Stella had to do was figure out how to make it work. Making friends always seemed so easy in books. Trying in real life was . . . strange. Like a curious-rumbly-feeling-in-the-pit-of-her-stomach strange. Should she ask? Say, "Hey, so you're mine now, deal with it," and see what happened?

What if Nicole didn't like pushy people, though? Stella could let her actions speak for her—put her skills on full display to show what a great catch she'd be. Nicole would fall right into her partner trap.

That could work. She could totally be subtle. Harlow didn't know what the hell she was talking about.

Up the stairs and around two left corners, they arrived at a T-shaped hall. Well lit, with white walls trimmed in gold and six closed doors. Each one had a plaque in the center with a name engraved on it.

Luna's and Alex's doors were on the right. Directly across, Nicole's door was next to Francis's—presumably, player six. And at the end of the hall, Stella's door was next to Harlow's. Because of course it was.

"This is where you'll all be staying. Think of them as hotel suites. If you need anything just give staff a call by picking up the phone and pressing zero," Ethan said. "I'm sure you're all tired, but as a reminder, anytime you want to wander around, be sure to take your tablets with you. I cannot stress that enough."

"Watch this," Stella whispered to Nicole, then raised her voice. "Why isn't mysterious player six here yet? I don't buy that 'they got delayed' excuse. There's no way an obvious control freak like Jewel would tolerate that."

Olive glanced at Ethan before hiding her smile behind her hand and looking away.

"That's actually the truth," Ethan said. "They're just not here yet."

"*Because* they were delayed."

"Is that a question?"

"Am I lucky?"

Ethan's amused half smile suited his freckled face beautifully. "Too early to call it."

"These word games sure are interesting," Stella said with a nod, walking backward toward her door. "But I'm on a different level. Adjust your expectations accordingly." She held Nicole's gaze and winked with her left eye.

See? Totally subtle.

Stella gasped, jaw dropping when she entered her room. Floor to ceiling, wall to wall, furniture, curtains, bedding—everything saturated in shades of red. Her laughter flitted quickly from a stunned whisper to staccato disbelief to finally, a throaty cackle.

Red. It matched the jewels on her tablet and her gem emoji on the map.

But *this* was so much more than that.

Red room of pain. Redrum. The Red Room. And on and on and on.

If everything was supposed to mean something and Jewel was telling a story, what exactly was she trying to say about Stella by giving her that room?

"Incredible." She started cackling again.

FRIDAY, 2:00 A.M.

"Oh wow." Luna all but floated from the door farther into her room.

Her feet were there, sure, but how could she be expected to feel them? She'd been assigned to the green room—pale green, to be exact. Her sleep-deprived brain imagined someone taking her entire room and dipping it in watered-down pastel food coloring like an Easter egg. A door on the left side of the room had been propped open. Luna wandered over to it, peeking her head inside.

Adjoining suites! As far as she could tell the room mirrored hers, down to the monochromatic paintings on the wall, but was pink instead of green.

It truly took her brain a few seconds to process what she was seeing. Pink.

The Pink Room, one of Jewel's preferred filming locations. Using it was a surefire signal to Goldspiracy—holy-impending-emotionally-vulnerable content, Batman!

If Luna had been given the pink room, she truly wouldn't have known how to act. Close proximity was good. Soothing pale green was for the best.

In the middle of the room, Alex was completely knocked out, fast asleep on the massive canopied bed. Face buried in the pillows. One socked foot hung off the side of the bed. Blanket wrapped tight around him. He'd left the lights on, so she clicked them off. He looked so peaceful, and Luna's very last brain cell, the sole survivor from her conversation with Jewel, appreciated it.

Luna hesitated while closing his door.

Would leaving it open violate the girlfriend boundary? It's not like they were sharing a room or a bed or anything like that. They were just sort of . . . next to each other. Suite mates, with direct access to the other's room. Which she might need.

It hadn't happened in a while, but waking up in unfamiliar places confused her. Luna forgot where she was, that she was safe, and not abandoned in her mom's old apartment. The first few nights after moving in with Tasha had been filled with nightmares, screams, footsteps running down the hall, and endless cups of hot chocolate while watching *Living Single* reruns in Tasha's room until the sun came up or she stopped snoring—whichever came first.

Tasha always rescued her. Every time. If she had an episode, if she couldn't have Tasha, she only wanted Alex.

Luna bit her lip and let go of the knob, door still open. "Sorry, Melody," she whispered.

Just like Jewel said, her suitcase had already been unpacked. Someone had put away all her clothes in the walk-in closet. Quickly, she grabbed her pajamas and headed for the bathroom, which was also entirely pale green. She ran a hand along the edge of the deep bowl sink with a chrome faucet. Smiled at herself in the wide mirror above it—and laughed at the double image of the reflection in the vanity behind her, its top covered with makeup and skin care products as if it had robbed a department store counter. In the nook parallel to her, a giant bathtub had been built under a window and lined with candles in ornate candelabras. Next to it, the triangular-shaped shower with glass doors and an incredible number of showerheads called her name.

Luna didn't know it was possible to be in love with a room—loved it so much, she couldn't even remember to feel jealous. The bathroom alone was bigger than her bedroom in Tasha's house.

Her toiletry bag waited for her on the sink, right in front of a small basket with complimentary toiletries like at a hotel, and another basket of mint-colored towels. While brushing her teeth she wandered to the window beside the vanity behind her. She had a perfect view of the breathtaking backyard—the open grassy field morphing into small rolling hills before hitting the edge of the forest.

Grainy, slightly out-of-focus pictures online had nothing on seeing it in person.

It honestly looked like a scene from one of the classic historical romance movies Tasha liked. Luna could imagine it—two people running toward the hedge maze, and each other, for a perfectly secret moonlight tryst. Just enough shadows to keep them safe. Just enough light to lead the way. Her heart filled with longing and hope for her imaginary couple.

A man was staring up at her window.

Luna gasped, accidentally swallowing foamy toothpaste. Her feet moved faster than her brain, and she tripped, crashing onto the floor with a solid *thud*. "Ow," she moaned in between coughs to clear her throat. Still coughing, she hauled herself up to the sink to spit and rinse her mouth.

Who the hell was that? Luna grabbed a towel—the shoulder she landed on throbbed in pain—and wiped her mouth as she inched toward the window.

Somewhere way in the back of the reasonable part of her brain, she knew going for a second look wasn't a good idea. But she wanted to see him again! It wasn't like he could do anything from down there. She was on the third floor, safe and sound.

Unless he had a gun. Were the security people armed? Surely, Jewel would have mentioned that.

Unless he *wasn't* security and just some random person who had managed to sneak onto her property. In that case, she had to get a good look at him. Just in case. To keep everyone safe.

A quick hop to the right later, Luna stood with her back against the wall. She used the cotton curtain as a shield, hoping it kept her hidden as she peered out. The man was still there, still looking up, just not at her window. She'd been wrong. His face was turned in her general direction, but his gaze shot straight past her. He wore a dark-colored trench coat with a reflective material sewn onto the hems and collar. His long hair was slicked back away from his face—wrinkled, pale, and angular.

"Oh," she said, slightly disappointed. How rude. Following his gaze, she strained to see what he could. Luna squinted, pressing her forehead against the window as if moving that extra centimeter closer would help her see better. When it didn't work, she rocket-launched caution to the wind and focused on him instead. "What are you doing, Mr. Super Creepy Man?" she whispered.

The man lowered his head as if he'd heard her.

No mistaking it this time. His dark eyes zeroed in on her window.

Goose bumps rippled across Luna's arms. Her heart rate kicked up to a smooth gallop, but instead of running, this time something wickedly defiant glued her feet to the floor. She raised her chin, ignoring the fearful shiver settling into her bones. Swallowing hard, she did the bravest thing she could think of: She waved at him.

Luna had a rule. When something scared her, she vowed to always scare it right back. Face it down and prove she was more than it would ever be.

I see you, she thought. If she could handle her sleep paralysis demon, a creepy man on the lawn in a shiny coat was nothing.

The man began to smile, sagging cheeks lifting like curtains for an old stage play. He waved back before walking away toward the forest. The same reflective material was sewn onto his back in the shape of a sickle.

FRIDAY, 6:00 A.M.

A Message from Jewel

Good morning, darlings! I trust you slept well.

I refuse to hear anything to the contrary, because it would be a blatant lie.

Please proceed to the Floral Sunroom for breakfast, which will begin at 8:00 A.M. sharp.

As promised:

A Nonsensical Recipe for Winning

Preheat oven to 314 degrees.

Mix all colors until batter is smooth.

Pour into sweet companion molds. Set aside all but three key ingredients.

Whip two partridges until a psychopomp
and circumstance forms.

Share and cut the Baker's dozen
chocolate bar into quadragrams.

In a pressure cooker, separate the royal flush
with red herrings wild. Bake for seven minutes.

Serve the chocolate concoction
scrambled atop a pie on a cloudy white
day under a winner's cursed crown.

MORNING
RESTLESSNESS

Nicole's tablet vibrated in her hands. A large image of a twitching purple envelope filled the screen. She tapped it once, and it unfolded into a letter, a reminder stating breakfast would begin in one hour. The screen switched to her map—the pathway to the Floral Sunroom tracked out for her with white dots.

"Ridiculous," she muttered. What was the point of having a house so big, guests needed a map to navigate it? Of having Jesus knows how many staff to maintain it and no family or friends to speak of to live in the empty rooms that just sat there?

People froze to death on the streets because they couldn't find housing, but having a Soda Room was an excellent use of space, money, and resources.

Sure.

Okay.

A grumpy morning restlessness had filled Nicole with snark and cynicism. Bodies didn't care about vacation. Her internal alarm clock had wound itself and woken her up, right on time for a 4:00 A.M. shift at Salty Sea that she didn't have to go to. Coincidentally, she shared a time zone with Jewel's outrageous family estate. The ninety-minute flight and thirty-minute car ride had barely inconvenienced Nicole's day, other than having to pack.

After waking up, lying in bed and staring at the pale yellow ceiling had felt wrong. So she'd gotten up, got dressed, and decided to use her map to wander the halls, a nice change from making lattes on auto-pilot. But the longer Nicole walked, the angrier she got.

A few of the doors were locked, but so far, she'd found the Holiday Wing, where each room looked like it had come straight out of a seasonal decorative catalog; two different pool rooms designed as a forest lagoon in summer and a hot spring in winter respectively; a whole room full of soda with bubbly wallpaper to match; and a fifties diner's ice cream shop, of all things.

Every room a perfect temperature.

Every room pristine and presentable.

Every room devoid of life.

Following the map, Nicole turned the corner as two workers walked out of a room, laughing with arms full of sheets and blankets. They placed them in a laundry cart next to the door.

All the staff Nicole had seen so far wore uniforms that reminded her of flight attendants—sharp, dark blue button-down dresses that stopped under the knee, matching pointed hats, and their hair slicked back into flawless buns. A large, circular gold brooch had been pinned to the left side of their chest. Nicole recognized it immediately because the same insignia had been welded to the estate's front gates: a wyvern wound into an infinity symbol eating its own tail, wings spread behind it. She knew it wasn't a dragon because it only had two legs.

"Oh, good morning," one of them said, noticing Nicole. She wore a white eye patch over her left eye, and her name had been stitched onto the dress in gold under the brooch. Taylor. "The breakfast event is starting soon. Do you need help finding the correct dining room?"

Correct probably meant there was more than one, because of course there was. "No, thank you," she said, politeness out in full force. "I have my tablet."

"You should hurry," the other worker, Fantasia, said. "Jewel doesn't like it when people are late." Nowhere near as friendly as Taylor, she looked Nicole up and down, a slight sneer twitching at her lips.

Okay.

"I know who you are," Fantasia continued. "I've seen your videos."

A small price of internet fame? Strangers would always have an immediate one-sided advantage. Nicole braced herself for no reason other than self-preservation. She never knew what would come next after hearing those four words.

Taylor let out an exaggerated sigh. "I'm gonna finish up." She headed back into the room.

"You're not better than Jewel," Fantasia said. "You're just a cheap, fame-seeking imitation."

"How omniscient of you to make assumptions about me, a total stranger, based on a painstakingly curated online presence." Nicole breathed and paused. She'd never been afraid to stand up for herself, but being strong didn't mean she had to be a jerk. "I'm not trying to start anything. There's something about my face that makes people get the wrong idea about me, but I swear I'm one of the chillest people ever."

Her face. Her ambition. Her talent.

Her dark skin. Her body.

Just . . . her.

There didn't seem to be a middle ground. People either loved her or hated her. She was a lot like Jewel, in that respect.

"You don't get it." Fantasia shook her head, turning to go back in the room. "I hope you do before it's too late."

The look Fantasia gave Nicole before closing the door felt like a magical shot to the heart. Every lick of common sense she had screamed GET OUT like she'd just been dropped into the heart of a horror movie. The hallway felt bigger and colder with sinister intentions looming in the shadows.

Nicole hurried down the hall without looking back.

Three gentle knocks in rapid succession sounded from across the room. Stella glanced at the adjoining suite door, deciding whether to answer Harlow or not. She was in the middle of reviewing the Winning Recipe that had popped up on her tablet while simultaneously deciding what kind of new and fabricated personality quirk her assigned red room of pain could inspire.

If Jewel expected her to play a role, she'd be happy to oblige. It's like Nicole said: *When in Rome . . .*

In one fluid motion Stella rolled off the bed, pausing to set her tablet on the nightstand, and walked to the door. "Greetings."

"You're not dressed?" Harlow asked.

Stella looked down at herself. She supposed her blue-and-white gingham romper could be viewed as pajamas. More than that, though, it had become an opportunity. "A question even though you can clearly see I'm not. Why are you like this? Who hurt you?"

"Is that supposed to be a joke?"

"Are you laughing?"

"No."

"Then it wasn't." Stella shrugged, turning back to her room. "Come in. If you dare."

Harlow continued to hover near the door. "Breakfast is in like thirty minutes."

Stella resumed lounging on the bed, turning on her side. The mattress hit a perfect sweet spot of plush firmness that had knocked her out cold the moment she had lain down after her shower. "I'm not the breakfast type," she lied.

"Meals are mandatory."

"So, then, go," Stella said. "I'm not stopping you."

Harlow rolled her eyes. "Whatever." Instead of walking back through her black room—the colors of onyx and ebony and coal—she used Stella's red door, opening it with more force than was necessary.

She probably would've slammed it too, if the padded red envelope waiting on the other side didn't make her pause. "What's this?"

"What's what?" Stella asked, watching her carefully. At the sight of the envelope, clearly labeled A PRESENT FOR STELLA, she rolled off the bed again, hurried to Harlow's side, and snatched it from her. "Did you get one?"

Harlow glanced at her door. "No."

Stella tore into it, upending the contents into her palm.

"A necklace?" Harlow asked.

"I do believe this is an Ouroboros." A rather large wyvern with wings eating its tail with a heart-shaped hole in the center of its chest. Stella held it by the chain, and read the inscription on the back aloud:

> For Red, I gift this medallion and chain
> Once unlocked it will show the way
> How to unite, lead, locate, and play
> Too bad for Black sacrifice is the game
> A White Key in the heart of blame

"Cryptic and low-key threatening. Seems par for the course of this weekend." Stella was about to return the necklace to the envelope when Harlow asked, "Can I see it? Please?" with her eyes too wide, too focused on the necklace.

The golden wyvern turned slowly between them.

"Sure." Stella watched Harlow, her naked desire for the thing, and noted the way Harlow's hands shook as the necklace landed on her waiting palms.

"Why did you get a present?" Harlow asked. "I thought we got them from challenges."

Stella considered that—she had a point. "We probably will, but Jewel never said we *only* get them for challenges. They like word games here." Whatever the Gamemaster Trio wasn't saying would be just as important as what they were. "It's equally possible there was a challenge when we got here and we just didn't know it. Maybe I earned this by agreeing to play."

"We all agreed to play, so we should've all gotten one."

"I don't like you," Stella said, deciding on the spot to not invest any more of her time in Harlow. Not worth it—too whiny and entitled for her liking. "You all were willing pawns, down for whatever. I'm not. We have contact with the outside because of me. I *challenged* Jewel, and I won."

"You're making that up. That's way too convenient."

"All theories are made up," Stella said. "And if my color was in the same sentence as the words *too bad* and *sacrifice*, I'd be worried about what comes next, not why didn't I get one."

"Whatever. Everyone else already went downstairs."

"Not so fast." She gripped Harlow's arm, yanking her to a standstill. "Give it back. It was in front of my door with my name on it. You may not steal another player's presents, remember?"

"I wasn't stealing," Harlow furiously whispered, looking around as if to check to see if someone else had heard the accusation. "We're supposed to work together for the game."

"Are we? Did *Jewel* say that?"

"She implied it."

"No, you interpreted it that way."

"Same difference." Harlow shrugged. "We need a leader to make sure everyone stays on track."

"And you think that's you?" Stella stretched her arms upward, yawning. "I don't know what kind of Sweet Valley High you came from, but you're not leadership material by any stretch of the imagination."

Harlow scoffed, rolling her eyes again—an interesting reaction and habit that *her* parents obviously didn't help her break. "You're such a bitch."

"Thank you."

"That wasn't a compliment."

"Are you sure? I think it was." Stella winked. "You need to calm down."

"Don't tell me to calm down," Harlow said, fuming. "From the second you got here you've been nothing but bitchy to me. And now you're going to hold us all back in the game."

Stella raised an eyebrow. "That was quite the little speech. Remind me to pay attention next time." She laughed, and then said, "Look. You can't out sass me, so don't try. If you want to talk about perceptions? We can do that. Your attitude has been absolute condescending and sycophantic trash. Let's be honest with each other: If I'm a bitch, so are you. I'm just better at it."

"Whatever. I truly hope you get sent home for not coming to breakfast."

"For your information, these aren't pajamas. I happen to be fond of rompers and onesies. I wear them all the time—outside, inside, it's all the same to me." Stella retrieved her Jewel-gifted satchel and tablet and slipped on her indoor shoes. "I never lose, by the way. I look forward to seeing your face three days from now after I've won." She selected the map app on her tablet and typed Floral Sunroom into the search bar. A white trail of dots appeared on the screen to lead the way to their destination.

FRIDAY, 7:45 A.M.

Nicole's map instructed her to make a series of left turns, convincing her she was running in circles, but no, there was a staircase *finally*. Her heart thudded in her ears, breath coming in short quick gasps while she loped down the stairs, two at a time.

Before Nicole arrived, part of her worried that she'd only meet people like Fantasia, who would have already made assumptions about her. They'd assume she was exactly like the character she played in her videos—expect her to entertain them and be witty 24/7 as their emotional-support comedian. Or hate her for some irrational reason. She'd read comments from voyeurs who said they were just waiting for someone to "expose" her.

But then there was Stella.

While Harlow had practically shouted her username and sweetly fangirled over JadeTheBabe's videos, Stella had introduced herself and said, "I don't care about any of that. I'm just here for the party." Her mocking smile was almost too much. "Congratulations on your face, by the way. It's a good one."

Nicole's tablet beeped softly. She stopped to catch her breath against the wall beside the propped-open door. Jewel's voice drifted into the hall—and someone answered. Definitely not Stella. Or Harlow or Luna. It didn't sound like Alex, but if Luna wasn't in there, she doubted he'd be found anywhere without her.

Outside, the gray morning looked beautifully mysterious. Fog drifted through the trees and clung to the grass. It must have taken a lot of water to keep the grass that green these days.

Many summers ago, Nicole's dad had all the grass removed from their front yard, replacing it with black and white stones, and cacti, because of the water shortage. "We can't do much, but we can do this," he had said. That was her dad—always thinking of ways he could personally make a difference, even if his changes amounted to the equivalent of a tiny drop of water in an ocean.

Why did the onus of saving resources fall on them when places like Jewel's backyard did more damage than their tiny lawn ever would have done?

She missed their house and her bedroom. Her parents had been thirteen years into a thirty-year mortgage. Banks, she'd found out, couldn't care less about orphans who didn't have any money.

She missed her block and her neighbors too. Well, kind of. Even before the bank took their house back, the weight of her neighbors' piteous stares had begun to reach unbearable territory. Everyone in her old neighborhood knew what had happened. A few had probably been morbidly curious and looked up the leaked crime scene and autopsy photos. Nicole could always tell the ones who had seen versus the ones who had not. Their pity hit her differently, like earsplitting ambulance sirens stuck in gridlocked traffic on a stormy night. Somewhere to be and no way to get there—desperately trapped without a shoulder to drive/cry on. She recognized it because she felt it too.

That was the tenor of her grief, most days. Anger and longing twisted together in hopeless, breathtaking fashion. Striking without warning, triggered by innocuous things like too-green grass.

"Nicole," Stella said as she approached. "You didn't wait for me. I'm devastated."

She instantly snapped out of her anguished reverie. "Hey." Lord Jesus, why did she sound breathless? Her smile felt too big, her feelings too eager. "I've been up since four, wandering around. I figured you were still asleep—otherwise, I would've asked you to come with me." She pushed off the wall and noticed Harlow, glowering next to and at Stella. "You okay?"

Surprise flitted across Harlow's face. "Not really." Her gaze flicked to Stella and then back to Nicole.

"Fine. I'm guilty," Stella said. "I don't do well with sensitive people. Lock me up if you must. I'd make an excellent queen of a prison."

"I've always been a fan of rehabilitation over prison. A little empathy goes a long way," Nicole said. "Where did you get that?"

Stella was wearing a wyvern necklace—same as the brooch the staff wore, same as the symbol on the gates. "Someone left a present outside my door."

"Really?" Nicole asked. "Any idea what it means yet? That recipe we got this morning was, um, interesting. Have you read it?"

"No to the meaning. Yes to the recipe. There's a riddle on the back of this too." Stella showed her.

After reading it Nicole tried to not sound worried as she asked, "Harlow, aren't you in the black room?"

"You're definitely a lot quicker than she is," Stella said with a laugh.

"Why are you all standing out here?" Jewel appeared in the doorway, hands on her hips.

Stella erupted with sound, cackling and trying to talk at the same time. "Oh, this is too *much*."

Jewel wore a floral contraption that had probably been modeled on some high-fashion runway in Paris. The strategically placed puffs, the rose print, the thin crisscrossed straps—it was *a lot* for 8:00 A.M. Nicole tried not to judge, but her eyebrows had no such qualms and refused to come back down.

"*Honestly.*" Stella approached Jewel, saying, "So far, everything about this trip has exceeded my meager expectations. Bravo. Just"—she kissed her fingers—"best trip of my life, hands down."

"My outfit tipped the scales for you?" Jewel asked, skeptical. "Really?"

"It's the total package. If it keeps going up from here, I might not survive."

Jewel said, "Out of everyone here, I know the least about you. I truly cannot tell if you're being sarcastic or sincere."

Stella's words consistently slanted toward harsh, but she always smiled while she spoke. Mischievously captivating, as if she had a secret she was dying to share, but—plot twist! The secret would be about you. And there'd be a 50/50 chance whether you'd like the secret or not.

Nicole absolutely wanted to know the secret. Was it possible to like someone *too* much, *too* fast? God, she needed a serious moment to check herself before she embarrassed herself. Or fell headfirst into jealousy.

"I can tell you with absolute certainty that it's always a little bit of both." Stella winked. "Love that dress. Really."

Jewel stood toe to toe with Stella and said, "I've decided I'm going to keep my eye on you, after all," before walking into the dining room.

Stella followed, keeping close. "You know who else does that? Sauron. I'm totally into that, by the way."

"Into what?" Jewel laughed—a real laugh, joyous and throaty. "Lord of the Rings? Or . . . ?"

"It's always a little of both," Stella reminded her.

"Is she *flirting* with Jewel?" Harlow whispered as she entered the room with Nicole, who answered, "I honestly don't know."

Jewel said, "Hmm, you might just be a bit too clever for me."

"Oh, don't let that stop you. Besides, you seem like the kind of person who likes a challenge."

"I like challenges I can win."

"Where's the fun in that?"

"Yep, definitely flirting," Harlow said in a small, scandalized voice.

Jewel said, "Oh, you'd be surprised. And if you're lucky, I'll tell you about it later." She pointed to a chair. "Have a seat."

"Yes, ma'am." Stella laughed and sat.

Harlow sighed, sitting in a chair, leaving a space between her and Stella for Nicole to sit in the middle.

Nicole gave Stella a questioning look.

"What?" Stella crossed her arms on the table and whispered, "I'm just messing around."

"Uh-huh."

"I don't get to do stuff like that in real life. It's just fun."

Harlow, visibly irritated, muttered, "And you called *me* a sycophant."

"Because you are," Stella said, "and clearly can't tell the difference between flirting and brownnosing."

"Enough, children. Stop fighting," Jewel said, clapping her hands once. "And where are the other two?"

As if on cue, Alex and Luna appeared in the doorway, breathless and more than a little disheveled. They stared at the room, unsure what to do.

Fifteen was barely four years ago for Nicole. She'd always been the biggest, the tallest girl in school but couldn't remember ever looking that innocent in the face or vulnerable. Then again, fifteen was the year she aged thirty years in a single moment and lost some of her memories to trauma response.

Luna had her scarf on, wrapped loosely around her neck. Alex was as gangly as they came, but Mother Nature kept his height at a reasonable level. Nicole thought they were . . . cute. She'd heard that saying "a head taller" before and never understood it until right then, seeing their complementary heights on full display, fitting together like nesting dolls.

"Huh. That's never worked before," Jewel said with a mischievous smile. "Good morning, please sit down sometime today," she drawled, finally putting them out of their misery.

"Sorry," they said in unison, and Alex added, "We lost track of time."

"I'd ask what you were doing that nearly made you late, but I don't want to risk embarrassing you, don't really feel like watching you squirm and sputter out excuses that we'll all know are lies, etc., etc.," Jewel said. "But I will say, I'm a stickler for timeliness. If an event starts at eight you should be here at seven forty-five. Am I clear?"

"Yes," they said together, tone so placating Nicole grimaced involuntarily. A song began to play, echoing through the room. Instrumental, light and airy, it had a classic, soothing rhythm to it. Ten seconds later, a clock chimed eight times.

"Welcome," Jewel said, "to Family Breakfast."

A FAVOR.
A PROMISE.

FRIDAY, 8:00 A.M.

"For the next twelve hours, the clock will chime throughout the estate, so you'll always know what time it is." Jewel threw a pointed look at Alex and Luna. "Eventually."

Luna nodded, eager as always to please. She truly was adorable. As was the room they were in—like a greenhouse ripped from a picture book made with soothing watercolor illustrations. Glass walls and metal panes. Green vines bursting with flowers climbing upward toward the domed ceiling. Sprouting, colorful plants in neat rows lined the room—more flowers and fruit bushes. The circular table was painted a muted orange, and the high-backed chairs were a deep brown.

"Hi, Luna," Stella said, louder than necessary. "Word on the street is I'm not good with being subtle. Good morning. I missed your cute little face."

"What about me?" Alex said. "My face wants to be missed too."

"Good to know." Stella winked at him. "I have enough metaphorical eyes for everyone. Except Harlow."

"Stella. Please," Jewel said. "Control yourself."

"Why?" Stella laughed.

"Because we have a schedule to keep and you're very distracting," Jewel said. "I want you all to meet someone. Player six?"

"Francis." He walked in from the door directly behind Jewel, taking the empty chair on her right. "My name is Francis. Not player six."

Nicole had an unparalleled skill for first impressions, and there were a lot of buts about him. His eyes, large and dark brown, were almost too big for his face, but somehow suited him. He had tanned skin and features that made her think he could've been Black, but probably wasn't. His thick but wiry black hair had been cut short on the sides and curled loosely on the top of his head. Their voices had a similar rasp, but his had a deeper tone and a harsher edge than hers.

"Do you use Golden Rule?" Luna asked. "Your profile wasn't on the home page with ours."

"Nope," he said.

"I asked Francis to join the game as a favor," Jewel said. "We're friends."

"We're not."

Luna exchanged a look with Alex, who then asked Francis, "So if you don't use Golden Rule and you're not friends, then how do you two know each other?"

"Ethan," Francis said, clearly eyeing Jewel. "No story. Just him."

Cute, *but* probably an asshole.

"Yikes," Harlow whispered.

"Fine." Jewel sighed, pinching the bridge of her nose. "I tried to be nice, but since you're dead set on being a pain in my ass, let's move on. Who's hungry?"

A small squad of staff in their stylized flight attendant uniforms filed in through the doorway directly behind Jewel with carts full of food. Their formation split into two—one for each side of the room—some wearing a pantsuit variant of the uniform.

Someone was saying something. Nicole heard the muffled tones of it, but the entirety of her being had hyperfocused on the creamy hollandaise sauce on the plate of eggs Benedict on the cart behind Stella.

Jewel had included a food survey with the GWX paperwork. The questions asked for food allergies, favorite dishes, and foods to avoid.

It hadn't occurred to Nicole that she could have asked for eggs Benedict.

She should've asked for eggs Benedict.

Hunger pains cut through her stomach. She'd been up since four and hadn't eaten since before her flight. Ignoring hunger was a skill she'd mastered out of necessity, but it only worked for so long.

An arm reached around Nicole—she looked up, reading the name *Prince* before seeing his face. He placed a plate of the fluffiest french toast sprinkled with powdered sugar and raspberries, and the most perfect pieces of bacon she'd ever seen, in front of her. It looked so amazing it could have been in a commercial for a restaurant.

"Would you like syrup?" he asked softly.

"No, thank you." Nicole's stomach tilted into full-fledged revolt, giving its acid free rein to travel to places it had no business being. Her salivary glands joined the revolution by springing a serious leak.

But no one else was eating yet. She clenched her hands in her lap, trying to pay attention to Jewel.

". . . you will also be expected to dress for our meals together. The wardrobe on the second floor is full of everything you could possibly want to wear, and if it's not, just ask. You'll know the theme in advance, but you're not required to stick to it. No matter what you choose, however, I expect you to express yourself and your creativity with fashion. Don't disappoint me," Jewel said. "Any questions? Good. Let's eat!"

Nicole closed her eyes as she chewed her first bite. It tasted even better than its appearance promised. If she wasn't careful, she'd inhale the entire plate in thirty seconds. She forced herself to eat slowly, to cut smaller pieces and take smaller bites. And to make conversation— she could make it last if she talked while she ate. She whispered to Stella, "I kind of blacked out for a second. I only caught the part about having to dress up. What did she say before that?"

"My God, why are you whispering at the table?" Jewel demanded.

"This is Family Breakfast Event. You don't whisper and have side conversations during family breakfast."

"There you go," Francis said, openly hostile and staring at Jewel. "I'm not your family."

"Ooh. I know that look," Stella said to him. "My mom does it whenever she wants me to shut the hell up."

"And I bet you listen to her every time, huh?"

"But of course. I'm no heathen." Stella raised her glass of orange juice, smirking over the top of the glass before sipping.

"Why is everything a joke to you?" Francis snapped.

Luna flinched, dropping her fork to the floor with a loud clang. "Sorry," she whispered, leaning closer to Alex. Her attendant, Cher, silently sat another fork beside her plate before picking up the one on the floor.

Stella set her glass down, smirk disappearing. "Not everything. I'm sure someday, something will come along and snatch the little bit of joy I have in my life clean away. Smother me until my light goes out so something far scarier replaces it. Until that day, I humbly"—she placed a hand on her chest—"suggest you let me get my jokes off and enjoy my weekend in peace. Also. It's quite *interesting* how you said 'everything' when you *just* met me." Her gaze slid to Jewel. "You're making this too easy," she said in a singsong voice.

Nicole sighed. All she wanted to do was eat and keep eating, but there was game stuff happening? Was that what Stella was implying? She'd gotten pretty good grades in school, but riddles and games like this definitely weren't her thing.

"Can we talk about The Cruelest Jewel? The rules said we couldn't ask staff, but you're not considered staff, right?" Alex asked Jewel. He had ordered pancakes. Even half devoured and drenched in syrup, they looked perfect too. As did the second stack on the cart behind him.

Seconds.

Nicole turned around, and yep, there was another plate of french toast and bacon waiting for her on Prince's cart. Her brain started sending signals to the rest of her: Food rationing was officially over for the weekend.

At home, every morning she ate the same thing—cereal and milk. She measured out exactly one cup of cereal and two thirds a cup of milk because it was the only way to make it last. Math was the one consistent universal truth of life: Each bowl was the equivalent of having spent $0.40 per meal. The box promised and delivered on twelve cups of cereal. If she ran out of milk and couldn't get some for free at work, she'd use water or eat it dry. Still, that was twelve days of at least one meal per day. Guaranteed.

But if she won The Cruelest Jewel, it could be over indefinitely.

Which meant she had to pay attention.

"No, I'm not staff," Jewel said, "but I did make the game and you brought up an excellent point. Addendum Number Two: There will be no discussions about The Cruelest Jewel during meals."

"Thanks, Alex," Harlow said, full of sarcasm. "Really."

"Sounds good to me," Nicole said brightly. And then promptly downed her entire glass of orange juice.

FRIDAY, 9:03 A.M.

Nothing sounded better to Nicole than a power nap.

But if she lay down, the sheer amount of food-coma energy pumping through her veins would render her unconscious for hours. Instead, she leaned against the wall in the hallway for support, semi-delirious and stuffed.

"So, hey, Luna," Harlow said. "Where were you guys this morning? Did you, um, find anything interesting?"

"Real smooth, Sherlock," Stella said. She crossed her arms, tilting forward in Luna's direction and back again, her necklace glinting as it came to a stop right in the middle of her forearm.

Harlow asked, "What? I can't ask questions now?"

"Not like that," Stella said.

"It's okay," Luna began while looking at Alex. "We just went for a walk outside and got turned around. That's all."

"That happens quite easily here," Jewel said, joining them with Francis in tow. She closed the door to the Floral Sunroom behind her. "I have some business to attend to, but I'll see you all at lunch. Stella. Harlow. Walk with me."

Stella's eyes practically sparkled at the invitation. Two steps in Jewel's direction later, she turned and said, "Nicole, I promise that I'll be thinking of you the entire time we're apart. I will *literally* count the minutes until we're reunited."

"You're lucky I like you," Nicole said, taking a chance.

"Don't I know it. And you're welcome."

God, Stella was insufferably perfect and precisely Nicole's type. Harlow groaned loudly farther down the hall as Stella ran to catch up.

"Um, well," Luna began, "we're gonna go . . . um. Do stuff. Bye."

Alex at least waved at Nicole as they set off in the opposite direction.

And just like that, she was alone. Unsurprising. Being routinely isolated or excluded had been a fact of her life for years. Sometimes, when quiet got the best of her, she wondered how it was possible to have a follower count in the actual millions but only two close friends in real life. Charlie would've thought this whole thing was wild—she hoped he was okay working double shifts. She wished she could've brought him with her, like Luna was able to bring Alex. He deserved a vacation too.

"So. Hey."

Oh lord, she'd forgotten about Francis. That fast.

He stood in front of her now, seemingly unbothered that he had to look up to meet her eyes. Her height bothered guys. A lot. If her massive online following didn't scare them off, her height did. She had a theory that they stopped being interested the second they realized they'd never be able to tower over her, never be able to use their size to intimidate her.

"Hi," she said.

"I'm Francis. I know you heard me say it in there, but I wanted to introduce myself."

She smiled a little. "Nicole."

"Were you going anywhere?" He smiled back. Nothing about it looked effortless. "Or did you plan to just stay here until that Stella girl came back?"

"That crossed my mind," she joked. "It's not like I have anything else to do. The game already started, but I didn't get anything. Stella got a necklace. I think Alex and Luna must have gotten something too since they ran off to go do 'stuff.'"

"Do you want to sit down, then? There's some couches in there." He pointed to a closed door at the end of the hall, nestled under the staircase.

"What room is it?" she asked, walking toward it. "Sofaland?"

"Maybe," he said, a half step behind her.

"I'm really full, though. I'll sit, I'll lie down, and next thing you know, I'll say I'm just resting with my eyes closed and be knocked out for three hours," she admitted. For some reason, she expected the door to be locked. The knob turned easily under her hand, and she peeked inside. The small room smelled dusty and clean at the same time, and a giant circular beanbag took up most of it. Weird and definitely not couches. "Yeah, it's way too comfy in there."

"Why did you eat so much?"

Nicole's head snapped around so fast it moved between moments. She looked him up and down, eyebrow daring him to try it. "Because I was hungry."

Francis blinked in surprise. "I didn't mean it like that."

"Uh-huh." Fat jokes were like earthquakes. You didn't know one was happening until the ground started rolling beneath you. She'd heard her coworkers hissing behind her back, *She can't be that damn poor. Look at her. Obviously, she has money to spend on food.*

The assumption that a person had to be emaciated to show they were starving was laughable. Bodies, genetics, were far too tricky for that. She was fat, she was constantly hungry, and food insecurity was an eating disorder waiting to happen. All true and existing simultaneously.

"Really. I swear." He held his hands up in surrender. "I'm not like that. I don't say shit like that to people. I just meant you knew there'd be a game we'd have to play and you wouldn't be able to sleep it off so"—he paused—"you know what? I'm sorry. Let's just leave it at that. I was wrong, and I'm sorry."

"We need to go to my room," she said, purposefully ignoring his apology. Forgiveness was a suggestion, not a requirement. "I forgot she said you'd be here this morning—otherwise I would've brought your tablet to breakfast."

"Oh, I don't need that. I know my way around."

"It's a part of the game. We have to carry them. Jewel specifically asked me to give you yours."

Francis exhaled, eyes rolling toward the ceiling. "Right. Come on," he said, leading the way.

Their wing didn't have a name on the map. Nicole had decided to christen it Crayola Hall to match the theme. Their tablets matched their room colors—her room landed in the shades between a pale yellow and a soft cream. It also had a door with a weird double lock and purple knob that led to Francis's room. That would absolutely be staying locked.

"What's this?" A small yellow package had been placed in front of her door. Nicole picked it up, weighing it in her hands.

"I don't know," Francis said.

"I wasn't actually asking. It was rhetorical."

"Then maybe you shouldn't have said it out loud."

Nicole side-eyed him. Judging by the half smirk and expectant look in his eyes, there was a 75 percent chance he was teasing her—and hoping to do it again. The thin ice under him had already begun to splinter. Instead of responding, she opened the package, pulling out an iron box no longer than her palm with a small star-shaped hole on the top. She shook it by her ear. "Doesn't sound like anything is inside."

"There's something on the bottom." Francis reached up, taking the box and turning it over.

> *And lastly, for you, a locked iron box*
> *Occupied by birds with skeletons of tin*
> *Keen eyes can solve the mystery within*
> *But not before finding a lost arctic fox*
> *The Green codex and the Red paradox*

Nicole stared at the words, willing them to magically make sense. *Green* meant Luna and *Red* meant Stella, but the rest? "What is it with her and riddles? Why can't she just make this easy and get it over with?" She opened her door and headed for her nightstand. The box soared after she threw it, bouncing on the bed before teetering to a stop, riddle side up.

"Because she likes to watch people struggle for fun." Francis sounded so resigned she nearly laughed. He retrieved the box, holding it loosely in his hand and out for her to take. "I really hate her sometimes."

"Who? Jewel?" she asked, trading his tablet for her present.

"Who else?" While the tablet booted up, Francis attached the strap and then slung it across his body. It landed near his hip. "We're really not friends. She's friends with my friends, and Ethan is my best friend. More than anything else we orbit around each other because we have to."

"Then why did you agree to be here?"

"Good question."

"And does it have an answer?"

"Yes," he said. "Why are you here? I heard you didn't come willingly either."

She wondered if she should tell him. He said *either*. Meaning he probably already knew about her side deal with Jewel or assumed she'd made one because he did too. If she told him her secret, maybe he'd share his.

"I did," she said, feeling bold. "Sort of. Jewel promised me a role in her next web series and a meeting with her agent. She even said there'd be a way for me to earn a bonus, which I know now is the prize money."

Francis surprised her again by looking genuinely concerned. "Be careful with that. Anytime she promises something, her puppet master strings are usually out in full force." He shoved his hands in his pockets, stepping closer and lowering his voice. "This isn't the first time she's hosted a game like this."

"I know. This is the tenth time," she said in a mock whisper, fully ignoring the way she allowed herself to lean in closer to him. Of course she had heard about the previous Golden Weekends and how nobody talked about what happened during them, as if it were some sort of secret club. A game made the most sense. The silence that followed didn't—not that she cared. She didn't join Golden Rule to solve puzzles. She joined to get famous.

"No, it isn't," Francis said. "About five years ago, way before she blew up with Golden Rule, she invited a group of us here, to this house, for a party, but really, she made us play a game. She had help, Ethan, some of our other friends, but the game was . . . hard."

Imagine that. Golden Weekend X was actually number eleven. She wondered if Francis had any other secrets to share. "How hard? Like on a scale of one to ten."

"Twenty. My team didn't even finish. If this game is anything like that game, this weekend is going to be hell," he said.

"A hell that you're willingly walking through. What did she promise you?"

Francis leaned against her bedpost, suddenly looking away and at the floor. "Something I didn't think she could actually make happen. That's why I wasn't here last night. I didn't believe her and refused to show up until she proved it."

"Are you *sure* you're not friends?" Nicole teased, holding up her iron box. "Your answer was just about as cryptic as this riddle."

Francis scoffed, a half grin out in full force. "Let's just say, it's nothing on par with five hundred grand. Winning *might* be worth that to me."

"Which one means more to you?" She matched his dry tone, watching him carefully. Something felt off about his answer, like he wanted her to believe the money was more important but meant the opposite.

Constantly striving to improve her acting craft influenced everything she did on the screen and off. And everything about Francis in that moment—his stance, his tone, his answer—felt like he was purposefully trying to mislead her.

She didn't get an answer.

Their tablets began vibrating as The Cruelest Jewel app opened on its own. "I'm supposed to go to Winterwonderland," Nicole said, switching to her map.

"Imagine that." Francis held up his tablet.

Please proceed to Winterwonderland.
Your key code: 14082309180525

Same location. Same code.

YOU DESERVE TO BE HAPPY

FRIDAY, 9:08 A.M.

Alex flopped down on Luna's bed, defeated by their failed search. And jet lag. "I don't think it's here."

"Then where else would it be?" Luna sat next to him with a pout. "We tried everything. She wouldn't have given this to me without a way to open it."

After her shower, Luna had tossed and turned, still too wound up to sleep. It took a while, but her brain slid into a nice slice of REM cycle that ended abruptly three hours later when she sneezed herself awake.

A green envelope had been placed next to her pillow. Someone had entered her room without her knowing to place it there. She'd slept right through the intrusion. And all the fear she felt drained away the second she'd opened her present.

A small book as long as her hand, from wrist to fingers, was inside. A crescent moon encased in a shimmering atom had been stamped on the front cover, and the back had a riddle:

> *Your gift, a hidden world for the silent girl*
> *A foolproof codex to find every door*
> *Passages in the walls & under the floors*

No need to wait for the trick to unfurl
With the Invisible Words of the Silent Girl

A lock with a diamond-shaped keyhole had kept her from opening it to read the pages. They'd almost been late for breakfast because they'd spent the morning searching for the key. Alex had the bright idea that "invisible words" meant invisible ink. They found a kitchen and tried to heat up the codex—in the oven at 314 degrees like the nonsensical recipe said—to see if maybe Jewel had used lemon juice to hide the location of the key. No dice.

At breakfast, when Luna had unrolled her napkin, she thought of *unfurl*—maybe the key was hidden in her room, wrapped in something. They unrolled all the perfectly folded towels in both their bathrooms. Tore through the guest socks in their closets. Checked inside the pillowcases, under their beds and flat sheets, behind the curtains, and nothing.

Nothing.

"Maybe there's another hint in the recipe?" Luna pulled it up on her tablet. "'Mix all colors.' That's us. We all have different color rooms, and we're supposed to work together."

Alex said, "It says 'all,' though. Maybe we should have asked the others for help."

"I really don't like that," Luna complained. "If only two can win, we should only work in pairs."

"Aye, aye, Captain," he said, falling backward on the bed. "How about a nap? Nap sounds good."

She lay next to him, staring at the canopy above her bed. "I think Stella wants to work with Nicole."

"Mmhmm."

"But I also think Jewel wants Stella to work with Harlow."

"Mm."

"Because they're the remainder. Francis pretty much stared at

Nicole the *whole* time at breakfast. I think he's here for her. Which is extremely suspicious."

"That's some hardcore deducing."

"I mean, I don't have any proof, but I have a feeling," she said. "And, you know, their rooms are next to each other, so that makes it kind of obvious too."

"How are you not tired?" he asked, amused.

"How are you sleepy? This is so exciting I can barely stand it," she said. "*So much* is happening. I can't let myself get tired. I know the second I close my eyes again, I'll miss something. Jewel is so amazing. This is the best day of my life."

"What happened after we got separated last night? Er, this morning. I tried to wait up for you, but . . ."

"I know. You fell asleep with your lights on. I checked in on you when I first came upstairs," she said. "We just talked in the den."

"About?"

"I thought you wanted to take a nap."

"Talk me to sleep. Like a bedtime story."

Luna snorted, wriggling closer to him to lay her head on his shoulder. That was probably also a violation of the girlfriend boundary—lying so close together on a bed. Why did Melody get to say whether or not touching Alex was allowed? She didn't *own* him. He wasn't her property.

"It was like"—she hesitated, reaching for a way to make him understand how momentous it had been for her—"like being with Tasha."

"Oh."

How could she describe the indescribable? Talking to Jewel felt like a dream, soft and blurry like a cloud, but sharp too, razor sharp as a knife's edge. She remembered every second and doubted herself about it.

"Yeah. And all she did was ask me about home and school and stuff. She said it was nice hearing me talk since I never do in my videos."

"You have a good voice," he said, matter-of-fact.

"And she said she's wanted to get to know me for a while, I guess."

"Something you both have in common. I guess."

"I guess." She giggled. "She's so great, Alex. Different from her videos. I was right—she definitely has a wall up, but it was like I could literally see it crumbling the longer we talked. She's so warm. And funny."

"I'm glad you're happy," he mumbled, almost asleep. "You deserve to be happy."

FRIDAY, 10:15 A.M.

Luna shot up into a sitting position, heart racing. She'd fallen asleep! NO!

Her tablet vibrated on the bed next to her, muffled but persistent, echoed by Alex's. She pulled it onto her lap with one hand and shoved Alex with the other. "Wake up, wake up! We have a challenge!"

"No, thank you," he grumbled, rolling over.

"Yes, thank you! GET UP!" she shouted at him, grabbing his tablet to read his message too. "We have to go to the library! There's a key code we have to use to get inside!"

Luna had never seen the library. She'd wondered about the design in the past because Jewel *loved* to read. Every so often her videos flew off the rails when she mentioned a book she had finished. Once, she uploaded a thirty-minute book talk for some fantasy about twins and alchemy.

Prerecorded Golden Rule diary entries had a ten-minute maximum. Jewel had broken her own app rules for a book.

"I have a headache." Alex groaned, sitting up with an intense frown.

Luna slid off the bed, grabbing his hands and pulling him into a standing position. "The map says we'll pass a kitchen to get there. We'll get some water on the way. Come on!"

They were already down the hall when Alex realized he'd forgotten his tablet and had to go back to get it.

Ten minutes and one pit stop later, they arrived outside their designated door. She entered their code and tried to get her expectations in check. Maybe it'd be a small and intimate room. A couple of bookshelves, some plush chairs perfect for lazy reading days, and some cozy window seats.

Alex whistled as they walked in. "*Je-sus.*"

Natural light from the glass ceiling spilled into the narrow three-level library. There was a staircase on the left and right, both leading to a second- and third-floor U-shaped landing with an open space in the middle. The built-in shelves were packed with books, the spines a mixture of old binding and new. But strangely, on the first floor, the wooden bookcases protruded from the walls.

"I wonder if it has one of those slide ladder things in here," Luna said. "I'm totally going to pretend to be Belle."

"Wait, does that mean I'm the Beast? Because there are two main characters in that story and that's not happening."

"No." She laughed as she walked to the left to search for their envelope. "I'm talking about the scene when she's in the bookshop. If anything, you'd be the wizened old bookstore employee who lets me have the book I keep borrowing before a sheep rudely eats some of the pages."

"That ain't it either." Instead of checking the right side, Alex had followed her, which . . . was unhelpful.

"Gaston, then?"

"How dare you."

"Running out of characters here."

"It's fine. I prefer Ariel anyway."

"Ah, so you're a Prince Eric?"

"If you ever need saving from a sea witch, I'm your man," he said.

"That's funny. Ariel and Prince Eric's daughter's name is Melody. You can save her instead."

"Or not," he muttered, pulling one of the books off the shelf. "We broke up."

"What?" Luna momentarily paused her search. "Why?"

"She didn't want me to come here." He shrugged. "And if I didn't, that meant you couldn't. I wasn't gonna do that to you."

"Okay, um, well, thank you. But that's not worth breaking up over?"

"It was. Melody said it was her or you," he said.

"Oh." She took a step back, realized what she was doing, and stopped.

"I know how that sounds. Relax." He poked her in the arm. "Ultimatums are gross. I don't want to be with someone who thinks like that, so I chose myself. I wanted to be here, and I am."

"And you're okay?" she asked. "I mean, you two were together for so long and you didn't even mention it. That seems like the kind of thing you should've told me so I can, you know, support you. Emotionally. Like you do for me when I'm having a hard time."

"You're sweet." Alex's bottom lip poked out while he looked away, thinking. "But I'm fine. Don't worry about me."

Luna nodded, deciding to distract him. "Where do you think the envelope is? Maybe you should check the second floor? We'll cover more ground if we split up."

"In movies, splitting up is always a terrible idea."

"*Horror* movies. We're not in a horror movie."

"And how do you know that?" Alex walked backward, giving her a questioning look softened by his know-it-all smile. He made it halfway up the stairs when he called, "Found it."

"Really?" Luna ran to him, plucking the offered envelope from his hands.

"It was just sitting there. On the seventh step."

"Hmm. That was easy." *Too easy*, she thought as she opened it.

> *Dreams are never out of reach as long as you climb*
> *Upward and onward, with a pinch of luck on your side.*
> *To unlock the moon codex, you must find the snowy owl key.*
> *Hidden in a single black book in an endless sea of green*

Alex said, "We could've slept in. We could've went back to sleep right after breakfast."

Luna giggled at how seriously annoyed he looked. "No, we couldn't have. We didn't know this was going to happen. We always have to try even if it leads nowhere."

"Saying that doesn't make me less cranky."

"I appreciate you," Luna said. "You're my favorite person who's my age."

"That qualifier. *Hmph.*"

"You're my favorite person who's not Tasha and not Jewel."

"Third?! You know, you're really bad at this," he said. "And now *you're laughing?*"

Luna's giggles turned into snorting cackles. "I promise I will make it up to you once we win and are rich beyond all reason." She laughed, holding her tablet up, finger hovering over the button. "Ready?"

Alex nodded.

The moment Luna pressed BEGIN, a great rumble began to shake the library. Alex grabbed her immediately, holding her to him with one arm and securing them to the banister with the other. With a sharp *clack*, thin strips of floor snapped downward in looping, circular patterns.

All the bookcases on the first floor swung away from the walls—and there were more behind them. An endless stream of green bookcases flowed out of the openings, turning and sliding and rolling on the newly created tracks. When the last one clicked into place, so did Luna's idea. "It's a maze."

The entire open floor of the library had been crowded with bookcases with a clear entrance. Right in front of the staircase where they stood. Luna grabbed Alex's hand, pulling him inside.

A uniform sea of green books on green bookcases. Nothing on the spines. No signs to guide them.

"This isn't happening," Alex said. "We're never going to find the key now."

"Yes, we are," she told him. "Don't say that."

Luna's heartbeat was erratic with excitement. Again. She would probably have to see a doctor when she went home to get checked out. The Cruelest Jewel wasn't any regular, degular game. Of course, Jewel would make them work for it. She looked up at him, speaking with conviction. "Everything has been practically handed to us so far. *This* is how we earn our spot. This is where we prove we're meant to be here."

At the maze entrance, she plucked a book at random off the bookshelf and set it on the floor. "Do you see the black book on either of these two bookcases?"

He searched the one, while she searched the other. Row by row, from top to bottom. Luna selected another book, placing it on the floor at the edge of the bookcases she'd just checked.

Alex smiled, catching on. "Bread crumbs." He did the same to make his side of the path.

"It might take a long time, but the challenge riddle basically told us to not give up. As long as we keep trying, we won't fail. Me and you. Till the very end."

"You and me," Alex agreed. "We got this."

KNOW YOUR PLACE

"**S**tella," Jewel said as they traveled down yet another seemingly endless hallway. "Why did you agree to come here?"

The more important question was, Who designed this house? Ghosts? No one in their right mind would possibly create something like this place. It didn't seem *that* big on the outside, yet the sheer number of rooms and corridors screamed haunted maze, like that Winchester place. Their gem emoji—hers, Jewel's, and Harlow's—moved at a steady pace, matching their movements step for step, turn for turn. Nothing seemed amiss until Stella actually watched where they were going.

Interesting.

"Isn't that obvious?" Stella said. "I wanted to get away from my parents. I said yes to your little trip and fought like hell to convince them to do the same. They've already emailed me four times this morning, by the way."

"How did you convince them?" Jewel asked, and Stella frowned for a hot second before fixing her face. She already knew exactly how because Lloyd and Diane told her.

Ah, so she wants to air my backstory, Stella thought. She glanced at Harlow, who was watching her and waiting for an answer. If they were all a part of the story, then Jewel must have needed Harlow to hear it. To play or not to play . . .

"I told them I'm going to write an essay about you. Maybe even a book," Stella said. "A tell-all bursting with every good, bad, weird, and intensely ugly fact I can dig up."

Harlow gasped, actually gasped, letting her mouth hang open.

"What?" Stella asked, all innocence. "She agreed to give me a no-holds-barred interview. It's why my parents said yes."

"People lie, Stella," Jewel said with a grin. "Why would I tell you anything about me?"

Stella decided to keep the innocent act going and added in a dash of faux confusion. "Why wouldn't you? Aren't celebrities always going on and on about how they can't be normal? How everyone knows them and they have no privacy and they can't trust anyone, waah!" She laughed lightly. "I don't know you. I don't care about you or any of this. Who better to be yourself with than little old oblivious me? Face it, we're a romance novel waiting to happen."

Jewel scoffed, blinking rapidly from shock as she looked away and back again. "Why would I want someone like you?"

Anyone else would have been insulted or instantly embarrassed. But not Stella.

Never Stella.

"Someone like me?" Stella mock-gasped and pressed her free hand to her chest. "You make me sound so scandalous and irresponsible. I love it. Though, truthfully, I've always thought of myself as the sheltered know-it-all with the tragic backstory, but I do have a soft spot for the corrupting bad-boy type. I can totally be that for you. If that's what you need."

Suddenly, Jewel smiled, nothing friendly about it. "What I need is for you to do a job for me."

Against her better judgment, Stella glanced at Harlow, who met her gaze with a question. She had no idea what was going on either.

Jewel led them straight to a pair of double doors, which she pushed open with both hands. Bookshelves, a fireplace, a desk, inspirational art on the walls—someone's dark cherrywood office.

"I'm listening," Stella said.

"Harlow's too seasoned," Jewel said, nodding to her while opening the desk drawer. "They know her. But you, Stella, don't have a leg in this race."

Stella squinted. "That's not how that saying works."

"My bank accounts disagree with you," Jewel said. "I want you to make livestreams for Golden Rule while you're here. Everything you do and see and experience, talk about it. As often as you can, but not more than once per hour." She held out a clear plastic case with a microSD card inside. "Insert it into your tablet and run the program. It'll give you access to the app and Wi-Fi."

"Why?" Stella asked.

"Because you're my only option," Jewel said. "I can't use Luna because she makes silent videos. If she suddenly starts talking on camera, Goldspiracy will have a field day in an empty parking lot. I can't use Nicole because it will interfere with her brand. She wouldn't have enough time to create a full production. That leaves you. Your following only exists because I chose you. I've seen that video you made. You don't have a style or the content to sustain it. No one knows you. Make the videos. Tell them everything."

"*Rude*. I have style." Stella's shtick had a 97 percent success rate in person, but something about video flattened her personality. Cameras transmitted her energy and reflected back everything she didn't want to see. It wasn't possible to hide from herself in stunning HD—a descendant of Dorian Gray, evolved but just as immoral and profane. "I just haven't figured it out yet."

Harlow moved, shifting closer to Stella.

"This should also please your parents, no?" Jewel asked. "A documentation of your time here that you'd be free to reference later."

Stella clicked her tongue to focus herself. Jewel had explained why Stella was her videographer of choice but not why the videos needed to exist. She could ask, should really, but . . . "You said it was a job. What do I get paid?"

"Whatever you want. If it's within my power, I will make it happen."

"And if you can't?"

Jewel sighed. "Name your price."

Stella whistled, low, long, and exaggerated. "Being rich must truly be amazing."

"You would know." Jewel seemed genuinely confused. No doubt the background check had revealed some Forbes-related truths about Stella's parents.

"You're confusing my paltry allowance with my parents' financial portfolio," Stella said. "Everything I want to do? Anywhere I want to go? If they don't approve, they don't pay. Really, it's a miracle I'm so well adjusted considering the fascist state of their parenting regime."

Jewel laughed. "You're quick. That's good."

"It's a gift."

"So, will you do it? The livestreams must be at least two minutes long with a maximum time limit of seven minutes." Jewel gestured with the plastic case still between them, waiting like a hand to be shaken. "What do you want for your time?"

"My time for yours." Stella would do her homework, fulfill the promise she made to her parents, but it would be on *her* terms. Why conduct an on-the-record interview when the challenge of wiggling around the NDA was *right there*. Because something else was going on in this outrageous estate. This game, Jewel's story, had to be about more than a bottom dollar. She continued, "For every video I make, I get seven minutes of exclusive alone time with you. No lying. No pretense. I get to spend time with the real Jewel in her unfiltered and natural state."

Jewel seemed stunned into silence. Harlow too—her eyes darting from Stella to Jewel and back again.

Stella continued, "I also want a bonus. An extra minute for every five thousand views the video has before I cash in the session."

"That's a confident bonus for someone who lacks screen presence. Making watchable videos is harder than it looks," Jewel said, recovering.

"I won't be promoting the videos to the main page. You'll be lucky if you break a thousand views total."

"Then my terms shouldn't be a problem."

Jewel considered the offer and said, "Deal."

Stella took the card with her left hand.

"Oh, and one last thing," Jewel began. "You cannot tell any of the other players what I've asked you to do. If either of you do"—she made eye contact with Harlow—"if they find out in *any* way, you're both disqualified."

"Why do I have to keep her secret?" Harlow asked, petulance on full display. "It's not my job. I'm not getting paid for it."

"Because I said so." Jewel's cold tone could make a penguin shiver. "Is the prize money not enough for you? I'm paying the winners in cash—what more do you want from me?" She walked from behind the desk, standing in front of Harlow. "Maybe you should focus on what you've already been given instead of whining about what you don't have."

"I didn't get anything," Harlow said in a tiny voice. Her hamster brain was no doubt spinning like a wheel being so close to Jewel. They were practically sharing the same breaths.

Jewel reached out, smoothing Harlow's shirt over her shoulders. "Do *you* know why you're here?"

"No," she admitted. "I haven't really thought about it."

"Your *job* is to be neutral. A touch of realism. Find your place, middle child," Jewel said with a soft seriousness. "Know your place." She lifted Harlow's tablet, placing it in her hands. It began vibrating.

So did Stella's.

"Please proceed to the wine cellar," Harlow read.

"Why are you doing this to me? I thought we had a *connection*," Stella said to Jewel. She had also been assigned to the wine cellar.

"You're already together. Look at that," Jewel said. "How convenient for you."

Tricky, tricky.

114

STELLA SAYS
EPISODE 1

Nine in the Afternoon

Hey, is this thing on?

[voice off-screen] I don't think I can look for you. I'm not supposed to be in them.

What are these gold-star things floating in the corner?

[voice off-screen] Pulse points. Like a thumbs-up. The more you get, the more notifications are sent to users who don't follow you to tell them about your livestream.

I see. Well. I think that's enough time wasted. Yes, I can see your comments, SpoopyRenaissance.

That's right, kids, my name is Stella and I am coming to you live from the hallowed Van Hanen grounds. Want to know the super-top-secret ins and outs and dirty details of our wild and rowdy Golden Weekend X? Then I'm your girl. I've been tasked with giving you all the inside scoop with a side of style.

You better strap in because believe you me, it's going to be a day.

First order of business: The Cruelest Jewel—an ambitious game with ambiguous stakes. We've been tasked with solving intricate riddles and completing Jewel-crafted challenges all in hopes of winning an obscene amount of money the likes of which most people wouldn't even dare to dream about.

Right now, me and my compulsory partner-in-crime, who shall remain faceless but not voiceless, are on our way to our first challenge in the—drumroll, please—wine cellar. To be honest, we have no idea what will happen once we get there other than we'll have to follow the instructions we're given.

Am I scared? Not really.

You?

[voice off-screen] In the middle.

Unfortunately, I have a seven-minutes-in-heaven time limit on our little live chats and am only allowed to make one per hour. Also, I'm not entirely comfortable bringing you into the dungeon of doom with us.

We just met. I can't have you seeing me in potentially vulnerable situations. I don't know you like that.

But I promise I'll be back with updates. Pinkie swear.

Now, *your* challenge, if you choose to accept it, is to get this video to over five thousand views. If that happens, I will devote episode three exclusively to a no-holds-barred Q&A. Tell all your friends.

This is Stella, signing out.

How's that for not having style?

[voice off-screen] Um, honestly, it was a little over the top.

See, that's exactly why I don't–

[video cuts off]

MONSTERS UNDER
THE BARRELS

FRIDAY, 9:37 A.M.

Two black flashlights sat on a small table next to the wine cellar door. Harlow picked one up and said, "There better be lights down there."

Stella raised an eyebrow, well practiced in the art of being both curious and mocking. "You're not scared of the dark."

"I don't want to accidentally fall or something." Harlow opened the door, shining her light against the wall. "No switch." And then down the wooden stairs. "Ready?"

The smell of sawdust wasted no time crawling into Stella's nose and mouth. She yanked a white cloth napkin from a rack filled with them and used it to cover the lower half of her face. "Born for it." She aligned her light with Harlow's to illuminate more space.

At the foot of the stairs, a row of giant brown barrels had been lined up on the far right. Bottles upon bottles of wine, resting at angles on wooden racks built inside the walls on the left, stretched in both directions in front of them.

"They don't actually make the wine down here, right?" Harlow asked. "Don't they use a factory or something?"

"I have no idea how to make wine," she lied. "Ask someone else."

An aircon unit whirred in the background doing its job and the absolute most. Stella shivered. She hadn't been expecting such a drastic temperature change since the inside of the house always felt perfect.

Harlow headed for the barrels. She squatted down, nearly having to lower herself to the floor to see underneath. "Nothing here." When she stood, her knees and hands were still clean. "Where do you think the envelope is?"

It took everything Stella had to keep a straight face. "Probably tied to that doorknob."

"What? Where? Why didn't you say something?"

"I was going to, but then you decided to check for monsters under the barrels and I decided to let you," Stella said with a laugh.

"Stop wasting time." Harlow marched to the door in question. Faded red paint clung to the split and warped wood. Carefully, she pried the wax seal on the envelope loose with her thumb and unfolded the flaps.

> *Twenty-six letters across the board, yes and no and numbers.*
> *Add a planchette to help you awaken the*
> *old ones from their slumber.*
> *Create your six questions thoughtfully,*
> *use the five W's and how,*
> *To find the key to unlock the wyvern's*
> *heart, in the here and now.*
> *Take turns seeking answers, be sure to stay patient.*
> *When all is said and all is recorded,*
> *you'll go back to inhumation.*

> *Press* BEGIN *when you are ready. Enter the room, don't*
> *break the circle, and remember to say goodbye.*

"Another riddle?" Harlow asked, frowning. "Do you think there's a clue in here about solving the nonsensical recipe?"

"There could be some overlap. The recipe has the word *key* in it, and so does this riddle. I don't think that's a coincidence," Stella said, deep in thought. "But let's table that and stick with C-P-R for now. I think this"—she held up the envelope—"is specifically for what we have to do right now, during this challenge, to earn the next present, which should be a key for my wyvern."

"That makes sense. One step at a time, then," Harlow said, and read the riddle again. "Do you know what *inhumation* means?"

"In this context? Nothing good." Stella thought it for the best to keep that potentially nasty tidbit from her. She hoped she'd jumped to a conclusion that would end up being way off base. "That clue had Ouija board written all over it."

"I got that part. It's not real, so it's fine."

Stella's eyebrows shot upward. Logical, she was. Rationality was her patron saint. Still, she'd grown up a believer in the idea of a soul, of energy existing after a body's death. She kept her tone cool. "Atheist?"

Harlow shook her head. "I'm not religious, but I'm equally not opposed to the idea of religion. I just don't think Ouija boards are real. It's a mass-produced board game with a registered trademark symbol. Hardly a gateway to the great beyond."

"Believing is the gateway, not the board itself. It's the law of attraction."

"I don't believe in that either."

"Unsurprising." Stella laughed.

"It's seriously just a stupid game designed to scare gullible people. Someone has to push the planchette thing to make it move. Some unseen force isn't controlling it. The players are." One hand hovered over the flashing BEGIN button on her tablet, and the other held the doorknob. "Ready?"

"I suppose."

Harlow had the nerve to look disappointed.

The room beyond the old red door was little more than a broom closet minus the tools. A small table faced the back wall with the board on top, planchette resting at an angle pointing to the letter *R*. The lit candles nestled in candelabras on the wall flickered and created shadows.

And once they were inside, the door swung shut—loud enough to make Stella jump. "It won't open," she said, thoroughly and absolutely *not* panicking. "Hey!" She knocked on the door. "I'm not claustrophobic, and I'd like to keep it that way, thank you!"

"It's fine, Stella, jeez. Sit down. It's probably remote controlled." Harlow pointed to the camera in the corner on the ceiling. "Once we were inside, they closed it. It'll probably open once we're done."

"Probably," Stella echoed.

"The sooner we do this, the faster we find out."

"You're way too cavalier about this." Stella narrowed her eyes. "You're not Black, are you?"

"Will you please stop wasting time? Do you want to lose?"

Stella exhaled through her nose, fuming with frustration. Reluctantly, she sat down next to Harlow and kept her hands firmly at her sides. The board screamed one of a kind, crafted with care. She took in the carved letters, numbers, and words. Pictures and symbols told a story she couldn't read along the border. It had been made from a thick plank of wood—the sides had been scorched in a fire and the top had been coated with a soft polish.

"The five *W*'s," Harlow said. "That's like who, where, what, and, um, when? And—"

"Who, what, when, where, why, and how."

"Right." Harlow placed two fingers of her right hand on the planchette. "I'll start. Come on."

Stella eyed the board. "I'm good, thanks."

"You're not scared of a Ouija board," Harlow said, clearly delighted to throw Stella's earlier words back at her.

"I'm not scared. I'm self-aware enough to know there are some things you don't mess with. Making a point isn't worth potentially being incredibly and supernaturally wrong," Stella said, anxiety breaking through the surface. "And this is the best damn Ouija board I've ever seen. Pretty sure this sucker wasn't mass produced."

"If you don't play, we get disqualified and have to go home. What was the point in making all that fuss about your parents if they're just going to pick you up anyway because you're too scared?"

Stella said quietly, "I did not sign up to get traumatized."

"You can't be if you don't let it."

"You have no idea how trauma works, do you? You don't get a choice."

"I think you do. I think it's mind over matter."

A small voice inside Stella's head whimpered *Help*. In the irrepressible spirit of not wanting to go home, and only for that reason, Stella slowly lifted her hand and copied Harlow's placement.

"We have to move it in a circle a few times," Harlow said, leading the way. "Are there any spirits in the room? We'd like to talk to you."

Stella had never been so instantly stressed out in her *life*. As soon as Harlow finished speaking, fear *slammed* into her like a freight train. She could *hear* herself breathing, *feel* herself shaking. She believed in ghosts. Not just believed, but was *afraid*—actually, genuinely afraid. When did this happen? *How?*

Harlow asked again, "Are there any spirits in the room? We'd like to talk to you."

The planchette tugged to the left. Harlow must have sensed what would happen—she clamped her free hand down over Stella's wrist to keep her in place. "You can't let go until we say goodbye. The rules said we can't break the circle," she whispered.

The planchette came to a stop over *Yes*.

"You go first," Harlow instructed, annoyingly unbothered.

Stella asked, "Who are you?"

"That's a terrible question."

"I disagree." If Stella had to do this, she wanted to at least know who the hell she was talking to, dead or alive. She refused to blink, watching as the planchette moved and paused on letters as it spelled out the answer.

M-E-R-C-Y

Harlow continued, "Remember, it's not real. They're probably using magnets to move it remotely once we've asked our question."

"Probably." Stella took a deep, rattling breath.

"What does the key look like?"

C-A-T-K-E-Y

Harlow said, "Your turn."

"When did you die?" Stella asked.

"Ask better questions," Harlow snapped.

W-I-N-T-E-R

"Where should we look for the cat key?" Harlow asked.

U-N-D-E-R-S-T-A-I-R-S

"It's *not* a ghost. A real person is watching and answering us. Focus on the game," Harlow said. "Ask a question *about* the game."

The game. The Cruelest Jewel.

Stella swallowed the little bit of moisture she had left in her mouth. It barely soothed her dry throat. Believing was the gateway and the question. The answer was choosing *what* to believe in. Even if she *were* talking to a dead person named Mercy (h e l p), that didn't change the fact that the answers would play into Jewel telling her story. Stella breathed in and out slowly, trying to find her calm and ignore the way Harlow stared at her.

Believe in the game, she told herself. *Rationalize your way out.*

If Mercy, Jewel by proxy, was telling the truth, what would help Stella help Nicole win beyond finding the cat key? What *why* did she need to know? She thought back to asking Olive why they were there. Why this game?

Stella's lips trembled so hard when she opened her mouth to speak she had to immediately press them together to regain control. She cleared her throat, painfully swallowing again, and said, "Why The Cruelest Jewel?"

The planchette didn't move. Before, the millisecond after the question was asked, the planchette was shooting around the board.

"Maybe they didn't understand the question," Harlow said, voice low and . . . impressed? "Try it again. Change it a little."

Stella sat up a little straighter, a touch of her familiar groove returning. "Why does The Cruelest Jewel exist?"

The planchette gave a false start, twitching to the left and going still for five seconds. This time when it moved from letter to letter it felt slow, sluggish with reluctance, as if it were revealing a secret it shouldn't.

W-A-R-D-E-N
S-I-R-E-N

Stella had no idea what that meant, but she had definitely asked the right question because Harlow gasped—all excited eyes and a barely hidden smile.

"My turn," Harlow said. "How do we beat Jewel's game?"

Stella *tsked*. "We know how to do that."

"No," Harlow said, grinning. "We know how to *win*, not outsmart her." She repeated her question, louder and with more confidence. The planchette moved with the same slowness—they'd definitely caught "Mercy" off guard.

F-O-L-L-O-W-T-H-E-M-O-O-N

"See? Completely different question," Harlow bragged.

EVERLASTING FIRELIGHT

FRIDAY, 9:20 A.M.

Above the pristine door handle, the connected keypad glowed soft green in the dimmed hall. Nicole took the lead, entering the egregiously long code. Gears inside whirred with intent before unlocking with an audible *click*.

The door opened out, not in.

Nicole stood on the top step of a short staircase inside the room. She rubbed her arms against the sudden cold, marveling at the breath pluming in front of her face and the state of the room.

Francis unleashed a string of creative swears, the likes of which Nicole had never heard before and probably wouldn't again.

Winterwonderland had not been an exaggeration.

A thick blanket of snow—no, it *couldn't* be—of something white and fluffy coated the ground. It dusted the tops of the giant silver armchairs, filled the blackened fireplace, clung to the ivory wall fixtures, and stuck to the ice-blue frames of landscaped portraits. In the center of the room, a silver light post's flame flickered in the cold and lit up as much as it could, which wasn't much. An envelope had been tied to it with ribbon.

"I've never seen snow before. That's not real, right?" Nicole shivered, teeth already chattering. Overhead, vents blew frigid air into the room, *whoosh*ing in earnest. She stood closer to Francis, drawn to him like a heat-seeking missile. "The amount of water damage would be ridiculous."

Francis loped down the three steps, dropping into a crouch. He grabbed a handful of the stuff. "It's not. It's some kind of clumping powder. It's not even cold." He rubbed his fingers against his palm to make it crumble and fall. "I think she turned the AC down to subzero for effect."

Nicole joined him, trying to step lightly until she was sure it would support her weight. She pressed some of it between her fingers. Grainy like sand, but also soft like powder.

Neither of them heard the door when it closed.

Francis trudged to the light post, fake snow crunching underneath his shoes. He broke the wax seal on the envelope, unfolding it quickly.

> Find the arctic fox key hidden beneath the snow.
> Use your hands and feet, you can even use your toes.
> But keep in mind that warm blood isn't
> terribly fond of the cold.
> Every three minutes the temperature will
> drop, along with more snow.

> Press BEGIN when you are ready.

"Instead of needle in a haystack, it's key in a snow patch," Nicole joked, feeling instantly disappointed in herself. "I'm cold. My brain has clearly stopped working already."

Francis laughed anyway. "The room isn't that big—if we start on opposite ends, we can go from side to side until we meet in the middle." He looked up, making her do the same. Fine black netting covered the ceiling. It bulged with the fake snow waiting to be dropped on them. "We need to be quick, though."

A BEGIN button pulsed on their tablet screens.

"Ooh, do you think we have to synchronize our tablets like *Mission: Impossible*?" Nicole asked with fake excitement.

He laughed again, bless him. "We're in this challenge together, so if one person starts their timer, the other will start too. Most likely. Ready?"

Nicole shivered violently again, exhaling in a frigid huff. All things considered, this wasn't that bad. And her partner was focused and tolerable.

Fine.

More than tolerable.

And slightly mysterious. With a nice face.

"I think I want to go to the bathroom first. And get a jacket," she said. "I'll be right back."

"Oh. In that case I'll wait in the hall, try to warm up a little."

"Good plan."

But when they tried to open the door, it wouldn't budge. Francis pulled and rattled the handle. He even placed one foot on the wall to yank it open before giving up with more colorful curses. "She locked us in. I can't believe her."

Nicole rubbed her arms. "For how long?"

"My guess is until we find the key or time runs out. Whichever comes first."

"Jewel didn't say anything about locked doors." Nicole took a deep breath to calm herself. She was in this now. No going back. No point in allowing herself to get upset and lose focus. There were 500,000 reasons why she wouldn't let a cold room, a locked door, and a full bladder break her.

Why did she drink so much orange juice?

"Really makes you wonder what else she didn't mention, huh? Let's get this over with." Francis pressed the button, which activated both timers. "So says one, so say we all. You can take this side," he said, voluntarily heading to the far side of the room.

Following Francis's system seemed like the best idea. Nicole started in the corner, nose against the wall. She brushed the fake snow to the side with her feet until she could see the dark floor underneath, steadily moving to her left. Behind her, Francis used his hands, also facing the wall.

They searched in silence until a scratching noise sounded overhead. The netting began to move, shaking gently back and forth until the fake snow drifted down toward the floor in a wave so thick Nicole had to keep her head down to keep it out of her eyes. Within ten seconds, the entire row Nicole had cleared filled back up. "Well, that sucks," she said once it stopped.

"Just don't lose your place, and keep moving toward the center of the room," Francis called. "The key is already under the snow."

Nicole didn't think it was possible to feel colder than she already was, but then her hands started shaking. She cupped them around her mouth, blowing into them. If she thought about how it felt like shards of ice were burrowing into her bones, it would only get worse. Her brain would overreact, and she wouldn't be able to do anything. She had to think about anything else except the cold.

They were trapped in a room together, so she might as well make use of it. She hadn't forgotten that he didn't answer her question earlier. If he wanted to keep it a secret, she could respect that . . . but would it be her fault if she innocently happened to figure it out on her own? To start, she didn't know much about him other than he said he didn't like Jewel (he played the part well so far, but she wasn't fully convinced), Ethan was his bestie (no doubts there—they had the same flavor of mischievous energy), and he didn't use Golden Rule. Hmm. No explanation for that one.

"So," Nicole called, teeth chattering. She'd read somewhere that talking helped stave off hypothermia. Or did it just make it obvious that you had it? "You really don't use Golden Rule? Ethan does."

"Why would I?" His voice was deep and clear, carrying across the room. "The last thing I need is for her to have more info about me than necessary again."

Again? Nicole's brain zoomed in on that admission but set it aside in favor of focusing on Ethan to keep her true intentions hidden. "Doesn't it bother him that you don't like his sister?"

"No, because he understands how she is. He's required to like her, I guess, plus he works for her company."

"Required because they're family?" she asked, assuming it was a joke. "What's his job?"

"Same as hers. They run BeJewel Industries together."

"Really?" Nicole stopped shuffling, turning around. "She seems like too much of a control freak to share anything, let alone a company."

"Oh, it's definitely hers. I think he can approve and sign for some stuff, but the company itself is *only* in her name. Ethan's her right hand, and Olive's her left," he said. "She says they're her kryptonite."

"'She says' meaning you don't believe her?" When he didn't respond, Nicole nodded to herself and returned to searching. "Ethan and Olive are dating, right? I think I read that somewhere?"

"Engaged."

"But they're so *young*," she said, absolutely scandalized.

Francis laughed lightly—a scoff mixed with a grin over his shoulder. "People fall in love. When you know, you know."

"Sure," she said skeptically. Finding someone she loved enough to want to marry seemed unfathomable.

Nicole couldn't remember the last time she'd been on a date or even opened a dating app to try to meet someone. She loathed being approached in person by strangers. No matter who asked, she always turned them down. It felt like an invasion of her space, forcing her into a corner to reckon with their desire, leaving no room to consider her own.

If she found someone online, it usually took her some time to talk herself into it. No, it wouldn't be a waste of time. Sure, you can leave after ten minutes if you want. No, you don't have to kiss them. Very rarely did she meet someone who made her eager and excited to see them again and again. Even rarer than that did she meet someone who captured her interest immediately. Those moments tended to catch her by surprise. For some reason, she never saw them coming.

A scratch, a shake, a shift. More snow fell, and the room got impossibly colder.

"I hate this I hate this I hate this." Nicole began to shiver so hard she had to bounce on the balls of her feet to keep moving. Bounce, scrape, slide. Cold, cold, cold. She had never felt cold like this in her life. Not even when she didn't have money to pay for her heating bill in the winter and had to sleep in three layers of clothes.

"I've seen your videos," Francis called out suddenly.

Nicole's heart sank into her stomach. *Not now, not now, not now. Don't tell me that right now!* Once again, she turned around to look at him. His back was still to her, and he'd made way more progress than she had, currently digging under one of the chairs. "But you don't—"

"Use the app, no. I've seen rips of them elsewhere." He glanced at her. "Keep searching."

Instead of turning around, she hopped behind the row she had created, kicking the fake snow behind her. She wanted to keep her eyes on him. The cold made it hard to think.

"Do you know what *The Everlasting F-Firelight* is?" He shook his head as if to shake off the cold and his stutter.

"No." She inhaled sharply, regretting it. Her lungs burned with a frosty ache. Even her toes were beginning to tingle.

Francis abandoned the chair, resuming his trek across the room in a straight row. "It's a story my mom told me when I was a kid. Basically, it's about these t-tiny people, like, um, in *The Borrowers*, but they lived underground. And on a different planet. Anyway. One day their light system breaks, and so Julip, the main character, goes off into the dark alone to steal this magical Firelight that will never go out. But when he finds it, he discovers that it already belongs to another group of tiny people who need the Firelight just as much as he does. He's kind of a jerk, so he tries to steal it anyway."

Nicole exhaled a shivering laugh.

"Julip is completely captivated by the Firelight. It's the most beautiful, shining thing he's ever seen. But remember, it's magical, so when he gets close to the Firelight it starts to talk to him. It convinces him that it's wrong to steal, and they come up with a plan together to save everyone. After talking to the leader, he has to prove himself by fighting for the right for his people to live there with them and wins. At the end of the story, they all gather around the Firelight that brought them together. You're like that in your videos. You're the Firelight that draws everyone else in."

For a startled, freezing moment, Nicole didn't know what to do with that. Was he messing with her? She'd gotten more than her fair share of compliments (and insults) in her life, but never anything quite so earnest and disarming. He sounded so *genuine*. Serious, even.

He had called her Firelight. Captivating and shining Firelight.

Nicole smiled, and the cold hit her teeth so fast it gave her an instant headache.

"Thank *fuck*," Francis exclaimed, standing up and hurrying to her. Standing so close to him, she could see how he was shaking too, how hard he was breathing and trying to blink away the cold. "Here." He handed her a white key with a fox-head bow and star-shaped tip. Fake snow clung to his hair and the tops of his shoulders. His nose and cheeks had turned a dull red. "It's your arctic fox to unlock your iron box."

"There you go again," Nicole said as the air conditioners audibly turned off. "Making rhymes just like Jewel."

FRIDAY, 11:13 A.M.

A Message from Jewel

Hello, hello! You all aced your challenges! Huzzah!

I expected nothing less, and therefore am *not* pleasantly surprised. If I may offer some constructive criticism: Feel free to move quicker next time.

Nonetheless, I do miss your brilliant faces, so how about lunch at 12:30 P.M. to celebrate? I'm sure this morning's search has left you all ravenous with hunger.

Please proceed to the **Wardrobe Room** for dress. Dazzle me, darlings, because the theme is **twisted tea party**. I can't wait to see what you all come up with.

See you then in the backyard at **Tea & Croquet**!

Oh, and as a reminder:

A Nonsensical Recipe for Winning

Preheat oven to 314 degrees.

Mix all colors until batter is smooth.

Pour into sweet companion molds. Set
aside all but three key ingredients.

Whip two partridges until a psychopomp
and circumstance forms.

Share and cut the Baker's dozen
chocolate bar into quadragrams.

In a pressure cooker, separate the royal flush
with red herrings wild. Bake for seven minutes.

Serve the chocolate concoction
scrambled atop a pie on a cloudy white
day under a winner's cursed crown.

CUT THEM ALL LOOSE

"Stop pouting," Alex said. They were following the map leading them to the Wardrobe Room on the third floor. It wouldn't be much farther.

"I am *not* pouting." Luna clutched her moon codex and snowy owl key to her chest. The key they'd found inside the all-black book had the diamond-shaped tip that opened her codex, as promised. But another riddle had been stamped on the front inside cover:

> *Some things change, while others remain*
> *On one true thing you might all agree*
> *The power of three might set you free*
> *And in the end, it might only be a game*
> *But only Red can decode the codex's aim*

Red. Stella. Group work.

"It's supposed to be me and you," Luna said, definitely still pouting. "I don't want to rely on them for anything."

"Doesn't seem like it's going to work that way." Alex gently swerved into her.

"And why *her*?" Luna continued, ignoring his gesture. "I hate how she keeps making fun of my lack of height."

"I think she likes you. If she didn't, she'd treat you the way she treats Harlow."

"You don't tease people you like, especially when you first meet them." She eyed him. "Would you like it if she teased you?"

He shrugged. "Maybe. It's not like I didn't give her a hint at breakfast."

"Wait, you were serious about that? I thought you were trying to help me. You know, deflect?"

"It was that too," he said, while pointing, "It's this door."

The Wardrobe Room turned out to be a full-service clothing boutique masquerading as a massive walk-in closet. Racks upon racks of clothes, color coded and sorted by style; enough shoes, jewelry, and accessories to rival a department store; a fully stocked makeup display; and changing rooms galore. The GWX paperwork Luna received asked for her measurements, and her clothes and shoe size. Jewel really had thought of everything.

Luna only allowed herself to gawk at the room for half a second before making a beeline for Stella, who sat at one of the vanities. Nicole finished putting eyeliner on her. "See the difference? With your eye shape, you don't want to go too far out."

"Unless I'm feeling dramatic. As you know, I live for the drama of it all," Stella said, examining her eyes. "You have an extremely steady hand."

"Hi," Luna said. She stood in perfect view of the mirror, hands behind her back, Alex by her side, as always.

"I'll let you do your own mascara so you can practice." Nicole handed Stella a tube.

"I hope they have eye patches here. Things are about to get dangerous."

Luna cleared her throat. "Hi, Stella."

"Hey." Nicole turned around. "How are you?"

"Good. Fine," she said, trying to catch Stella's eye.

"Any ideas for your lunch costume?" Nicole asked. "Need help?"

"No," Luna said. "I'll probably just pick out whatever."

"Hmmm. Are you sure about that?"

Harlow said, "They're not going to do what you want unless you let them dress you up."

Luna did a double take—Harlow was a rabbit. "Why are you dressed like the Easter Bunny?" She wore a full-on white body suit, complete with mittens and booties. The pullover hood even had pink ears.

"Easter Bunny is for April. I'm the March Hare." Harlow didn't seem too upset about being a sentient cotton fluff with ears, but *happy* wouldn't exactly describe her either.

"Dress me up how?"

Nicole and Stella wore matching smiles. *And* matching fur-lined pantsuits. White and Red respectively, with crown headbands.

Luna took a step back. "Um, no?"

"Um, yes," Nicole said, holding up a small gray box. "Unless you don't want to know what this is. I found it outside my room this morning."

"My wyvern seconds that sentiment," Stella said.

Ten minutes later, Luna stood glowering and miserable in a blue dress with a white petticoat, pinafore, and lace wrist cuffs.

"Your scarf kind of ruins the look," Nicole hinted.

"I'm *not* taking it off," Luna said. "And I hate you both."

"Why do I have to be the cat?" Alex had gotten off easy—a black shirt, black jeans, and cat ears.

"Because you're very adorable and my third favorite. Now stop complaining." Stella held out a pair of white tights and black Mary Janes for Luna. "Go on. Hurry up so we can start group work show-and-tell."

Luna, regretfully, did as she was told. When she returned from the changing room, as promised, Nicole handed over her present. "There's a riddle on the bottom."

And lastly, for you, a locked iron box
Occupied by birds with skeletons of tin
Keen eyes can solve the mystery within
But not before finding a lost arctic fox
The Green codex and the Red paradox

The key sticking out of the box resembled the one Luna had found during her library challenge—small, white, and with an animal head at the top. "Is this the arctic fox?"

Nicole nodded. "Francis found the key during our challenge, but I'm pretty sure the riddle is saying I can't move forward without you or Stella."

Luna twisted the key, and the top popped open. Two metal bird skeletons were inside.

"You can't take them out," Nicole said.

Both birds, stuck fast to the bottom of the box, had a small empty rectangle in front of them, as if something were missing. A string of white numbers had been engraved inside the top of the box—the same exact length as the code she'd used to open the library door. Luna removed the key. The bottom part was star shaped.

"What did you find?" Luna asked Stella.

"I also got a key, but Harlow found it. Turns out my wyvern is a cat lover." Stella inserted her white cat key into the wyvern's empty heart and turned. Something rectangular popped out of its head. "Ta-da! A flash drive." She plugged it into her tablet. "Presto chango." The screen turned white, then back to the blueprints of the map with red markings connecting some of the nearby rooms. "We think the red markings are the secret passageways." She pointed to the wyvern. "This little guy is a map expansion."

Luna had to take a hit of her scarf. She'd hoped they couldn't hear her breathing. That happened sometimes. When she got too excited, she began to wheeze. She pulled her snowy owl key and codex out of her bag, showing them the chart written by hand on the pages. The left column had the name of the room. The right had a one-line clue to find a door.

"I have a guide to find the secret doors. Nicole probably has the key code to open said doors. And Stella has a map so we don't get lost while we're in the passageways." Luna spoke carefully, as calmly as she could.

"Nicole's number has exactly the same amount of digits as the one we got for our challenge," Alex said after he finished counting. "I think you're right. This all fits together."

"This *sucks*," Harlow said. She stood off to the side with Francis, who didn't look nearly as irritated. Probably because *he* wasn't wearing a costume. "Why didn't we get anything? What's the point of us being here if we don't even get to play?"

Francis spun a top hat in his hands, saying, "Be careful what you wish for. You don't want the Eye of Jewel upon you."

"I made that joke earlier, thanks," Stella said. "We don't have time now since our tea party awaits, *but* we should put this to the test as soon as we can."

"What do you think, Francis?" Nicole asked. "You've played before. Does that sound right?"

Luna turned to face him, eyeing him warily. She could recognize every single Golden Rule user who'd been invited to Golden Weekend. He was a stranger. A complete stranger. She didn't even remember Jewel, Olive, *or* Ethan ever talking about him before.

"No. I didn't." Francis focused on Luna. "Stop looking at me like that. You're tiny and terrifying, and it's extremely jarring."

Stella said, "Hmm, I'd go with intense over terrifying."

Nicole said, "Wait, but you said she made you play a game."

"Yeah, The Scavengers Initiative, a cut-and-dried scavenger hunt with some horrible dares thrown in. I had a partner, and we didn't work with other teams. We weren't even allowed to. Whatever information you're after I don't have it. I'm in this just like the rest of you."

Luna didn't think he was lying, but that didn't mean he wasn't. That might have been the truth—just not all of it. She made a mental note to talk to him later. Alone. If need be, she could be very charming to get her way. Being small was the bane of her existence, but it did come with some perks. She could probably con some clues that he didn't even know were clues out of him.

"Somebody make her stop," Francis said. "I'm serious."

Stella cackled. "This is so much fun. I'm glad I decided to stay."

"Were you thinking about leaving?" Nicole asked.

"It briefly crossed my mind," Stella said. "But then I realized I didn't have your phone number yet and powered through."

Alex said, "We also still have to figure out how all these presents relate to the nonsensical recipe."

"We obviously need each other. That's what the first line is talking about," Harlow said. "Remember how it says 'mix all colors'? That means we have to work together. No one would have been able to solve what we have so far on their own without stealing presents, which isn't allowed."

Luna objected to that, but kept her mouth shut. Group work was *a* solution, not the only one. Jewel never said they couldn't spy on other teams or *borrow* clues. Because the last line of the first part also said *set aside all but three*. And her codex referred to the *power of three*.

"Maybe that's the point. All together until it's everybody for themselves. That sounds like something Jewel would do." Francis bit his lip, focusing on his feet. "Did she happen to mention something about Addendums?"

"Yes," Luna said quickly.

"Stop that or I stop talking."

Stella giggled and whispered, "Oh my God."

"You asked a question, and I answered. That's all." Luna shrugged, looking away.

Francis said, "During Scavengers, Jewel would make Addendums to the game, adding things and changing the rules last minute when she thought it was necessary. I wouldn't be surprised if she did that again."

"Okay," Luna said. "After lunch, we'll meet back here, pick a secret passage, and see what we find. Let's promise to work together to solve this thing. Everybody in?"

Luna smiled as everyone agreed, one hand behind her back. Fingers crossed.

She'd cut them all loose the second the game told her to.

STELLA SAYS
EPISODE 2

Bad Noon Rising

Hello, lovely internet ether.

It is I, Stella, here to give you a super quick two-minute update before my super friends notice I've temporarily flitted off without them.

I'm in a closet.

That's not a metaphor.

Whoa—these comments move lightning fast. Uh, hi, xxCreepsterxx.

That person wanted me to say hi. So, hi.

Thank you, by the way, for getting my last video to almost ten thousand views. I'll host the Q&A later tonight when everyone is asleep so we won't be interrupted.

Anyway, I'm happy to report that my first challenge is in the ghostly bag. Fun fact: Turns out, I'm a believer in the supernatural. Didn't know that before I got here. It's, uh, been a day.

While I can't speak on if any other pair found some new traumas to contend with, in Jewel's words we all aced our challenges and got some nifty presents in return. Next step: deciphering a nonsensical recipe one step at a time, but first? I need your help again.

I know, I know. I'm asking for a lot. I've heard it all my life, but have you seen Nicole?

I mean, come on. *Come on.* I gotta bring the goods to get the girl. Help me help myself.

So, during my first challenge, two words popped up that I didn't understand. Harlow did, but she refuses to tell me. Which is just so like her, you know what I mean?

Do the words *Warden* or *Siren* mean anything to any of you?

    [pauses]

I'm seeing Ethan . . . and . . . Olive? Okay, but how? I don't understand.

    [pauses]

Wait, the comments are moving too fast. I can't–

[pauses]

Okay, stop! Everybody stop! Will someone please type a full sentence and explain? And then if you must, everyone else copy that one sentence so I can see it.

[pauses]

Huh.

Well, that's interesting.

BEWARE THE IDES OF MARCH HARE

Jewel had the inspired idea to host lunch outside. The air had warmed up, the misty morning long gone, and a partly cloudy sky stretched overhead. With the map leading the way, they walked as a group across the too-green grass toward Tea & Croquet.

"This feels like walking in an arboretum," Nicole said. "I can't believe all of this is someone's backyard."

"I block it out. Pretend like it's not," Francis said. "I've had a lot of practice. Growing up with rich friends really messes with your head when you have less than nothing."

Stella said, "That sounds dreadful. I wouldn't know, though. I'm not allowed to have friends."

"That's probably for the best," Francis said.

"Lloyd and Diane would like you. So, therefore, I do not," Stella said, light and airy. "It's the principle of the thing, you see."

Francis asked, "Who are they?"

"My parents," Stella said.

"You call your parents by their first names?" he asked, stunned.

"Not to their faces. Obviously."

"Obviously." Alex laughed.

Always ready, Stella had another retort locked and ready to go, but decided to . . . not. When she let the friend secret purposefully slip,

Luna's bright eyes found her. The compassion in them was matched only by her curiosity.

Stella had decided to leave just enough of a trail to entice her. Luna wouldn't be able to resist a good mystery—and person puzzles seemed to be her specialty. A few more cryptic remarks and she suspected she'd have her.

Harlow could keep her Warden and Siren secrets. A little more information and the tiniest of pushes, then the moon would be the one to follow Stella.

A few more minutes of walking later, they reached the long table with high-backed chairs in the middle of the green field. It had been set up to look like a disaster—overflowing teapots, cups stacked into towers threatening to topple over, an assortment of jams and jellies in odd-shaped containers, and mice. Actual mice safely running around inside a winding tube system attached to the tabletop.

Jewel, however, had toned herself down, opting to wear a cute summer dress that looked like someone had thrown blue, yellow, and green watercolors at it.

"Welcome, welcome," Jewel said. "Please remember that there will be no discussion of challenges during family meals."

"Not your family."

"Shut up, Francis."

"Where's Ethan?" he asked instead of doing as he was told. "I thought he was going to be here."

"Since when am I my brother's keeper?" Jewel rested a wooden flamingo mallet over her shoulder. "Anyone up for a game of Wonderland Croquet?"

"I am!" Luna shouted before anyone else had a chance. Stella watched her run to Jewel, grabbing the other mallet. "Oh, um. I don't know how to play?"

"I'll teach you," Jewel said, wrapping an arm loosely around Luna's shoulders. "Come along, Ace."

Oh, ho, ho, ho. Stella's plan to ensnare Luna was absolutely going to work. She didn't bother hiding her confident grin as she sat at the table. A customized playing card printed on pearlescent paper had been placed on every seat. Every member of the GWX squad got one with a fantastically drawn portrait of themselves as the face of the card. The back had their name written diagonally across the length of the rectangle, striking through an image of the Van Hanen wyvern crest. The words KEEP ME were printed at the bottom in small blocky letters.

"Do you guys think these are presents?" Harlow, the Ten of Hearts, asked, beaming at her card. "If it's like last time, there's probably gonna be another challenge to unlock what they mean."

"Odds are good," Francis said. Jewel had given him the King of Hearts card to match Nicole's Queen.

Stella twirled hers—the joker—in between her fingers. "I can't help but think this means Jewel doesn't take me seriously. I'm a *joke* to her? The nerve."

The flight attendant staff were missing in action, but among the chaos there were orderly food trays of finger sandwiches, colorful macarons, and tiny cakes with tiny labels attached. Stella loaded her plate with a bit of everything and stole a whole teapot and milk for herself.

Out of nowhere, Francis commented, "She's like a puppy. A vicious little Chihuahua wearing a frilly blue dress and bow."

"Who?" Nicole asked while arranging her sandwiches by color on her plate. He gestured to the game, and she asked, "You mean Luna? She's a sweetheart. What are you talking about?"

The vicious puppy in question was talking a mile a minute, all but hopping around Jewel in an excited circle. For her part, Jewel seemed engaged, replying, laughing, and looking at Luna as if she actually cared about her. Maybe she did.

Stella thought they could be mistaken for sisters—the adorable mini-me and the big sister she idolized. "What's with the scarf?" she asked Alex. "Why won't she take it off?"

"It's her sister's."

"I think it's cute," Harlow said. "She's nice, and it's not hurting anybody."

"Yet," Stella said, intentionally drawing everyone's attention. "What? I'm just agreeing with Francis. He might not be wrong."

"Luna wouldn't hurt anybody," Alex said, defensive.

"Oh please," Stella said, pouring another cup of tea. "I like her, truly, but you'd be stupid and get exactly what you deserved if you underestimated her. She's surprisingly aggressive for someone so small."

Was that 100 percent true? Probably not, but the statement served its purpose. Francis had broached a subject Stella had been pondering since seeing puzzle-solving-extraordinaire Luna in action in the Wardrobe Room. She said one thing with her words, something different with her body language, and her eyes gave her true intentions dead away.

The moon definitely had a calculating, dark side.

"Aggressive how? Because she wants to win?" Harlow asked. "Honestly, I'm with her. I'm not convinced any of you are taking the game anywhere near serious enough."

"We're not supposed to talk about the game," Francis said.

Stella said, "We're not. We're talking about Luna."

"There's more than one type of aggression," Nicole said. "I'm not saying Stella and Francis are right, or even that I agree with them, but just because Luna's not in your face, bossing you around, doesn't mean she's not quietly plotting your downfall."

Oh dear. Alex was seconds away from steam shooting out of his ears. Anger made people reckless, made them say things they probably wouldn't under less stressful circumstances. He had a button named Luna, and Stella was about to lean on it as hard as she could. She said, "Oh, she's definitely plotting. It's like Harlow said: Luna wants to win. That ambition is naked as a newborn baby."

Francis said, "Stop talking about the game."

Stella continued, "Not to mention she's ruthless as hell and very skilled at hiding it. Look at her"—she glanced at the ongoing croquet game—"look at the way *she* looks at Jewel. She'll betray us all the second Jewel gives the word. Remember only two can win and there's no way of knowing if Jewel will pull a Head Gamemaker, turning that two into a one. We're all inconsequential and disposable to her. Every last one of us."

Not quite the truth. Not quite a lie. The last line was a bit unfair—Harlow would probably *also* betray everyone when the time came.

Still, the bait worked. Around the table, everyone watched Luna, forming their own opinions about what Stella had said, drawing their own lines in the sand. Everyone except for Alex.

"You don't know her," he said to Stella, fuming with a quiet and impressive rage. "You don't know *her* or about *anything* she's been through. Don't ever talk about her like that again."

"Please relax," Stella said with a laugh designed for damage control. "We've all got a story. No one is passing judgment. She's short, cute, and calculating. Color me intrigued. She's definitely my kind of girl."

Nicole said, "I guess when you think about it like that, it's not surprising that she looks up to Jewel so much.

"That's a bad thing," Francis said. "Jewel is low-key awful."

Harlow bristled. "No, she isn't."

Francis sighed loudly, rolling his eyes. "There's always one."

"She isn't!" Harlow said. "People always judge her because she's young and rich, but that's not fair. She works really hard, and she's super kind. Did you know all the staff here are felons? It's super hard for them to get a job when they get out of prison, so she decided to set up a program to get them employed through her company. They get health benefits and retirement and everything. There was this big story about it a few years ago."

Stella thought she might just change her opinion about Francis after all. She hadn't figured out his place in the game yet, but he could be useful. She asked him, "Is that true?"

"Yep."

"And," Harlow continued, "she gives away so much money that the *New York Times* even wrote about all the different charities she supports. I even heard about a hospital that was being strong-armed by their landlord so they were going to close because they couldn't afford the rent. Who does that to a hospital? Jewel bought the building and sold it back to the hospital for one dollar."

"Also true."

"She even randomly gives money to users on Golden Rule. Everyone knows that if you're having a hard time, like really having a hard time and not faking it for views, Jewel will give you what you need."

"Good deeds don't automatically make someone a good person," Francis said. "Yeah, she did all of that and more. She also made sure that everyone knew about it. The kindness of her heart has a lot of ulterior motives."

Harlow said, "I don't get it. If you hate her so much, why are you here?"

"Ding, ding, ding," Francis said, and Nicole added, "That's the million-dollar question."

Hello, hello. Stella sat up straight, watching the two of them while biting into a frosted cupcake. It seemed her new best girl and Francis had some secrets between them.

Harlow asked, "Wait, did you know about the prize money before you came here?"

"Stop." Francis didn't even bother to finish the sentence.

"For the record," Stella said, watching as Jewel and Luna made their way back to the table. "I don't think Francis knew about the money. He's here for something else."

All smiles, Jewel said, "I won. Who's next?"

"Me!" Stella laughed like a demented hyena. "Sit down, Harlow. I'm next."

Luna passed the mallet to her. "Watch out. She cheats."

"I do not," Jewel said, still grinning. "You're just a sore loser."

"I am," Luna admitted with a laugh and a euphoric smile. "But you also cheat."

Stella followed Jewel down the small slope. Unlike the others, she had only watched exactly two videos of Jewel on Golden Rule. She hadn't seen any of Jewel's TV shows or movies either. Some things about her were obvious—she liked being in control, manipulation was her best friend, she had a creative soul, and she had to be made of at least 90 percent secrets.

And she was beautiful, which was neither here nor there.

"We start here." The balls had been painted to resemble hedgehogs. "Do you know how to play?"

"No, and I don't plan to learn," Stella said.

"Oh?" Jewel's skin had hit that delicate balance between dewy glow and sweaty.

"We can just say you won. I won't even call you a cheat," Stella said while checking her Golden Rule app. "I'd like to cash in the payment for my first video. Almost fifteen thousand views and counting, so let's round up—ten minutes of your undivided and honest attention."

"If you must." Jewel sighed, setting her mallet down. "Ten minutes is enough time to walk to the vineyard and back."

Stella fell in step beside her, keeping the leisurely pace. "You should know my goal is to make you regret making a deal with me," she teased.

"Not possible," Jewel said, voice losing some of its brightness. "You're annoying and not anywhere near compelling enough to have an impact on my life." She looked at Stella, stone-faced with one perfect eyebrow arched. "Change my mind."

Okay. Wow. Right on cue, Stella's heart shouted, *Yep! Still gay!* "I'd call you rude, but I know that wasn't your aim. I'm sure you've figured out by now that you can't hurt my feelings."

"I have," Jewel said. "I'd like to get to know you, Stella At All Times. You wanted me honest and unfiltered. This is me—I like talking to people, getting to know them and their story. It's why I started my app."

"I thought it was because you liked puzzles."

"That unexpectedly came later," Jewel said. "You can learn a lot about a person from what they post online, but there's hardly anything about you."

"Just the way Lloyd and Diane like it. Can't get catfished by a misogynistic internet predator who likes to rape and murder young girls if they can't find you," she said all in one breath. "Are we trading life stories, then? I'm very interested in yours."

Jewel laughed. "We can trade, but only if you'll be honest and unfiltered too."

"Lying isn't my style."

Jewel scoffed. "Sure."

"It's true. Perception can be manipulated by details and delivery, but that doesn't mean I'm telling wholesale lies. I can't control someone else's assumptions. Surely, someone of your stature and circumstances can appreciate that," Stella said. "I like to tell jokes. I take my fun where I can get it, but beyond that? It stops being my problem."

Jewel regarded her for a moment before turning away. She chewed on her index fingernail, no doubt trying to figure out how to fit someone like Stella into a box for her little game.

The problem was, Stella realized suddenly, that Jewel hadn't anticipated someone like her being there. A match that rode too close to being an equal.

Leaning into that could be . . . fun.

Switching gears, Stella decided to enhance her plan by adding in some earnest revelations. She'd give Jewel a few more pieces to work with, make her feel like she had a way to keep things exciting and according to plan. "You should know that I'm not allowed to date," she said conspiratorially.

"Is that what we're doing here?" Jewel said, distracted.

"We're not *not* doing that. I figured it was best to let you know before we opened that very obvious door."

"Do you think you're my type?"

"Do I think? Hmm, what an interesting way to phrase that question. Do I think so? No. But do you think I am? Maybe."

"Maybe." An echo, not an admission.

"I think you're trying to justify why you think I am. Trying to make it make sense."

"Sure. Let's play," Jewel said, nodding. "You're intelligent and very forward. Confident and relentless. Usually people who are sheltered past the point of reason end up as shy and awkward sweetheart wallflowers."

"But not me."

"Not you."

"You should be careful," Stella said. She had Jewel right where she wanted her. "You might not think so now, but the novelty of me will never wear off."

The VAN HANEN VINEYARDS sign had a simple design. The name. Some grapes. A couple of squiggly lines. Dry as the sun-bleached wood it had been stamped on. Considering the rest of the house, Stella had expected something a whole lot more dynamic and not quite so pedestrian. The symmetrical rows of tethered grapes behind it weren't anything to write home about either.

"I'm not offering, and I'm not interested, but why aren't you allowed to date?" Jewel asked as she stared at the hills in the distance. "Tell me more about your parents."

As they turned back around, Stella made a mental note: Unfiltered Jewel made far less eye contact than her crafted-for-public-consumption counterpart. "You mean the people who would snatch me out of society and lock me in a tower if they could see me, here, being gay as hell."

That surprised Jewel. "Because you're gay?"

"Oh, no. No, no, no, no, no. Don't get me wrong, they have a lot of issues, but that isn't one of them. They don't care about my sexuality," she said. "The problem is they don't want me connecting with people, period. No dating. No friends. No acquaintances."

"That seems"—Jewel paused—"abusive."

"It is. Just not the kind the government cares about."

"Do you need help?"

"Oh yes. Lots. I go to therapy every week. We even have family therapy once a month. We had a breakthrough, which ended with the agreement that I would be allowed to use Golden Rule, which is how I ended up here ruining your little game. What a fun coincidence."

"That's not what I meant." Jewel remained unfazed and endearingly serious. "Do you need help getting away from them?"

Francis's earlier warning replayed in Stella's head: *The kindness of her heart has a lot of ulterior motives.*

Why was Jewel offering? What would she gain by helping Stella?

"They're not bad people," Stella said. Great. Now she had to redeem her parents. "They just exist with a tremendous amount of anxiety about their only daughter and her untimely demise. They had a Black, dark-skinned kid in a world that hates Black people. They can't control school shootings or drunk drivers or hate crimes or sex trafficking. Instead, they try to control me, who I talk to, where I go, the things I do. They need me to be safe, and they're convinced I'm safest when I'm kept under their thumbs."

"Then why did they let you accept my invitation? I know they're in town and they want you to interview me, but if everything you just said is true? You being here seems beyond the pale."

"Because of the first-class ticket and chauffeur and bodyguards and extensive security detail you have in place here. I convinced them it would be the safest first solo trip that I'd ever be likely to have," Stella said. "We're making progress. Slowly. Painfully. But it's still progress."

"That still doesn't make it right," Jewel said. "Do you love them?"

Right for the jugular. Stella considered dancing with a lie for a split second but changed her mind. "My therapist, Joan, claims I do. She says it's possible to love someone, deep in the irrational and unknowable parts of your heart, and not be able to stand the sight of them. I don't particularly like my parents. There are days when I'm positive I've slid into full-blown hate.

"But there are times when I miss them. Not right now, but sometimes I get sad if Diane is gone too long on a research trip. Or when Lloyd is on deadline. He turns into a nocturnal writer, and we have to stop having breakfast together every morning for a couple of weeks. If anything ever happened to them, I would probably be devastated," she said with what she hoped was nonchalance. "I figure if one part of what Joan said is true, the other could be too."

Jewel laughed softly. "I think your therapist is right."

"You don't know that." Stella sniffed, looking away. "It could be Stockholm syndrome. I'm still deciding." She turned back to Jewel. "Your turn. I demand secrets of equal value."

"Later," she said, gesturing with her chin. They'd made it back to the Tea & Croquet lunch party. "I think this is the end of our first date."

"You gotta give me something. That's only fair," Stella said.

Jewel sighed as she picked up her mallet again. "One. You may ask one question for now."

Stella considered her options. There'd be plenty of time to ask questions about Jewel's life—her second video was racking up views and she still had the third one scheduled. She needed to start small. Something simple. Something that appeared to be innocuous. Jewel probably wouldn't answer any questions about The Cruelest Jewel . . . unless she didn't know she was answering about the game.

Stella had a good, long memory. Her mental notes were practically etched in stone. She asked, "What's with all the cameras in the house? Really? According to the internet, you don't live here full-time. Doesn't it get super uncomfortable knowing you're constantly being watched? I've been here less than a day, and I think about the cameras all the time."

"I see you, Stella At All Times," Jewel said with an amused laugh. "The house cameras are a necessary evil. You're right, I don't live here, but everyone knows this place is my home. Safety has been an issue in the past. People getting in, hiding out, waiting for me to show up, threatening my family and the staff. It's better to see everything than to let anything be hidden."

"And being watched doesn't bother you?"

Jewel shrugged. "It's better to be seen than to be forgotten."

A CONVERSATION ABOUT CAKE

Nicole had been absolutely wrong about Luna.

The SilentStar of Golden Rule talked *a lot*. Luna began recapping her entire game she played with Jewel the moment she sat. The whole thing. Not a single detail skimped or skipped.

Francis lasted thirty seconds before he dramatically gave up on life. He cleared the space in front of him and put his head down on the table, closing his eyes. Before that, every so often, he'd catch Nicole's eye. He'd give her a forced, tight smile before looking away to stare at the forest in the distance. She still couldn't get over *Everlasting Firelight*. Knowing herself, she'd never get over it, honestly. He didn't feel shy, but it was like he suddenly couldn't talk to her.

Or wouldn't.

Nicole tried her hardest to focus on Luna, but her attention inevitably wandered to the croquet game.

Empty. Mallets discarded. Where did Stella and Jewel go?

No one else seemed to notice—Harlow, Luna, and Alex were still talking about croquet.

She sat up straighter as if that would help her see farther down the field—it didn't—before giving up. Not interested in the conversation (and with Francis ignoring her? Lying down was certainly a choice when she was right there?), she busied herself with experimenting.

The food wasn't nearly as decadent as breakfast had been. A good spread, nothing outrageous, but the tea.

The tea.

An assortment of small porcelain honey pots filled with different kinds of dried leaves and spices sat on an elaborate glass tray. Nicole all but created a ritual for trying the different combinations listed on the fancy recipe index cards—pausing to smell each ingredient before carefully packing it in the infuser, counting the seconds turning into minutes while it steeped, and finally taking a conservative sip to concentrate on identifying both the obvious and unfamiliar flavors. Then she experimented by adding milk to some, sugar to others, dollops of honey here, cinnamon cream there, and even a syrupy fruit jam once to see how well the flavors would mix.

Harlow shot a disgusted look at her for that last one.

Nicole shrugged and drained the cup. An unexpected pang of sadness rushed through her as she realized she didn't know *what* she liked because it'd been so long since she'd had a choice that went beyond buying the same cheap groceries week after week. She wanted to try everything, really give her palate a chance to enjoy the experience, no matter how strange it looked. Odds were good she'd never get another chance like this again.

Besides, it would all most likely go to waste anyway. There was way too much food and drink for seven people on the table. Might as well get creative with her choices.

Stella's irrepressible cackle echoed through the open area. Nicole watched as she strutted from the playing field back to the table. Her supermodel walk needed work—way too much hip, and it sort of looked like she didn't know what to do with her arms—but she got full marks for confidence.

"Nicole," Stella said as she sat. "I'm assuming you missed me. Feel free to lie to me if you didn't."

"I did. No lying required."

Jewel, who had lagged a few steps behind, asked, "Who's next?"

Harlow shot to her feet before anyone could beat her to it, and they walked off together.

"Where did you and Jewel go?" Nicole asked.

"Just for a little stroll down to the vineyard," Stella said, plucking a bright pink macaron from the spread. "I'm not the athletic type, so I opted out of croquet. Are you jealous?"

"No."

Stella huffed. "I *said* you're allowed to lie to me."

"You're truly something else. You know that, right?"

"I've been called worse." She sat back in her seat, slightly turning away. Knees pulled up to her chest, she began using her tablet. "I'll take a 'something else' from you any day."

It took Nicole a few heartbeats to realize Stella had ended their conversation. She stared, waiting patiently for her to look up, but she didn't. What was she doing, anyway? The tablet only had three active apps: The Cruelest Jewel, Mapped Up, and Touch Base—their only way to contact the outside. Everything else on the tablet had been disabled, including the Notes app.

Across the table, Alex and Luna shared a bowl of strawberries, speaking quietly to each other and laughing. Francis was still sleeping, or at least pretending to. All at once, she realized that if they didn't have The Cruelest Jewel to talk about, nothing else held them together.

Nicole had thought they had a good group vibe going, and she'd obviously thought wrong.

No one wanted to talk to her?

People liked the idea of JadeTheBabe, or the other characters she played, more than the real Nicole. Coming to terms with that dissonance had wrecked her for an entire week a few months ago. Her worst fears had come out to play, telling her everyone she met could sense something broken inside her, something they instinctively knew to avoid—or try to take advantage of.

Just as Nicole began to settle into the doldrums of feeling sorry for herself, Stella looked up and said, "Nicole, you're breaking my heart.

You have a magnificently expressive face, and it is bellowing sadness at me."

"I'm not sad," she lied, purposefully winking her left eye. "I'm thinking very, very hard."

"Aww, you remembered."

"It's barely been twelve hours since you said that."

"Ahh, you're right. It feels like I've been here forever. Probably because of the sleep deprivation."

Nicole laughed at herself—she'd shot straight to paranoia for no reason. Why was making new friends always so anxiety inducing and stressful? She needed to relax.

"Hi, everyone!"

Nicole turned to see Olive and Ethan approaching the table wearing matching denim overall outfits—a dress for her and pants for him—and a black collared shirt with short sleeves.

"Sorry we're late," Olive continued. "We had to call an emergency staff meeting."

"Everything okay?" Francis had miraculously risen from the dead.

"It will be," Ethan said as they sat.

"What did we miss?" Olive beamed around the table, filling up a plate with food. "Is she really making you all play twisted croquet? She always cheats when we do."

"See? I told you she was cheating!" Luna said.

Olive grinned at her. "Minus the cheating, are you having a good time so far?"

"I am," Luna said. "I love the house and the game and everything. Everything's really perfect."

"This house is wild," Stella said. "And probably haunted."

"It's not haunted." Olive laughed. "But I know what you mean. The first time Jewel invited me over so we could study, I had a string of small heart attacks. And that was before the renovations."

On the app, Olive always seemed cheery and helpful. Nice in small doses, but at the table with no reprieve it made Nicole uncomfortable.

Her behavior felt . . . fake. Plasticky. As if she were trying to over-compensate or cover something up.

"Renovations?" Nicole asked, trying to shake her discomfort. "Is that why there's a Soda Room?"

Ethan shrugged. "MJ created Neverland Ranch. Dolly Parton has a theme park named after herself. Jewel inherited Van Hanen Winery and reached for her wildest dreams." Now he seemed exactly the same as on the app. Unsurprising. As the Warden, he intentionally kept all the users at an unapologetic arm's distance. Parasocial relationships weren't his thing. He'd made that perfectly clear on more than one occasion.

That didn't stop some of his fans from being the most notorious on the site—the Warden Wives were *devoted* to him.

"Oh, um, Ethan?" Luna said. "You're in charge of security here, right?"

"I supervise all the staff, security included, yeah."

"Okay, um, 'cause I was really, *really* tired and I don't really trust my memory, but I think I saw someone outside my window last night. They were just standing on the lawn doing nothing."

Ethan gave Luna his full attention. "What did they look like?"

"An old white guy with greasy, slicked hair. He was wearing a long blue coat, and it had shiny, reflective stuff on it."

"Oh, oh, he's fine. He works for me," Ethan said, clutching his chest and exhaling in relief. "You scared me for a second there."

"Sorry! It's just you said there were incidents and stuff, and my sleepy brain got carried away."

"Honestly, thank you. If you see anything strange or off, or something you're not sure about, always tell me immediately. I'd rather be safe than sorry."

"Okay. I will."

"I see you two finally decided to show up late to my party," Jewel said.

Nicole had a sneaking suspicion Harlow was a member of Ethan's unofficial fan club. She returned to the table, bypassing her original seat next to Luna to sit by Ethan instead.

Jewel set her mallet down and draped herself over Olive. "Move over." They fit inside the chair together, but just barely. Jewel ended up practically in Olive's lap, crouched like a gargoyle-barnacle chimera. Jewel looked right at Stella and said, "She's mine. You may not have her."

"Actually, she's mine," Ethan said.

"I don't know what's going on, but this might be a little too complicated for me. My parents would never approve," Stella teased.

Olive, who appeared to be in good spirits about being claimed left and right, said, "Boyfriend." She pointed to Ethan, then Jewel. "Best friend."

"And by the end of the weekend, one of them will betray me." Jewel laughed—and was the only one to do so.

Olive said to Stella, "You really hurt Jewel's feelings when you said that thing about the religious imagery."

"That's not true," Jewel said, giving Stella a pointed look. "I don't have feelings to hurt."

"Sure. Well. Anyway," Olive said with a sigh. "I really like your necklace, Stella. Where did you get it?"

Nicole registered Stella's slight pause, quick as a flinch or an idea clicking into place. Stella asked, "You don't know?"

Olive shook her head. "Did you have that made? It's just that it looks a lot like the Van Hanen crest, so I was just curious."

"I didn't realize the Van Hanens had a monopoly on legendary creatures," Stella said.

"Not all of them," Ethan said. "Just that one. Where did you get it from?"

Nicole accidentally locked eyes with Luna—who had seemed to stop blinking. She gave a wide-eyed gentle head shake, gaze darting to Stella and back. Nicole frowned as a near-perfect silence descended on the party. Everyone was waiting for Stella to answer.

If the necklace was part of the game, why were they being so insistent on asking about it? Was it a test to make sure they abided by the Addendum?

Oh no. Were Ethan and Olive setting Stella up so they could give her a penalty?

Stella, for her part, seemed wholly unbothered, smiling lazily.

"Stop, oh my God," Jewel said. "Why are you interrogating her over nothing? It's just a stupid necklace. It's probably not even real gold."

"Excuse you," Stella said. "As if Diane would let me wear fake jewelry."

"Who's Diane?" Olive asked.

"My mom."

"You call your mom by her first name?"

Stella sighed. "*Not* to her face. Why do I have to keep explaining that to you people?"

"Oh, sorry." Olive laughed, glancing at Jewel before shifting her attention to Nicole. "I've watched a lot of your videos. You're really talented."

Well. Jewel had certainly ended that test. "Thanks," Nicole said.

"We've never seen someone get so popular so fast on the app before. We were all pretty shocked when your metrics came in."

"Someone would have eventually," Nicole said. She wasn't exactly downplaying her accomplishments. More like trying to get away from admitting how calculated every move she made was. Breaking the Golden Rule algorithm had only been the first step.

The best and most viral-prone diary entries on Golden Rule? Cathartic, emotional porn.

Nicole had plenty of copycats now, but everyone knew JadeTheBabe was originator of the SkitShow style. Nowhere in the terms did it say she had to just sit and talk to the camera. Nowhere did it say she couldn't edit her videos. Nowhere did it say she couldn't wear costumes and do impersonations.

However, she did have to tell the truth. If her entries reeked of too much effort, too many embellishments, voyeurs would stop watching. Voyeurs noticed anything and everything less than genuine and responded accordingly. And they wanted daily updates.

Nicole managed to get as close as she could without losing her creative edge. All videos had to be posted within twenty-four hours of the events occurring, and she posted three days a week without fail. She lumped that schedule announcement in with some honesty: orphan with no extended family, broke-as-hell college student, working two jobs plus making videos. She kept her struggle transparent. Relatable. Authentic.

That was the final trick of Golden Rule: Voyeurs didn't want to be lectured. They wanted to be entertained. They wanted to experience sympathy. Even if they had never experienced racism in their daily lives, they wanted to feel like they did, through her. Sally, who lived on a farm in Nebraska, wanted to know what she was missing and found comfort that she would never experience it. And then shared the video on her platform for ally cookies.

Sometimes, you had to play the game designed to break you. Just like her parents taught her: *You play the game before it plays you.*

Changing the subject, Nicole asked, "Stella, did you know Olive's a singer who is also really talented?"

Stella's eyebrows perked up like an excited puppy's ears. "Singer, you say? How interesting. I had no clue about that. None whatsoever."

"I'm getting tired," Jewel said, fake yawning. "Want to do the raffle honors?" She repositioned herself, pulled a small deck of cards from her dress pocket, and handed them to Olive, who began shuffling them. Jewel continued, "Each of you received a playing card at the beginning of lunch. If Olive draws your doppelgänger, you win a special prize."

Shortly after, Olive set the cards down and drew the top one. "Queen of Hearts."

"Oh," Nicole said, holding her portrait card in the air. "Me."

"Congratulations," Jewel said. "Hand me your tablet, please." She didn't have it long, rapidly tapping across the screen before passing it back with a warning: "Avert thine eyes. No one is allowed to look at Nicole's screen until she's done."

Stella, who sat right next to Nicole, snorted and made a show of looking away. "This cake was disgusting," she said to Jewel, pointing toward the end of the table. "Terrible. Positively vile."

The rumblings of the cake conversation surrounding Nicole faded away as she read the instructions:

Congratulations on your good fortune!

You have been gifted one (1) Free Challenge Card:

Good for one (1) penalty-free afternoon
off from The Cruelest Jewel.

Please select one (1) player to spend the
afternoon with by discarding the others.

Five playing card portraits lined up in a row underneath the text. A trash can appeared on the bottom right.

Well, then.

She eliminated Alex and Luna first. They had each other and probably wouldn't want to be separated.

Harlow went next. She didn't know her well enough to want to spend an afternoon together.

Francis's and Stella's cards began to glow, backlit in shimmering silver.

Her finger hovered above the screen, going back and forth between them. Oh no.

Oh no.

Jewel was watching her with a coy smile on her face. "Problem?" she asked.

"No." Nicole returned her attention to the screen. A timer had appeared—she only had two minutes to decide.

When there was literally nothing stopping Stella from talking to Nicole, from really trying to get to know her, Stella immediately started using her tablet instead. She told Nicole repeatedly that she liked her, but why did she? Because she was pretty and tall? Those were literally the only things Stella commented on.

If Nicole really wanted to be friends, she should pick Stella so they could have official bonding time, right?

But after the first challenge, Nicole had walked into the Wardrobe Room with Francis and he just kind of . . . clammed up. Stella had an intense energy about her. Larger than life and literally impossible to ignore. Whenever they were together, she usually aimed most of her focus straight at Nicole. Maybe Francis felt like he couldn't compete. No point in trying to win a battle for Nicole's attention if Stella would never cede.

Now she had a chance to be alone with him again. A free pass for a free afternoon built into the game.

Thirty seconds left.

There'd still be time to meet up with the others to strategize and talk about the recipe later. They'd have all night to run around the secret passageways to find what came next. Afterward, maybe she and Stella could have a sleepover together. There weren't any rules about sharing rooms.

Twenty seconds.

She wouldn't be risking anything to spend a few hours alone with Francis and could even try to get more information out of him—like if he knew why Ethan and Olive had just tried to sabotage Stella.

Fifteen.

If she didn't do it now, would she get another chance?

Ten.

Nicole took a deep breath and made her choice.

SOMETHING WICKED THIS WAY COMES

FRIDAY, 1:30 P.M.

S taff began to clear the table and break down the setup as they all stood in the middle of the field.

"As a consolation prize for losing the raffle, I will allot you all one hint for your next challenge," Jewel said. "Olive?"

"Everything is connected, but bird is the key word."

"And with that, we bid you adieu," Jewel said.

"Good luck!" Olive waved as the three of them left, Ethan's arm draped over her shoulders.

"So," Harlow said, "secret passage time?" right as the tablets began to vibrate.

Alex sighed. "She's really trying to keep us busy, huh?" Luna pulled on his arm, standing on her tiptoes to see his tablet screen as he checked it. She gasped, grinned, and excitedly showed him hers.

Nicole had no trouble playing it cool. She went through the motions, silently checking her tablet for a message that wasn't there.

Harlow announced, "I'm off to somewhere called the Bone Room."

"My luck. It forsakes me," Stella said. "Nicole, don't forget me. I will be viciously jealous if you do. She winked and grinned—her usual parting—and then took aim, pretending to shoot Francis with a finger gun. "To the Bone Room."

"Wait, you too?" Harlow asked.

"That's what I just said," Stella said, walking away. "Really, Harlow, you could at least try to keep up."

Luna led Alex away by the hand, scampering off together to their secret location. No *goodbye*. No *see you later*. No *let's meet up and strategize later*.

Francis hadn't torn his steely gaze away from Stella's retreating form. He didn't look angry. He didn't look anything at all, really. That was something unique to him—a perfected stoic passiveness that hid whatever he felt. Stone cold. Impenetrable.

Nicole wondered how long it would take someone to truly get to know him. Better yet, how long it would take for him to let someone in.

He exhaled into a sigh, raising his shoulders near his ears, and then let them drop. "Funny story," he said, showing her his tablet. "I think I'm just supposed to follow your lead."

Enjoy your afternoon with the Queen.

"That's what the raffle was for," Nicole admitted. "I get a free afternoon off from the game."

"Ahh, and since we were partners earlier, I get to come along for the ride. Got it," he said. "What would you like to do?"

Nicole chose to not correct him. She honestly just wanted to talk to him, almost saying so before changing her mind. "Since you know this place so well, what's your favorite room? Let's go there."

He blinked in surprise and smiled—quick and with teeth. The most effortless one she'd seen from him so far. "Sure, but it's not a room. It's a place."

FRIDAY, 1:45 P.M.

Both of their tablets read

Please proceed to the Bone Room

But strangely, their key codes didn't match. Stella's was the usual string of numbers, too long to be worth memorizing, while Harlow's was a much simpler B340.

"The keypad doesn't even have a *B*," Harlow said while they stood outside the door. "Yours must be to let us in, and mine is for something inside the room."

"Sounds legit." Stella pressed the numbers. A whir, a click, and a whoosh of the door opening automatically later, she said, "By the pricking of my thumbs." Skeletons galore filled the room. Stacked and bound to make furniture like chairs and tables. Skulls and femurs and pinkie bones alike had been fashioned into artwork and figurines and statues. Hung from the ceiling, they twisted in the air like mobiles. Three walls each had a black square bordered by a bone frame at their centers. The fourth wall had a gold-plated door with a keypad.

"Holy wow, this is morbid." Harlow shivered with the heebie-jeebies.

"Ouija boards are fine, but fake bones, oh no, that's a step too far," Stella said. While mildly overwhelming to look at, the bones had a distinct plastic sheen and were covered in telltale seams. She inspected what looked like an octopus figurine constructed of tiny, tiny bones strung together with craft wire. "Someday, some *hour* soon, this house will stop impressing me."

"Skeletons belong inside bodies," Harlow said. "Not as furniture."

"Until the body dies and then it's our bones' time to shine." Stella moved to the open space in the center of the room. The rug, deep red in color in the otherwise light gray room, had been stitched with an optical illusion. It took her a few moments of squinting and walking in a circle to read it: MEMENTO MORI. "Remember you are mortal. Remember you must die. Little on the nose, but it works."

Ethan had said Jewel made this place into her sanctuary. Stella's guess? Jewel built a room to remind herself that death was inevitable, no matter how famous someone was.

Living in a million different memories was not the same as being alive—*ooh*, Stella liked that conclusion. It could be a whole chapter in her book, if she ever really wrote one.

"Found the envelope," Harlow said, opening it without waiting for Stella to join her.

> *This time there are two treasures to seek*
> *One is hidden and the other must hide*
> *The first is a picturesque evening grosbeak*
> *The second relies on time being on its side*
>
> *Step One:*
> *Separate. Designate the seeker and the sought.*
>
> *Step Two:*
> *The seeker will follow the bird in the bones.*
> *The sought will walk through the golden veil.*
>
> *Step Three:*
> *Use your present as you see fit.*
>
> *Press* BEGIN *when you are ready.*

Stella did not like the sound of that. She eyed Harlow, careful not to betray her concern, but her partner had already zeroed in on the golden door across the room. "Let me go," Stella said.

"What?" Harlow asked.

What indeed. What in the hell was she doing? "I'll go through the veil. You find the bird."

Okay, apparently a part of her brain had plans it didn't let the rest of her know about.

"No," Harlow said. "It's my code. I'm supposed to go."

"It said 'designate.' That means we can choose. I think you should stay here in this room."

"And I think"—she pushed Stella's hand off her arm—"you just got used to getting all the presents. It's my turn."

"Look, I don't know what's going to happen, but I don't think you want that present."

Harlow scoffed.

"I'm serious. I have a really, *really* bad feeling about this. Bad enough for me to amend my rule to only be serious about three things in my life."

"You had a bad feeling about the Ouija board too, and that turned out okay, didn't it? And if it's so bad, why are you volunteering to go?"

For that, Stella didn't have an answer. Speechlessness didn't strike her often, but it had landed with the full force of a train derailing.

Too bad for Black sacrifice is the game.
When all is said and all is recorded,
*   you'll go back to inhumation.*

A Ouija board to talk to the dead.

A Bone Room with an obvious warning.

Was it really Stella's responsibility to help Harlow, who hadn't connected the dots of the game?

Or maybe she had and just didn't care. Winning must have meant something to her to make it worth it.

Harlow began to enter the short code into the keypad, complete with a *B*. "I'll be fine. Worry about yourself." She looked back with a teasing smile as the door closed slowly behind her. "See you on the other side."

"That's not funny." Stella shook her head, turning away. Some people just didn't have the sense they were born with. "Okay, bird. Let's get this over with. Show yourself."

Bird in the bones.

Stella circled the room twice, trying to take everything in, noticing as much as she could. Once the initial shock of *bones!?* wore off, one chair—a bone throne—caught her eye. She kept coming back to it because it was weirdly in a corner by itself. The rest of the room felt like one cohesive set piece, every bone item staged intentionally to fit a larger, complete picture.

The seat resembled a flattened rib cage, the back had a spine (naturally), and spindly fingers flared out at its sides like a small pair of wings. Stella crouched in front of it, inspecting the arms and legs, which were probably constructed with their literal counterparts.

Bird in the bones.

Something about that kept tickling Stella's brain.

"Bird in the bones," she whispered to the empty room. Why did that sound familiar? But it was off—like it should have been something else.

Bird in the bones . . .

. . . birds in the box.

Nicole had metal bird bones in her iron box.

How was that supposed to help her now, though? She didn't have the box with her. It wasn't her present.

Stella stood up, scanning the room again with a frown. Initially, she had thought there would be secret bird etchings on the bones that would guide her around the room to find the present. "*Bird in the bones* is so specific," she said, thinking out loud. "Not on the bones. *In.*"

Well. Jewel probably had insurance.

Not that that would stop Stella—not her house, not her problem. The only piece of property she had agreed to protect was the tablet. Not stopping to question her sudden glee at the idea of property destruction, she took another stroll around the room. "Where to start," she said in a singsong voice. "Bird in the bones. Birds in the box."

Stella selected a bone flute. It weighed almost nothing, and when she shook it, nothing rattled inside. Holding one end, she slammed it into the wall as hard as she could. It *popped* open like a plastic Easter egg because of the *seams*. The bones had been meant to snap apart the whole time.

"That's encouraging." She broke a few more items—an owl figurine, what looked like a camera, and an airplane—only to find nothing.

There had to be another clue. Something she was missing.

Olive had said, *Everything is connected, but bird is the key word* as a clue. Where else had she seen or heard about birds? Nicole's box. The riddle for this room.

And the nonsensical recipe.

Was she supposed to use that too?

Stella walked back to the bone throne and sat, placing her tablet on her lap to pull up the nonsensical recipe. The fourth line said:

Whip two partridges until a psychopomp and circumstance forms.

A partridge was a bird. "Whip the birds? Gotta find the dead things first," she joked.

Psychopomp and circumstance was an interesting mash-up. *Psychopomp* was, like, a guide to the underworld. "Pomp and Circumstance" had to be a reference to the graduation song.

"A guide to help someone graduate to the underworld?"

What?

Stella had to be missing something. She stared at the golden door for a moment, pausing to let her brain reset. "C-P-R," she reminded herself, and reread the challenge riddle.

This time there are two treasures to seek
One is hidden and the other must hide
The first is a picturesque evening grosbeak
The second relies on time being on its side

A picturesque evening grosbeak? Could that be literal? Something like a picture. A portrait? There *were* three frames on the walls. She didn't know what a grosbeak was, though, had never even heard that word before, but birds had beaks. Maybe it was a made-up word to mislead her, just like Olive had tried to. She searched the room again, taking her time, moving from right to left.

When she made it back to the bone throne, she sat down. Something caught her eye, but only when she didn't look at it directly.

The bone throne was only a couple of feet away from the bone frame on the wall. Leaning forward and keeping the black square in her periphery, another optical illusion began to appear: an outline of a landscape—a setting sun over a small body of water next to a cabin, smoke curling out of the chimney. Picturesque evening, indeed.

Stella jumped to her feet, running for the portrait. As expected, the image disappeared when she stood in front of it, but when she pulled, the right side swung open like a cabinet. A small square had been cut into the wall.

Empty.

"So *rude*," she grumbled in disappointment, moving on to the next one. The third bone portrait turned out to be the charm—an optical illusion of a small bird sitting in a nest made of bones. And behind it in the wall, she found a small human skull dyed black.

Stella's smile should have been criminal. "I bet you thought this was so clever when you made this up." The skull popped open when she smashed it against the wall, same as the others had. A gold bar bracelet inside had a bird engraved onto one side, while the other side said, MEMENTO: FOR THE BIRDS.

A loud whirring noise sounded from the golden door, now directly behind her. It clicked and began to open slowly—an invitation to join Harlow since Stella had solved her part of the riddle. Obviously.

"Surprising no one, my intellect remains undefeated," she bragged, walking as she put the bracelet on her wrist.

The smell of dirt hit her immediately. It cushioned her steps as she walked. Overhead, a fluorescent light buzzed in and out. The room was bigger than the broom closet in the wine cellar but much smaller than the Bone Room.

A red door with the same bird in a nest of bones engraved into the wood was on the wall directly in front of Stella, across the room. This time, however, the bird held a bracelet in its beak.

"Harlow?" she asked, confidence evaporating like water on a hot sidewalk. If she wasn't in there, where did she go? Faintly, almost as if it were an auditory hallucination, Stella heard muffled, soft crying. "She didn't," she whispered under breath, looking down in disbelief. "She absolutely did *not*."

This time there are two treasures to seek . . .
. . . The second relies on time being on its side

Harlow was the second treasure. An incredulous laugh bubbled out of Stella. "Literal buried treasure, okay, okay."

. . . follow the bird in the bones . . .
Use your present as you see fit.

Stella's gaze automatically drifted toward the door—the *red* door. Her color, her door.

Jewel was giving her a choice. She could choose to leave, choose to follow the bird with her bracelet in its beak, choose to abandon Harlow.

The crying continued. Underground. Under *her* feet.

Stella closed her eyes and breathed in, counting to five. And then went looking for the shovel she knew was somewhere in the room.

FRIDAY, 1:45 P.M.

Although Francis led Nicole back toward the house, they didn't go inside. Instead, he steered them parallel to it toward the hedge maze. Composed of blocky sections of green foliage, it promised multiple paths and intricate patterns. A white trellis woven with light blue and white flowers with pink garden roses mixed in stood at the entrance.

"I like to walk in here," Francis said as they passed under the trellis. "It looks nice, but it's low-key dangerous. Keeps me in check."

"Dangerous how?"

"The bushes. They'll irritate your skin and give you rashes if you touch them."

The leaves had serrated edges and were covered in a slight fuzz. Nicole kept her hands to herself as they continued walking in silence. It was . . . nice. Peaceful. Birds chirped. The wind blew. Everything smelled soft and delicate, like sweet peas. The white stones shifted under their feet with each step. They headed toward a giant stone statue in the center of the maze.

"I'm glad we're partners," Francis said. "You have good energy."

"Thanks. I try."

"Oh, for real? It's not, like, a natural part of you? You know, just exuding positivity and 'I care about people 24/7' vibes."

He laughed. She didn't.

Instead, Nicole looked him in the eyes to make sure he knew she meant what she was about to say. "You said you've seen my videos, right? I'm not like that all the time. I'm playing a character—an exaggerated and scripted version of my best self. Yes, I care about people. Yes, I try to be positive. But sometimes that's not possible. There are definitely people I hate and make a point to make sure they know it. Not everyone deserves kindness or to be forgiven."

Like her neighbors or rude customers. And the man who murdered her parents. There was quite a bit of hate in her heart for him.

"A saint with a heaping dose of wrath," he said, holding her gaze. "Got it."

Nicole paused, looking away. *Everlasting Firelight* was great—that really meant something to her, but *saint?* How could she make him understand what she was trying to say? She wasn't going to ever be some perfect online fantasy come to life.

"Being online, being so public can get really weird, really fast when people assume they know me. I'm careful about what I share and how I share it," she said. "I'm not a saint. I'm a person. I'm sorry if that's disappointing, but this is me. Ambitious but barely surviving, and trying to do my best. I'm a very well-constructed disaster."

And depressed and grieving and she didn't have the luxury to stop living, stop hustling long enough to deal with it. Survival mode had kept her alive—was *still* keeping her going. Knowing she was in it didn't mean she knew how to make it better.

Francis frowned, eyebrows drawing together. "Why in the hell would I be disappointed? *Nothing* about you has been disappointing," he said. "I hear you and I'm listening."

Nicole had made the right choice. She felt it in her bones. Together with the others in a group, Francis always seemed to fade into the background. Something she suspected he did on purpose. She'd seen that before. Not everyone could be Stella and command a room with a single sentence. But she couldn't quite explain why she felt so compelled to find him. Or how his eyes found hers while she was looking.

FRIDAY, 2:15 P.M.

Still buzzing from spending time with Jewel, Luna couldn't help but skip and dance down the hallway as she and Alex walked to their next challenge location: the Dead Van Hanen Hall of Fame.

"You know how in books when characters say they feel like they were struck by lightning when something good happens and they get really excited?" she asked. "I've always wondered about that because *I* think getting hit with lightning would be heart-stoppingly bad and painful."

"Sure," he said.

"*But* I kind of get it now. Isn't Jewel the best? Every time I get to spend time with her it's like my entire body resets. Suddenly, I'm wide awake. I'm invincible, and I can conquer anything."

"Sounds fun."

Ever since they'd separated from the others, Alex had seemed kind of down. She didn't ask him what was wrong because if he wanted her to know, he would've told her. That's how it'd always been between them. Instead Luna tried filling the space with noise to distract him.

"I've also been thinking a lot about the recipe. I tried to ask Jewel some questions about it, but she shot me down." On her tablet, she pulled it up. "Do you know what a psychopomp is?"

"Nope."

"Me either. Jewel loves wordplay, so I think some of these phrases have double meanings," she admitted. "Do you think we're allowed to go back to the library? I want to look up some of this stuff. We should have grabbed a dictionary while we were in there. I don't know why I didn't think of that."

"Not sure," he said, "but it won't hurt anything to check."

"Stella probably knows. She's so smart." She frowned. "I don't want to ask her, though."

"Good plan," he said.

"Good? I thought you wanted to work with everyone else?" Luna grinned up at him. "What changed your teamwork tune?"

Alex didn't smile back. "While you were playing croquet, they kept saying stuff about you."

"Oh? What kind of stuff?" she said, calmly as she could manage, smile still forcibly in place.

"Stuff." He shrugged. "I just don't think we can trust them. If there's a way to win without them, we should do that."

"That's fine. So, what did they say?"

Alex glanced at her quickly before looking ahead again. She recognized that motion: him deciding whether or not to tell her the truth. "Francis started it. I think you kind of scared him in the Wardrobe Room. I didn't think he was serious at first, but then Stella started in, calling you ruthless and stuff, like you'd double-cross everyone if Jewel asked you to."

Luna snorted. *That's it?* Of course she would. She might not have liked that Stella saw her plan so clearly and warned the others, but it wasn't a *lie*. With a little more time, she'd be able to come up with another way to trick Stella into letting her guard down. Easy peasy. She was about to say so, to tell him not to worry about stuff like that, but then he continued.

"And she kept looking at me when she said it. Like she was implying you would do that to me too."

Shock and fury ripped through Luna so fast she couldn't tell them apart. "Alex, I would *never*—"

"I know," he said. "I know that."

Luna sensed a *but* in there, a pause that smothered everything else she felt with overwhelming sadness. He knew it . . . but did he?

Bad things happened when Luna cared too much. She loved her dad, more than anyone else, and he died. She loved her mom and got abandoned. It was better if she stayed apart from everyone. Kept to herself. Stayed silent, in the background.

But sometimes, she couldn't help it, like with Tasha and Jewel and Alex. Her feelings rebelled and said, *No. They're ours.*

So, one night she prayed God was listening and made a deal.

My life for theirs. Let the bad things happen to me, anything you want. Just let me have them, please.

Luna always teased Alex, pretending that she cared way less than she actually did. That was them—*their* dynamic. It always made him smile and laugh and look at her in a way that nobody else did. How could he not know?

How could he ever doubt her, even for one second?

"Hey," she said, softly touching his arm. He stopped walking and so did she. "I would never do that to you. I told you we're partners, and I meant it."

Alex wouldn't look at her. "It's just I know how much Jewel means to you and you really want the money for Tasha and—"

"And nothing," she said firmly. That was part of her deal too. They were equal—she was never supposed to choose between them. "We're in this together. Full stop. Stop being silly and listening to people who don't know *us*. Okay?"

He inhaled through his nose, a deep reverse-sigh, and let it out quickly. "Yeah. Yeah. Sorry."

Luna held his hand, leading him forward. Same as always.

When their challenge arrived on their tablets, they hadn't been given a code to enter the room because there wasn't one. A long rectangular hallway, clinically clean with soft lighting, stretched before them.

"It's like a museum in here," Alex said.

Each portrait had its own spotlight and the same deep gold frame. Luna read some of the names as they passed them—Philistine, Gertrude, Augustus, Agatha—and stopped counting when she reached twenty. How many generations of Van Hanens could there possibly be?

At the end of the hall, empty black squares framed in gold, arranged in a grid of ten by ten, covered the majority back wall almost up to the ceiling. There was a clear line of extra space before the last row of frames began—animal portraits. Luna reached out and touched one of the black squares. "It's velvet."

"One of these portraits is not like the others." Alex's mischievous smile had returned. He pointed to the portrait in question. It was slightly larger than the others; the nameplate read ROGUE AND MERCY VAN HANEN UPON THE OCCASION OF THEIR WEDDING. Rogue looked so pleased with himself, standing with his chest puffed out in pride in a black suit and bow tie with a white shirt and very large gold cuff links. Mercy's white dress was huge and ruffly, nearly swallowing her whole. She wasn't smiling. Instead, she looked like a cat who had just knocked a glass off the counter while looking you dead in the eye.

And their envelope had been tucked into the corner waiting to be found.

> *Nepotism and inherited wealth are never fair*
> *But all are equal in the land of the dead*
> *This time there is one treasure to share*
> *A bracelet hidden in the hall of the dead*

Step One:
Fly with the bird to the correct fallen soul.

Step Two:
Unlock the sweet secret hiding in plain sight.

Step Three:
Use your present as you see fit.

Press BEGIN *when you are ready.*

Luna read it again, then once more to be sure. Reaching out, she tested one of the black portraits, trying to move it, but the entire thing had been secured firmly to the wall, all four sides. Just as she suspected.

"Are you thinking what I'm thinking?" She shoved her tablet at him to hold along with her satchel.

"I highly doubt it." He took the items anyway.

"I'm going up."

"*Up?* Up where?"

"See that corgi?" She pointed to a portrait. "That's Jewel's dog, Dulce. She died from cancer a year ago. That's where the bracelet is."

"Whoa, hold on," he said, grabbing her by the elbow to stop her. "You wanna maybe explain how you know that?"

"Dulce!" she said as if that one word should have explained everything. When he didn't catch on, she added, "*Dulce* means 'sweet' in English! Sweet! Like in the nonsensical recipe!"

"Still don't get it."

Luna tried not to let her frustration and impatience show. She took a breath, made eye contact, and spoke as slowly as she could manage, which wasn't very. "Okay. The recipe says, 'pour over sweet companion molds.' It's wordplay! You know how much Jewel loves wordplay. "*Pour over* sounds like pore, p-o-r-e, over. *Pore over* means to examine something in great detail, you know, like you're searching for something."

Alex sighed, staring at the ceiling for help. "Go ahead. Bring it home."

"Dulce was literally Jewel's *sweet* companion. Why else would it say '*sweet* secret' in the envelope if Dulce wasn't the correct fallen soul? The portrait is a *mold* of her image in the hall of the dead. 'Fly with the bird' means we have to go up. I don't have wings, so I gotta make it work with my hands and feet."

Alex thought quietly for a moment, then said, "We're supposed to use C-P-R, but you're using the recipe now."

"So? Jewel never said we couldn't, and Olive gave us a clue, remember? Everything is connected."

"Yeah, but . . ." He paused. "Would anyone else have known that besides you?"

Luna hesitated. "Maybe?"

"That just seems like quite the reach. We haven't gotten any other *actual* clues or information about Dulce. If you weren't here and that was the answer, how would the rest of us have solved that?"

"You wouldn't even be here without me," she reminded him. "I know what I'm doing."

"Wow. Really feeling that partner vibe you were talking about earlier. Thanks."

"I'm just saying that you should trust me on this," she said. "The whole point of Golden Rule was for Jewel to share her story with us and for us to share with her. I don't think it's too odd that a clue is a throwback. Kind of like it's a reward for being faithful to her for so long? Or a test—something only someone like me, who's used the app since the beginning and loves Jewel, would know."

He didn't look convinced at all.

"If I'm right, we'll find our present. If I'm wrong, then I'll just have sore arms tomorrow. No harm, no foul. I'll come back down, and we'll keep looking."

"I don't know. It just seems really off to me."

"At least let me test the first row? Give me a boost. If it's not safe, we'll try something else."

"Promise?"

"Cross my heart."

Alex slung her tablet and satchel across his torso and helped lift Luna up onto the first row. Her foot fit perfectly in the space between the wall and the frame of the portrait. She reached for the row above her head, testing how it felt to lift herself up. The frame held fast. Her hands stung a little, but nothing too bad. "I think it's fine. It feels sturdy," she said.

"I really don't like this, Luna." He hovered around her, arms extended in a semicircle of protection near her hips. "What if you fall?"

She looked over her shoulder, smiling with manic excitement. "What if you catch me?"

"Of course I'll catch you," he said with confidence, but looked nervous. "But you could still get hurt."

"I won't," she said, heaving herself upward.

Unfortunately, climbing the wall turned out to be more difficult than she'd thought. By the time she reached the fourth row, she was huffing and puffing, hands turning red from holding the frames in a death grip. She paused to catch her breath.

"Everything okay?"

"Yep. Just deathly out of shape," she said in between breaths, squeezing her eyes shut in case the urge to look at him overpowered her. Luna didn't think she was afraid of heights, and now was not the time to put that thought to the test. Standing on bridges and looking down was one thing. Free soloing up a portrait wall was on a whole different level. She kept her gaze focused on Dulce. "I guess to be out of shape, I'd have to have been in it at some point."

If I were tall, I'd be there already, she thought bitterly, gritting her teeth. Row after row, using frame after frame, she continued hauling herself upward. *Okay. I got this. Almost there.*

The animal portraits were slightly smaller than the black ones. She tested Dulce's portrait—secured just as tightly. She straddled two black portraits on the top row, one under each foot, balancing her weight. Holding on with one hand, she searched with the other, feeling the edges and running her hands gently over the textured surface. "I think this is a real oil painting," she said.

"Anything else?" Alex sounded so nervous she almost broke her no-peeking rule.

"No," she admitted while double-checking. "Maybe I should try the parrot portrait? Since it's a bird?" Three portraits away. No big deal.

"Or maybe you should come down?"

"But I'm already up here. Might as well be thorough." She extended her foot, resting it on the top of the portrait, steadied herself, and swung herself to the left.

The black portraits directly under Julius the golden retriever shifted downward, knocking her off balance. Luna's heart all but stopped as she lost her footing.

That fast, *so fast*.

She heard herself gasp, felt the protesting ache in her tired arms as Julius's frame suddenly had to support her. Feet scrambling, trying to reach the closest frame, but she just couldn't—

And then it was like she was astral projecting again. Watching herself fall straight down, down, down, in a blue dress, white pinafore, and thick gray scarf.

Just like Alice tumbling down the rabbit hole to Wonderland.

FRIDAY, 2:15 P.M.

Francis seemed to know his way through the maze by heart. He didn't hesitate or pause when they reached a fork in the path. He didn't even have to look forward—for most of the walk, he kept his gaze on the pebbles under their feet while Nicole watched him. She kept waiting, expecting he would tell her to stop at any second.

"Are you still in school?" she asked.

"No," he said. "College wasn't for me."

"Do you just work, then?"

"Yeah. I'm an electrician apprentice. Two years of trade and then I signed with a union. I also do some IT and security work on the side."

"Do you like any of it?"

"I wouldn't do it if I didn't." He grinned. "If I have to sell my labor, it should be worthwhile, right?"

"That's one way to look at it," she said. "Family?"

"Mom. Sister."

Nicole laughed. Since he knew the basics about her from her videos, it was only fair that she got to ask what she wanted to know about him. All his answers had been short and to the very abrupt point. "You don't like talking about yourself, do you?"

"Not particularly," he said, glancing at her. "But I'll tell you whatever you want to know."

Finally, at the center of the maze, they sat on a bench underneath a statue of a woman kneeling in quiet contemplation. "On a scale of one to ten this is hardly a twenty," Nicole said, recalling their earlier conversation about the Scavengers Initiative while gazing at the sky. An airplane glided over their heads. "Minus the lethal bushes, it's negative two at best."

"Last time there were spiders, a paintball-gun firing squad, jumping out of windows, and Olive almost drowning," Francis said.

"Really? That sounds horrible."

"You asked why I don't like Jewel. It started that night. She figured out what we were all afraid of and used it in the game. Even Ethan didn't talk to her for a few weeks afterward."

"Why are you here, then? Why make yourself go through her games twice?" There she was, openly staring again while he kept his face turned down and away. Avoiding her.

Francis didn't respond immediately, gently tugging at some leaves without ripping them away. She wanted to slap his hand—weren't they poisonous?

Had he lied to her? Why would he do that?

"I have a good reason." He sounded like he regretted it, and let go of the leaves. Holding his hand palm up, he showed her his reddened fingertips. "And I know Jewel better than all of you combined. Once she knows you're desperate, it's game over."

"Acting isn't what most people think it is," Nicole said. "I don't just read lines and try to make it convincing. It's a craft. And for me, that means watching people closely. I can't mimic what I don't understand."

"Okay?" He looked at her, confused, while blowing on his hands to soothe the inflammation.

"I watch everyone. All the time. Including you. What aren't you saying?"

He smiled—the corner of his mouth pulling into a reluctant half grin. "I thought Stella was the one I had to watch out for."

"Francis."

Sitting, their height difference didn't feel as drastic. Inches away from her face, he leaned back, lifting his mouth to her ear, and whispered, "I can't give her more ammo than she already has. Neither should you."

STELLA SAYS
EPISODE 3

Afternoon Delight

Mmm, hello. I promised you all a Q&A, didn't I?

First, let me fill you in on what you've missed, as is my civic duty to do.

We had lunch, fantastic; I spent some time with Jewel, enlightening; Ethan and Olive made an appearance, charming and tricksy as ever; and then we had an afternoon Cruelest Jewel challenge, and, uh, that's where things took a very questionable turn.

Failure doesn't exist for me, so obviously we rocked the Bone Room—yeah, you heard that right. Got this pretty thing as a reward [holds up a gold bracelet]. However, my partner is [pauses] indisposed at the moment and probably scarred for life. Please keep her in your thoughts and prayers. All religions welcome as well as nondenominational best wishes. Pretend you're politicians. It seems to work fine for them.

Yes, I see your comments. I am *talking*. Wait your turn.

Where was I?

I haven't the faintest idea where anyone else is. I miss Nicole. I'm hungry. My back hurts like you wouldn't believe. I need a nap.

Currently, I'm in my room safe and sound and showered. All our rooms are color coded, by the way. Mine is red and just brimming with connotations that I'm not entirely oblivious to.

Oh! The screen is flashing a five-minute warning at me. How convenient.

I'm assuming that little number at the top means how many of you are watching. That's a whole lot of you, there's only one of me, and these comments are flying by, to be honest. I'll read what I can catch for the next four minutes and forty-five seconds and answer with the utmost honesty as promised and *[pauses]* go!

Umm, how much money will we win? Two winners, five hundred grand each.

Can you give a tour of the house? No. Don't ask that again.

What's Jewel really like? Not as smart as she thinks she is. Creative—I get serious tortured-artist vibes from her. Perceptive. Intriguing. I've only spent a handful of minutes alone with her so far. I don't really have any expectations to compare her to.

Is Luna okay? Wow, okay, I see your question now, I see it. Luna was fine the last time I saw her.

Okay, having some trouble here—your inquiries must be in the form of a question with a question mark if you want an answer. Otherwise, it just reads like a statement. Plus y'all are using some syntax and abbreviations I have never seen in my life and I do not understand a lot of it. Which, all things considered, makes sense. Questions with questions marks. Please.

Uhhh, let's see, are you really gay? Wow *[laughs]*, I knew I shouldn't have made that joke about being in the closet earlier. I don't know. Maybe. Probably. Jury's still out. Literally. Imagine there's a trial and the jurors are in deliberation. There isn't quite a unanimous vote just yet, but the dissenters are rapidly losing ground. My therapist—yes, I go to therapy, *hello*—says it's perfectly fine to not know or to have a label yet, and I trust her. So. Next question.

Have you seen the silver scythe? No, I don't even know what that is.

What is the Bone Room? It's a room full of bones and skeletons. Jewel's very literal like that.

Are Luna and Alex dating? No idea.

What do you think of each player? Love Nicole. Harlow is [pauses] Harlow. Alex is very adorable. I want my parents to adopt him. Francis is gunning to be my enemy. And Luna is [pauses] intriguing.

Why can't we see Luna? I told you earlier. I'm not allowed to share the app with anyone. I was told to keep this a secret between me, Harlow, and [pauses] three thousand of you. Holy God. Okay.

The little timer is saying thirty seconds to go. It's been real. It's been fun. It hasn't been real fun. I'll check back in after dinner.

In the meantime, I've earned my nap.

Until next time.

Tell all your friends.

Announcement

Please proceed to the Wardrobe Room for dress.

The theme of the evening is summer pool party.

Dinner will begin at 6:00 P.M. at the Blue Lagoon.

For your convenience:

A Nonsensical Recipe for Winning

Preheat oven to 314 degrees.

Mix all colors until batter is smooth.

Pour into sweet companion molds. Set aside all but three key ingredients.

Whip two partridges until a psychopomp and circumstance forms.

Share and cut the Baker's dozen
chocolate bar into quadragrams.

In a pressure cooker, separate the royal flush
with red herrings wild. Bake for seven minutes.

Serve the chocolate concoction
scrambled atop a pie on a cloudy white
day under a winner's cursed crown.

SOMETHING FOR HERSELF

As soon as Stella walked into the Wardrobe Room with Harlow, she spotted Nicole and Francis sitting on a round orange ottoman together, already dressed for the theme of the night.

Almost immediately, she began wondering if their challenge had been anywhere near as harrowing as hers had been. Quite frankly, it couldn't have been.

Their closeness—heads bent, and bodies turned toward the other—spoke volumes. Whispers and hushed laughter. Out-of-control heart eyes. Followed by quick, fleeting moments of eye contact as if they weren't quite ready to fully commit to something that intimate. None of their behavior landed under *D* for devastated.

Interesting.

And deeply, deeply irritating.

"Stella," Nicole called, seeing her. She stood up, smiling at Francis, before walking over. Her all-black one-piece bathing suit had strips of fabric missing in interesting places, and she had paired it with a lilac-colored sarong and matching strappy heels.

"Be still my heart," Stella said with all the drama she could muster while fanning herself. "You're just too hot for me. I cannot take this. I need you to change immediately."

"Funny," Nicole said.

"Who's being funny? Surely not me."

"Uh, is she okay?" Francis nodded to Harlow.

Not wanting to speak for her, Stella said, "This afternoon took a turn for the intense." Harlow hadn't spoken a single word all afternoon. Objectively, she looked like death warmed over with a zombie parasite attached to her brain as she perused the clothing selection. Stella was still deciding what, if anything, to do about that. She had a plan because that's what she did—make plans and stay ready—but it wasn't time to play her cards just yet.

"Did you finish your challenge?" Francis asked, still eyeing Harlow.

"We did. No idea what this means yet." Stella held up her arm to show the bracelet. "I needed sleep, so I slept until my tablet woke me up. What did you get?"

They exchanged a glance, and Stella's eyebrow reacted immediately.

"Nothing," Nicole said. "We did what we were told, but no present to show for it."

Francis said, "I'm gonna head down now. See you."

"Goodbye," Stella said quietly to his back. "Good riddance."

"Stella!"

"What? It's my turn. I'm an only child, and I never learned how to share." Besides, she had a feeling Nicole would be easier to get information out of if he wasn't around. What they were doing all afternoon had just become the mystery du jour. "I'm assuming you're in charge of wardrobe again?"

"In charge? Definitely not." Nicole laughed. "But I'll help you if you want."

"Oh, don't act like you didn't have fun this morning," Stella said. "Dress me, darling. I want to be beautiful."

One hour later, Stella sashayed into the Blue Lagoon feeling completely at home in a halter sundress and sandals with an excessive amount of platform and calf-binding straps. Nicole had also picked out a lush floral crown and done her makeup again—something she never wore at home.

Being a Fancy Lady for the night felt surprisingly comfortable. On the scale of super-duper femme to baby stud of the year, she'd always felt like she belonged dead center, too lazy to care about anything other than a proper skin care routine, ChapStick, and the occasional dress to twirl in.

"Someday, some hour," Stella said. "At this point, rooms like this shouldn't affect me. And yet."

"I found it this morning. I walked in and walked right back out. Ridiculous," Nicole said.

Lush green foliage covered the walls. Leafy plants crowded the room—tall, squat, and thick. Twisting rope vines hung from the ceiling in erratic patterns. Flowers in a plethora of vibrant colors bloomed and filled the warm humid room with tropical scents that mixed with the smell of dirt. A paved cement path curved in a meandering arc, separating the plants from the pool.

A darkened grotto, created by craggy faux rocks, made a mini waterfall at the deep end. The water spilled over the edge and roared straight into the main body of water. Jewel, Olive, Ethan, and Francis stood at the shallow end near yellow pinstriped tents.

"It's too quiet in here. Where are the birdcalls? The annoying buzzing insects? Where is the ambience?" Stella noted. "Criticisms aside, shall we go mingle?"

"Sure," Nicole said.

"Uh, not me. I think I'm going to get something to eat," Harlow said, pointing to and leaving for the buffet spread, which just so happened to be on the opposite side of the room as Jewel and the Gang. Nicole had worked her magic on a reluctant Harlow too—a pair of jean cutoffs and a loose floral top. She'd paired her look with a large pair of black sunglasses that swallowed half her face.

"Is she all right? Really?" Nicole asked.

Instead of getting food, Harlow shot straight past the table to sit in the corner, on the ground, under a particularly perfect cove of giant leaves. She pulled her knees up to her chest, wrapping her arms around her shins.

"No. I don't think she is."

"What did you do?"

"Me?" Stella scoffed. "I'm not the one she's running from. Never meet your heroes and all that." Linking arms with Nicole, she tugged her forward. "Besides, I have a plan. Follow my lead."

"Uh-oh?"

"Oh no, this is going to be good."

"Is it about the game?"

"It's not *not* about that." She grinned. "Everything's connected here."

When they reached Jewel, after exchanging pleasantries, Stella asked, "I have a question. Harlow and I were talking, and she was explaining how everyone has a category on Golden Rule. Like you're the Warden"—she gestured to Ethan—"and you're the Siren"—then to Olive—"Jewel's the Queen, obviously. What is that? What does it mean?"

"Oh my God," Olive said, excitement kicking into gear. "It's so funny that you asked that because I've been trying to figure out *your* call sign."

"I have one?"

"Everyone does," Nicole said. "The community gives it to you. It's like a rite of passage. Sometimes, it's individualized like theirs, but usually it's just a way to associate you with an already-established video style or way someone participates in the app."

Harlow hadn't told her anything. No one seemed to suspect the lie for what it was.

And that explanation made sense. *Warden* meant security team. *Siren* was obvious. Olive was the virtual Golden Rule guide, welcoming users to the app, drawing them in with her cute red glasses and perfect voice.

Olive continued, "You only have the one video, so I've had a hard time placing you."

One video? Surely, Stella had created enough content to earn a category-call-sign thingy with her livestreams. Unless . . . did Olive not know about the livestreams?

"I gave you one, Stella," Jewel said, "but I want to know what Olive thinks before I share."

Olive said, "Nicole practically revolutionized the way people tell their stories on Golden Rule now because of SkitShow; Luna was one of, if not *the* first to make silent films; and Harlow is one of the best quicksilvers on the app. And then there's you. What do you think your specialty is, Stella? Like, if you could pick any word or phrase for yourself, what would it be?"

Stella regarded Olive for the briefest of moments, no longer than a pause on the surface, as she attempted to quickly parse through the situation at hand, because something was definitely happening. Jewel seemed a bit too smug, standing next to the earnest Olive, riddled with holier-than-thou vibes.

Never one to back down from a challenge, even if she couldn't precisely identify the flavor of it, she said, "I'd like to think of myself as a verbal assassin."

"I can see that working. I'd have to see a few more videos before I'd agree, though," Olive said, smiling a million-dollar grin that nearly knocked Stella backward.

Would every girl she'd meet that weekend be inhumanly attractive in some way? Or in Luna's case, criminally cute as a button? Which reminded Stella— "Where are Luna and Alex? We waited for them in the Wardrobe Room for as long as we could, but they never showed."

Olive's entire being changed into a picture-perfect example of discomfort. Ethan's expression mirrored hers. Conversely, Jewel remained stoic as she said, "Luna had an accident."

"Accident? Hmm, don't like the sound of that," Stella said, surprising herself.

"Is she okay?" Nicole asked, sounding worried. Francis began to switch sides, standing closer to her, eyes throwing daggers at Jewel.

"She will be," Jewel said. "You all signed the waiver *and* Olive gave you several chances to opt out. I'm not forcing anyone to do anything. Choices have consequences."

"Wow. Okay. No." Nicole scoffed. "Luna is basically a naive little kid who's extremely excited to be here. You need to remember that in whatever it is you're planning."

"I don't need to remember anything," Jewel said. "And the last thing I need to do is take advice from you. I know what I'm doing here. Do you? Because Luna does."

Olive looked confused. "Did you know Luna before you came here?"

"I don't need to know someone to care about them. What is wrong with you people?" Nicole seemed truly astounded. "Agreeing to be here doesn't give you the right to hurt anyone."

"I'm shocked you care so much," Jewel said, looking anything but. "Maybe you should spend less time worrying about Luna and more time on the competition."

"I refuse to think of a fourteen-year-old kid as my competition."

"She's fifteen, and that's not what I said."

"Why don't we go check on her?" Olive volunteered, grabbing Ethan. "We'll be back."

No time like the present; Stella kicked the second part of her plan into second gear. She didn't *like* thinking about their second challenge. It had taken almost fifteen minutes to get all the dirt from under her fingernails so she wouldn't have to *see* it. It *upset* her, and then she got mad at herself for being upset.

But it was time. It had to be now.

"*Well,*" Stella said with perfect theatrical calm. "I know I'm worried about the competition. After spending the last part of my afternoon digging Harlow out of a dirt hole in the ground because you buried her alive in a glass coffin, I'm downright terrified for tomorrow. I think she might be traumatized."

Bombshell dropped, so did Nicole's jaw. "I'm sorry, you did *what*?"

Jewel said, "Oh, it was only three feet deep."

"My lower back and arms would like a word with you about that *only*," Stella said.

"*Oh my God.*" Nicole turned on her heel, marching away from the group and swearing up a storm. Stella didn't have to turn around to know she headed straight for Harlow.

"Yeah, that sounds about right." Francis left too, following his partner.

Once they were alone, Jewel said, "I knew she'd be a problem, but you? You definitely didn't strike me as the caring type."

"How would you know? You said it yourself: Out of everyone here you know me the least."

"Touché. Sit with me." Jewel walked into the closest tent and lounged on one of the beach chairs.

"I hope you don't think you can flirt your way back into my good graces." Stella chose to wait by the entrance. "I second the Alex and Luna Outrage Act. They're far too small and cute for me to remain calm if they're hurt."

"Oh, I'm willing to do way more than flirt." Jewel tapped the beach chair next to her, then said, "I asked Luna if she wanted to leave. She declined. I arranged for her to receive proper care and attention in the meantime, which is where she is now. If she were truly hurt, I would've made her go to the hospital, penalty-free."

"Why didn't you tell Nicole that?"

"Because I like it when people assume the worst about me. Keeps my skin clear."

Stella cackled. She hadn't expected that. "And Harlow? Did you make her an offer? Where are her arrangements?"

"Oh, now I know you don't care about her."

When she closed her eyes, Stella still saw Harlow's face through the dirty glass, nasal cannula giving her oxygen, tears covering her cheeks. She could smell the dirt too. The sound of the buzzing fluorescent light wasn't far behind.

"I'm still deciding. Answer the question." Actually, she *had* decided.

She wouldn't allow Harlow to get hurt on her watch again. Wearing her emotions too close to the surface wasn't an option. Knowing the truth meant people could use that against her. Lloyd and Diane had taught her that.

Jewel sighed. "I suppose I could talk to her."

"Nicely," Stella clarified. "Be nice to her with all your money bags and resources in tow."

"Fine. Now, will you please sit with me?"

Stella looked over her shoulder and across the room. Nicole plopped down right in the dirt next to Harlow, placing a plate of food she must have made in front of her. They'd be okay for now.

Jewel smiled as Stella sat down. "I've been thinking about you all day."

"That's not surprising. I have that effect on people."

"One day, that mouth of yours is going to get you in a lot of trouble."

"You're assuming that hasn't already happened."

"My apologies." Jewel's laughter ended in a smile. She bit her thumbnail, holding it between her teeth. "Your videos have been good so far. I'm almost impressed."

"Almost doesn't count," Stella said. "You owe me secrets."

"Not for free I don't."

"Stella Says Episode Two has almost reached fifteen thousand views. You do the math."

"No, thanks. I'll give you until Ethan and Olive come back. We have a schedule to keep."

Stella considered her options. Her plan had entailed getting information about The Cruelest Jewel without anyone realizing it and cashing in the views on her next video for some alone time with Jewel, both of which had panned out. But that was as far as she'd gotten.

Now, she needed a reason. Something for herself. She knew what she wanted—and knew enough about herself to realize she probably shouldn't. She asked, "Why are you really doing this? I've heard a version of an explanation from Olive, from Luna, Harlow, Francis—even Nicole shot a theory into the ether. But not you. You've never said why. Why does The Cruelest Jewel exist?"

Jewel side-eyed Stella with a smile. "Didn't you already ask that?"

"So, you were watching?"

"I monitor everything. It's my game."

Stella let the silence stretch to a count of ten. "That wasn't an answer."

"Because the answer solves the recipe and I'm not giving you that."

"That's fair. Moving on," Stella said. "You don't trust them, do you? Ethan and Olive."

"What are you talking about?"

"They're running the game with you, right? It's like there's certain things they don't know. Why is that?"

"You tell me. You're the one playing," Jewel said. "I thought you wanted to talk about me."

"I did. And then you buried Harlow alive."

"That bothered you," Jewel guessed.

"I wouldn't say that. *Bothered* is an ugly word," Stella said. "You just didn't strike me as a sadist. I'm wondering how I was wrong."

"You called me Sauron."

"That was a joke. I had no idea I was right on the money."

"I don't enjoy inflicting pain on people, but I do like to test them. Find what makes them tick. See what they're *really* made of when their greatest fears come knocking. See how they change because of it." Jewel's wicked grin crawled right under Stella's skin. "You're in my house now, Red Queen. Watch yourself. It's been fun getting to know you, truly, but it's time for you to understand who's in charge here."

Something sharp and merciless began to cut its way to the forefront of Stella's brain. She was raised to be nothing short of the best. Her parents controlled her every move, ensuring they raised her to not only know her worth, but to worship it. She balanced it with skill, executing everything she did with precision and grace. It would have been all too easy to turn into a rebellious teenage dropout runaway. She didn't for a reason.

Stella reveled in her superiority because she'd worked so hard for it. Made her peace with sacrificing everything to have it. She had leaned so far into her parental suffocation it became fuel that would always drive her to be better than the best.

No one would best her. Ever.

Jewel continued, "I wasn't able to dig up, as you so aptly put it, enough on you in time to incorporate it into the game. Any distress you experience is purely your own doing."

"You caught me off guard, I can admit that," Stella said. "That was a mistake on your part, though. I hope you're ready."

"Ready for what?"

"Me. Because I'm playing for real now."

"The End isn't set in stone." Jewel sighed. "Unfortunately, I don't think I'll see you there. Sorry."

"Stop flirting with me when I'm being serious," Stella shot back. "It's not fair to the others. They'll think you're playing favorites and pretending that you aren't."

Once more, she had made Jewel laugh. "I've decided I do like you, Stella At All Times, but you're all wrong for what I'm trying to do here. I need someone who will make me a better person. And here she comes."

Stella followed her gaze toward the door, landing on Luna just as she exclaimed, "Oh wow!" while walking into the room, her left arm in a dark blue sling with a very harried Alex next to her. They'd taken the time to change into matching pink and baby-blue floral jumpsuits—probably Jewel's creativity and not their own. Ethan and Olive weren't far behind them.

"All good things," Stella said, standing up. She made it to them at the same time as Nicole, and asked Luna, "And how did this happen, young lady?"

"I fell," Luna said. "I'm toooooootally fine, though."

Nicole bent down in front of Luna, hands on her knees. "Hey, look at me for a second?"

"Okay." Luna had trouble focusing, blinking too often. "How are you so pretty?"

"Genetics," Nicole answered, and then whispered to Stella, "She's high as shit."

"I'm not high! I have a prescription! The doctor gave it to me!"

Stella cackled, threw her head back and everything. "You bring me so much joy. So much." She turned to Alex. "The doctor should have given you one too. You look stressed."

Alex sighed. "I honestly wouldn't have said no."

Stella laughed again and grabbed his wrist. "Talk to me." He followed when she pulled him toward Harlow's sorrow corner. Whatever Luna did must have been bad enough to make him forget how mad he was at her during lunch. "Tell me what happened." She caught Nicole's eye, who nodded in silent agreement.

Stella would take care of Alex. Nicole would take Luna. Francis was still sitting with Harlow. A well-oiled comfort machine.

Nicole said, "Why don't you come sit with me and Harlow? I'll make you a plate."

"Okay," Luna said. "How are you so tall?"

"Genetics strikes again."

"Before you all get settled, we have a small matter to attend to," Jewel announced. She, Olive, and Ethan remained standing a few feet away.

Ethan said, "Per the rules, if you fail a challenge you will be assessed a penalty that can include disqualification. Unfortunately, this afternoon, Luna and Alex failed."

"Fortunately," Olive chirped, "after reviewing the footage, we decided that neither of you will be disqualified."

"Unfortunately, you're still getting a penalty," Ethan said, grinning expectantly at Olive.

"Is talking like that a weird couple thing? I don't like it," Stella whispered, and Jewel tried to smother her laughter.

"They're playing a game," Francis whispered back.

"Fortunately, I've decided to waive it," Olive said. "Luna, even though you were wrong, you didn't hesitate to pursue what you thought was right."

"Unfortunately, while brave, it was also kind of stupid and is going to cause me to drown in paperwork on Monday morning," Ethan said. "If we wanted you to climb the wall, we would've given you proper gear to do it."

"Climbed a wall? What wall?" Nicole asked. "You climbed a wall and you fell?"

"To the very top of a wall of portraits," Jewel added. "Alex mostly broke her fall."

Olive continued, "Fortunately, instead of penalizing your *poor* choice, we're going to reward your bravery."

"Really!?" Luna asked around a mouthful of potato salad.

"Unfortunately, it won't be until tomorrow," Ethan said. "For tonight, we want you to eat and try to relax a little before the game resumes. Dinner, and all mealtime rules, will last until ten P.M."

THE TODDLER TRICK

The bells for 9:00 P.M. hadn't even finished chiming before Jewel left, unceremoniously dragging Ethan and Olive away with her.

"Was it something we said?" Stella joked.

Nicole, who had spent the last few hours drowning in guilt, tapped Stella on the shoulder and whispered, "Can I talk to you for a second?" She stood up, motioning for her and Francis to follow, not far, just a few feet away behind a rather thick and leafy plant.

"I know this morning we said we'd do the secret passage thing ASAP, but that was before." Nicole leaned around a leaf to make sure Harlow, Alex, and Luna were still where she'd left them. "I'm worried about what will happen to them if we go back to playing the game in an hour."

"I've been thinking about that too. I'm in it to win it as much as the next person"—Stella glanced at Luna—"maybe slightly less, but you do have a point. Harlow is practically catatonic. Alex is dead on his feet, and Luna . . . Well. Someone needs to save her from herself and from Jewel."

"We really don't have a lot of time," Francis said. "If there's anything else we're supposed to solve today, we should do it *today*, as in before midnight. I think that's the reset point. Otherwise we'll fall behind."

"We still have two whole days. You don't think that's enough?"

"I honestly don't know," Francis said. "But letting obvious next steps pile up is a mistake."

"Well, I'm the only one who got a present today," Stella said. "I don't know what it is. I have nothing to contribute to group work. I vote we rest and regroup."

"We'll have to convince Luna." Nicole figured a change of plans wouldn't go over well with her. The girl broke her arm and refused to go home. That's a specific kind of desperation Nicole didn't want to fight with. "Or we could trick her into it. I know she's tired—she has to be. Let's get her upstairs and have her lie down for a bit. I think she'll fall out."

"The Toddler Trick. I'm into it."

Francis actually laughed. "All right. I guess it's two against one, then. Go, team." He walked away, leaving their small group, and joined the others. "Hey, I know we were going to go exploring tonight. Maybe we could rest up for a bit first? I'm like a Snorlax—I always need a power nap."

"I love Pokémon!" Luna's eyes widened with happiness. "I'm like a Cubone. You know, just sitting in a field—wailing for my—my dead mom—while wearing a skull on my head." The room got quiet. "That didn't sound right, did it? I just meant Cubone's my favorite. My mom's not dead, she just doesn't want to be around me anymore." She closed her eyes, grimacing.

Alex whispered in horror, "Oh no."

"Um, can you forget I said that?" Luna asked Francis as if she hadn't realized everyone else had heard it too.

"Didn't hear a thing," he said kindly.

"Okay," Luna said. "Thank you. My arm hurts."

"Where's your, uh, prescription?" Stella barely managed to hold back her laughter.

"In my room."

"How perfect and not at all coincidental. Francis needs a nap. I'm going to take Harlow upstairs so she can lie down too."

Harlow said, "I don't need an escort."

"Well, hello. Welcome back," Stella said. "And too bad because you're getting one."

"What time would we start, then?" Luna asked. "I don't think we should waste too much time. I'm fine staying up for as long as it takes. I'm not even tired yet."

Oh dear God, Nicole thought. She'd spent the afternoon gallivanting around with Francis while they were being buried alive and getting their bones broken. The least she could do was make sure they ate and got some rest after what they'd been through. Someone *had* to take care of them.

But who was she to decide that for them? They'd sacrificed so much, maybe they *should* all just keep playing. Maybe she should just let them win. She didn't deserve that much money when all she did to earn it was get to know a cute boy.

Everything felt off balance. The guilt spiral had kicked up again, trapping her in a whirlpool of doubt. She couldn't *think*, couldn't see reason.

Stella said, "Resting isn't wasting time. That's capitalism talking—break the cycle."

"I definitely want to change out of this thing," Alex said, pulling on his jumpsuit. His words sounded garbled, like he was thirty seconds away from collapsing from exhaustion. "I'm in for upstairs too."

"Majority rules." Stella locked eyes with Nicole. "Let's go."

Back in Crayola Hall, Nicole followed Luna to her room, the adjoining door to Alex's suite noticeably open. "Hey," she said, "do you need help getting changed because of your arm? You can say no."

"Oh, um." Luna looked around her room as if she were searching for something. "Yeah. Olive helped me earlier." She walked to her closet first, grabbing a pair of sweats and a T-shirt, and then to the bathroom, where Nicole followed and asked, "Do you want to take a shower? I can go find a bag to wrap your arm, so your bandages don't get wet."

"No, I just want to change my clothes. Alex needs me."

"You two are so cute," she said, undoing the straps to Luna's sling.

"I think he's mad, though."

"At you? Why?"

"Doesn't matter." Luna winced taking the jumpsuit off. "It's really starting to hurt again."

"Almost done," Nicole said, kneeling. "Step out." The shirt was a bit harder to get on. Maneuvering it around her arm without making her straighten it took a few tries. "Maybe we should steal you some button-up shirts from the Wardrobe Room. Sit down, I'll do your hair."

"Can you put it in a ponytail? Don't comb it out, please. It'll just get poofy."

"I got you. Don't worry."

Nicole used the trick her mom taught her, wetting the brush first and then brushing the hair. Luna had a lot of it too—long, fluffy ringlets that had probably seen better days. After pulling it back into a ponytail, she sectioned off a portion of the loose hair and began to twist all the way down.

"Can I ask you something?" Luna said in a tiny, sleepy voice. "Do you trust Stella?"

"I just met her. Same as you," Nicole said. "But I'd like to."

"Alex told me what she said about me. And she's kind of weird. She talks like she grew up in a TV show."

"I don't know her well yet, but I don't think she was lying when she said she didn't have any friends. Friends can normalize you. No, not *normalize*, that's not the right word. They balance you out, I guess. Really amazing friends can enhance the good parts of you. They can shape and sharpen your personality into something that fits in while still being unique. I think she's only had herself."

"*I* don't have that many friends."

"But you're not her. Everyone adjusts differently. You make silent videos, but you also write a lot, so you found your people online. She's really sheltered, talks too much, and copies behavior she thinks is right. She's just so aggressive and good at pretending, most people can't see how hard she's trying."

"Did she tell you that?" Luna yawned, long and loud.

"No. I'm one of the people who can see it."

"Are you studying to be a psychologist or something?"

"I'm—just an actress who takes her craft seriously. I could be wrong. It's just what I think. All done."

Luna inspected her hair in the mirror. "Thanks. Um, I'm gonna go talk to Alex now."

"Okay, if you need me, for anything at all, I'm right across the hall."

As they walked back into the bedroom, one more thing tugged at Nicole. She warred with herself, deciding quickly if she should say something. Sometimes, all someone needed to break free was permission. Someone couldn't make a different decision if they didn't know they had options in the first place.

"Hold on," she said, waiting. Luna stopped immediately, turning those big trusting eyes on Nicole. "You know it's okay to say no to Jewel, right?"

"About what?" Luna frowned.

"Anything. You don't have to do everything she says."

Nicole focused on reading Luna's reaction—her gaze shifting to the left as she looked off to the side. She disagreed but wasn't going to say it.

"Golden Rule can make it easy to feel like you have a personal connection to someone, especially after watching so many of their videos for so many years," Nicole pressed. "Jewel isn't the person any of us think she is. That's not necessarily a bad thing—it's okay if the Jewel in your head doesn't match the Jewel in real life—but being loyal to an idealized version of her *is*." She gestured to Luna's broken arm. "You have to put yourself first, even if that means going against Jewel's plan."

"I think you're nice," Luna said, but then shook her head. "Maybe you're right about Stella, but you're not right about me."

WHAT A STAR

Nicole was just about to put on her satin bonnet to finish getting ready for bed when someone knocked on her door.

"Hey," she said after opening it.

Francis stood on the other side, hands in his pockets. "Hey."

"Everything okay?" Nicole looked past him, out into the hall. All the other room doors were closed. He was alone.

"As far as I know," he said. "I had a feeling you might be up still."

"Yeah, I don't really sleep much. I was going to give it a shot, though." She gestured to her pajamas—a matching short set she lifted from the Wardrobe Room. It was cute. She wanted to wear it. So.

"Oh," he said, nodding. "I was, um, wondering if you would want to maybe watch a movie. With me. The theater's not far from here."

The fact that her immediate gut answer wasn't *no* took Nicole by complete surprise.

Yes. She wanted to say yes.

"Let me tell Stella first. I promised to answer some questions she had about making videos. Just want to make sure she doesn't look for me since we're all supposed to be 'resting.'" But when she knocked on the red door, no one answered.

"Maybe she's in Harlow's room," Francis offered.

Nicole hesitated, wincing. "I don't think I want to bother them, then. Let's go." They left together, Francis once again navigating without using his tablet. Try as she might, she just couldn't stop thinking about Harlow. At first, the afternoon off had seemed great. Felt great. She truly had a good time getting to know more about Francis. Meanwhile, poor Harlow . . .

"Does it bother you that we had the afternoon off?" Nicole asked. "Nothing bad happened to us."

"No."

Her heart sank with disappointment. If he didn't want to care, she couldn't make him, but she had hoped he would. Worry hadn't stopped gnawing on her insides, giving her a stomachache for the ages. Why did she always end up being the only one who cared too much?

"Do you think Jewel hurt them on purpose?" she asked. "I can't believe she really put Harlow through that."

"Everyone has to make their own choices. That's the point of the game. Jewel sets the stage, and we play our parts," Francis said, shrugging. "I don't like it, but I get it. Harlow made the choice to go through with it."

But she'd been manipulated! Didn't he see that? Harlow wanted to win—had said so multiple times now. Maybe Nicole was just different. Maybe she just didn't want the money bad enough (which was a hot take she hadn't been expecting *at all*). If that had been her challenge, she would've taken the penalty. There was absolutely no way in hell she'd agree to being put in her grave early for a *game*.

"I can't even imagine what that must have been like. Being buried is one of my worst nightmares," she admitted. Her stomach began to bottom out just thinking about it. "Both of my parents are dead. Watching their caskets being lowered into the ground kind of broke me."

Her brain refused to shut up about it. *One day, that's where you'll be too. Cold and in the ground with a faded headstone, no one to remember you.*

Nicole had never told anyone that. If Jewel had known, would that have been her part to play instead of Harlow? "Would you have done it?" she asked him, carefully watching his reaction.

"I already did," he said, surprising her.

"During Scavengers Initiative?"

He nodded. "I wasn't buried, but I was in a glass coffin full of tarantulas. I got bit by a spider when I was seven, ended up having a severe allergic reaction, and almost died. All Jewel knew was I didn't like spiders, not why. Don't give her anything else."

"My *God*."

"But you don't have to worry," he said quietly. "Just be careful."

"What do you mean?"

Francis glanced at her quickly before looking away. "I mean exactly what I said."

Had Francis just tried to give her a hint? But how would he know? He'd been so adamant that he was playing the game too, that he didn't know more than they did. Had he been lying this whole time?

Nicole eyed him warily, trying to decide what to say next. Her mom used to say: *You catch more flies with honey than vinegar.* If she were like Stella, or even Luna, she'd immediately go on the offensive, but that wasn't her style.

Disarm him, Nicole thought. She'd confided in him about her parents and her fear. And he reacted, letting his mask slip to tell her, in his own way, that she'd be fine.

She got him to slip once. She could do it again.

"This way." He pointed to the right. They made the turn into a hallway, entering the first door on the left into a dimmed room. The theater had the usual expected staples. Four chairs, red and plush, by five rows. Wall fixtures with soft yellow lights. An overhead projector and a large curtained screen. At the theater entrance, a touch-screen monitor had been built into the wall, displaying the extensive movie catalog.

"How about this one?" she asked him. "Have you seen it?"

Francis's features crumpled with disgust. That was the most emotion she'd seen on his face so far, and it was *delightful*. She laughed, uncontrollably tickled by his expression.

"What's wrong with it?"

"What's right with it?" He sounded offended, truly, but softened his tone as he said, "Come on, Miss Actress. You're gonna have to do better than that."

Nicole blocked the monitor with her body so he couldn't see and made the selection, navigating back to the main menu after. "The deed is done." She chose the third seat in the middle row. The movie began almost immediately, the first sepia-toned shots filling the screen.

"What is this? I don't think I've seen it," he said.

"It's a romance about a mermaid who falls for a human. Wait until we get to the shots where she's swimming underwater. The actress did all of her own stunts. They look amazing. You're going to love it."

"We'll see." He side-eyed her with a knowing grin.

Fifteen minutes later, his quiet, "Holy shit," filled her with triumphant joy.

"Told you so," she whispered.

Something small soared past her—right in between their faces. Francis saw it too, immediately turning around.

Ethan sat alone in the back row, looking a little too pleased with himself. "I thought you two might want some snacks." Taking aim, he threw something again, making the same accurate shot right between their heads. "I need to borrow you." He climbed over the seat instead of walking around and sat directly behind them.

"We're kind of in the middle of something," Francis said, scowling.

Scowls could be cute. Imagine that.

Ethan looked at Nicole for permission. "Twenty minutes. I promise I will bring him right back. You can time me. I'll even let you give *me* a penalty if I'm late," he said, taunting her with his lopsided grin.

"Sure," she said with a shrug.

Francis's sigh turned into a grumble in the back of his throat. He followed Ethan without complaint, but playfully pushed him as they walked up the short set of stairs. Ethan laughed, pushing him out the door in retaliation.

Nicole was alone for exactly ten seconds.

"I love this movie," Jewel said, emerging from the shadows on the right side of the theater. She'd changed her clothes again—a simple pair of jeans and a cute top this time. She sat in Francis's empty seat. "It's one of my favorites. You too?"

Nicole didn't answer, choosing to stare at her instead while she tried to stay calm. She'd been set up. Because of course she had.

"Oh, are *you* giving me the silent treatment now?" Jewel laughed. "They're fine, Nicole. They are fine, and they will continue to be fine. Luna's accident was just that—an accident."

Nicole believed that. Luna had told them all exactly what happened. Her choice to climb the wall. A portrait that her feet were never supposed to touch gave way because it hadn't been installed properly. No one knew she'd choose to go up there.

"And Harlow?" she asked.

Jewel tapped her chin and bounced her crossed leg in time, like a metronome. "People like to forget that I'm human too because it's convenient for them to do so. They forget that I have feelings, a good memory, and damn-near-unlimited resources at my disposal. Sometimes they need a reminder."

In the silence that followed, Nicole found her answer. Jewel had always planned to put Harlow in the ground. What in the hell did Harlow do to her to deserve that?

"And sometimes," Jewel continued, "people give me a reminder. I stopped breathing when security called to tell me Luna was climbing the wall. My entire body froze on the spot. Just like that." She snapped her fingers and turned her attention toward the forgotten movie still playing on the screen. Her concern began to morph into a soft grin. "Can you imagine being so driven by the power of your beliefs that you'd be willing to do anything to succeed? Luna didn't even pause to second-guess herself, not even when Alex rightfully pointed out how wrong she was." Jewel's smile continued to grow. "Fifteen and fearless. What a star. The worst thing that can ever happen to her is losing that belief in herself."

"I don't think that's the worst thing," Nicole disagreed, leaving no room for debate.

"Luna thinks she's doing all this for me, but she's not. She just hasn't figured that out yet," Jewel said, glancing at Nicole. "You're a lot like her, but with five years of growing up and common sense on your side. I had that kind of fire once. Nothing was going to stop me from building my empire. And then I did. Want to know what I believe in now?"

"Sure."

"You."

Nicole snorted with laughter. "Me. Right. Okay."

Jewel didn't laugh or smile. She had spoken with a completely straight face. "Why is that funny to you?"

"Because you don't even know me. You just think you do, which is pretty ironic."

"Really, Nicole, it's like you pick and choose what you want to hear whenever I talk to you." Her tone oozed with frustration. "Let that go and listen to me." She leaned forward, eyes boring into Nicole's. "I know what happened to you. I know what happened to your parents. I know what you want because of it."

Nicole's actor brain struggled to find the words to capture the feeling seizing her in that moment. Charismatic didn't come close to describing what Jewel was. Magnetic? Compelling? No, those weren't right either. In her diary entries on Golden Rule, Jewel had an intense level of authentic sincerity—she'd tell you the sky was green and you'd believe her because you *knew* she would never lie to you.

Up close and personal, it felt like Jewel had the power to stare your deepest, darkest desires right in the face. Somehow, they appeared in the forefront of Nicole's mind—she couldn't think about anything else. The only child of two only children. No aunts, uncles, cousins, or grandparents that she knew of. The last in her family's bloodline. If Nicole didn't make a name for herself, her parents would fade away into nothingness.

That's why she wanted to be famous—as long as people knew her name, she could force them to know theirs too.

"Nothing will stop you from leaving your mark on this world," Jewel said. "*Nothing.*"

FRIDAY, 10:15 P.M.

Stella balanced her tablet on her chest. She'd have a crick in her neck soon if she didn't sit up, but Golden Rule was just. So. Addictive. No wonder her parents refused to let her idly scroll on the internet.

An hour ago, she opened the app fully intending to make the next episode of Stella Says and had been utterly ensnared. It hadn't occurred to her that she had access to the entire app, not just the livestreaming function. Her voyeur count had skyrocketed. Her notifications were bursting with video replies from people introducing themselves and asking questions for another Q&A.

Stella didn't know how many videos she'd already burned through. Click. Watch. Give them a Gold Star. Repeat. Most weren't longer than thirty seconds—easily consumable like potato chips. One chip, two chips, and before you know it the whole bag is gone.

Her pulse jumped when she spotted a somewhat familiar face in the frame of the next thumbnail. She clicked on it.

"Hi, Stella! I'm Harlow's sister, Winnow."

Both had burning gold-tinted hazel eyes and that ethnically ambiguous look yet still white-passing skin tone, but Harlow's face was rounder, her body softer. She had jet-black hair and a mole just below the right corner of her bottom lip, while her sister had purple hair and severe cheekbones.

"Why can't Harlow be on camera with you? Is she okay? Tell her hi for me and that I love her and that she did so good! Post again soon, please!"

Winnow ended the video by blowing kisses and waving. Meanwhile, Stella frowned as she stared at the screen before hitting the REPLAY button. Twice.

So good with *what*?

Her notifications list had been set to "oldest replies" first. She'd been watching them in the order they were received.

Winnow sent the video at 2:17 P.M. No. It couldn't be . . . could it?

Following her hunch, she reset her notifications to "newest replies" first and clicked on the first video in the queue.

"Hey, Stella. I, like, never do video replies, ever, but I wanted to say, um, that I know exactly how you feel about your parents. Mine are like that too. At my school, this kid, he, well, um. It's still really hard for me to talk about it. Sorry. I'm in therapy too. I've been working really hard, you know? I just can't yet. Um, but yeah, now my parents are super overprotective too and they won't let me do anything. I barely get to leave the house now. If you ever need someone to talk to, I'm here. I'm rooting for you and Luna to win the game."

"Sneaky, sneaky," Stella whispered to her room. Laughter that sounded like she was hyperventilating bubbled out of her mouth. Her skin prickled with goose bumps as she went hot and cold at the same time. She stared at the camera in the corner of the bedroom. At the solid red dot in the center of the small black dome to remind her the camera was on.

Forget Big Brother, Golden Rule was *watching*.

But where were they watching? Stella went back to the landing page, scrolling, scrolling, scrolling—nothing. When she searched for The Cruelest Jewel, the only videos that popped up were about them. Theories and reactions and shipping—what the hell was shipping? She clicked on a video with her name in the title.

"Okay, guys, so I just spent the last two hours catching up and it's totally

not my place to speculate about her sexuality because she hasn't said it, but it's very obvious she's not into any of the boys. I don't buy that whole jury analogy she tried to sell. Ethan is hot as hell and she's barely glanced at him?? Okay, like, wtf? But at the same time, is anybody else getting serious enemy-to-lover vibes between her and Francis? Yeah, I know he's into Nicole, but I think he has the most chemistry with Stella. Breakfast was tense as heck, but at lunch he kept staring at her! I don't think she even noticed—"

Stella closed the window. "Nope. Not doing that," she said quietly, going completely still. That video had over nine thousand views.

Somewhere on the internet, the entirety of Golden Weekend X was being livestreamed to the masses.

A million questions ripped through Stella's brain. The hows, the whys, the whats, not to mention the ethical dilemma of whether or not to tell the others. They had a right to know, didn't they?

Except she couldn't tell them.

Jewel must have known Stella would find out about the broadcast. If she told them, they would ask her how she knew and she'd have to tell them about the livestream, which she'd been expressly forbidden from doing.

Loophole closed.

Never in her life had she ever been so blindsided. Nobody one-upped her, ever. That was something that happened to *other* people.

Two soft knocks sounded on the red door with the black knob. Harlow.

Harlow. Stella could tell her! Excited, she tossed her tablet down, running to the door. "You will never guess what I figured out," she said, then snapped her mouth shut.

Harlow took gasping breaths through her mouth as she sobbed. Her runny nose would give Rudolph a run for his reindeer money, and her eyes were equally red. "Can—I—please—" She dissolved into a cough-inducing sobbing fit.

"Not going to do the thing where I ask if you're okay because you're clearly not," Stella said carefully. "So, what do you need?"

Harlow must have been truly desperate to knock on Stella's door. She wrapped her arms around herself as she visibly trembled. "I—want—my—sister—I—"

"Ah, Winnow, yes."

"H-h-how do you know her name?"

"Funny story about that. You probably won't laugh," she said with a sigh. "You can come in. If you want."

One of Stella's favorite words was *distraught*. She'd say that to her mom before dramatically throwing herself onto the nearest surface while pretending to wail. She thought it was hilarious. Actually, seeing it was anything but. Harlow embodied every sense of the word, truly beside herself with distress. She walked into Stella's room and just stood there. In the middle of the room, still sobbing.

"You can also sit down," Stella said, wrestling with her patience. "On the bed. Come on."

While Harlow sat, Stella ran to the bathroom to get some tissues. She picked up the box, thought better of it, and grabbed a towel instead. Less wasteful. "Here," she said, handing it to Harlow. "Would you like to, uh, talk about what's bothering you?"

Harlow wailed in one long breath.

"Was it the challenge? Too much?"

She started crying harder.

"We could also not talk. I'm fine with that. Silence doesn't bother me at all—and we're touching. Okay, okay." Harlow had flung herself onto Stella. She wrapped her arms around her shoulders and buried her face in Stella's neck.

"You know, maybe we should find Nicole? She's the reigning queen of comfort here."

Harlow sucked in a breath and continued wailing, right by Stella's ear.

"Wow. Okay."

Stella hadn't planned on spending her night with someone else's salt water making her skin wet and her favorite new dress soggy, but there she was stuck with no clue how to make Harlow feel better. This naive girl who got buried alive and just wanted to see her sister.

Something, Stella realized, she could actually help with. Reaching back and straining a little, she grabbed her tablet and placed it on her lap. She replayed the message Winnow had sent to Stella.

Harlow hiccuped, gasped, and amazingly stopped wailing.

Winnow must have been the most important noun in Harlow's life. The one thing she thought about while she was underground. The only thing she needed to make her world right again.

If Stella had gotten buried instead, and if she thought for even one second that she was going to die down there, her last thoughts would have been regret.

Regret for all the things she hadn't done, hadn't seen. All the places she'd never been and all the people she'd never meet. All the experiences her parents had stolen from her. And all the reasons why she allowed herself to care about her parents anyway. Because living as a blank, malleable space filled with snarky rage felt best because it was easier. It made her forget and let go of all the things she wanted.

All at once she realized the world would always be bigger than her anger. And she would always long to hold it, no matter how much she tried to convince herself it wasn't true.

"When I'm upset," Stella began when the video ended, "I hate when people tell me it will be okay, because sometimes, it truly won't be. When they say things happen for a reason, I want my fist to happen to their face.

"I don't think there's anything I could say right now to help you not hurt. I'm not good with this. I don't know how to help you. But you're here, and if you want me to, I will sit with you for as long as you need." To prove her point, she wrapped Harlow up in a hug and pressed her cheek against the top of Harlow's head. "If you tell anyone about this, I will deny it and call you a liar to your face."

Harlow laughed, watery and breathy.

Stella navigated to Winnow's profile page. They watched another one of her videos, but it wasn't long before Harlow's sobs started again.

STELLA SAYS
EPISODE 4

In the Midnight Hour

This is my bathroom. It's red, opulent, and unnecessarily garish, but the tub is nice. Greek inspired, sunk into the floor with pillars. You too can bathe in the waters of Olympus and be transformed into a goddess. That kind of vibe.

[deep exhale]

Apparently, you all know how this works. We play The Cruelest Jewel. A team wins the money at the end.

Today, Harlow had to make a sacrifice. It cost her quite a bit.

I had no idea comforting people could be so stressful. She cried for an hour. A whole hour until she fell asleep and I almost had to carry her back to her room. I . . . *[pause]*

I've been wanting a reason to be here. It's hard not to compare myself to the others, how invested they are. I didn't actually think I'd get one. *[laughs]* There's more to this game than what I initially thought. Winning, for me, will look very different than it will for someone like Luna. I'm quite upset that I'm being forced to feel my feelings during my inaugural wild child weekend—stop being rude. Yes, I can see your comments. This time I ask the questions. You give me answers.

Question one: How much can you see exactly?

[pauses]

Everything is an extremely troubling answer. You can see me on this livestream, but you can't see me in the bathroom right now on the other app?

[pauses]

Okay. Good. At least she didn't lie about that.

Oh. Now that's interesting. Thank you, DollyVicious. Can *anyone* see inside Francis's room? *No?* Any idea what makes Francis so special?

[looks off-screen]

[stands up and walks off-screen]

[video ends]

PART III

VIEWER DISCRETION IS ADVISED

"I do have some level of self-awareness. Not much. But some."

—JEWEL VAN HANEN

WAKING
NIGHTMARES

Nothing gentle resided in the darkness. It had been saturated by emptiness, grown thick with fear powerful enough to both stop a heart and restart it.

Nicole knew exactly where she was—standing at the bottom of an open grave, too deep and too muddy to climb out. She screamed for help, throat going raw from strain almost instantly. All she got for her efforts was dirt thrown in her face. Over and over and over and over . . .

Gasping for air, Nicole bolted upright in bed. Stiff, clammy hands bunched in her soaked sheets. She writhed in placed, legs twisting— confused and still trying to climb out. Her eyes burned, but she refused to blink herself back into that endless darkness. She recognized this moment punctuated by aching bones, straining muscles, and chattering teeth for what it was.

And she knew how to crawl back into herself, second by second.

Nicole inhaled, filled her protesting lungs, held it for three infinite seconds, and then exhaled. She repeated that process until it stopped hurting to do something so normal. Until the murky shadows regained the original shapes of her suite on Jewel Van Hanen's estate.

She threw the blankets to the side, running to the bathroom to get dressed. Twenty minutes later, she knocked repeatedly on the red door at the end of Crayola Hall.

Stella's eyes were barely open as she leaned against the doorjamb. "Nicole, I adore you, truly." Her voice had lowered into a gravelly vocal fry. "But the *sun* isn't even up yet. This better be good."

"It is," Nicole said. "I need your help."

SATURDAY, 6:00 A.M.

Announcement

Please proceed to the Wardrobe Room for dress.

The theme of the morning is flower child disco.

Breakfast will begin at 8:00 A.M. in the Cat Café.

A reminder:

A Nonsensical Recipe for Winning

Preheat oven to 314 degrees.

Mix all colors until batter is smooth.

Pour into sweet companion molds. Set aside all but three key ingredients.

Whip two partridges until a psychopomp and circumstance forms.

Share and cut the Baker's dozen
chocolate bar into quadragrams.

In a pressure cooker, separate the royal flush
with red herrings wild. Bake for seven minutes.

Serve the chocolate concoction
scrambled atop a pie on a cloudy white
day under a winner's cursed crown.

PARTNERS

Waking up felt like dragging herself through the mud, one dirty fistful at a time. Luna had a headache right in the middle of her forehead. Her skin felt too tight on her face, and her eyes itched—and she could only use one hand to touch them.

Because she'd fractured her arm. Right. A dull ache pulsed inside her forearm.

After Luna had lost her footing on the portrait and fallen, everything had shifted out of focus. The pain in her arm and in her back had been immediate and unrelenting. She didn't remember screaming, but she knew she had cried.

And then, Jewel was there, asking if she wanted to go home.

Of course, she didn't. She wanted to stay.

After Nicole had left last night, Luna had found Alex already asleep in his room. She lay down next to him. Not *on* him. Which was where she was now. He was awake, reading something on his tablet. His other arm was wrapped around her shoulders, holding her to him.

She sat up. "Did I sleep on you all night?"

"I dunno. Maybe."

"Oh. Sorry."

"Apology not accepted. That's not worth being sorry about."

Was she supposed to feel weird or something? She'd never slept with a boy before. She'd never even shared a bed with anyone except Tasha—obviously very different circumstances.

Her friends had always made it seem like something like this would be a big deal. She'd watched enough Golden Rule videos to know that people would turn this into a Big Deal if they found out. If Melody was still his girlfriend, she'd *definitely* have something to say about it.

So why didn't she feel weird? Embarrassed? Shy? Nervous? Alex seemed fine too. The hand that had been on her shoulder was now draped over her knee. Maybe things were fine because she was keeping her distance. Morning breath would make it weird. Definitely. She pressed a finger to the back of his hand—and noticed a gold bracelet on her wrist.

"That's not a buzzer." Alex sighed.

"Did you put this on me?"

He inspected it and said, "No."

The bracelet had a thin chain connected to a gold bar with a bird engraved on it.

"Where did you get it?" He laid his tablet facedown next to him.

"I don't know." And then she did. "You know, I thought it was exciting the first time they gave me a present while I was sleeping. It's actually really not?"

"Oh." Alex gave her the longest of long-suffering looks. She held in her giggles, while he said, "I thought we'd have to do a makeup challenge or something for it."

"Me too. Guess they changed their creepy minds. Can you take it off for me?"

He did and asked, "How's your arm?"

"It hurts." The dull pulsing hadn't stopped since she noticed it. "But I don't think I want to take those pills again. They make me feel . . . off. Like I can't think. Too foggy. I need my brain."

He sat up too, frowning. "I've been thinking."

"Nope, don't do that."

"Maybe we should go home."

"What? Why? You don't want to win? It would make your family so happy."

"Not all money is good money." He rubbed his hand roughly up and down his face. "I remember every second of what happened. You fell in slow motion, and I swear I heard your bone crack when we hit the ground."

"I'm sorry."

And she was. Sorry that she wasn't more careful. Sorry that she fell and that he had to try to catch her. Sorry that she hadn't thought about how he felt. She hadn't even considered he might not be okay.

Luna wanted to tell him that, to open her mouth and let everything in her heart pour out, but she knew if she tried, she'd mess it up. Everything would be diminished and lost in translation.

"I don't want to be here. I want to go home and be safe. With you." He sighed again, shoulders sagging.

"I know everything feels terrible, but we can't leave. Not yet." Luna chewed on her lip, trying to decide what to do. She was sure he knew some of what happened with her mom—there's no way his mom didn't tell him what Tasha had probably told her. "And I'm not saying that because of Jewel, I promise. She doesn't mean more to me than you or anything like that."

"I'd hope so," he said with a sardonic laugh. "You just met her, and no offense, she really doesn't seem all that great to me."

Luna decided to let him have that. He was upset, not trying to hurt her feelings. "I want to win for Tasha. I really mean that," she said. "My mom doesn't give Tasha any money for me. Last year, Tasha asked if she could claim me on her taxes and my mom said no because she was going to do it. Tasha got so mad, I thought she was going to kick me out, but she didn't. She just got another job. Winning is the only way I'll ever be able to pay her back for taking care of me."

"You don't have to do that." Alex looked alarmed, but his voice was so, so soft. "Tasha would never ask you to do that."

"She doesn't have to. I owe her my life. I don't know where I'd be if she didn't agree to be my guardian," Luna said. "Being here was supposed to be my dream come true. I love Jewel, like, I know I'm obsessed. And I thought that if I could make everyone else think that was all I cared about, they wouldn't take me seriously, you know, like as a strategy. I'm naive and starstruck so nobody would watch me too closely. They wouldn't see me as a threat so I could do anything to win and they wouldn't know about it until it was too late. I didn't want anyone to know how badly I need that money. Including you."

Alex was quiet for a long time. "First of all, you should've told me that earlier. Partners don't keep secrets from each other. But I understand why you did it. Second, your plan is ingenious. I had no idea you were that devious."

"I wouldn't say devious."

"I would and am because it's working. Francis told me Nicole and Stella practically turned into Mama Bears when they found out you got hurt."

"Really?"

"I'm still on the fence about Stella—she's slippery, you know? But I think Nicole is good."

"Me too! Last night, she helped me change and did my hair." She showed him the twists Nicole took the time to do for her.

Someone knocked on the door. Alex said, "I'll get it," rolling off the bed to go answer it.

"Hello, Romeo. Do you have my Luna?"

"Your Luna?"

"That's what I said." Stella peeked around him. "Good morning, little one. How are you feeling? I'm up early and I don't like it."

Luna bristled at being called *little one*, but shrugged it off. "I'm fine."

"Hi," Nicole said from behind and above Stella. "We had an idea. I thought you might need help getting ready, so we decided to bring the wardrobe to you." She held up a stack of neatly folded clothes.

"And as a bonus"—Stella held up her bag—"we'll strategize how to catch up in the game while we get ready. Harlow and Francis are still asleep. We figured we could just fill them in when we see them."

Alex stepped to the side to let them in, while keeping eye contact with Luna. They walked in single file, to check in on her, to help her get ready, to play the game. Together.

A grateful lump felt stuck in Luna's throat.

Oh.

Oh no.

SATURDAY, 6:45 A.M.

Stella sat on the floor in Luna's room, tablet and their combined presents in front of her. "So, we're in agreement. Olive intentionally lied to us. Everything might be connected, but C-P-R supersedes everything. Each recipe step is telling us something we have to do *with* our presents."

"That's how I messed up," Luna said, also on the floor, in between Nicole's knees, while getting her hair french braided. "I thought everything mixed together and you had to try to make any part of it apply to your challenge. Alex was right. I should've listened."

"It was a good guess," Nicole said kindly. Luna had explained her doggie debacle logic in detail. Combined with the "pour over" vs "pour into" mistake, she'd created her own recipe for disaster.

Luna continued, "I think the first step references Jewel's announcement post. She posted it on March fourteenth. Not sure what we're supposed to do with that, though."

Alex twisted the snowy owl key in his fingers, sitting in between Luna and Stella. "I think we're past steps two and three. We were each given a color, some of us got freebie presents, and we decided to work together as a group. Harlow was right. We *had* to mix our colors."

"Freebie presents. Ooh, I like that," Stella said. "Presents come in two classes: freebie and challenge. Continue."

"Then," Alex said, "Jewel paired us up, made us each have a *companion*, and we got *keys* from the challenge, which unlocked the freebie presents. I think the pairs she put us in might be a requirement for winning. For example, I can *only* win the game if it's with Luna."

"I *like* him," Stella said to Luna. "He's my second favorite now."

"Thoughts on going in the secret passageways?" Nicole asked. "If everything is intentional, us not having any spare time to actually explore them might be as well. Maybe we're not supposed to go in them because we're supposed to set the *freebies* aside for the time being."

"It was a pretty elaborate reveal. Why bother giving it to us if we can't use them?" Alex asked.

"It's almost as if she was trying to hide them," Stella said quietly to herself. She was sure that was in fact the case. Jewel didn't want *someone* to know they had access to the passages. Their getting caught running around in there would be a dead giveaway, so Jewel kept them out by scheduling challenges directly after meals and extending mealtime rules to 10:00 P.M. That was too controlled to be a coincidence. But she couldn't put her finger on *why* it needed to be a secret. Not yet.

"Maybe it's written like that because she wanted us to focus on the function of the keys first," Luna said. "They exist to unlock the freebies. Recipe step solved; please wait for further instructions."

"I can second that," Nicole said. "It sounds plausible."

"Onward," Stella said. "Step four: for the birds."

"Wait, what did you say?" Luna asked.

"I'm sure you heard me," Stella teased.

"Yeah, I did, I just—um, never mind. That's what my bracelet says."

"Bracelet, you say? Like this one?" Stella pushed up her sleeve to show hers. She'd never been the gold-wearing type, and now look at her. Two different pieces of gold jewelry that looked fabulous on her skin.

"Yes! I was wearing it this morning when I woke up and asked Alex to take it off for me," Luna said.

"I'll get it," he said, and ran to his room.

"Obvious choice"—she picked up Nicole's iron box—"birds on the wrist have something to do with birds in the box."

"The bracelets have chains. That could be the whip."

"Can I see?" Luna asked. Stella passed the box and her bracelet, just as Alex returned with the second one.

"Anyone know what a psychopomp is?" he asked.

Stella said, "It's a guide to the underworld."

"Jesus," Nicole breathed, shaking her head.

Luna yelped, shrinking back toward Nicole. Her mouth hung open as she stared upward.

One of the metal bird skeletons hovered above their heads, eyes glowing red. The wings didn't flap. No hum of a motor keeping it airborne. And yet, there it was, mocking gravity.

"Now, how did you get up there?" Stella mused.

"Okay, that's really cool," Alex said, smiling.

"It's the bracelets!" Luna pointed inside the box. "That little empty space right there? The bar part of the bracelet fits inside perfectly!" She passed the box to Stella—and the bird moved.

"Wait." Stella moved the box back and forth and then in a circle. "The bird's following the box."

"Put my bracelet in," Luna urged.

Luna's bracelet was nearly identical to Stella's, except the back of hers said MORI: FOR THE BIRDS.

Memento mori again.

The bracelet clicked into place, and the second bird shot into the air, this time with green eyes. The two birds spun in a circle around each other before flying toward the closed door.

"I wonder how they're flying," Nicole asked. "Drones are usually loud as hell."

"I wonder where they're trying to go," Luna said, hopping up. She opened the door, but they didn't make any moves to fly out of it.

"Slow your roll, small wonder," Stella said. When she stood up, box in hand, the birds moved forward as she drew closer. "Oh, I get it. They're tethered to the box. They'll lead as long as the box is moving with them. Shall we journey to the underworld?"

"I'm not sure if we have time for this," Alex said. "We don't know where they're going or how long it will take to get there."

"Maybe we should split up," Nicole offered. "Just in case, so we're not all late."

Luna said, "It's my bracelet. I'm going."

"Guess that means I'm going too. It's Nicole's box so she should probably come with," Stella said. "And someone needs to stay behind to fill Harlow and Francis in when they wake up."

"Guess that leaves me." Alex looked at Luna, who said, "I'll be super careful. I've definitely gotten being a daredevil out of my system."

Tablets and satchels full of their presents, Stella, Nicole, and Luna set off without Alex. The birds flew a steady few feet ahead, and just as Stella concluded, if the box stopped moving, the birds paused.

"They're kind of freaking me out," Nicole said. "I don't see an engine of any kind. But aeronautics isn't my thing."

"Jewel has a whole tech company. I know they make more than apps. It probably came from there."

"Thanks for the tidbit, little bit," Stella said.

Luna glared at her. "You know, you tell people they can only call you Stella."

"And?"

"So stop calling me little! Or any other nickname you come up with about my size. My name is Luna."

Stella pretended to consider it. "Do you want to know why I do it?"

"Because I'm sh—um, I'm not tall?"

"No. Well, yes." Stella smiled as sweetly as she could manage at her. "But it's also because I don't have any siblings. It's just me and my parents all the time. I've always wished I had someone like you around. So, I've decided to adopt you. We're sisters now. Me, you, and Nicole."

"What—"

Stella shushed Nicole. "Relax. Go with it. Let it happen."

Nicole scoffed but smiled as she shook her head.

Perfect.

"Sisters?" Luna asked warily.

Stella didn't know if she was allowed to claim the people she wanted to be *her people*. Her severely stunted social skills told her it was probably a bad idea. But she liked them! They probably liked her! And they were stuck together for the time being!

And more important, Luna had a very obvious big sister complex. There was no way she didn't care for Alex—Stella refused to believe otherwise—but it was clear Jewel, a stranger, came first. Luna's mom wasn't in the picture, but she lived with her older sister, whose scarf she continuously wore.

Stella wasn't going to take Luna head-on in order to win. Taking Luna under her wing would be a far more effective approach.

"I never asked for this, but I fly into mysterious and inexplicable homicidal blood rage if I even think about you being hurt in any way," Stella said. "I have given up and accepted my sisterly fate."

"Um, okay?"

"You may also just go with it," Stella said. "But in the name of sisterhood you are allowed to give me one, count it: one nickname."

"Really?" Luna perked up.

"Really."

"Anything I want?"

"Within reason." Stella shrugged. That was enough. No need to keep pushing.

"Okay," Luna said after a few beats of silence. She glanced up at Nicole, who gave her an encouraging smile. "Sisters. Yeah. Okay."

Stella aimed her cheesiest smile right into the closest camera as they passed under it. She hoped Jewel was watching.

The massive black oak door carved with fleurs-de-lis and cherubs miming for you to *Shhh* claimed the entirety of the short hall. No other rooms or doors were visible. The path began and ended there.

"Where's the keypad?" Nicole asked as she searched. The door didn't even have a handle. "We're supposed to go in, right?"

Luna stared at the birds, hoping they would do something else. They only continued to hover. She tried to tamp down on the hot flash of frustration ripping through her. What more did they need to do? She took a deep breath to center herself. The scent on her scarf had begun to fade.

"There appears to be a secret passage on the map connected to this room. I'd vote yes," Stella said while looking at her tablet.

Luna examined the door again, hoping to spot something new. "All the locked doors have opened with a key code so far. Even the ones we haven't found yet are supposed to open with a key code. Why not this one? Why is it special?"

Nicole said, "Well, it's the only colored door besides the ones in Crayola Hall. Almost everything else is just glossy wood."

Stella said, "Black isn't a color. It's a shade."

"Oh, and there's a white door too," Nicole said. "I found it in the Holiday Wing."

"Do I even want to know what that means?" Stella asked.

"I didn't, and if I have to suffer, so do you." Nicole laughed. "The rooms were sort of like small cubicle-type offices, but each one was decorated as a different holiday. The white door was the only one that wouldn't open."

Luna pressed her fingers where the doorknob would have been. She found a hole right under a cherub's foot. A star-shaped hole. "Our keys open the door?" she whispered to herself before repeating it again, saying it louder. "Which key had the star shape on it?"

"Mine," Nicole said, digging in her bag. When she inserted it into the hole Luna had found, a quiet *pop* sounded from inside the door. "Now what?"

"We have to find the next one," Luna said, trying to feel for another indentation. Stella found the diamond-shaped hole for the owl key right between the eyes of a cherub. The next one took longer to find and was so high, Nicole had to step on her tiptoes to use the cat key.

Once the last key clicked into place, the door swung open. Silently gliding across the floor.

Just as their rooms had been decorated in a single solid color, this one had claimed muted grays—every single inch of the room, including copious amounts of skeleton-themed artwork. The birds went in first. They flew toward the center of the room, hovered for five seconds, and then crashed to the floor. Lifeless once again. Nicole scooped them up, placing them back in her box and returning the bracelets to Stella and Luna. "What is it with Jewel and cold rooms?" she said, already shivering. "I hate being cold."

Luna said, "This is Jewel's office. She's made videos in here before. I recognize the pictures."

Behind the desk, enlarged black-and-white photos, nine individual images positioned into a grid, hung on the wall. The only thing they had in common was Jewel. She appeared in every picture.

"Computer's on," Stella said, sitting down. The wallpaper was a close-up shot of a raven. "Password protected. Any guesses?"

"Is there a hint?" Nicole leaned in close to see the screen.

"'Remember you are mortal' no space," Stella read after clicking on it. "'For the birds' wins again." She typed *mementomori*—the computer unlocked.

Nine video files were readily available on the desktop. Nothing else.

Luna stood on Stella's other side and said, "Too easy?"

"No," Stella said, "I'd say consistent. The worst games are the ones where the players never stand a chance. Jewel definitely wants someone to win. There might be something else in here too. We'll come back and search when we have more time."

Stella clicked on the video named *GWI*.

Luna recognized the room because she'd seen it in one of Jewel's videos. She recognized the faces sitting around said room on the expensive furniture. She recognized Jewel's purple dress, and Ethan and Olive in blue.

The video was composed of clips from the inaugural Golden Weekend. By the time they'd watched the last of the five-minute highlight videos, *GWIX*, Luna had been sitting on the floor for quite some time.

In every previous year, Golden Weekend had been a *coaching* retreat. Participants sat around talking about their dreams and goals, making plans, learning skills, and connecting with one another. And at the end Jewel funded whatever they wanted to do. She gave them the money and resources—whatever they needed, she made sure they had it.

None of the other groups had played The Cruelest Jewel. Not one.

WE HAVE
SOME NEWS

Running was the work of the devil. Watching all the videos had been a mistake because now Stella, Nicole, and Luna were *running* so they wouldn't be late for breakfast in the Cat Café. Well, any *later*. When they rounded the last corner, she was surprised to see the others still waiting outside.

"You made it," Francis said to Nicole and Nicole alone.

Hmph.

"Why haven't you gone in yet?" Nicole panted, hands on her knees.

"Solidarity. If you were late, we'd be late." He shrugged.

"Group work until it's not. Huzzah," Stella said, air wheezing back into her strained lungs. "Let's go. I need some water."

"Find anything good?" Alex asked.

"Definitely," Luna answered.

Stella walked through the door and immediately began shrieking in abject glee. She had never seen so many cats in one place. Curled inside cubes, wrestling with plastic bags, chasing toy mice, sunbathing on carpeted towers and bridges. Brown cats and black cats and tuxedo cats. Cats with squishy faces and stumpy tails. Some with long hair and others bald as the day they were born. "This is the best day of my life," she squealed, scooping up a curious kitten with folded ears.

"Not to be that person, but isn't it a little unsanitary to eat in here?" Francis asked.

In the far-right corner near a window, a table had been set for nine. There wasn't a single human in sight.

"If you're so worried about it, don't eat," Stella said.

Some rather friendly cats began to twist and rub around Luna's ankles. They followed her as she walked, doing everything they could to get her attention. When she sat, a large black cat jumped on her lap. "Hi, kitty. Nice kitty."

"He's *so* big," Stella said, eyes wide. "Look. At. Him. *Oh my God.* I need him." At 8:20 A.M., when Jewel still hadn't arrived yet, she said, "I call dibs on chastising her for being late to her own party," as Ethan and Olive strode into the room, heading straight for the table. The usual army of staff was behind them, wheeling in covered trays of food.

"Good morning. We have some news," Olive said, worrying at her hands. "There was an emergency meeting this morning."

"Insurance," Ethan said quickly.

Stella assumed it was because of Luna's arm. Her fall had probably sent the insurance agents into a capitalist tizzy. Voyeurs got to witness the accident firsthand. A cover-up wasn't going to save them.

"Jewel isn't, uh, she won't be joining you for breakfast," Olive said. "Everything else should be according to plan."

Ethan added, "Unfortunately, we won't be joining you either. There's some things we have to take care of."

"Everything okay?" Francis asked.

"Still figuring that part out," Ethan said.

"Have a good breakfast," Olive said.

"There goes my morning," Stella said after they'd gone. "I hate when I look forward to things. It only ever ends in disappointment for me."

"I'm sure you'll see her later," Nicole said.

"You think?"

"It's her house. Odds are good."

"I was hoping to see her too," Luna said.

"You're not missing much," Harlow muttered around a cheek full of eggs. That was the first time she'd spoken all morning. She was wearing her giant sunnies again, her clothes didn't match, and it didn't look like she'd brushed her hair. Things were rough for the newly liberated.

"That didn't take long," Francis mused.

"I've always been an overachiever," Harlow said.

"Did something happen?" Luna asked.

Silence. As if everyone at the table agreed to let Harlow decide how much was said next.

"You could say that."

"You weren't the only one who got—hurt yesterday," Nicole said.

"I'm fine."

Stella's eardrums said differently, but millions had probably seen Harlow's extended meltdown. She wouldn't out her in front of the few who didn't know yet. "You know who else is fine?" Stella said, purposefully trying to draw attention away from Harlow. "Jewel. I can't believe my luck. First trip out of my house and boom—romance. I've always heard it happens when someone least expects it, but I never thought it would just slap me in the face like this."

Francis dropped his fork and covered his face with his hand. "Why is this happening to me?"

"We're a classic love story in the making," Stella said. "A digital queen running out of territories to conquer. And there I was, a surprise and a delight to light up her life."

Stella almost broke character by laughing at everyone's faces. Luna's jaw had landed somewhere near her plate. Alex's face had the precise cadence of *Sure. Okay.* Nicole looked concerned, per usual, and Francis looked like he was two blinks away from a migraine.

Only Harlow seemed to get the joke. It took her a second too long to cover the beginnings of a smile with her fist.

Stella continued, "Can you imagine the power couple we'd become? Me with my brains. Her with her money and connections."

Luna recovered first. "Jewel's really smart too."

"Her with her money and connections," Stella repeated. "We'd be unstoppable."

"That's not nice," Luna said, grinning. "You shouldn't talk about your future wife like that."

"Although I genuinely appreciate your enthusiasm and support, it's way too early to be thinking about marriage," Stella said. "And I wasn't insulting her. I'm just saying we bring different skill sets to our future relationship and that's mine. She may be 'smart'"—Stella put air quotes around the word—"I mean she planned all this, so obviously she has vision and the resources to pull it off, but she isn't 'smarter' than me."

Francis said, "It's sad that you actually believe that. You don't know her. You'd be 'smart' to stop thinking you do."

"What's sad is my obsessive and uncontrollable desire to prove that I'm the most intellectually dominant person in a room at any given time. And full offense? I haven't had to work very hard here." Her words were for Francis, and she didn't care how they sounded to the others, but then her gaze rolled to Luna. "But I am watching you."

Luna sat up a little straighter, a little prouder. "Since she's not here, does that Addendum still apply? Or can we talk about the game?"

"Still applies," Francis said.

"Fine," Stella said to him. "Did you know that the other Golden Follows hadn't been subjected to The Jewel of Cruelty? We watched some home movies about the other Golden Weekends while we were away, and they had a normal, non-puzzle-based grand time."

"Yeah," he said, unsurprised. "I thought you all did. I told you this was the first time. Twice."

"See, you keep doing that, though," Stella said. "The way you present the information, it's like you're intentionally trying to mislead us. It's quite suspicious."

Francis couldn't even be bothered to stop looking out the window next to him. "What are you trying to say?"

"Nothing yet. But I am wondering about what else do you just *happen* to know."

"Believe what you want. It's like I said, I'm in this—same as all of you," Francis said. "Now, *stop* talking about the game."

SATURDAY, 9:30 A.M.

Midway through breakfast, a mean-looking bald cat had forcibly evicted the one with folded ears from Stella's lap, and made itself comfortable. "Do y'all think it'd be okay to take him with me?" she asked as they were leaving the Cat Café.

"In the video Jewel made after she adopted them all, she said they're not allowed outside this room," Luna said. "This is their space. They're really well taken care of."

That café had to be at least twice the size of Nicole's entire studio apartment with much better lighting. Those cats were probably waited on, paw and paw, too.

Stella picked up the cat, holding it close to her face. "I'm going to kidnap you. Don't tell the others." Surprisingly, the aggressive cat meowed and then licked Stella's nose. "Did you see that? I've been chosen. This really is the best day of my life."

Back in the hallway, they stood around waiting for their tablets to vibrate.

Nothing happened for several minutes. Nicole even opened and closed her app a few times to make sure it was working. Finally, Stella joked, "Well, we've certainly been trained."

Alex asked, "I guess there's no challenge, then?"

"I hope Jewel's okay," Luna said. "First she's not at breakfast, and now there's no challenge. Do you think something happened?"

"Like what?" Alex asked.

"I don't know. It just seems weird. It doesn't seem strange to you?"

Francis said, "I can check later. Ethan will tell me what's up if y'all aren't around."

"Uh-huh," Stella said. "I wonder what else he'll tell you."

"Do you guys want to go to the office?" Nicole asked a little too loudly. She didn't know what happened, but Stella absolutely had Francis in her sights in a bad way. "We wanted to go back anyway to search for something else besides videos."

Luna led at the front, eager to go. Alex stayed with her, asking, "And the videos said no one else played this game before? We're the first."

"It was like a highlight reel of each weekend," Nicole said as she slowed down her stride to walk at the back of the group with Francis. Harlow and Stella ended up in the middle.

"It even had music. Someone took the time to make those edits," Luna said. "The question is, Why? And why leave it for us to find? How does it fit into the game?"

"That seems to be the question of the weekend," Stella said. "I can't seem to get a straight answer from anyone about it. Why The Cruelest Jewel? Why now? What do you think, *Francis*?"

"I don't. I make it a point to not make Jewel's business, my business."

Stella turned around in midstep and began walking backward. "I'm watching you. I want you to know that."

"Is that supposed to mean something to me?"

"Cross me at your peril." Stella turned back around.

"I'm not dealing with this," he said under his breath, and then touched Nicole's arm softly. "I'm gonna go find Ethan. I'll see you later, okay?"

"Yeah, okay," Nicole agreed as he broke off from the group, turning down a hallway going in the opposite direction.

What in the hell was going on between Stella and Francis? Even Harlow, who'd been present physically but mentally off somewhere else for most of the morning, was openly watching them. What had Nicole missed?

She didn't have to wait long to find out.

After they opened the black door to the office, Stella pulled her aside. "Watch video seven again. He's in on it. Trust me."

What? Nicole didn't remember seeing him. Harlow beat her to the computer, sitting in the seat, so she kneeled down next to her. "I'll watch with you. Can we play number seven, please?"

"Sure."

Nicole kept her eyes focused on the video, skipping around trying to catch every scene and pay attention to the background. He must not have been in the forefront—she wouldn't have missed that.

"Why isn't our weekend like that?" Harlow said quietly. "This is what I thought it was supposed to be."

The guilt spiral slammed into Nicole again, shattering her focus. "I don't know," she said. "I wish it had been too."

Nicole had been alone in the theater with Jewel for twenty minutes, just as Ethan had promised, and left the theater believing in every single word Jewel had said about her. That was the kind of experience Harlow had been expecting this weekend—one-on-one time with someone she idolized. Someone who had the uncanny ability to zero in on exactly what you wanted and tell you exactly what you needed to hear. Someone who had the resources to help make your wildest dreams reality.

God help the world if Jewel ever decided she wanted to start a cult.

Harlow said, "She just gave them everything. Why is she torturing us with this stupid game?"

"Don't know that either. What can I do? I want to help."

"Why?"

"Because you're hurting." Nicole shrugged. "If there's something I can do to make that easier for you to bear, I'd be happy to."

"Can you go back in time and slap some sense into past me? Then, no. You can't," she said. "Sorry. I know you're trying to be nice. I'm just really mad at Jewel right now. It didn't have to be this way, and watching this isn't helping." She pushed back from the desk, walking away.

Nicole couldn't imagine what she was feeling—and to be fair, after her nightmare that morning, she didn't want to. That kind of pain would rip her to shreds until there was nothing left. She'd already been there and had zero intentions of ever going back. She slid into the chair and restarted the video.

There, at 3:14, was Francis walking with Ethan while everyone else took a group picture.

314. Just like in the nonsensical recipe. Was this what they were supposed to find?

Nicole opened her mouth, ready to call the others over, but stopped herself.

If Alex's earlier theory was correct, Francis was Nicole's partner—she could only win The Cruelest Jewel with him.

Was this another test—this time to see if she'd rat her partner out to the group?

Yesterday afternoon, she had chosen Francis over Stella.

Last night, he asked her to a movie, only to leave when Ethan appeared, a likely plot to set her up to be cornered by Jewel.

Nicole put her face in her hands. She was being manipulated again.

Francis had given her multiple warnings, as if he knew something the others didn't, with no real explanation as to *how* he knew. Her stupid lizard brain made her gloss over those facts every time he looked at her because she liked his face. A lot.

But Stella saw through him, and had been relentless this morning, constantly questioning him.

Nicole needed answers. She watched Stella and Harlow and Luna and Alex, searching and theorizing, trying to figure out what their next step should be together. Asking them for help didn't sit right with her.

Francis was her challenge. Not theirs. She felt the truth of it—all signs pointed to Jewel pushing them together. Before she said anything to the group, she would find out on her own.

If the videos were real, and Luna was *sure* they were, why was Francis in them? That's where Nicole had to start.

And she would end by asking if he was a part of The Cruelest Jewel. Point blank.

"I don't think anything is here," Luna said, approaching the desk with Alex. "Maybe we should try the passageway now? What do you think?"

"Sure," Nicole said, looking up. Her poker face was exquisite. She gave away nothing. "Let's do that."

"Great!" Luna laid her codex flat on the table. "Do you have your map open? What's the official name of this room?"

"It just says Office Space," Nicole said.

Luna flipped through the pages, scanning them quickly. "Oh, okay, here it is. Office Space Two: Misty Mountains. It says, 'Find a tabletop with X marks the spot. There'll be a switch underneath it. Flip it to make the keypad reveal itself on the door.'"

"On it!" Alex shouted. Nicole got up to help too, although it didn't take him long. "Easy peasy," he said, pointing to a side table against the wall. "Lemon squeezy."

A replicated pirate treasure map had been carved into the top. The landmass in the center, named Lapidary, was bordered by four seas: Carnelian, Malachite, Chrysocolla, and Pyrite. A lone full-rigged ship traveled westward on the Pyrite, following along the dotted line heading straight to the heart of the mountain region of Lapidary. It had a giant X painted in the center.

Alex lowered himself into a crouch, feeling under the table until it clicked. A sound resembling a dead bolt sliding back drew their attention to a leather couch nestled in a nook on the far side of the office.

Stella moved first, reaching the couch and hopping onto it. When she pushed the wall, a panel lifted next to her hand. "Nicole, my dearest, I require your numerical assistance."

As soon as the door opened, Stella leaped over the couch. "Harlow, come on! I don't like being the excited one alone. It's dangerous, and I could hurt myself. This is your job," she teased.

"I've never been so unexcited in my life," Harlow said, holding on to Stella, who helped her over and down. "My whole world is a lie."

"Not the whole thing. Just a tiny part of it. You know what the best way to heal from this kind of disappointment is? Revenge. Cold, premeditated revenge."

Harlow scoffed, almost *laughing*. "Yeah, 'cause that's likely."

Stella truly does have a way with people, Nicole thought as she climbed over as well.

"Next?" Stella said, arms open to help Luna over.

Yellow lights had been strung up on both sides of the walls to keep the passageway from plunging into complete darkness. The path was anything but straight. Every few feet the tunnel either made a sharp right or left and used more than a few S-curves.

"Anybody else notice what's missing?" Nicole asked.

"Missing?" Stella asked, looking around at the group. "Did we lose someone?"

"No, but the house lost us," Nicole said. "There aren't any cameras in here."

"Oh wow, you're right!" Luna said, checking the ceiling for cameras that truly weren't there. "That's a pretty big security flaw. Why *wouldn't* they put any in here?"

Stella said, "Excellent question, my dear Shortson."

"*No*," Luna said, and Stella cackled in response.

They reached a fork in the path breaking off into two different tunnels. One of the tunnels promised glowing teal and green lights while darkness filled the other.

Luna asked, "Where do these lead?"

Stella consulted the map expansion, wyvern plugged in. "On the left, the green light will go to the tennis court, so outside. And the right, hello darkness, goes to"—she zoomed in on the map—"Jewel's room? Uh, it says it goes to Jewel's room."

"That'd be really invasive if we went there, huh? We should definitely not go there, right?" Luna asked, looking like that's precisely what she wanted to do.

"She doesn't care about us, so why should we care about her privacy?" Harlow asked. "Anyways, we don't have flashlights. I'm against the darkness right now. Extremely so."

"Green sounds good to me," Stella said.

They never got the chance.

All five tablets began vibrating *and* beeping.

Emergency Announcement

11:00 A.M.

There has been an incident.

All guests please proceed to **the White Drawing Room** immediately.

All staff please proceed to **bunker two** for briefing.

Thank you for your swift compliance
and cooperation.

NOBODY KNOWS

SATURDAY, 11:13 A.M.

"Thank you all for coming so quickly." Olive had begun to pace back and forth in a small line. "I don't want to alarm anyone, but we decided it would be best to tell you. Jewel is missing. We don't know where she is."

"Normally we wouldn't worry except she's not answering her phone and things aren't adding up," Ethan said. A man in a blue trench coat with silver hems and cuffs stood next to him. The name tag read SIMON G.—JVH SECURITY.

"What kind of things?" Stella asked.

"We can't—" Olive's voice broke, and Ethan had to finish for her, "Things that required us to call the police."

Olive burst into tears, covering her face. "I'm sorry, I'm sorry," she said as she fled the room, Ethan helplessly watching her go.

Simon spoke next. "Last night, there was a breach. We think they got in when you all did. Usually they're harmless. They take pictures and leave. We change key codes, have safety meetings, contact the police, and then we move on. Unfortunately, we don't think this person was here to just take pictures."

Luna said, "Um—"

"No," Francis snapped. "Let him finish."

"I understand you may have questions, and I'm sorry but we're not at liberty to discuss them at the moment. For now, we've decided it's safest for you all to stay here to keep up appearances. In the meantime, the police would like to ask you some questions individually."

Ethan said, "We were able to verify where everyone was around the time we think she went missing. They're just trying to get a more accurate picture of what happened yesterday, so anything you could tell them would be extremely helpful."

"We've also added a panic function to your tablet home screen," Simon said. "You may have seen it previously as the ABORT button. If you see anyone or anything suspicious, please don't hesitate to push it. We'd appreciate it if you all stayed in your rooms. Lunch will be brought up shortly, and after the police have everything they need, we'll begin to think about travel arrangements to get you home."

INTERROGATIONS

Interviews were conducted in collaboration with JVH Security and the local sheriff's department. Names of minors are redacted for their protection.

Suspect: Rhodes, Nicole

JVHS: We've been informed that there was a pool party last night. Can you walk us through what you did after it ended?

NR: Am I under arrest?

JVHS: No. We just want to ask—

NR: Am I a suspect?

JVHS: Miss, this is simply—

NR: I don't care what it is. Please answer the question.

JVHS: Now, there's no need to be difficult.

NR: I am not being difficult. I'm asserting my rights.

JVHS: Miss, we just want to ask you a few questions.

NR: You may ask and I will decide if I want to answer.

JVHS: Can you please walk us through what you did after the pool party ended?

NR: Pass. Next question.

Suspect: Jane Doe 1

JVHS: We've been informed that there was a pool party last night. Can you walk us through what you did after it ended?

JD1: There are cameras everywhere in this house. You know exactly where I was, what I was doing, and who I was doing it with.

JVHS: We'd like to hear it in your own words.

JD1: Oh, I see, so you know that we know that you know but are hoping to catch one of us in a lie. Human memories are extremely unreliable. Let me save you some time: Use the video. Unless you don't have any.

JVHS: What makes you think that's the case?

JD1: Why else would you be wasting time here?

JVHS: Standard procedure. Just covering our bases. So, if you don't mind—

JD1: I do mind. Greatly. My guess is you have the video but for some reason, there are missing pieces. Someone was with her, and you can't move forward without any proof of wrongdoing. You set up this little charade to smoke them out by using what we tell you to trick them into confessing.

JVHS: That's quite the story.

JD1: My God, you really need to work on your poker face. I can't believe you're going with something that basic.

Suspect: Jane Doe 2

JVHS: We've been informed that there was a pool party last night. Can you walk us through what you did after it ended?

JD2: Are you cops? You're legally required to tell me if you're a cop.

JVHS: You're not under arrest. We just want to hear what you did last night in your own words.

JD2: I have the right to remain silent!

JVHS: Again, you're not under arrest.

JD2: I plead the fifth!

JVHS: You're not on trial.

JD2: There's a camera in this room. You can't hurt me because security will see it!

JVHS: What? We're not going to hurt you. Please, relax. Take a deep breath. All we want to know is what you did last night. That's it. Just walk us through it.

JD2: I had a prescription!

JVHS: *[deep sigh]*

Suspect: Cruz, Francis

JVHS: We've been informed that there was a pool party last night. Can you walk us through what you did after it ended?

FC: I don't talk to cops.

JVHS: You're not under arrest. We—

FC: Don't. Talk. To. Cops.

JVHS: Thank you for your time.

Suspect: John Doe

JVHS: We've been informed that there was a pool party last night. Can you walk us through what you did after it ended?

JD: I went to sleep.

JVHS: Right after?

JD: Yeah. We went upstairs. I changed my clothes. I went to sleep.

JVHS: What room were you in?

JD: Mine. The *[REDACTED]* Room.

JVHS: Where did Nicole Rhodes and Francis Cruz go after you all went upstairs?

JD: How should I know?

JVHS: Do you know where Harlow Bailey went?

JD: Again, how would I know? I was asleep.

JVHS: Before you left the pool party, did you hear anyone else say where they were going?

JD: Ethan and Olive didn't say anything other than good night.

JVHS: And Jewel?

JD: I didn't hear anything.

JVHS: Is there anything else you can tell us that you think might be helpful?

JD: If you're looking for something specific, Francis is probably your best bet. He barely talks. All he does is watch us.

Suspect: Bailey, Harlow

JVHS: We know there was a pool party last night. We've reviewed the security footage. Can you walk us through what you did last night?

HB: [silence]

JVHS: I should add that you're not under arrest. We only want to get more information.

HB: [silence]

JVHS: It's okay to talk to us. We're here to help.

HB: *[silence]*

JVHS: Everyone else cooperated. For example, we know you went upstairs with everyone. Sometime later, Nicole and Francis went off on their own. You spent some time with *[Jane Doe 1]*. We've got their sides of the events. Now, we would like to hear yours.

HB: *[silence]*

JVHS: Is there anything we can do to make you more comfortable? Would you like some candy? Here. Take it.

HB: *[silence]*

JVHS: Would you mind taking your sunglasses off?

HB: *[silence]*

JVHS: I'll level with you, we know you were the last person to see Jewel. At 3:14 A.M., you both walked into her bedroom and you walked back out alone an hour later. It would be better for everyone if you just told us what happened while you were in there.

HB: Why don't you both go tell Jewel to [REDACTED] herself.

JVHS: You seem angry at Jewel. Did something happen between you two?

CHALLENGE
ACCEPTED

Everyone had gathered in Nicole's room.

It hadn't been an active decision. After each interrogation, they hadn't been allowed to rejoin the others. A member of security escorted them back upstairs, putting them in their rooms. And exactly no one stayed put.

For years, Luna had been the SilentStar of Golden Rule. Being quiet had saved her. She learned how to make friends with it, found a solace to soothe the chaos inside her. It had felt like fate when she found Golden Rule around the same time. Her identity became inextricably linked to her persona and to Jewel.

And now, everyone else had gone dead silent too. Only Stella said something as she entered: "Confined to Crayola Hall. I cannot believe I traveled over four hours just to be put on house arrest again."

They had scattered themselves around the room, lounging on chairs and sitting in corners and staring out the window, all lost struggling with their own thoughts.

So serious for no reason.

Well, the police and security team were scary. They almost convinced her.

Luna untucked herself from Alex and crawled to the edge of the bed. She wondered what he was thinking, figuring it wasn't anything good. He had wanted to go home, stayed for her and Tasha's sakes, and now, they were all suspects in a missing person's case. The second she had seen his tired, worried face, after his interrogation ended, she almost broke down and told him. Almost.

They needed to sit with their thoughts. They needed to find their own quiet.

If they would be any help in finding a way to win, they had to bring something to the table for Luna to work with.

Because The Cruelest Jewel was far from over.

Standing in the middle of the room, Luna cleared her throat, loud enough for everyone to hear. She began walking toward the bathroom, motioning for them to join her, not stopping until she stood between the sink and the window, in full view of everyone.

Stella caught on first, as expected. She shot straight past Luna inside the bathroom, choosing to sit in the bathtub. Tablet balanced on her knees, she tapped the screen a few times before looking up.

No one else had followed.

"Nicole," Stella said, shattering the silence. "Get in here."

And that was all it took. Not just Nicole, everyone entered the bathroom and found a comfortable place to sit. Luna closed the door and joined Alex sitting on the sink countertop.

"So, what are we doing?" he asked.

Luna smiled. "No cameras in the bathroom, remember? We can talk in here."

Nicole asked, "Is there a reason we're avoiding cameras now?"

"We can't let them know what we know."

Harlow said, "And what do we know?"

"That we're still in the game." Luna took a breath, tucking her face into her scarf for a beat longer than usual.

"What are you talking about?" Francis asked.

"Jewel disappearing, the police, the interrogations—all of it is a part of the game. We're still playing."

Five pairs of eyes stared at Luna as if she'd grown a second and third head.

Nicole said, "Oh, Luna, sweetie. No."

Harlow said, "Did she miss the part where there are literal, actual cops here?"

Francis said, "I have a headache. Why is this happening to me? Why am I even here?"

Alex took Luna's hand. "I know this might seem like something Jewel would do—"

"No," Luna said. "There's no *might*. This is part of the game. Jewel isn't really missing or hurt—she made herself a challenge."

"Luna."

"Don't Luna me, okay? I know I'm right. I can feel it."

"I'll give you that the timing on all of this is fishy," Francis said. "I think she wants you to believe it's a game, but really she's setting us up to take the fall for what those police believe is a very real crime."

"They're actors," Luna said. "They're not real cops."

"They looked real," Harlow said.

"It's a moot point since we have no way of checking badge numbers," Francis said.

"Why would she do that?" Luna asked. "What possible reason could Jewel have for setting us up?"

No one had an answer for her.

Luna turned back to Alex. If she could get just one person to believe her, she'd be okay. All she needed was one. "Think about it. The timing isn't just fishy—it's controlled. Remember how we all just stood in the hallway after breakfast waiting for the challenge notification this morning? We assumed that structure—meal, challenge, meal, challenge, meal—would apply to today. We filled in the blanks because Jewel conditioned us to. So, when it deviated, we immediately assumed and believed the worst."

"That's a really good point," Alex said, and her heart grew three sizes.

"Everything is exactly as it seems in The Cruelest Jewel," Luna said. "They even activated the ABORT button. They just changed the name, thinking it would fool us."

"All right. Fine," Francis said. "If this is a challenge, how do we complete it with no envelope telling us what to do?"

Luna had an answer for that. On her tablet, she pulled up and recited the exact game language: *For some, you will receive a notification and instructions through your tablets at the designated time. If asked to enter a challenge room, once inside you must locate your envelope.*

"There's no envelope because we didn't enter a room. This challenge, let's call it *Jewel Is Missing*, is happening estate-wide. Look at the recipe," Luna said, waiting for everyone to do so.

Preheat oven to 314 degrees.

Mix all colors until batter is smooth.

Pour into sweet companion molds. Set
aside all but three key ingredients.

Whip two partridges until a psychopomp
and circumstance forms.

Share and cut the Baker's dozen
chocolate bar into quadragrams.

In a pressure cooker, separate the royal flush
with red herrings wild. Bake for seven minutes.

Serve the chocolate concoction
scrambled atop a pie on a cloudy white
day under a winner's cursed crown.

"We've figured out steps two through four. Now we're on step six! Don't you get it?" Luna paused, trying to rein in her excitement. "A pressure cooker? That's the interrogation. Separate the royal flush from red herrings wild? That's us. We're the royal flush because of the freebie present playing cards we got at lunch yesterday! The recipe is telling us we have to decide how we want to move forward. We've already been given everything we need to solve the recipe."

"You skipped step five," Francis said.

"*I* didn't," Luna said, confidence waning. She knew the next part would be a hard sell. "I think someone in here received a freebie present. They have the answer to number five."

"What gave you that idea?" Harlow asked.

"It's just a hunch."

"Who has the present, then?" Francis asked. "Don't all speak up at once, now."

"Maybe they can't yet," Luna said softly.

"That's convenient."

Alex sighed. "I'm with you, you know that," he said, "but last time you reached this hard because of that damn recipe, it didn't exactly go well."

"That was a mistake," she pleaded. "I'm right this time. I know it."

Harlow asked, "What about you, Stella? What do you think? Are we still playing the game?"

Nicole added, "You've been strangely quiet this whole time."

"That's true." Stella locked eyes with Luna. "It is strange."

Stella was the only person in this room who could change everyone's opinion with virtually zero effort, the only other person who stood a chance of winning, and now she was looking at Luna like she was about to eat her alive.

"I think that's enough for now. Tell all your friends," Stella said, tapping her tablet.

"What?" Luna asked.

"What?" Stella slung one leg over the rim of the bathtub, turned onto her side, and barrel-rolled into a standing position. "I think it's time to address the elephant in the room. I'm just going to come out and say what we're all thinking: Nicole is way too pretty to go to prison. There I said it!"

"Stella, please," Nicole said with a pained expression. "This is serious."

"I am being serious. We have two options: one—figure out what in the hell is happening in this house, or two—go to prison. I'm assuming I'm the only one here with any kind of connection to financial affluence, if you will. Lloyd will definitely lawyer us up with a Johnnie Cochran type, but that's no scot-free guarantee."

"Lloyd's your dad?" Francis asked. "That's what you said, right?"

"Indeed. Now, a body doesn't have to be found to convict someone of murder. Jewel is a megacelebrity, which means there will be an aggressive hunt to find her and make an arrest."

Stella paused—Luna almost shouted *but it's a game!* Stella must have sensed her objection because she looked at her and imperceptibly shook her head.

"It's time to address elephant number two: Dumbo's Revenge," Stella continued. "All the colors have been mixed, and our batter is smooth as butter. We're in this together. So, in the event that *Jewel Is Missing* is not a challenge, and someone in here had anything to do with her disappearance, fess up and we'll figure out a way forward. Together."

Everyone had returned to quiet.

"Good, because the second one of you stepped forward, I was going to sell you straight down the river." Stella laughed.

"How do we know you didn't do it?" Francis said. "Your parents keep you on lockdown because they know you're a repressed ax murderer or something. Inaugural wild child weekend? Sounds like a perfect opportunity to let out some homicidal rage."

Stella stared at him. "That is exactly the kind of skeptical thinking we need on our team. Love that. So glad you're here. However, you're a crappy detective. If I were going to kill someone, do you really think

I'd use something as imprecise and messy as an ax? On someone else's turf with no way out? Give me some credit here. I'm obviously way too clever for that."

"She does have a point," Harlow said.

"That's just what she wants you to think," Francis said.

"Also probable," Stella agreed.

"This isn't getting us anywhere," Luna said. "Do you believe me or not?"

"Of course I believe you. I never said I didn't," Stella said, as if it were the most obvious thing in the world. "You were absolutely right to have us meet in here. We can't let them know that we know something is up, and we can't let them know what we know about it. However."

Luna involuntarily sat up straighter as Stella approached her. Tablet in hand, Stella flipped it around to show her the slide that explained C-P-R. "You're not entirely wrong, but you're also not right. You're conflating challenges and the recipe again. Stop that. It's very disappointing."

"I am?"

"Think about it," Stella said. "You said the interrogation was the pressure cooker. No. Wrong. Incorrect. The interrogation wasn't something we had to solve. It was something we had to survive. Sure, no one got arrested, but no one got a present either."

Luna's eyebrows scrunched together as she thought. "The challenge is still happening?"

"And if the challenge is happening . . ." Stella trailed off.

"Then the interrogation can't be in the recipe. *Damn it.*"

"Language, little one. We try not to swear in our family," Stella teased. "You gotta slow down. You get too excited, and you start making mistakes."

"Right." Luna nodded. "So, what do we do next?"

"Yeah, what should we do next?" Francis called. "Sorry, didn't mean to interrupt your little meeting, but the rest of us are kind of waiting for an answer too."

She looked at Francis. "I'm so glad you asked, Double Agent."

"I'm not a double agent."

"You are now, comrade," Stella said. "They told us to stay in our rooms. You're the only one who can wander around without it looking suspicious. You're their friend. You're concerned and want to help. Unless you had something to do with this, they should have no problem telling you what they know."

"Oh, that's good," Luna said. "I didn't even think of that."

"By the by, I can also spot a lie from across the room, so if you try to double-cross us, I hope you know how to fight."

"How do you spot a lie?" Harlow asked.

"That's for me to know and you to research on the internet," Stella said. "While Francis is off being his best super spy self with Nicole to keep him honest, the rest of us will stay here and put the game versus reality theory to the test."

RECONNAISSANCE

SATURDAY, 2:08 P.M.

Francis waited until they had made it down the hall before asking, "What are you thinking?"

"About?" Nicole refused to read between his lines anymore.

"All of it. Back there, almost everyone offered up some kind of guess or rebuttal. You didn't."

So, he *had* noticed her intentional silence. Honestly, she'd been super lost in the bathroom. Luna and Stella simply moved faster than she did. Nicole needed time to compile data and process things one step at a time. More of a slow, calculated burn than lightning fast and whip smart like them.

But that didn't mean she was useless.

"Luna and Stella had it under control. I trust them," she said.

"You just met them."

"I just met you too."

Francis blinked at her a few times, mouth forming a silent and surprised, *oh*.

"I want to see the best in people for as long as I can," she said. "Usually right up until they do something to convince me that I shouldn't."

Stella had sent her off with Francis for a reason. It was so strange—even though parts of the game still weren't clicking for her, she knew precisely what Stella expected her to do.

Nicole hadn't had time to come up with a solid plan of action. Between the JEWEL IS MISSING announcement, being interrogated by what she hoped were rent-a-cops, and trying to figure out exactly what was going on, all the questions and inconsistencies that had formed around Francis had been put on involuntary hold.

"Do you know where Ethan and Olive are?"

Francis shook his head. "We have to make a stop first. I know they won't talk to me if you're there, but I have an idea." He had led her back to the main foyer. She hadn't seen it since they'd first arrived.

Nicole expected him to take her to one of the staircases, but at the last second, he curved to the right.

"This hallway has a nook that the cameras can't see," he whispered. "Unless security is watching our every move, it'll take them a while to figure out where we went." They stopped in front of an empty space of wall tucked into a corner, and he started counting, stopping at thirty. "They're not coming," he said with a pleased grin. "If they were watching us, the second we dropped out of sight they would have immediately started tracking us through the tablets. They would've found us by now to escort us back to our suites."

"Thirty seconds?"

"Jewel demanded it." He pressed a button she couldn't even tell was a button in the wall. A panel appeared—he entered a code and the wall slid apart, revealing an elevator. Inside, he pressed the *3*. "If *anything* off plan happened, whoever was on shift had thirty seconds to get there. Luna's guard got fired last night. That's what Ethan needed my help with."

"Firing someone?" she asked, managing her surprise.

He shook his head. "Revoking their access. I told you, I do security and some IT work on the side."

Nicole sighed, careful not to let her reaction slide into overexaggerated territory. "You didn't mention that it was for Jewel."

"Because it's not." Her sigh had worked—his expression changed to confusion mixed with worry. "I work for Ethan. He's in charge of staff."

On the third floor, the elevator doors opened directly into an attic. The floor sparkled despite the musty smell of neglect and dust that lingered in the air. Overhead, the ceiling sloped at a 45-degree angle and one entire wooden panel had been replaced by a skylight. Sunlight beamed through, curling into every square inch it could reach.

The only thing inside the room was a computer station with three monitors and a wheezing desktop tower.

"This is what's left of the old server room." Francis held the chair out for her to sit down. "I'm going to patch into the security system and show you how to make the cameras follow me."

"Won't they be able to detect that? An intruder alert or something?"

"Not if I use the back door that I built," he said, leaning close to her while he typed too quickly for her to follow on the keyboard. "Ethan and I designed the system together. We're the only people who know about it. I'll just tell him I wanted to double-check to make sure everything was running the way it should, all things considered."

The screens clicked on, each with a grid of nine cameras and a list of available feeds. "That is . . . overwhelming to look at it." Every room in the house really was monitored.

"I'll simplify it. Don't worry." He handed her a pair of dusty, old headphones. "They won't know you're watching. By the time they figure out you were, it'll be too late to do anything about it. You'll get a front-row seat to the truth."

"And you're really okay with this? Letting me spy on you and your friends?"

"Not particularly," he said. "But if this is how Jewel wants to play it this time, then so be it."

This time.

The fact that they were the first group to play The Cruelest Jewel had been quietly haunting her. The fact that Francis appeared in one of the videos meant something. And now, not only did he work for Ethan, he had access to the security system.

He was going to tell her the truth, whether he wanted to or not.

"Francis," she said, voice low. "How many Golden Weekends have you attended?"

He stopped typing, eyes still on the screen. She watched him begin to chew on his bottom lip. "Define *attend*."

"I saw you in one of the videos."

"They're my friends," he said quietly. "I go where they go."

Nicole turned in her seat to face him. To his credit he did the same, meeting her eye to eye. The first time she'd seen him, she'd thought he was cute. There was no denying that. It always amused her how once the surprise wore off, how fast a face could become her favorite. Starting at his hairline, she let her gaze drift downward, lingering over every feature. When Golden Weekend was over, Nicole wanted to see him again.

She truly hoped the next handful of minutes didn't ruin all chances of that happening.

"Are you helping them with The Cruelest Jewel?" she asked. "Have you been lying to me this whole time?"

"No, of course not," he said.

Nicole sighed again; eyes downcast. "I just"—she paused to let some frustration build in her chest and leak into her voice—"I don't think I can believe you. All those little cryptic warnings you gave me, every time it seemed like you were holding back from telling us the truth—how can I trust you if you won't even be honest with me now, when it's just us?"

"I'm telling you the truth. I didn't help them plan anything."

"Alex thinks we can only win if the person Jewel paired us with is at our side." She lingered over his features again, ending with looking into his eyes. "That's *you* for *me*. We're supposed to be together."

"Nicole, I *swear* I didn't have anything to do with it."

"*It?*"

"The Cruelest Jewel," he clarified quickly. "I'm supposed to play the game. That's the deal."

"So, you don't know if Jewel is really missing or not? They didn't tell you *anything* beforehand?"

"No. Not about that."

"Then what did they tell you?"

Francis hesitated, biting his lip again.

"I knew it." Turning away, she shook her head. "I can't *believe* this. The *one* time I let my guard down, and this happens to me."

"Wait, wait," he said, taking her hand. "I can explain."

Nicole looked at him, forcing herself not to blink. If her tears fell, it would be too much. Threatening to cry always trumped actually crying. She needed to appear on the brink of broken—he could pull her back and be her hero or push too hard and break her heart.

"What *deal*?" she asked, voice pitching. "What does that mean?"

"The Scavengers Initiative really happened." He dropped into a crouch, and Nicole almost lost it. Francis looked like he was proposing—holding her hand, looking up at her with the most earnest expression she'd ever seen him wear. He continued, "I played that game, and I swore I would never let Jewel do something like that to me again. But—I don't hate her. We really are friends."

Nicole suspected as much from the very beginning. She knew an antagonistic love-based relationship when she saw one. "Okay? And?" she asked. The way he revealed the truth felt like it had been a big deal for him. Needing him to focus, she decided to let that part go.

"When she asked me to play The Cruelest Jewel, I said no. Because no. And then a few days later, she told me she planned to invite you, and I said maybe." The longer he spoke, the quieter his voice got. "I swear I'm not some obsessed stalker. I just wanted to meet you."

Nicole's shock temporarily overpowered her plan to disarm him. "Me?"

"That's why I didn't get here at the same time as everyone else. I didn't believe her until she sent me a video of you in the house."

She tried to figure out what to say because even though his admission had taken her by surprise, there wasn't really anything to feel violated or betrayed about. Or angry.

Technically, he hadn't done anything wrong. Jewel, his *friend*, had invited him to her house.

If anything, Nicole needed to have a long talk with Jewel. There was no doubt in her mind that Jewel knew Francis had a crush on Nicole and used that to her advantage. She'd set them up on a date neither of them knew they were on. She continued to stare at him even though he'd long since stopped looking at her. His skin had a reddish tint—he was *embarrassed*, oh God. She almost laughed. How could she be mad at him? He was so cute when he wasn't trying to be a stoic player.

"Jewel could've put you in another coffin of spiders or worse." She held him lightly by the chin, lifting his face to make sure she had his undivided attention.

"You were here." He shrugged. "I tried to be as up front as possible. That's why I told you I'd seen your videos. I wanted you to know that I knew you. Anytime you asked me something, I always told you the truth."

"And you implied that I'm more important than five hundred thousand dollars to you," she teased.

He closed his eyes, groaning and rubbing his hands over his face. "I'm sorry. This is all going *so* wrong."

"Maybe. Maybe not." Nicole smiled at him. She turned back to the computer. "Now, show me how this works, comrade. I'm ready to earn my spy stripes."

RANSOM

Truth be told, Stella was still undecided.

Her bright plan had been to twirl dramatically into the room to boost morale and say, *Raise your hand if you believe Jewel isn't actually missing and this is all a part of the game!* She'd then use their responses as a guide on how to move forward.

But she had spotted Luna first, hiding in plain sight. She had curled around Alex as if she were a koala and he was a bamboo tree. Cute. Innocent. Eyes on everyone. Luna took her time moving from person to person, watching them process what had happened. When she finally stood up and walked into the bathroom alone, Stella knew that little Einstein had come up with a plan.

And it was good.

But not great.

"We should just—leave," Harlow said. They had migrated to her room to keep things fresh and exciting for the cameras. Not that anyone besides Stella knew that. "We have everything we need to escape. We can use the secret passageways to get off the estate. Or—your parents are here, right?"

Stella nodded.

"Can't you call them? Tell them Jewel's lost her fucking mind and ask them to come get us?"

Luna said, "Running away would only make us seem like we have something to hide."

Harlow looked elsewhere in annoyance.

Whatever were they going to do with Harlow? Stella didn't fault her for checking out so early. If their circumstances were reversed, she couldn't swear to probably not doing the same. But make no mistake about it, Stella fully planned to win The Cruelest Jewel. And she was going to do it by beating Jewel at her own game. If there was more than one ending, like Jewel had said, Stella wanted to find the one that would cause the biggest upset.

But first, she needed more information.

"Running away. Bickering. Waiting patiently for my love to return from the war. It's all the same and intensely boring," Stella said, staring at each of them in turn. "It's time to work. This godforsaken recipe will not solve itself. Luna?"

"Yeah?"

"Assemble our goodies, here on the floor so we can see everything laid out." Luna was in motion before Stella even finished her sentence. "Alex?"

"What?"

"Sit next to me. You have a good brain in that big head of yours. I need it."

"I don't have a big head," Alex grumbled while Stella smiled to herself. He also did as instructed.

"Harlow?"

"No."

"Good. Just checking to make sure you're present and conscious. Your job is to sit there and look pretty."

They had collected

- An iron box with a skeleton key code and two metal homing birds inside.
- A wyvern medallion map expansion.

- A moon codex with a list of doors.
- Three white animal keys: a fox, an owl, a cat.
- Six playing cards: King, Queen, Jack, Ten, Ace, Joker.
- Two bar bracelets that read MEMENTO MORI when put together.

They spent the next hour going back and forth debating possible different interpretations for each line of the nonsensical recipe. Stella was getting cranky, desperately trying to beat back spite and impatience. What came next? And why was it taking so long to show up? Even Luna appeared to be getting bored theorizing in circles.

Just as Stella was about to announce her cover story so she could go make her next livestream in relative peace and quiet, Harlow's room door flew open.

"Stop talking," Francis said. "Right now." He was holding Nicole's hand as they walked through the room, heading straight for the bathroom.

"Uhh, no one was saying anything," Alex said, getting up.

Stella's eyebrows spoke for her. Francis and his heart eyes for her new best girl annoyed her, but she decided to follow him. Just this once.

"We have a problem," he said once they were all inside.

"Oh, I'd argue we have several," Stella said.

Francis's face never went blank because it stayed that way. He had an eerie stillness about him that could be hard to read. Hard, not impossible. This was the closest she'd ever seen him put out—almost like he was flustered.

"I've known Ethan my whole life. Either he doesn't know what's happening or he does and it's really bad." Whatever he'd learned had agitated him to the point of pacing. "I don't know if it's true, but they *believe* Jewel is really missing. They think she's still on the property, but they don't know where."

Stella hazarded a guess that he was telling the truth. Nicole watched him, full of concern—she believed it too.

"I'm not doubting you," Luna said carefully, "but Jewel's an actress. Maybe Ethan can act better than you think he can."

Francis shook his head. "It's not just him. Olive can barely lie without stuttering, and she was crying so hard they were talking about sedating her."

Uncomfortable with how that last revelation settled around the room, Stella said, "That's certainly dramatic. Did you find out anything else?"

"There's a ransom note," Nicole said. "Whoever has Jewel instructed Ethan to tell us Jewel was missing. It was their idea to conduct fake interrogations using the security guards and fake cops."

"Wait, they wanted us to know she was missing?" Luna asked. "Why?"

"Because in the note they demanded exactly one million dollars," Francis said.

It was like a giant overpowered vacuum sucked all the air out of the room.

"They want the money already in the house," Harlow said softly. Stella knew exactly what she was remembering. "Payable immediately. Jewel told me and Stella it would be cash."

"Why won't Ethan just give them the money, then?" Alex asked.

"Because they can't," Francis said. "The safe can only be opened by whoever wins The Cruelest Jewel."

"So, the 'kidnappers' need us to keep playing the game because it's the easiest way to get a million dollars without raising suspicion outside the house!" Luna said, practically jumping up and down. "I don't know for sure, but if you tried to withdraw a million dollars from a bank, cash or digitally, that would raise some serious red flags. They think that if we know she's missing, we'll just hand it over to get Jewel back."

"Exactly," Francis said. "Ethan is trying to decide whether or not to ask us to keep playing, but there's another problem." His gaze shifted to Harlow, who then said, "Goddamn it."

Stella happened to look at Luna at the exact moment she looked at her. One confused face mirrored the other.

Harlow removed her sunglasses, placing them on the counter. She sat down under the window. Her entire body slumped in defeat—shoulders sagging, chin barely raised, hands limp in her lap. "I never should have come here."

"Too late for that? Yeah?"

"Shut up, Stella," she said with a weak smile. "Jewel woke me up this morning, saying she wanted to talk to me. She asked me to go to her room."

"Why didn't you just talk in your room?" Alex asked.

"Because there aren't any cameras in Jewel's room. Shit." Francis rubbed his face.

"We both walked in, and only I walked out," Harlow said, nodding. "And now she's missing."

So Harlow *knew* the last place Jewel was seen was her bedroom. No wonder she didn't want to go down the dark passageway earlier. Well, that and the whole being-traumatized-from-being-buried-alive thing.

"*And* they think you're in on the kidnapping. That you helped," Francis said. "That's the other reason why Ethan hasn't sent us home. They're trying to keep you here."

Luna asked, "What happened when you were in her room? What did you talk about?" Was that jealousy Stella heard in Luna's tone?

"Jewel said she wanted to ask me if I was okay, off the record, and Stella told her to be nice to me because I was upset."

Alex asked, "Wait, if she wanted to talk in private why didn't she just go into your bathroom? It's closer."

Harlow said, "That occurred to me when that fake cop started yelling in my face. When I left the room, she was there, fine, alive, breathing, and very much not missing, sitting in this stupid half chair thing."

"It seems like our choices are play the game to rescue Jewel or play the game because it is a game," Stella said. "I'm a little concerned about the C-P-R element. If the challenges are over and that no longer applies, it means we're in a free-for-all. We have to defer to the second rule of Cruelest Jewel conduct: *Everything is connected*, but we have no idea how to reach the endgame other than by solving the recipe."

"It's like I said," Luna began. "We already have everything we need to solve it."

Everything except the final answer, Stella thought, cranky mood returning.

"If everything is connected, maybe the recipe is *how* we find Jewel," Alex said. "The last step in the recipe will lead us to her. Or it could be the location of the safe."

"We still have to figure out steps five and six," Stella reminded him. "Let's not get ahead of ourselves."

"We have until eight A.M. tomorrow," Nicole said. "The kidnappers only gave Ethan twenty-four hours to decide if he'll pay the ransom."

Outside the room, someone shouted, "Hello? Kids? Are you in here?"

Alex opened the door to check. "Oh, they brought food."

"Thank God," Francis said, hurrying out. "I already ate with cats. I'm not eating in the bathroom. We can take a break."

Stella waited until everyone else left. Only Harlow remained. She got up from her bathtub perch and sat next to her under the window. She still had questions that she wasn't going to ask the group. It would only make things more complicated, but they were good questions that deserved answers.

Like, how did the kidnappers know about the game?

How did they know about the money in the safe?

Why ask Stella to livestream the weekend when it was being broadcast anyway?

Something wasn't adding up.

"You were livestreaming earlier, weren't you?" Harlow asked.

"Guilty as charged."

Harlow nodded. "Do I look as terrible as I feel?"

"Yes."

Harlow put her sunglasses back on. "Okay."

Stella laughed. "You look fine. Your eyes are just puffy like you've been crying for several hours, which coincidentally, you were."

"Yeah."

"You could've at least brushed your hair. It would've helped. A little."

"Why bother? Life is meaningless."

"I'm not laughing because it's funny," Stella said, laughing because she obviously thought it was funny. "I'm laughing because I'm uncomfortable. I like you a lot more than I did yesterday, and it's throwing me off. I don't usually change my mind about people."

"Oh. I haven't changed my mind about you."

"See? That is exactly what I'm talking about! Empathy is gross! I don't like it!"

Harlow snorted, looking away. "I am glad we're partners, though," she said softly. "I don't like you, but I appreciate you."

Stella stared at the back of her head. "I'm okay with that."

"I didn't tell them everything," Harlow said quietly. She pulled a square, loosely wrapped in gold foil, out of her pocket and handed it to Stella. "The cop gave it to me during my interrogation. You can have them."

Stella peeled it open. Six oversized letter tiles: G, E, N, R, I, S in a rich chocolate-brown color with white lettering. "Chocolate," she said.

Share and cut the Baker's dozen chocolate bar into quadragrams.

"Congratulations, Harlow," Stella said with a small laugh. "You just helped me solve step five."

Luna had been right after all.

STELLA SAYS
EPISODE 5

Black Steel in the Hour of Chaos

Hello, again.

Hello, goodbye.

This will be my last episode of Stella Says.

We're winding down, and I have a feeling I will no longer be paid for my services. My labor is far too precious to be given away.

[pauses]

Jewel Is Missing is quite the hot topic, I see. No, I will not be answering any of your questions.

[pauses]

You'll just have to tune in and see, Filia20.

[pauses]

Anyway, before we go our separate ways, true to form, I am in need of one more favor. As I understand it, Luna's brood, you Goldspiracy folk, create transcripts for all of Jewel's videos. Have you been doing that for our Golden Shindig as well?

[pauses]

Excellent.

On our first night here, Olive said some interesting phrases to me. I don't remember all of it—she was very cute, and between her and Nicole I was very overwhelmed—but I do remember this: If you find the key, you can unlock the game.

What was the rest of it? What else did she say?

I'll wait.

HEART OF GOLD

SATURDAY, 7:30 P.M.

Nicole had no idea what she should be doing.

As a group they had decided on a plan: When Ethan summoned them at eight tomorrow morning, they would call his bluff. They would all ask to go home. Everyone agreed his response would be the deciding factor in what came next.

They play the game so the ransom money could save Jewel.

They play the game because it *was* a game.

Unfortunately, that wasn't for another twelve hours.

"How are you holding up?" Francis asked.

They sat alone outside. His suite was the only one with a balcony—a cute table-and-chair set took up the entire left side. The weather was so nice. Partly cloudy with a delicate breeze as the sun began to set.

"I'm not. I wish there were something else I could do to help Luna and Stella," she said. "Last I checked, they were holed up in the bathroom again."

"Guess that means we're in third place," he said. "Honestly, I don't see how we can beat them."

"I've been thinking about that too. At some point, the game is going to force us to separate since only two of us can win," she said. "Part of me feels like maybe I didn't want it bad enough, which feels really weird to admit out loud. Every fiber of my being knows exactly how that money can change my life for the better. But I didn't have a strategy. I was content to let Stella lead—still am. That's not how a winner plays."

"You played the game your way," he said with a shrug. "There's nothing wrong with that. You're not Jewel. You're not Luna or Stella. Sometimes losing is okay if you were able to stay true to who you are."

And who was she exactly?

JadeTheBabe. Nicole. Her father's daughter and her mama's mini-me.

An orphan with two jobs, big dreams, an even bigger heart, and an iron will.

"It took me a long time to get comfortable wanting things for myself. I still struggle with it, honestly. I have to live so minimally—I wouldn't be able to survive otherwise—that I just stopped hoping. This place is too much, but is it bad to want a balcony that faces the west with a nice view of trees or the ocean? I would love to have something like that someday," she said. "We can't give up yet. We have to play until the end. Whatever happens, we keep going."

"When this is over, if we don't end up in jail, I was wondering if you would want to go out sometime?"

Surprised, Nicole tore her gaze away from the beautiful sunset.

Francis continued, "I know I'm here and you're a few hours away, but if you wanted to keep in touch, that'd be cool too." He cleared his throat and wouldn't look at her. "Yeah."

Nicole laughed, softly, heart fluttering all on its own. "Francis, this whole weekend with you has felt like one long weird, and at times wonderful, date. I think we've passed the 'let's keep in touch' stage."

SATURDAY, 8:15 P.M.

"Stella?" Nicole opened the red door while knocking. "Can I come in? I brought cookies."

"Even if you didn't have cookies, you'd be welcome," Stella said. She'd already changed into her pajamas—a matching set of chilly penguins kissing. The presents had been spread out on one side of her bed, while she lay on the other, staring up at the ceiling. Her tablet had the nonsensical poem open.

Everyone had a different method of playing The Cruelest Jewel. The rules were clear—only two could win—and yet, every single one of them had been fine with giving Stella access to *all* the presents. Even Luna's codex and bracelet were there. Stella could up and disappear in the middle of the night, much like Jewel had, double-crossing them all. There'd be nothing to stop her from winning because they had freely given the presents to her.

If Stella had the chance, would she take it?

"What are you doing?" Nicole placed the cookies on the nightstand and pointed to the empty spot next to Stella. "May I?"

Stella nodded. "Trying to absorb the answer through osmosis. I thought if I stared at it long enough, it would appear in my brain. That didn't work."

Nicole stretched out next to her, but not before grabbing the letter tiles. She arranged them on the bed, moving them around, making words and trying to memorize them. This was the first time Nicole had access to the tiles since their appearance earlier that afternoon because Harlow had given them to Stella—and *only* Stella. She made it clear no one else could have or borrow her present. "I can't believe Harlow hid these from us," Nicole said. "We all shared our presents as soon as we got them."

"I don't think she was hiding them. More like it was the last thing that made her feel special. The videos from the previous Golden Weekends crushed that feeling and the tiles brought it back," Stella said. "She doesn't care anymore. She just wants to go home, so I'm going to make sure she gets there."

"You sure are something, Stella At All Times," Nicole said, grinning. Her plan would take time, but it would work. She couldn't be nearly as heavy-handed as she had been with Francis. "I wouldn't have been able to solve any of the stuff you and Luna did. I have no idea why I'm here."

"You're the talent." Stella turned on her side to look at her. "That's why you're here."

"What do you mean?"

"I'm still working on it. You're the talent. I'm the outsider with the inside edge. And Luna, well." She whispered even though they were alone. "Don't tell anyone, but Jewel wants Luna to win."

Nicole had figured that out as well. The way Jewel had spoken about Luna in the theater had given her dead away. Apart from Francis, no one knew that she'd met with Jewel privately. Their meeting didn't *have* to stay a secret, but it was going to.

"How do you know?" she asked.

"She told me. In a way," Stella said. "I'm still deciding if I'm okay with that or if I'm going to beat Jewel to prove a point. I don't know which one is more important to me."

Nicole paused for a beat to collect her thoughts. She still had some difficulty reading Stella. Almost everything she did was so erratic and unexpected, pinning her down anytime soon seemed unlikely. Sure, Nicole could tweak the pitch of her voice, speak faster with long-winded sentences, casually insult everyone around her in a baffling, endearing way, but the heart of who Stella was wouldn't be there because Nicole still hadn't seen it.

If Nicole were going to lose to this girl, she'd better be worth it.

"I think the fact that there's even a choice says something," she said, keeping her voice soft, contemplative. "You don't owe Luna anything."

"And I owe myself everything. I'm very selfish. Can't you tell?"

Nicole laughed. Stella did have a selfishness about her, but it didn't feel malicious. What had she said to Nicole before? She was an only child who never learned how to share? The Cruelest Jewel had given her a crash course in that lesson. She thought Stella had risen to the challenge beautifully. "I don't think you give yourself enough credit."

"Excuse you, I give myself all the credit. I'm incredible. Haven't you been watching me sleuth everybody under the table all weekend? That was for show."

"That's why you're our leader. The way you hopped out of that bathtub and backed Luna up? I hope you were serious about being her sister. That really meant a lot to her."

"I am a good leader," Stella said. "Iron fist all the way."

"Iron fist. Heart of gold."

Stella nodded, rolling onto her side and taking the tiles from Nicole. She shuffled them quickly, spelling out the words Nicole had made in rapid succession. "I was serious about being your sister too, you know."

"Oh. I wasn't sure because . . ." She trailed off.

"Mmm, yeah. I figured your type was short brown boy with nice hair. I adjusted my course," she said. "That's all."

"I like him," Nicole admitted.

"I object."

"I like you."

"Sustained." Stella laughed. "One door closed for me, so I opened the window."

"See? That's how I know you'll make the right choice about Luna." Nicole wondered if Stella had trouble sleeping at night. Always looking for an alternative route to get what she wanted, always thinking of her next steps that would ensure she stayed five steps ahead of everyone else—living like that must have been exhausting. She was calculating, but far from cold. Her complete turnaround with Harlow stood as a testament to that. She cared about others when she wanted to, on her terms, and wanted them to want her back. No, *needed* them to. That small distinction felt closer to the truth.

Stella needed everyone on their team just as much as they needed her.

We can trust her, Nicole thought, feeling good about her decision. Stella would do right by them—she was sure of it. "Whatever you plan or want to do, I'm in. I hereby resign myself to joining your machinations."

Stella froze, hand hovering in midair still holding a tile. "You are so, so talented." Her head turned slowly, grin growing at the same snail pace. "I've been trying to figure out why Jewel wanted us to watch the videos from the previous Golden Weekends. It's because she's starting over. *We're* the new chapter. Think about it."

"Okay," Nicole said. "I'm thinking, but remember I'm not Luna."

"That's fine, that's fine. Sometimes, I just need to think out loud. Stay with me." Stella sat up, sitting on her knees, eyes wild. Her brain must have felt like it was on fire. "When the game started, Jewel referenced a bunch of portal stories, remember?"

Nicole pulled the opening poem up on the tablet just in case Stella needed it. "I do, yeah."

"And then, Olive confirmed it first. The Cruelest Jewel is a story," she said. "Jewel has always been obsessed with stories, and she *told* me the game has more than one ending. That's the *key*. And"—she hesitated—"I can't tell you why, but I have a very good reason for knowing that."

Nicole waved that away. "Pretend like I know what you're talking about and keep going."

"The purpose of the recipe is to build a new narrative one step at a time," Stella said. "The Cruelest Jewel is a story. The Queen has been abducted. The players must choose which route to take to save her. So, what if we choose wrong? What if we went off script and wrote our own ending?"

"But why would we do that? How would we win if we don't follow the rules?"

Stella didn't answer, instead leaping off the bed and running for the door. She yelled into the hall, "Crayola Hall Coalition, assemble! We're making a new plan!"

PART IV

THE REVOLUTION WILL BE TELEVISED

"This was definitely the result of me having one of those 'just because you can doesn't mean you should' moments and then me completely ignoring it."

—JEWEL VAN HANEN

SUNDAY, 8:00 A.M.

Announcement

All guests: please proceed to the
White Drawing Room immediately.

WILD ROYAL FLUSH

"It's happening," Luna said, breathless and bouncing on her tiptoes. "It's happening!"

Stella said, "We'll need everything—all our presents. Harlow?"

"Already packed," she answered, and handed Alex her bag. "Can you hold on to everything for me? I'm on tablet duty."

"But we know how to get to the drawing room," he said, taking it anyway.

"I'm using Stella's tablet to catalog all the secret passageways we pass on the way down," Harlow said.

Alex frowned. "It works when the necklace isn't plugged in?"

"We—"

"Huddle up," Stella shouted. "Sorry to cut you off there, Harlow, except I'm not. Come on, hustle, hustle, hustle! Huddle, huddle, huddle!"

"She can't be serious," Francis said.

"Huddle. Up," Stella threatened, content to leave the *or else* implied. Once they formed a friendship-is-magic circle, she continued, "We stick to the plan, which means you all sit back, relax, and enjoy the show. Let me handle everything. Luna, I know this will be hard for you, but stay silent until it's time. Eyes on me."

"Excuse you, you're talking to the SilentStar of Golden Rule. Show some respect," Alex said, smiling.

"And just like that, you're third favorite again," Stella said. "Such a waste."

When they opened the door, burly men with bad haircuts wearing earpieces that coiled down and under the collars of their jackets waited for them on the other side.

"Just a safety precaution," Guard Number One said, standing at the front of the group. His partner brought up the rear.

Nicole whispered, "I hope you're right about this."

Stella regarded her new best girl and sister with a cool, mocking look—the first time she'd used it on her. "I'm not *not* right about it."

That weekend Stella had learned quite a few new and shiny things. Like the fact that she was slightly afraid of ghosts. She craved having friends who would become more like sisters. She could care about people like Harlow (and she deserved cookies for that one). She had a romantic type, and it would probably cause her a hefty amount of tender heartbreak later on.

Attending Golden Weekend had also confirmed something she already knew. She would always be insufferably and violently herself.

The one and only Stella Beauregard.

Unexpectedly, Ethan and Olive waited alone in the White Drawing Room. Considering the bodyguard escort, Stella had assumed there would be a more obvious security presence to up the intimidation factor.

"Hi, everyone," Olive said. Bloodshot eyes and croaking voice—someone was sure committed to winning the Oscar for grieving best friend. Such a cute little liar.

And somehow, Stella managed to not laugh at her. She made sure her team all sat next to one another, on one couch, and that she sat closest to Harlow at the head.

Olive continued, "We've been thinking about everything and how to move forward. I don't know if Francis told you this, but Jewel"— her voice cracked, wow—"really loves these kinds of games. We even played before a few years ago. She made some really big promises to you all, and if it were me, I would be disappointed. So, while we've decided to send you home early, we're going to give you the prize money to split among yourselves."

Stella decided to roll with it. "Oh, how generous." She looked to the right at her ducks in a row for effect and back to Olive. "Wow. Thank you."

"The only problem is that the safe is locked," Ethan said. He looked a bit raggedy, as if he hadn't changed his clothes or slept in days, but not nearly as destroyed as Olive. "It can't be opened without the present someone would've received from the last challenge today. In order to pay you, we would have to ask you to play."

Olive said, "We understand if you don't want to. This is an extremely unconventional and stressful situation we've put you in. There would be security with you the entire time."

"I'll play," Stella volunteered, raising her hand. "But first, an Announcement." She stood up, careful to stay close to her group.

"Seven," Harlow said.

"Everything we've done since The Cruelest Jewel started has been broadcast online," Stella revealed. "All of it. Every challenge, every meal, every whispered secret in a hall when you thought no one was listening. Say hi to the viewers at home, because we're all stars now."

Confusion, followed by shock, replaced by anger, rippled down the line, just like they'd practiced. "What are you talking about?" Nicole asked.

"Ask Francis," Stella said kindly. "He knows all about it."

"No. I don't," he said to Nicole. "I swear."

Stella turned back to Ethan and Olive. "Our substitute hosts definitely know. They helped Jewel plan this whole Golden Shindig. That's why they're going to let me monologue, because I know how to put on a show. Ratings, am I right?"

"Um, actually," Olive said, "I was going to ask you to sit down."

Stella shushed her. "Now, in order to make sense of this opportunistic airing, we have to start at the beginning."

Luna jumped at her cue, speaking as fast as she could. "Jewel created Golden Rule as a way to connect with fans, share her story, and so they could share theirs too. Then, she started hosting top-secret Golden Weekends, exclusively for users on the app to spend time with her."

"But then, she stopped. Completely left her own app, and nobody knew why." Stella began to stroll toward the fireplace. "She took a break to 'find herself' until she decided it was time to make her triumphant comeback. She called on her best and brightest to help her plan what would be her final Golden Weekend."

"Six," Harlow said.

"No, it's ten," Luna whispered.

"Luna. We talked about this." Stella eyed her. Carefully, she plucked a red flower from its vase on top of the mantel and twirled it between her fingers. "Admittedly I'm a little fuzzy on the details, but all signs point to something going south. My theory? Jewel uncovered a sinister plot to take her out of commission during Golden Weekend. Side note: Can you imagine the audacity, the gumption, someone would have to possess to even think they could pull that off?" She scoffed and shook her head in pity. "Whatever Jewel discovered wasn't a threat to her—it was a challenge. So of course, Jewel, being Jewel, decided to beat them with her own game."

Olive turned to Ethan, stricken with alarm. He said, "Okay, that's enough—"

"It is not enough," Stella said. "I'm about to break this case wide open, and if you care about your sister half as much as you claim to, you'll let me finish."

Ethan shook his head. "You don't know what you're talking about." He lowered his voice until just enough of a whisper carried across the room. "Don't make this worse. Please."

Stella hesitated for three whole seconds. "Jewel created a game within The Cruelest Jewel."

Their reactions, surprise and then confusion, happened exactly as Stella believed it would. Smiling, she readied herself to rocket launch the next bombshell at them.

"The culprits had planned the perfect crime," she continued as she approached the love seat. She sat, crossing her legs at the knee and leaning forward. "Jewel would go missing in the middle of her grand event, whisked away with only a ransom note with very specific instructions left behind." She sat back, emphasizing her point with the flower. "But Jewel knew what she was doing. She set it up so that if everything went sideways, no matter what happened to her the culprits wouldn't get away with it."

Stella paused, waiting to make sure she had them.

"Five," Harlow said at the same time Ethan asked, "How?"

"I'm so glad you asked," Stella said. "First, Jewel selected Nicole aka JadeTheBabe, Golden Rule's newest Queen and my new best girl, to ensure there would be an audience eagerly watching *their* best girl in the game. Next, she selected Harlow—a controversial choice, for sure, because she was used as a proxy to send a message to Jewel's detractors. Mess with her, and she'll bury you too." Stella paused, locking eyes with Harlow.

"I'm fine," she said.

"Good," Stella continued. "Luna was selected to ensure the entirety of the Goldspiracy Forums would watch to support their Founder. If anyone would analyze every single frame of video from this weekend to help discover the truth, it would be them."

Luna nodded in agreement. "We would've never given up."

"And then, there was Francis," Stella said.

"Whatever you're about to say, don't." Francis's stillness had broken again. "This isn't the plan we agreed to—"

"Of course it's not the plan that we agreed to, because I lied." She stood up only to throw herself onto the next love seat, lounging like a mildly irritated cat. "Whose side are you on? That's a real question by the way. Nicole, cover your ears."

"Stella—"

"Stop interrupting me." She paused again for effect, rolling into a sitting position. "Jewel wanted an inside man on our team. Someone who would ensure we got all the information we needed. Francis, she knew you would do your honorable best no matter the circumstances. And she also knew you would do everything in your power to help us, even if that meant spying on your friends. Face it, you're predictable and she likes you."

"Wait." Francis's gaze drifted slowly from Stella to Ethan. "No."

Nicole must have given him some acting pointers—he looked convincing as hell.

"Don't jump ahead of me now. After Jewel secured the players, she had one more trick up her sleeve. The proof is in the presents, because we got two sets: challenge and freebies." Stella could feel how unhinged her smile looked. "The culprits knew about the challenge presents, but they didn't know about the freebies. Jewel gave those to us directly in secret."

"But wait, there's more," Harlow said. "Four."

Stella pointed at Olive. "I figured out that neither of you knew anything about our freebie presents when you asked about my wyvern necklace. At first, I thought you were laying it on thick, because right before that Jewel said, 'One of them will betray me.' Them being you and Ethan. But Jewel wasn't being facetious.

"So I asked myself, Why would someone who helped plan the game, who helped host it, not recognize an integral part of it? Because Jewel intentionally hid it from you. And pray tell, why would she do that? Because the culprits *work* here. They didn't need to break in because the call was coming from inside the house."

Stella walked back to her starting place next to Harlow.

"The staff would never do something like that. Ever," Olive said, righteous as rain in the summer. "They wouldn't have any reason to."

Ethan agreed. "That's ridiculous."

"Is it, though?" Stella teased. "I told you the proof is in the presents. On the last night Jewel was seen alive, she gave Harlow a freebie present: six letter tiles that would form *quadragrams*—a portmanteau meaning four anagrams."

"R-S-G-N-I-E," Harlow said in a singsong voice.

This wasn't true—Harlow had definitely gotten the tiles from the cop, but neither Ethan nor Olive corrected her. She even waited, giving them time to catch the inconsistency, and they didn't rise to the occasion. Confident her plan would work, Stella continued, "Jewel told us who the culprits were. First anagram: SIGNER. Ethan, Jewel's brother and business partner. Coincidence? I think not. You said it yourself. *You* supervise the staff. *You* are in charge of security. The *Warden* of Golden Rule. Jewel would have never been abducted if you didn't give the go-ahead."

"*Wow*." Ethan laughed in disbelief. "I knew I should've stopped you before you got started. You can't seriously think that I had my own sister kidnapped. Why would I do that? I love my sister. We share everything and—"

"*Don't say that*." Olive's voice nearly hit a shrill pitch that only dogs could hear.

"—she's one of the most important people in my life. I would never do anything to hurt her."

"Why? *Why?* Why?" Stella said, ready to bring it home. "Second anagram: RESIGN. After a year of soul searching, I think Jewel was ready to walk away from everything. You may be partners, but Francis told us that it's not in equal shares. If Jewel decided to dissolve whatever you built together, there'd be nothing you could do about it. Once you recruited the staff to your side, you promised them the million dollars as a bonus—the first of many to come once you inherited Jewel's share of the company by default once she's never seen or heard from again."

"Three," Harlow said.

"Bravo." Ethan began the most sarcastic slow clap to ever exist. "That was good. Quite the show. But speculation without proof doesn't mean anything."

"For the last time, the proof is in the *presents*—are you just not listening to me?" Stella said, grinning again. "Third anagram: SINGER.

Olive, the Siren of Golden Rule, the beatific soprano, and Ethan's fiancée and accomplice. You stand to gain just as much as he does once you kooky kids tie the knot."

Olive's jaw dropped. She sputtered in shock and outrage, staring from Stella to Ethan and back again. "*How— What— I— No!*"

"Yes," Stella said. "It was the Lovebirds in the Bedroom with the Security Guards. I rest my case." She finished with a bow and sat back down next to Harlow.

"You don't *have* a case," Ethan said. A shock of red had begun to creep up his neck and face. "Again, you didn't prove anything. You just talked for five minutes—"

"Two."

"—about what you *think* happened by connecting nonexistent dots."

"Maybe," Stella admitted. It had been far too easy to cast Ethan and Olive as villains.

Jewel had primed them to take the unexpected fall from the very beginning. When Stella asked the Ouija board why The Cruelest Jewel existed, it answered WARDEN and SIREN. When she asked Jewel if she trusted them, Jewel never gave an answer.

The viewers, who saw everything, would remember that too. Stella made sure of it by specifically pointing it out during her last livestream.

There was too much evidence, too many instances that Stella could twist to her advantage. She took a moment to consider, to make sure she was sure, because she'd reached the point of no return. One more step and it would all be over. She nodded to Harlow, who nodded back in solidarity. "But in the court of public opinion you've been found guilty. Golden Rule is where people go to tell their stories. And I've just told mine."

Harlow pushed a button on Stella's tablet and turned it around. "Surprise."

"I'm here for a very specific reason," Stella said. "I know there's a delay on the broadcast, just enough time for you to edit and censor what you don't want seen. Like this—I'm sure you cut the cameras the moment it became clear I wasn't going to follow your plan. Want to know how I know?"

Olive, who looked near tears, again, exchanged another look with Ethan, who was boiling with fury.

"Because Jewel asked little old wild card me to make livestreams, as many as possible, in the Golden Rule app in secret. We didn't have our phones—Jewel knew it would never occur to you to check the app. *'In a pressure cooker, separate the royal flush with red herrings wild. Bake for seven minutes.'* Jewel set my livestream time limit to exactly seven minutes."

Stella sat back in her smugness and watched as silence descended. They needed time to process, to absorb the greatness she had just laid at their feet.

"Okay. Um. So," Alex said, right on time. "What happens now? I mean, I guess everything you said could be true, but what are we supposed to do about it? Citizen's arrest or something?"

"Oh! Right! The End. Sorry. I was internally reveling in my greatness a little too hard there," Stella said. "Francis, I know you're probably feeling betrayed by your besties right now. If it helps, they didn't really lie to you."

"What?" Scrunched face and pinched eyebrows, Francis looked like he was fighting off a killer headache. He was also holding Nicole's hand, something Stella zeroed in on.

"When I sent you to go spy for us, you came back with the truth," Stella said. "Ethan and Olive fooled you because they were telling the truth too. They really don't know where she is." She leaned forward to see around the group, focusing on the person sitting at the end of the line. "Jewel doesn't win until we find her, and neither do we. It's time to call it quits. I've laid my cards on the table, and it's a wild royal flush."

A shot suddenly rang out.

FEARLESS

Luna had never heard gunshots in real life before.

Everything happened so fast—the shouting, the screaming, the scrambling. Alex had tackled her to the ground, covering her body with his.

The rapid-fire *pop pop pop pop* sounded fake. The squishy, wet splatter sound that followed did not.

"*What's happening?*" Luna clutched at Alex's shirt as he picked her up. One second, she was on the ground and the next he carried her, running with Harlow and Nicole. Both of them screaming, "Go! Hurry! Go! Run!"

Alex ran through an open dark doorway. Luna looked over his shoulder just in time to see the secret passageway close behind them. The electric string lights clicked on, as weak as she remembered— barely enough light to see five feet in either direction. Security guards pounded on the door from the other side. "*Open this door! How do you open this door?*"

"We have to run," Alex whispered as he put her down. "Which way?"

"I don't know, I don't know." Each inhale felt like an uncontrollable gasp. "I don't have the map for the secret passages. My codex is only to find the door."

He grasped her hand. "Come on." And with that, they ran to the left, leaving the angry shouts behind.

They ran and ran, turning every corner and following the paths whether they sloped downward or tilted upward. Luna's lungs stretched and filled with the cold, damp air. Everything smelled like dirt and dust, filling her up and wrapping around the endless *what's happening* stuck on repeat in her head.

Security had shot at them.

They were alone.

They had left everyone else behind.

"Alex," she panted, "I can't—"

While they ran he had taken the lead, keeping his back to her. A quick glance over his shoulder later, he slowed to a stop, still holding her hand.

There in the almost dark, Luna could finally see his face. Pinched with worry and uncertainty. Straining and failing to hide it from her. His shoulders rose and fell with each deep breath he took, but he wasn't winded like her. She leaned against the wall, chest heaving and throat burning.

"What do we do?" he asked. "What do we do now?"

Luna's eyes stung with waiting tears. A lump filled a space in her throat. Her chest tightened, and her skin prickled. Was that real? Were they in danger? Was it up to them to call for help? To find a way to save everyone?

Alex's thumb swiped away the first tear to fall. He pulled her into a hug, and, face buried in his shirt, she asked, "What are we supposed to do?"

"Stop stealing my lines," he murmured into her hair, his arms once again trying to protect her.

Because he was right—that was his line. And now it was her turn to come up with an answer. She hugged him harder, holding him to her as tightly as she could, as if he would be the last person she would ever touch and she needed to remember it forever before it was too late.

"I don't know." She hoped he could hear her muffled words. If he couldn't, he might let her go, might look at her—might see the truth.

Maybe she'd been born that way, maybe something had changed

inside her a long time ago. Either way, somehow she became fearless. She could and would risk her life without a second thought. Climbing walls and bookcases, exploring darkened passageways, and taking a nap with spiders wasn't even enough to make her blink.

But she would never risk other people.

Luna had convinced Tasha to let her come to Golden Weekend. Promised her it would be safe, told her about the money she might come back with that would change their lives. Without a second thought, she decided she would put her life on the line for it. No matter what happened, she would rise to Jewel's challenges and complete them all so Alex wouldn't have to. He would never be in danger.

And now they all were.

Stella and Nicole and Harlow and Francis—she left them *behind*. She convinced them it was all a game. They were still back there because of her.

It was supposed to be me, she thought. *Not them. Me.*

Except she hadn't made the deal to include them. Alex was with her and Jewel was hiding—and *oh no*. It had only been two days! How was that enough time to start caring about someone, let alone two people?

"Why would they do that?" Luna asked, heart heavy with her worst nightmare coming true. "Why didn't they come with us?"

Nicole constantly looked out for everyone. Luna didn't get special attention—but it felt like she had. The moment they'd first met outside, she looked right at Luna and never stopped. She fussed over her, made sure she ate, cared if she got enough rest, dressed her up, took the time to comb her hair, listened to her, and gave advice.

Stella made jokes about Luna's height, always teasing her and laughing, but had called her a sister out of nowhere. Proved it by believing in Luna before everyone else. By helping her lead instead of taking over, teaching her how to stand up and present with confidence.

All of that mattered to Luna in ways she'd been unable to admit to herself.

"Did they know that would happen?" Alex asked. "They couldn't have, right?"

Luna flinched as the pop of the gun echoed in her mind again. She forced herself to keep her eyes open, because if she blinked she would cry. She would fall to the floor into a blubbering heap and cry until there was nothing left.

"It wasn't real," she said, trying out the feel of the words. Stella had done the footwork and tossed the baton back to her. *Jewel doesn't win until we find her, and neither do we. It's time to call it quits. I've laid my cards on the table, and it's a wild royal flush.* "It's still a game. Stella thinks it's still a game."

She felt him swallow, could feel the pulse of his jaw on the top of her head. "Okay," he whispered, squeezing her tighter. "I'm with you, Moon Princess."

"Because there can only be two winners," she said, pulling back and holding his gaze. "Stella must have guessed there'd be a plan to separate us? Maybe not weapons, but something? Like the police to arrest Harlow, or they thought they'd have to distract Ethan and Olive while we ran? Otherwise they would have come too? They wouldn't have stayed behind?"

Alex looked away, staring at the ground.

"I know that sounds weak," she admitted, flinching again. "I'm trying. I just can't—it's hard to focus."

Lost in his thoughts, Alex let her go. Cold despair began to well up inside Luna, but she didn't pull his arms back to her. Instead, she watched him reach for the bag he was wearing. "Before we came downstairs, Harlow asked me to carry her bag," he said, holding it open between them.

The presents, *all* of them. Harlow had even given him her tablet. Luna pulled it out of the bag—Stella's wyvern was plugged in, altering the map. Hands shaking, she passed the tablet to Alex and retrieved her codex.

There it was: White Drawing Room—*remove the red rose from the white vase*. Stella had opened the panel. Nicole or Harlow must have entered the code.

They had planned an escape for her and Alex.

Tucked into the back of the codex, there was a loose sheet of paper:

> *Sorry we left you out at the end there. We know*
> *they're not going to like our story—Francis thinks the*
> *aftermath won't be pretty, so we've taken necessary*
> *precautions.*
>
> *We decided to give you all our presents.*
> *Solve the recipe. Save Jewel.*
> *Make us proud.*
>
> *—The Crayola Hall Coalition*
> *(Especially Stella. It was my idea. Mine.)*

Luna raised her chin, squared her shoulders, and spoke with every ounce of confidence she possessed. "Stella bet on the game. And she's betting on me to end it."

"Us," he said, looking up from the tablet. "*We* have to end it." While she was searching her codex, Alex had opened The Cruelest Jewel app.

A twitching purple envelope waited to be pressed on the prompt screen.

> Please proceed to wherever you think is best.
>
> Your key code: (heavy is the head
> that wears the crown)

"There they are!" a high-pitched voice shouted from their left.

This time, Luna grabbed Alex's hand.

SUFFOCATE

"I hate you so much right now."

Francis.

Was he talking to her?

Stella turned her head toward his voice. She couldn't see anything through the black bag over her head. The cloth loosely clung to her nose and mouth each time she breathed in—how long would it take to suffocate? As she marched forward, the tip of something cold occasionally pressed between her shoulder blades to keep her moving.

"I'm not wrong," she whispered. For them. For herself.

"We should've gone home." Harlow.

"I'm not wrong." She was losing feeling in her hands, tied behind her back.

Were the cameras even still on?

I LOVE YOU /
I KNOW

The security guards were fast, but Alex was quicker. He carried her while she navigated, and he ran like the wind.

It had been at least two right turns and a long hallway since she'd seen them, but she knew they were in pursuit. Their angry voices carried through the empty halls.

Her best friend, the genius track star, truly was something.

"There! The red one!"

Alex stopped a few feet before a small, square door on their left and put her down. Kneeling, she quickly found the secret white button hidden under a panel in the floor and entered the key code from Nicole's iron box.

"My back hurts looking at that," Alex complained as she crawled through. He followed her in, continuing to complain, this time about his knees. Luna hit the corresponding button to close the door behind them, which also opened the blue door in front of her.

"Is it clear?"

"Yeah. We're in the upside-down." Luna laughed. The room beyond had been flipped, with the ceiling as the floor and the floor with all its attachments as the ceiling. "But there's probably a camera, so let's stay in here as long as we can. Hopefully, it isn't pointed at the opening."

"We need a plan," Alex said, moving into a sitting position in front of her. He had to duck his head in the small square-shaped space. "What did Stella say?"

"Something about calling it quits? And a royal flush?" Luna placed the cards on the floor, side by side, and then pulled up the nonsensical recipe on her tablet.

A Nonsensical Recipe for Winning

Preheat oven to 314 degrees.

Mix all colors until batter is smooth.

Pour into sweet companion molds. Set aside all but three key ingredients.

Whip two partridges until a psychopomp and circumstance forms.

Share and cut the Baker's dozen chocolate bar into quadragrams.

In a pressure cooker, separate the royal flush with red herrings wild. Bake for seven minutes.

Serve the chocolate concoction scrambled atop a pie on a cloudy white day under a winner's cursed crown.

"What about 'Preheat oven to 314 degrees'? We haven't done anything with that yet?"

Alex typed in *Room 314*: Location Not Found.

"That would've been too easy, I guess." Luna sighed. "I didn't expect her to make it easy, but she could at least stop doing stuff that makes me get my hopes up."

"What about a winner's room? A trophy room? Somewhere she

would keep awards and stuff?" Alex asked, and began to check. "There's an awards room, which has to be the most unsurprising thing of this entire weekend. Want to head there?"

"No, that doesn't feel right." She sighed again, shaking her head. "It doesn't fit anything else."

"Yeah. I think so too. It's probably a trap. There's easy and then there's stupid easy."

"The second we walk in we'll get ambushed." Luna grimaced. "Not really in a rush to live through that again. Even if it was fake, it was still kind of terrifying." That memory would probably turn into yet another event hell-bent on haunting her REM cycle. "Thank you, by the way. For trying to save me."

"Yeah," he said. "It's funny. I don't even remember doing it. I just moved, you know? I mean, it's like my body knew what to do before I could even think your name."

Luna knew what she would've liked to say to that but didn't.

"It's probably not the time, but I think it's safe to say that I definitely love you," Alex said.

"I figured that out a while ago." Alex's skeptical eyebrows shot up, and Luna gasped, "That came out wrong. Don't say anything yet."

Alex made a show of pressing his lips together, tucking them inside his mouth to make an impatient "I'm waiting" face.

"I meant me. I figured that out about me for you," she said. "I don't really let myself care about people. It doesn't work out for me, so I just decided to stop. With you I feel like I didn't have a choice. One day you were there, and then, I always wanted you to be there."

"That was a nice save."

"I've been holding that in for a whole year." She picked up the ace card with her face on it, noticing for the first time that it was the heart suit, and placed it in front of him. "I didn't want you to think that it meant I wanted to date or something, and I didn't know how else to explain how I felt, so I just kept it to myself."

"I get that," he said. "I don't think we would be good together like that. At least, not right now. It would mess everything up, and I like things the way they are between us."

"Me too." She nodded for everything she was worth. "Just like this is what I want. More than anything."

"I think"—he paused, face screwed up in concentration—"since we're being honest, I think I would like to kiss you one day. Someday. Again, you know, not right now, but it's something I've thought about enough that it's worth mentioning."

Luna took her time to make sure her answer felt right. "I think I would like to try that. Someday. If it's you."

"Someday."

"Someday," she agreed. And she knew in her heart that it wouldn't matter to him whether or not that day ever came.

Alex inhaled a deep, shaking breath and blew it out as hard as he could. "I'm glad something good came out of this."

"Fantastic detour. 10/10 would recommend. Didn't help us at all with the game, though."

"Too bad it's not 'Preheat oven to 214 degrees.' Two-one-four. That would be easy. Valentine's Day. Chocolate squares." He picked up the tablet. "Plug your ears, because if there's a Valentine's Day or Love Room I'm going to scream."

"Wait." Luna sat up, holding her hands out. "Wait a minute, wait a minute. Okay, hear me out. If I admit I'm really bad when it comes to guessing the meanings of this recipe, can we at least try my idea?"

"Sure. We're not really doing anything else."

"Thank you," Luna said, packing up their presents. "I haven't seen it, so I don't know if it's true, but Nicole said every door in the Holiday Wing opened except for the white door. The recipe starts with 'Preheat oven to 314 degrees.' Serve scrambled atop a pie on a cloudy white day. Three-one-four is pi. It's a pun. So maybe Pi Day is the white door in the Holiday Wing." She covered her mouth with her hands, eyes wide as she waited for him to react.

"Soooo," Alex said, "White Day is March fourteenth in Asia. It's like reverse Valentine's Day. If someone you like gives you a present on Valentine's Day, you're supposed to give them chocolates on White Day."

"*No.*"

"Yeah. It's a thing. Watch enough slice-of-life anime and stuff starts to stick," Alex said while searching for the Holiday Wing.

"That's not what I mean!" Luna said. "In the announcement video, Jewel said it was White Day! She asked if she should give us *chocolate* or something else. She posted the video on March fourteenth—I was right! Everything really is connected!"

The familiar line of dots marked out the trail using the secret passageways until it forced them to exit out of another crawl space. Once upright they stood next to a door with HALLOWEEN engraved onto a small pumpkin-shaped plaque and affixed to the center of the door.

At the end of the hall, facing out, the white door waited for them. No knobs, no handle, no key code. WHITE DAY had been engraved onto a shiny crown-shaped plaque.

There were six empty squares below the crown.

"I guess this is where we use the tiles," Luna said. "What word should we try first?"

"Stella said four anagrams," he reminded her while dumping the tiles in his hand. "SIGNER, RESIGN, SINGER. And cursed or not, a crown REIGNS. I think that's what Stella was trying to say. Cards on the table—a wild royal flush must reign too."

"You're a genius, and I love you." She took the tiles from him and placed them into the slots, one at a time. The door unlocked with an audible *click* and began to drift open. "You and me."

"Me and you."

"And me," a voice said.

THE END

Nicole knew Stella stood next to her. A wall at their backs and masks over their heads, the surprisingly tender "Harlow, please. Stop crying" gave her away.

There were others in the room. Feet shuffling against the floor as they walked around. Whispering. Heavy items being dragged, judging by the high-pitched scraping sound. Nicole inhaled, concentrating on the feel of her lungs filling and chest expanding, and exhaled for as long as she could until the tightness begged for more air.

No panic. No fear. Just an unfortunate resignation to whatever would come next. Part of her believed in Stella—most of her really. A smaller section filled with doubt was ready to start screaming.

When this was over, she would say goodbye, go back home, and delete everything. She wanted nothing to do with Golden Rule or Jewel Van Hanen. If starting over from scratch meant burning everything down, then she'd be a phoenix. Her life had already gone up in flames once before.

Somehow, she survived then. This time would be no different.

"And me," a voice undoubtedly belonging to Jewel said. "Congratulations. We've been expecting you. Please wait right there."

A finger snap later, the bag was gently lifted from Nicole's head. Taylor, the staff member she'd met Friday morning, stood in front of her, smiling and brandishing a pair of scissors. "Turn around, please."

Nicole let her cut the ties.

A dark, round table and nine chairs had been placed in the center of a universe. Just like inside a planetarium, the walls and ceilings and floors moved with the breathtaking realistic images of a shimmering and thriving galaxy. Moons revolved around their planets. Asteroids coasted at their own pace. Enormous colorful clouds pulsated. And surrounding it all were small pinpricks of distant star clusters and burning giants like the sun.

Even though she hated to admit it, she'd always been quietly impressed that someone possessed the kind of creativity needed to design each of the rooms with such care. They were wasteful and they were marvelous.

Jewel sat in one of the chairs at the table, gaze fixed on Alex and Luna, who stood in front of an open door.

Nicole stepped away from the others, moving toward the table. "I'm not a violent person." She wrapped her hands around the back of the chair, fingers holding the soft leather tightly. "Which is why I'm putting you on notice before this chair meets your face."

Jewel had the nerve to cackle. "Oh, stop being so serious. Sit down and I'll explain everything. Everyone, please sit. We have all day, but I'd prefer if it didn't take that long."

"Let's not be brash here. Details first, assault and battery later." Stella pried Nicole's fingers loose from the chair. "If you behave, I'll even think about helping."

Reluctantly Nicole sat, the weight of Stella's stare helping her get there faster. It didn't take long for everyone else to follow. Francis sat on her other side with murder in his eyes too. Gold-colored leather folders had been placed in front of each seat with a fancy ink pen on top. Each one appeared to be a different color—hers was yellow with her name engraved onto the side.

"Before we get started," Jewel began, "I want to say congratulations to the winners of The Cruelest Jewel—Luna and Alex, who impressively figured out the nonsensical poem. As promised, you are one million dollars richer."

"We want to share it," Luna said quickly. She didn't look any worse for wear.

"Yeah," Alex said. "We wouldn't have figured out anything without everyone else. They deserve the money too."

"I have no problems with that." Jewel glanced around the table. "Congratulations. You are all collectively one million dollars richer."

Nicole picked up the fancy pen, weighing it in her hand—Stella was there again to stop her, gently pushing her wrist to the table and shaking her head.

"I'd also like to extend a special thank-you to my staff and security team, who brilliantly played their parts as instructed." Jewel clapped for them. "You may go now."

As they filed out, Ethan and Olive walked in, heading straight for the empty chairs at Jewel's side, just like they did when they had first arrived at the house. Jewel leaned forward, placing her elbow on the table and her chin on the back of her hand. "The cameras are off. No one knows what's happening right now." Jewel looked at Luna. "Your forum is currently on fire. Everyone is burning to know what happened when you walked through that door."

Luna nodded. "I figured that."

"That part will still stand." Jewel addressed the table again. "As you've discovered, past Golden Weekends weren't anything like this. There wasn't any competition. We talked to coaches, spent time figuring out what they were truly passionate about, what kind of impact they wanted to leave behind as their legacy, and then I gave them everything they needed to get started with three caveats. One: To pay it forward. Two: They had to stop using Golden Rule. Three: They could never talk about what happened. If they broke the rules, there would be consequences."

"Why?" Luna asked, and then immediately winced. "Sorry. I didn't mean to interrupt. It's just that we could never figure out that part. Why did they have to leave Golden Rule?"

"Because I love symbolism."

Stella snorted.

"My app," Jewel continued, throwing an irritated glare at Stella, "had become a safe haven. No bullying. No threats. No hate. Anything and everything we wanted community and reality to be. Leaving the app meant it was time to face the real world and do their part to fix it. Now, it's time for me to do the same."

Luna gasped in alarm.

"It's okay," Olive promised. "Just hold on."

"I definitely and graciously must give credit where it is due. Stella guessed correctly. Almost nothing got past you. Stories have always been the heart of Golden Rule, and I wanted to create a new one for a new beginning. You didn't deliver the option I thought you would, but your interpretation of step five was very entertaining, nonetheless. Separate the team with a story of your own creation. I honestly did not see that coming."

"Neither did we." Olive laughed. "You were so good, so convincing, we started to think that maybe Jewel really *did* make a game within the game and didn't tell us. I started crying because I thought I would have to play the game to prove we were innocent."

"Because that's absolutely something she would've done. I love you and I hate you and I love you," Ethan said to Jewel, and then turned back to Stella. "We didn't know what was going on or how to react to it, how to stop you—*whew*. You really got us good."

"I do aim to please." Stella preened.

"Detour aside, you would have earned a final present after the challenge that would have solved step five in a different way," Jewel said. "Naturally, The Cruelest Jewel had more than one possible ending that ultimately would lead to White Day. Everything was always meant to connect back to my announcement post."

Olive said, "You guys figured out two of them: Play the game to rescue Jewel. Play the game because it is a game."

"When we figured out those were the options you decided on, we had a plan in place ready for each one," Ethan said.

"But then, you went rogue," Jewel said. "I tracked you, Stella, as you showboated your way around the White Drawing Room and watched you prepare the secret passage opening. I decided to play along and sent in the paintball brigade to punish you for breaking my story and to reward your initiative."

"Reward? You think being held at paintball gunpoint is a *reward*?" Harlow asked.

"Every choice each of you made changed the potential ending. Your choices would then be used against you. Stella's ending could be no different. I honored her by playing along," Jewel said. "I'd also laid the groundwork for a possible revenge ending based on a party game I hosted years ago, a really fun one involving a murder, a haunting—I'm really looking forward to seeing that one someday."

"Someday?" Luna asked. "There really is going to be another Golden Weekend?"

"Everything's in there." Ethan gestured to the gold folders. "You will each have to sign an agreement that you will uphold the cover story, which you will be compensated for. Going forward, Golden Weekend will become an extension of tonight. You select your players. You craft the story. They play the game to win their heart's desire with a promise to pay it forward and make a difference in the world."

Jewel said, "Luna, you will be in charge of weekend planning. You, Nicole, will be the host."

"No."

"Yes. I promised you a role in my next web series. What do you think you've been doing all weekend?"

Nicole said, "But you shouldn't have to compete for charity. You shouldn't have to compete for entrepreneurship and money for college. *That's* the problem with the system now. Scarcity isn't real."

"Then change it. *That's* the point—it's your show, your game. Your only requirements are to follow the cover story, select your players from Golden Rule, and it must be hosted here."

"So you expect us to lie for you?"

"I expect you to act," Jewel said, tilting her head to the side.

The *talent*. She was the talent.

Nicole opened the folder and began reading. She must have blinked thirty times in surprise before she made it past the first page.

She needed a lawyer. ASAP.

Maybe Stella's dad would help, or she could even hire one now with some of the prize money Luna shared with them. Because if what she was reading was correct, then Jewel was not only giving her and Luna Golden Weekend, she was also giving them Golden Rule—both would be under the newly formed company called Golden Chaos, LLC.

Nicole stopped breathing. Her brain skipped so hard it literally forgot to send the message to her lungs.

Jewel, Ethan, and Olive would retain shares of the company but nothing else. When she looked up, Luna was watching her, hopeful and excited. Francis, *Francis*, he was grinning at her. "Did you know about this?"

"Some of it. I knew Jewel was stepping down," he admitted. "But nothing about the game or the story other than I was told to talk about The Scavengers Initiative as often as I could and pretend like I hated Jewel because of it."

"I was *right*." Stella smacked the table. "You don't actually hate her, do you?"

"Nah." He shook his head.

"Wait, what about Stella?" Harlow asked, folder still open. "Why doesn't she get part of the company? She's the one who actually solved the game."

Jewel said, "She was disqualified. You both were."

"What?" Nicole focused on Jewel, happy shock rapidly being replaced by upset. "Why?"

"They were warned," Jewel said calmly. "If any of the other players found out about the livestreams, they knew they would both be disqualified."

"I don't care," Harlow snapped. "None of this would have worked without Stella. She knew there was more than one ending. She decided to let Luna win. You can't cut her out."

"You still talk too much, even after all this time," Stella said fondly.

"That was a choice she made, and as you've learned choices have consequences," Jewel said, and then looked at Stella. "It ends here for you."

"That's fine. I'm leaving with exactly what I want," Stella said.

"And what's that?"

"The bald cat, of course." Stella grinned. "You're going to give him to me."

PARENTHETICALS

Jewel had really outdone herself.

Brunch had been served in a massive golden ballroom for everyone—staff and security included. The theme, of course, was Graduation.

Tables with elaborate floral centerpieces and chairs had been set up on one side, enough brunchy foods to feed a small army on the other, and in the center, the dance floor was already in use. The DJ played an interesting mix of music—some old, some new, and some things Stella had never heard that would make her parents lose their minds if they knew she was listening to them. Opulent velvet curtains bordered the windows and sunlight streamed in, creating dazzling prismatic patterns with the crystal chandeliers.

"I still owe you an interview," Jewel said, sitting with Stella at her empty table.

Truth be told, Stella wanted to be alone. She had gone from severe isolation to spending every waking hour for over forty-eight hours with strangers who became so much more. Surprisingly, she'd had her fill of people for now. It wouldn't last, most likely, but she just really needed a little break.

Stella asked, "Can I have a rain check? I'm decompressing." Even her brain felt tired—a wholly new experience for her.

"No," Jewel said. "Why did you let Luna win? You had everything. Why did you give it away?"

Stella sighed theatrically. She let Luna win because that's what big sisters did. "The game meant more to her than it did to me. I got the ending I wanted."

Jewel narrowed her eyes. "You did all that just to prove you're better than me? Better than everyone? Really?"

"Yes," she said. It was true. She'd outsmarted the Gamemaster, but she never would have pulled it off without the others. Her people. Her friends and her sisters—*that* was the ending she wanted and risked everything for. Maybe Jewel was rubbing off on her—maybe she liked it when people thought the worst of her after all.

"At least you're honest about it."

"Why did *you* do it?" Stella decided to throw the question back at her. "People like you don't just wake up and decide it's time to go Full Wonka. What really happened? I genuinely want to know."

"That, actually." Jewel laughed. "It was time to send the torch back down."

Stella squinted, sure Jewel had combined *send the ladder back down* with *pass the torch* but didn't care to correct her.

In return, Jewel smiled softly. "You know what I mean. Really, I woke up and I had an idea."

Stella laughed. "Look at us: a pair of simpletons with simple answers."

"The simplest solution is usually the correct one," Jewel said, laughing too. "We're quite the pair, Stella At All Times."

"Don't tell my parents that," she joked. "What will you do now that you've given away a sizable chunk of your empire?"

"Disappear again. Give school a second chance. Prepare for the future."

"By doing what?"

Jewel grinned. "I've always found it interesting how actors somehow manage to make the seamless transition to becoming politicians. The world isn't going to change itself."

"How noble. I'll look forward to your scandalous headlines once your past comes back to haunt you."

"I'll be ready."

"Oh, but before you pull a Houdini? I will absolutely make sure Nicole's and Harlow's therapy bills are forwarded directly to you for putting black bags over their heads and marching them through your house at paintball gunpoint. Among other things."

Harlow needed therapy and lots of it. The second she agreed to go in that coffin, her happily ever after vanished. The story was never going to end well for her, no matter which path she took.

When she had told Harlow the plan to include using the livestreams against Ethan and Olive as "evidence" she didn't object, saying, "If we can't destroy them for real, might as well do what we can." Jewel had been right—they knew they would be disqualified. Thank God for Luna and Alex's kindness. At least Harlow would be going home with some money instead of just trauma and bad memories.

"Go away," Nicole said. She and Luna had appeared on the other side of the table.

Jewel laughed at her. "This is still my house. Watch yourself."

"We need to tell Stella something. In private," Luna said. "Please?"

"For you? Sure," Jewel said, standing to leave. "Goodbye for now, Stella At All Times. I've changed my mind about that rain check."

Stella nodded in acknowledgment. Rain checks could be leveraged for more time. Her goal had been lofty at best, she knew that now. A puzzle like Jewel could never be solved with a single sit-down interview, or even an exclusive series that lasted three days.

Her essay about Golden Weekend would be *everything*, told in a way only Stella could. But the small snippets of Jewel Van Hanen she'd managed to capture would never paint a full picture. Because Jewel was ever unknowable by design.

Jewel said, "Luna? Come find me when you're done."

"Okay," she agreed brightly. After sitting, she asked Stella, "How come you look so tired?"

Nicole answered for her, "Because scheming is hard work."

"That it is," she said. "I'm quite proud of us. Mostly me. But also us. How are you feeling? Still ready to break some faces?"

Nicole scoffed. "No. I'm a little less mad with each passing second."

Once they joined the party, everyone scattered to the four corners, essentially. Ethan and Olive sat with Nicole, answering her questions about Jewel's offer because she didn't trust herself to talk to Jewel directly yet.

Luna had already accepted but hadn't signed yet, thanks to Stella ripping the pen out of her hand and ordering her to let Lloyd look at the contract first. She and Alex had decided to make the rounds, introducing themselves to each staff member. Luna wanted to make sure she knew everyone's name.

"It's a good deal," Nicole continued. "She's really giving us everything. I can't stand the sight of her right now, but I also can't ignore how generous this is. I wish she didn't feel like it was necessary to manipulate us all to get us here."

"I don't feel manipulated. We had to agree to play. We had a choice. We could've walked away at any time, but we didn't and *we won*," Luna, ever the optimist, said. "Didn't you guys have fun? I did. I mean, the guns weren't fun at all. Neither was breaking my arm. Hmm."

"It definitely wasn't all bad," Nicole said, voice a bit too dreamy for the conversation. Stella followed her gaze to Francis, who had seemingly put himself in charge of keeping Harlow company.

"I object."

"Sustained." Nicole giggled. "Sorry."

"Anyway. Stella," Luna said. "We wanted to ask you something." She looked to Nicole, who nodded.

"Luna and I have been talking. After we sign, Golden Chaos will officially be our company. We don't have a plan or structure or anything more than vague ideas about what we're gonna do, but we realized, again, that it'll be our company. Meaning we can hire whoever we want."

"It's time for a new era of leadership on Golden Rule," Luna said. "The Crayola Quintet."

"And there's just no way we could do this without our Quicksilver and our Assassin."

"And Alex," Luna added. "He's going to help too. And also my sister because legally she has to sign the contract with me. It'll be like a family business."

Stella had to laugh, because if she didn't, she would cry, and she *never* cried. She'd convinced her parents to let her come to Golden Weekend in order to be a part of the Beauregard family business, and now, she was leaving with a second one. "Well," she said, truly happy for the first time in a very long time. "How could I possibly say no to that?"

"Who are they?" Luna asked, gesturing with her chin toward the door. "I don't think they're staff. Me and Alex met everyone already."

In six seconds flat, Stella made it from her table to the entrance. Her *parents* had arrived. "What are you doing here?" she demanded. "It's not time to leave yet! We had a deal! You said the whole weekend! You promised!"

Diane lunged forward, capturing Stella in a bear hug.

"What are you doing? I am yelling! You can't hug me when I'm mad and yelling!"

But her mom didn't let go, hugging her tighter. "I'm so proud of you." She sniffled and said it again. "Brilliant. Just—brilliant and perfect. You handled yourself so well."

". . . what?" Stella looked at her dad and noticed his extremely loud face had gone uncharacteristically soft. He opened his arms and hugged them both.

Stella nearly fainted. All the blood left her head because she realized Jewel had given them access to the livestream.

"You will never in your life, ever call me Lloyd, ever again," he said. "But I'm proud of you too. You did good, kiddo."

They'd seen *everything*. Oh no. Oh God.

"You were watching," Stella asked. "But you emailed me *multiple* times a day. You never said you were watching."

"Jewel asked to keep it a secret for the game," he said. "We agreed it could be a good learning experience for you. And for us."

"We watched the whole thing. We slept when you slept, and if you were up, we were up cheering you on," Diane said. "We even saw the ending in the planetarium. Jewel told us she cut the stream off before that but wanted us to know what you did."

"Oh," Stella said, for lack of anything better to say. "This is probably a good time to tell you I have a cat now. He's bald and possibly hypoallergenic. I don't actually know, but he's very cute and wrinkly." She continued to stand there while her parents hugged her. No, she wasn't crying. Much. (Leave her alone.) "I have friends now too. Really good ones. And a job. They're going to hire me."

"We know," her mom said, pulling back. She wiped her tears. "I'd like to meet them. If that's okay with you?"

"That's why we asked to come to brunch," Lloyd said. "We wanted to meet your friends."

Family *and* friends. What a concept.

Goldspiracy Forums

Transcript #1015

Original <u>Golden Rule diary entry</u> by Jewel Van Hanen
June 8, Year Three
🗨 Transcribed by **Oreo524**

FAMOUS LAST WORDS | Remember me.

Here we are. There you go.

This will be my final Golden Rule entry. After this video posts, my archive will automatically begin to delete. Systematically, one by one, self-destructing until only this video remains. It might seem like it, but nothing on the internet lasts forever. It's possible to make things disappear. With the right resources.

[pauses]

There's nothing I love more than having the last word. So, here are mine:

You'll never find me where it all began.
But for a lucky few this isn't the end.

I've done my time. The Quintet will live on.
And the Queen will reign with a long con.

[pauses and smiles]

Let the games begin.

ACKNOWLEDGMENTS

Three. I made it to three published books. Imagine that.

Usually I use this space as a blogpost confessional filled with thank-yous for everyone who made an impact on my life in some way during whatever year I wrote said book. But this one took two very long, very difficult years—and I spent a lot of that time alone and isolated while being betrayed. (You didn't really think you were getting out of this drama-free, did you? You should know me better than that by now.)

Thank you to the entire Swoon Reads/MacKids Books team, especially Liz, Kelsey, Ilana, and Kat. Lauren, thank you for helping shape this story when it was as chaotic and unfocused as I always am. To my copy editor for commenting "lol" on a couple of my jokes: That sincerely made me ridiculously happy. My greatest wish is that this story makes people laugh and they have a good time while reading it. Thank you for the confirmation giggles.

Wattpad HQ: Thank you for deciding to feature *The Scavenger Hunt* all those years ago and giving it a Watty Award. This book wouldn't exist without the love you showed that one.

Wattpad Readers: After I removed *The Scavenger Hunt*, at least a few times a week someone sent me a message asking where it was, if I planned to publish, would I bring it back . . . I'm sorry I couldn't give you a satisfying answer at the time. I hope this makes up for it.

Mommy, Mama, Moooooooooom: Hi. The only person who believes in me more than me is you. I hope you know how much I love you.

Macy: My snail sister, my goldfish-in-arms. You were the one who yelled at me to upload *The Scavenger Hunt* to Wattpad when no one wanted to represent or buy it. Not to be dramatic, but this book probably exists because of you. We still need to go swimming in our pennies!

Anna: Thank you for reading my Golden rough drafts an ungodly amount of times. Thank you for the missing stair (you're so brilliant it's painful). Thank you for listening to me whine and cry and yell in frustration. Thank you for commiserating with me when things outside of my control fell completely apart. Thank you for entertaining the size of my ego as I cackled about how much I loved this book. Thank you for everything.

Sarah: You won't remember this, but I do—"*Shut up, Randy.*" Ask me about it sometime.

SHINee & Shawols: You make my increasingly dark days brighter.

I spent an egregious amount of time on research for this story. If you've created content about the history of social media and YouTube, about the inexplicable rise (and downfall) of public figures, the nature of celebrity, parasocial relationships, and any content about ARGs and transmedia storytelling, I've most likely consumed it. Almost all the writing that resulted from that work got cut in edits because that's the way it goes. Anyway. A special thank-you to Clarkisha Kent, InsideAMind, TwinPerfect, Tiffany Ferguson, Emma Chamberlain and Joana Ceddia, Lil Nas X, and Jenna Marbles—the likelihood I'll ever meet any of you in person is abysmal so this will have to do.

And lastly, I want to thank Stella—yes, one of the stars of this book. If it wasn't for your voice coming to me in the midnight hour when I was dreadfully close to my next deadline, I don't know if I ever would have finished *The Marvelous*. You helped me rediscover the kind of writer I want and need to be, helped me solidify the kind of narratives I want to create. Thank you for always being violently yourself, Stella At All Times, and for teaching me how to be as well.

If I missed you, know that I still love you. Probably. I'm still deciding.

Check out more books
chosen for publication
by readers like you.

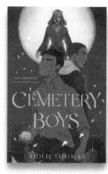

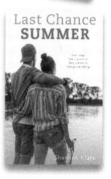